Catch Me When I Fall

Nicci French is the pseudonym for the writing partnership of journalists Nicci Gerard and Sean French. The couple are married and live in Suffolk.

There are now eight bestselling novels by Nicci French: *The Memory Game*, *The Safe House*, *Killing Me Softly*, *Beneath the Skin*, *The Red Room*, *Land of the Living*, *Secret Smile* and *Catch Me When I Fall*, all published by Penguin.

Also by Nicci French:

The Memory Game
The Safe House
Killing Me Softly
Beneath the Skin
The Red Room
Land of the Living
Secret Smile

Catch Me When I Fall

NICCI FRENCH

PENGUIN BOOKS

PENGUIN BOOKS

Published by the Penguin Group
Penguin Books Ltd, 80 Strand, London WC2R ORL, England
Penguin Group (USA) Inc., 375 Hudson Street, New York, New York 10014, USA
Penguin Group (Canada), 90 Eglinton Avenue East, Suite 700, Toronto, Ontario, Canada M4P 2Y3
(a division of Pearson Penguin Canada Inc.)
Penguin Ireland, 25 St Stephen's Green, Dublin 2, Ireland (a division of Penguin Books Ltd)
Penguin Group (Australia), 250 Camberwell Road, Camberwell, Victoria 3124, Australia
(a division of Pearson Australia Group Pty Ltd)
Penguin Books India Pvt Ltd, 11 Community Centre, Panchsheel Park, New Delhi – 110 017, India
Penguin Group (NZ), cnr Airborne and Rosedale Roads, Albany, Auckland 1310, New Zealand
(a division of Pearson New Zealand Ltd)
Penguin Books (South Africa) (Pty) Ltd, 24 Sturdee Avenue,
Rosebank, Johannesburg 2196, South Africa

Penguin Books Ltd, Registered Offices: 80 Strand, London WC2R ORL, England

www.penguin.com

First published by Michael Joseph, 2005
Published in Penguin Books, 2006

3

Copyright © Joined-up Writing, 2005
Set in 11.75/14 pt Monotype Garamond
Typeset by Rowland Phototypesetting Ltd, Bury St Edmunds, Suffolk
Printed in England by Clays Ltd, St Ives plc
ISBN-13: 978-0-141-00652-9
ISBN-10: 0-141-00652-8

To Jackie and Tomàs

I died twice.

The first time, I wanted to die. I thought of death as the place where the pain would stop, where the fear would finally cease.

The second time, I didn't want to die. In spite of the pain and in spite of the fear, I had decided at last that life was where I needed to be: messy, scary, tiring, lovely, hurting life, with all its failures and its sadness, with all its sudden and unlooked-for bits of joy that make you close your eyes and think: Hold on to this, remember this. Memories can carry you through. Dancing in the dark; seeing the sun rise; striding through the city, lost in a crowd; looking up to meet your smile. You saved me when I could no longer save myself. You found me when I was lost.

I didn't want to be dead, but someone else wanted me to be. They tried very hard to make me die. I'm a person who people seem to either love or hate. Sometimes it's been hard to tell the difference between the two. Even now, when it's all over and I can look back at it like a landscape I've walked through and left behind, there are things that remain hidden, secrets lost to me.

Dying takes you to another place. All alone, you cross a line and nobody can join you there. When my father died, I was sixteen years old. I remember the spring afternoon when he was buried. My mother tried to make me dress in mourning clothes but my father always hated black, so I put on my pink dress and my reddest lipstick and wore high heels that sank into the soft earth. I wanted to look like a hussy, like a tart. I smeared blue eye-shadow on my eyelids. And I remember the words the vicar said – 'Ashes to ashes, dust to dust' – and that people were crying and holding on to each other. I knew they wanted me to cry as well, and then they could have put an arm round me and comforted me, but my father hated people weeping. He always liked us to show the world we were happy. So I smiled through the service, and I think, because of the way everyone was looking at me, I even laughed a bit. My mother put a single white rose on his coffin when they lowered it into the ground, the way you're supposed to. I took the bracelets off my arm and tossed those in, so for a few seconds it felt more like a pagan burial than a respectable English funeral. One of the bracelets broke, and its bright plastic beads rolled around crazily on the cheap wooden lid. Rat-a-tat-tatting on my father's face.

For a while I thought I would go mad with loneliness and rage, although I never told anyone about that because I didn't have the words. For ten years, I tried to get back to him. In despair. In love. In disgust, hilarity, loathing and revenge.

I died twice. Only twice. You'd have thought that with all my frantic striving I could have done a bit better than that.

So here they are, then. The people who loved me and hated me, who wanted me to live and who wished me dead, who tried to save me and who let me go. They all look happy. They are gazing at each other, holding hands; some of them are kissing.

I can tell that they are making promises to each other for the life ahead. That great and mysterious journey. Only one is missing.

Dying Once

I

'I'm attracted to danger,' he said. 'Always have been. What can I get you two?'

I thought for a moment. Pace yourself, Holly. It was an hour since Meg and I had left the office but I was still buzzing. Fizzing. I once had a friend who was working as an actor. He'd told me how after a show it would take him hours to wind down, which was a bit of a problem if the curtain fell at half past ten and you had any ambition to fit in with the rest of the world. Mainly he found himself fitting in with other actors, who were the only people who felt like heading out for dinner at eleven and sleeping until noon every day of the week.

Another friend from college is a long-distance runner. She's impressive. She almost got into the Olympics. She runs ridiculously fast and far just to get her body going. Then she runs a properly serious distance and punishes herself up steep hills. After that, the difficulty is to bring her body back to normal. She does more running simply to wind herself down. Afterwards she puts ice on her muscles and joints to cool them. I could do with that. Sometimes I feel I'd like to put my whole head into a chinking barrel of ice.

'It's not that difficult a decision,' he said. 'Meg's already asked for a white wine.'

'What?' I said.

For a moment I'd forgotten where I was. I had to look around to remind myself. It was wonderful. It was autumn, but it was a hot evening and the crowd in the Soho bar was spilling out on to the street. It felt like the summer was going to go on for ever, winter would never come, it would never rain again. Out in the countryside fields needed water, riverbeds were dry, crops shrivelling, but in the middle of London it was like being by the Mediterranean.

'What do you want to drink?'

I asked for a white wine and some water. Then I put my arm on Meg's shoulders and murmured into her ear, 'Did you talk to Deborah?'

She looked uneasy. So she hadn't.

'Not yet,' she said.

'We need to talk about this. Tomorrow, OK?'

'Still or sparkling?' asked the man.

'Tap,' I said. 'First thing, Meg, before anything else.'

'All right,' she said. 'Nine o'clock, then.'

I watched her and she watched the stranger walking over to the bar. He had a nice, open face: what was his name? Todd, that was it. We'd all staggered over from the office. It had been a hard day. We'd arrived as a group but gradually been diluted by the crowd. I saw familiar faces around the room, which was full of happy people who had escaped from their offices. Todd was a client who had come in to check our proposal and he'd tagged along with us. Now he was trying to buy the drinks at the crowded bar. He was having difficulty because one of the women behind it was being shouted at by a rude customer. She was foreign – something like Indonesian – and the rude customer was yelling that she had given him the wrong drink. She was having difficulty understanding what he was saying. 'Look at me when I'm talking to you,' he said.

Todd came back clutching the drink for Meg, the two for me, and a beer for himself. 'They wouldn't give me tap water,' he said. 'It's from a bottle.'

I took a sip.

'So, you like danger,' I said.

'You make it sound stupid but, yes, in a way.'

Todd proceeded to tell us about a holiday he'd taken. He was cheerily proud of it. He and a group of friends had been celebrating something so they had undertaken a succession of dangerous sports across southern Africa. They had whitewater-rafted in Zambia, canoed past hippos in Botswana, bungee-jumped from a cable car going up Table Mountain and scuba-dived with Great White sharks.

'Sounds amazing,' said Meg. 'I don't think I'd have the nerve to do that.'

'It was exhilarating,' he said. 'Terrifying as well. I think maybe I liked it more in retrospect.'

'Did anybody get eaten?' I asked.

'You go down in cages,' he said, 'and we didn't see any.'

'Cages?' I said, pulling a face. 'I thought you liked *danger*.'

He looked bemused. 'Are you kidding?' he said. 'I'd like to see you jump from a cable car hundreds of feet up with just an elastic band for protection.'

I laughed, but not meanly, I hope. 'Haven't you read our brochure?' I said. 'We've arranged bungee-jumps. We've done the risk assessments, we've organized the insurance. I can tell you that it's less dangerous than crossing the road.'

'It's an adrenaline rush all the same,' Todd said.

'You can get adrenaline off the shelf,' I said. Was he going to be offended, or was he going to smile?

He shrugged self-deprecatingly and smiled. 'So, what's your idea of danger?' he said.

I thought for a moment. 'Real things, where it matters. Searching for unexploded mines and defusing them. Working as a miner – but not in Britain. I mean in Russia or the Third World.'

'What frightens you most?'

'Lots of things. Lifts, bulls, heights, bad dreams. Almost everything about my job. Failure. Talking in public.'

Todd laughed. 'I don't believe that,' he said. 'It was a good presentation today.'

'I was terrified beforehand. I always am.'

'So you agree with me. You like challenges.'

I shook my head. 'Your bungee-jumping and

canoeing past hippos, that was in a brochure. You knew how it was going to turn out.' I heard a noise behind me and turned round. The man was complaining to the woman again, but worse this time. She was trying to explain and she was almost crying.

'What about you, Meg?' Todd asked, turning towards her. She smiled up at him shyly and opened her mouth, but I interrupted her reply.

'You're saying you like risk?' I said.

'Yes.'

'Adrenaline?'

'I guess.'

'Do you want to show me?'

'Holly!' said Meg nervously.

Todd's eyes flickered from side to side. I detected a flutter of excitement, but also of nervousness. What was coming?

'What do you mean?'

'You see that man at the bar, the one being rude to the girl?'

'Yes.'

'Do you think he's being a bully?'

'Probably. Yes.'

'Go and tell him to stop it and to apologize for his behaviour.'

Todd tried to speak, but started to cough instead. 'Don't be daft,' he said finally.

'You think he'll hit you?' I said. 'I thought you were attracted to danger.'

Todd's expression hardened. This wasn't funny

any more. And he had stopped liking me. 'It's just a way of showing off,' he said.

'You're scared of doing it.'

'Of course I'm scared.'

'If you're scared of it, the only way to get rid of the feeling is to do it. It's like scuba-diving with sharks. But without the cage.'

'No.'

I put my two glasses down on a table. 'All right,' I said. '*I'*ll do it.'

'No, Holly, don't . . .' said Meg and Todd together.

That was the only encouragement I needed. I walked over to the man at the bar. He was wearing a suit. Every man in the room was wearing a suit. He must have been in his mid-thirties, balding, especially on the crown of his head. He was florid-faced from the heat of the day and maybe from the week's work and his agitation. I hadn't noticed how large he was. His jacket fitted awkwardly across his broad shoulders. And I hadn't noticed that he was with two other men. He was still saying something basically unintelligible to the woman.

'What's going on?' I said.

He turned, startled and angry. 'Who the fuck are you?' he said.

'You need to say sorry to this woman,' I said.

'What?'

'You don't talk to people like that. You need to apologize.'

'Fuck off.'

He pronounced it with particular emphasis on the *k*, so there was a pause between the two words. Did he think I was going to walk away? Did he think I was going to cry? I picked up his drink from the bar. It was a tumbler. I brandished it at him, holding it barely an inch from his chin. It would be good to say that the whole bar fell silent, like in an old Western, but there was no more than a ripple of attention just around us. The man looked down at the glass, as if he was trying to see the knot of his own loosened tie. I could see he was thinking quickly: Is this woman mad? Is she really going to smash a glass in my face? For this? And I should have been thinking much the same: If he could insult and shout at some poor woman behind the bar for giving him the wrong drink, what would he do to me for physically threatening him? And I might have been thinking, as Todd had probably been thinking, that this man might be just out of prison. He might have a propensity for violence. He might especially enjoy picking on females. None of this occurred to me. I was just looking into his eyes. I felt the throb of the pulse in my neck. I had the vertiginous feeling of having no idea what would happen in the next five seconds.

And then the man's face relaxed into a smile. 'All right,' he said. Delicately he took the glass from my hand, as if it might explode. He downed it in one. 'On one condition.'

'What's that?'

'I buy you a drink.'

I started to say no and looked round for Todd. He was gone, as was Meg. I wondered at what point they had fled the scene. Was it in anticipation of what might happen? Or was it when they saw what actually had happened? I gave a shrug. 'Just do it,' I said.

He was quite gentlemanly about it. He gestured to the nervous barmaid. He nodded at me. 'This woman – what's your name?'

'Holly Krauss,' I said.

'Miss Holly Krauss tells me that I was rude to you and that I ought to apologize. On reflection I think she is right. So, I'm very sorry.' The woman looked at me and then at him again. I don't think she understood properly what was going on. The man, whose name was Jim, ordered me a double gin and tonic and another for himself.

'Cheers,' he said. 'And, incidentally, she really is a bloody awful barmaid.'

I gulped back my drink and he ordered me another, and from then on the evening speeded up. It was as if I had been on a big dipper and it had climbed and climbed all day, and at the moment when I held the glass under Jim's chin it had got to the highest point where it perched for a moment, then began to descend more and more quickly. The bar began to feel like a party where I knew quite a lot of the people or wanted to know them or they wanted to know me. I talked to Jim and his friends, who found the whole episode with the glass very funny and kept on telling it, teasing him about it.

I was talking to a man who worked in the office across the courtyard from us, and when he headed off with some friends along the road to a private club for supper he asked me along and I went. Events occurred quickly but also in snapshots, like moments illuminated by a strobe light. The club was in an eighteenth-century townhouse, all shabby wood panelling and bare boards. It was an evening where everything seemed easy, available and possible. One of the men at the table where we ate was the director of the club so he was joking with the waiter and getting special food for us to try. I had a long, intense conversation with a woman who worked for something amazing, a film or photographic company or a magazine, and later I couldn't remember a word of it. The only thing I remembered was that when she stood up to go she kissed me full and hard on my mouth, so that I tasted her lipstick.

Someone suggested we go dancing. He said a new place had just opened not far off and it would be getting going about now. I looked at my watch and saw that it was past midnight; I'd been up since half past five. But it didn't matter.

We all walked there together, a group of about ten people who, until an hour or so ago, had been strangers. A man put his arm round me as we walked and started singing in Spanish or Portuguese or something. He had a beautiful voice, very deep, which boomed out into the soft autumn air, and I looked up and saw there were stars in the sky. They shone so bright and near I almost felt that if I reached out I would be able to touch them. I sang something too, I can't remember what, and everyone joined in. People were laughing, holding each other. Our cigarettes glowed in the darkness.

We ended up near the office again. I remember thinking I'd come full circle and that I was less tired than I'd been when I left. I danced with the man who'd sung in Spanish, and with someone who said his name was Jay, and then I was in the women's toilets where someone gave me a line of coke. The club was small and crowded. A black man with soft eyes stroked my hair and told me I was gorgeous. A woman, I think she said she was Julia, came up and said she was going home now and maybe I should as well, before something happened, and did I want to share a taxi, but I wanted something to happen, everything to happen. I didn't want the evening to end yet. I didn't want to turn out the lights. I danced again, feeling so light on my feet it was almost like flying, until the sweat poured down my face and stung my eyes and my hair was damp and my shirt stuck to me.

Then we left. Jay was there, I think, and maybe the singer, and a woman with amazing black hair who smelt of patchouli and other people I remember only as silhouettes against the sky. It was so beautifully cool outside. I pulled the air into my lungs and felt the sweat dry on my skin. We sat by the river, which looked black and deep. You could hear the tiny thwack of waves on the bank. I wanted to swim in it, to lie in its dark currents and be swept away to the sea where no one could follow me. I hurled in a handful of coins, though only a few reached the water, and told everyone to make a wish.

'What's your wish, then, Holly?'

'I want it to be always like this,' I said.

I put a cigarette into my mouth and someone leaned towards me, cupping the lighter in their hands. Someone else took it out of my mouth and held it while he kissed me and I kissed him back, pulling him towards me and gripping his hair in my hands, and then a different person kissed me as well, his lips on my neck and I tipped back my head and let him. Everyone loved me and I loved everyone. They all had tender, shining eyes. I said the world was a more magical place than we knew. I stood up and ran across the bridge. With each step I felt that I might never land on the ground again, but I could hear the sound of my footfalls echoing around me, and then the sound of other footfalls too, following me, but they couldn't catch me. People were calling my name, like owls hooting. 'Holly, Holly!' I laughed to myself. A car swept by, catching me in its head-lights and letting me go again.

I stopped for breath at last, near an arcade of shops, and they found me there. Two of them, I think. Maybe, maybe not. One grabbed me round the shoulders and pushed me up against a wall, and said he'd got me at last and wasn't going to let me go. He said I was wild, but that he could be wild too. He picked up a brick. His arm arced back over his head, just a few inches from me, and I saw the brick sailing through the air. There was a loud crack and a violent star spread in the plate-glass window in front of us and a pyramid of tins collapsed on their shelves, and for a second it was as if we were going to step through the perfect star into a different world and I could be someone entirely new. New and fresh and whole.

Then the alarm broke over us, nasal shrieks that seemed to be coming from every direction, and he took me by the wrist. 'Run.'

We ran together. I think there were still three of us but maybe there were only two by then. Our feet seemed in time. I don't know why we stopped running, but I know we were in a taxi, speeding along empty streets, past shops with metal shutters and dark houses. A fox froze as the taxi approached, orange and still under the street-lamps. It slipped into a garden, a slim shadow, and was gone.

After that, there are things I remember and don't remember at the same time, like something happening to someone else, in a film or in a dream you know you're having but can't wake up from. Or, rather, it was like something happening to me, but I was someone else. I was me and not me. I was a woman laughing as she went up the stairs in front of him; a woman standing in an upstairs room with one dim light in the corner, an old sofa heaped with cushions and, hanging from the ceiling, a turquoise budgerigar in a cage. Was there really a budgerigar piping away, looking down at her with its knowing eyes, or was that a strange hallucination that worked its way into the bright fever of the evening? A woman looking out of the window at roofs and night-time gardens that she'd never seen before.

'Where the fuck am I?' she said, letting her jacket slide to the floor in a puddle of darkness, but she didn't really want to know the answer. 'Who the fuck are you?' she asked next, but she didn't want to know that either. It didn't matter at all. And he just laughed anyway and pulled the curtains closed and lit a cigarette, or perhaps it was a joint, and passed it to her. She could feel excitement throbbing loose and deep along her veins, and she sat back in the sofa, against the cushions, and kicked off her shoes and curled her bare legs up under her.

'What shall we do now?' she asked, but of course she knew what they would do now. She undid a button on her shirt and he watched her. The budgerigar watched her too, daft sharp trills coming from its beak. She drank something transparent and fiery and felt its heat bolt through her body until she was molten at her core. There was music playing and it felt as if it was coming from inside her skull. She couldn't tell the difference between the beat of her feelings and the notes of the song. Everything had joined with everything else.

For a bit she was alone in the room with the music, and then she wasn't alone any longer. I wasn't alone any longer. I lay back, feeling soft as the river we'd sat by, and let him take off my skirt. We were on the sofa, then on the floor. Fingers fumbling with buttons. If I closed my eyes, lights flashed behind my eyelids and it was as if there was a whole strange world, over which I had no control, waiting to explode in my brain. So I kept my eyes open on this world, but I don't know what I saw. Cracks in the ceiling, the leg of a chair, a wall a few inches away, a face coming down against mine, the twist of a mouth. I tasted blood and ran a tongue against my lips. My blood: good. The carpet burned my skin: good. Hard fingers on my arms, on my body, digging into me. Me and not me; me and this other woman who was pulling off her shirt, buttons spraying on the floor, falling back on a bed, hair spreading beneath her; hands pulling off her bra; a weight on her. Closing her eyes at last and finding herself in a bright-lit world, full of shapes and exploding colours and rushing darkness.

'This is so strange,' she said. I said. 'Don't stop.'

2

There was something crawling along my cheek. A fly trickled down towards the corner of my mouth. Without opening my eyes, I moved my hand and brushed it off and I heard it buzz sluggishly away. I could tell without seeing it that it was one of those fat, late-summer flies, heavy with blood and decay. If I were to squash it, it would leave a purple-brown stain.

I didn't stir, but I knew something was wrong. I managed to squeeze one eye open and felt pain screw its way into my brain. I touched my lips with my dried-up tongue. They felt puffy and cracked. There was a foul taste in my mouth: stale, smoky, greasy, dirty.

All the colour had gone now. My one eye was looking through the gloom at a door with a scruffy grey towelling robe hanging from a hook. I swivelled my gaze to the left and saw the dull grey half-light of dawn coming in through the thin curtains. I held my breath and kept absolutely still. I heard the sound of steady breathing behind me. I closed my eye and lay there while the last shreds of dreams dissolved, until at last I was face to face with this day and this self. I touched my face, which felt numb and rubbery, like a mask. Silently I counted to fifty, then opened both eyes and gently shifted my head, feeling a queasy pain ooze round behind my forehead and flood into my temples.

Gradually I made out objects around me. I was lying on the left-hand side of a double bed, under a crooked pale duvet with a large L-shaped rip in the middle. There was a single square window quite high in the wall, an exercise bike under it that was draped with a pair of jeans and a bra. A nylon sports bag lay near the door with a squash racket on top of it. A wardrobe stood half open to reveal a few shirts on hangers. A pile of magazines tottered in the corner. A bottle of wine had tipped on to its side. The toe of a trainer poked out from under the bed. A tissue was screwed into a ball. An ashtray, a few inches from my face, overflowed with cigarette ends, which had spilled across a pair of striped boxer shorts. A digital clock showed a sickly green 4:46.

As I inched myself up into a sitting position, I saw there were smears of blood on the sheet as if painted on it in a couple of delicate brushstrokes. I stared straight ahead, then gingerly swung my feet to the floor. I stood up and the floor tipped under me. I instructed myself not to look round, but it felt as though an invisible wire was tugging my gaze and I couldn't stop myself darting a glance backwards to the shape in the bed. I saw hairy legs poking out from the duvet, a shock of darkish hair, an arm over the eyes, a mouth slackly open. That was all. I turned away again. I didn't know who he was. Didn't want to know. Mustn't.

I needed a pee, so I crept towards the door and pulled it open cautiously, wincing at the little groan it gave. There were gritty floorboards underfoot and opposite me a door, which I pushed. It didn't give on to the expected bathroom though. There was a carpet, a bed, a figure that shifted, then lifted its head and mumbled something thickly, out of deep sleep. I closed the door. I felt clammy, nauseous.

I found the tiny lavatory and sat down shakily on the toilet. My cold, sticky body felt as if it didn't belong to me, and I had to make an enormous effort to stand up again and make my way into the living room. I was hit at once by a locker-room smell of bodies and a late-night pub smell of smoke and beer. The room was strewn with clothes – his, mine. The table lay on its side, a broken mug beside it; another ashtray stood among spilled butts; crumpled beer cans rattled against my feet and a bottle of clear schnapps lay on its side. A garish picture was tipped sideways on the wall, and there was a red smear daubed beside it. There was also a strangely neat circle of what looked like brown rice on the floor. With a stab of memory, I looked up and saw the budgerigar's cage hanging above the spilled seed. The bird was asleep.

I picked up my skirt from behind the sofa and found my shirt, crumpled in the corner. Only one button remained and it was ripped along the armpit.

One shoe was under the table, its heel wobbly. After nervous fumbling I found the other in the corridor outside the bathroom. Holding my breath, I edged my way back into the bedroom and collected my bra from the exercise bike. It reeked of alcohol – schnapps, maybe. There was something sticky under the ball of my foot and when I looked down I was standing on a used condom. I peeled it off and dropped it on to the floor.

I couldn't find my knickers. I knelt down and peered under the bed, then retraced my steps along the corridor without success. I'd have to go without them. I needed to get out before the man or the person in the other room – or the bird, for that matter – woke and found me. Skirt, bra, flimsy torn shirt, whose hem I knotted round my waist. Sore feet into wobbly shoes. Jacket over the top over everything, but it was one of those stupid affairs with a single decorative button and scarcely concealed the mess underneath. I longed to be in a pair of flannel pyjamas under clean sheets, minty breath, clean limbs . . . Bag, where was my bag? It was near the front door, its contents slopping out in a heap. I shovelled everything back in, opened the door and closed it softly behind me, scuttled down the stairs and out into the grey street, where weariness hit me. For a moment I had to bend over to catch my breath.

Where was I?

I made my way to the end of the street and read the

name. Northingley Avenue, SE7. Where was that? Which way did I go to get anywhere else? My watch – still miraculously on my wrist – told me it was 5:10. I looked up and down the deserted street, as if a taxi would suddenly appear and scoop me up, then took a deep breath and set off in a random direction. It took so long to cover any distance; nothing seemed to get any closer. It was cold before the sun came up properly and I was crawling like a mucky slug along the road of unlit houses.

At last I came to a road where there were shops and one, a newsagent's, was just opening. I ducked under its half-lifted grid and approached the man behind the counter. He looked up from the papers he was stacking and his eyes widened. 'What . . . ?' he stuttered. 'Have you been mug – ?'

'Can you tell me the way to the nearest Underground station, please?'

His gaze hardened into something like disgust. I put up a hand to pull my jacket closer together and tried to look nonchalant.

'Straight that way for about half a mile.'

I bought a bottle of water and a little pack of tissues, then fished in the bottom of my bag for change.

'Thanks,' I said, but he just stared at me. I tried to smile, but my face wouldn't obey me. My mouth seemed too tight to move.

Strange people travel on the Underground at dawn. People stumbling home at the end of the previous day overlap with people at the beginning of the next, still bleary from their beds.

A man with gorgeous long dreadlocks came and sat beside me at the station while I was waiting for the first train out and played his mouth organ. I tried to give him some change but he said he wasn't a beggar, he was a wandering minstrel and I was clearly a damsel in distress. So I gave him my packet of cigarettes instead and he kissed my hand. My knuckles were grazed, my nails dirty.

When I was on the train I poured water on to a wad of tissues and dabbed at my face. Mascara, blood. I tried to see what I looked like in the window, but I was just a pale blur. I dragged a brush through my hair, and changed for the Northern Line and Archway.

I arrived at my dark green front door at ten to six and felt as if I'd climbed a mountain and run a marathon to get there. I opened the door with the double set of keys and eased my way into the hall. I dropped my bag on to the floor by the metal step-ladder and the tins of unopened paint. I kicked off my shoes and went into the kitchen, where I drank two glasses of water in quick succession. Outside, it was grey and windless. The tree in the back garden hardly stirred. I took off my shirt and pushed it deep into the rubbish bin, pulling tins and coffee grounds over the top to cover it.

The stairs seemed so steep that I went up on all fours. I crawled into the bathroom and took off the rest of my clothes. I bundled them up and shoved them into the bottom of the laundry basket, under the others. I looked at myself in the mirror and it was hard not to scream at the sight of the person looking back at me: the bleary, grubby, stained, smeary, bloody woman with the swollen lips, reddened eyes and a bird's nest of matted hair. I was like something that had been left out for the bin men to take away.

I made the shower as hot as I could bear, and then I made it hotter, burning needles of water puncturing me. I washed my hair till my scalp stung. I soaped my body and scrubbed it as if I could rub off an entire layer of skin and emerge renewed, uncontaminated. I brushed my teeth until my gums bled. I gargled with mouthwash. I rubbed cream into my face, sprayed myself with lotion, shook talcum powder wildly, rolled deodorant under my arms.

I went into my bedroom, where through the curtains the dawn had become day. The alarm clock showed 6:11. I made sure it was set for 7:10 as usual, then slid under the duvet and wrapped my arms round my knees.

'Holly?' muttered Charlie. 'Time is it?'

'Ssh. Go back to sleep. Everything's fine.'

As I fell asleep, I remembered I had forgotten to put my wedding ring back on.

3

'Holly. Holly, I've brought you some coffee. It's twenty past seven.'

For a moment I lay with my forearm over my eyes to shield them from the glare of the morning. My limbs were heavy, my mouth was parched, my head throbbed and my throat ached. I couldn't face the day; I couldn't face Charlie.

'Holly,' he said again.

I moved my arm, managed to open my eyes and look into his nice face, his brown eyes, and could see no disgust or surprise. 'Good morning, Charlie. You're up early.'

He looked warm and solid, in a shabby, unshaven, homely way. He worked at home, so he didn't have to put on a suit and a public self like I do every day, standing in front of the mirror and applying a glossy face, lipstick and lying eyes; smile, Holly, smile. He was just wearing his old grey cords and a long-sleeved, mustard-coloured shirt with a fraying neck.

I heaved myself up on to one arm and took a gulp of the coffee. Harsh, hot, black.

'Late night?' he asked.

'It just sort of went on and on.'

'I didn't hear you come in.'

'You were fast asleep. God, is that the time? I must have slept through the alarm. I'll be down in a second.'

I closed my eyes once more and heard him leave. I'd had a couple of hours of fragmented sleep, and now I had about three minutes before I had to become a person again among all the other people pretending to be people. I pulled the duvet over my head and made myself consider the events of the previous evening. It wasn't really like thinking. I felt I was being punched by someone who was skilled in such things, the blows aimed at the soft areas of my body where they would leave no mark. I found it difficult to breathe. I gasped and coughed, as if I had been washed ashore by a large wave. I thought of that woman last night – me – laughing and flirting and being so reckless and yielding to every temptation. No, not 'yielding', *courting* every temptation. The life and soul of the party. Now she just seemed like a ghastly, trashy bore. I thought of myself in that room, that other bed, with that man – whoever he was.

That's the thing, with love and sex: people write songs and poems and make movies and we swoon and fantasize about it and we all want it or we want it to be better. But in the end when it happens, when you've left the club, when the clothes are off, it's just a spotty back and a stained sheet and an awful flat somewhere in a nasty bit of London you've never been before and a slimy, crinkled-up condom on the carpet, which makes you want to throw up. I thought about going downstairs to the kitchen, sitting down opposite Charlie, telling him what I'd done last night while he'd been peacefully sleeping in our bed. The sheer stupid, squalid, ugly, nasty pointlessness of it. I imagined the way the expression would change on his face as I told him, and I squirmed further into my duvet and groaned out loud in the muffled darkness, sickened by what I'd done. If I could turn back the clock, leave the bar when Meg had done, leave the noise and lights and laughter, and come home to my husband, go to sleep innocently curled up at his side between clean sheets, wake this morning with a clear conscience . . . If only, if only . . .

Part of me knew quite well that I'd changed my life. There was a little voice in my head saying, 'You've committed adultery.' I remembered religious education lessons in school, fragments from the Bible about how you could commit adultery in your heart just by looking at someone with lust. But I hadn't committed adultery in my heart, or even in my head. I'd committed it with my body, the body I'd scrubbed so ferociously in the shower, as if I could wash it all out of me. I couldn't tell Charlie about it. It would be cruel and, like a great stain, it would pollute everything in our life.

I'm good at lying. I always have been. Since that autumn day eleven months ago, so blustery and bright and full of promise, when I tugged him into the register office, followed by the two bewildered, shy witnesses we'd grabbed from the street, I've lied lots of times, lied and pretended and faked, but never like last night. That was a first.

I heard Charlie downstairs, the clink of china, a clatter of mail falling through the letterbox on to the bare boards of the hallway, and I pulled the duvet off my face and squinted out into the room. My legs ached and my eyes ached and there were swollen glands in my neck. Perhaps I was getting flu, I thought hopefully. Then I'd have a reason to hide from the world just a little bit longer. But I knew I didn't have flu, just a hangover and a guilty conscience.

'Out of bed, Holly,' I ordered myself and, like an automaton obeying its master's command, I sat up, headache clanging round my skull, and put my feet on the floor. I waited for the room to steady, then shuffled into the bathroom where I washed my face in cold water. I stared at myself in the mirror: the darkish blonde hair that Charlie used to say looked like a lion's mane, the grey eyes that gazed back at me candidly from under thick brows, the wide mouth that smiled out at me so brightly. How was it possible that my mind should be covered with a layer of sooty grime while my face looked so fresh and happy?

'You can't fool me,' I hissed at myself, wrinkling my skin in a hideous grin. 'I know you, Holly Krauss. You can't fool me.'

'Are you going in to work at the usual time?' Charlie pulled a letter out of its envelope, glanced at it, then crumpled it into a ball.

'I've got to. I'm seeing Meg at nine. And there's someone I need to deal with first.'

Charlie looked round. 'That sounds ominous,' he said.

'I know,' I said. 'And then we're going to be frantic, preparing for next weekend. It's going to be a nightmare. Who was that letter from?'

'Next weekend? I didn't know about next weekend. What's happening?'

'I told you. Twelve executives crossing a pond on a raft. To help them bond. What are you doing today?'

'Stuff, you know. You want breakfast?'

'Maybe,' I said dubiously.

I had woken up thinking I would never need to consume anything more than coffee as long as I lived, but suddenly I felt the sort of ravenous shaky hunger that makes you think you'll faint. Had I eaten anything last night? I went through the evening as if I were fast-forwarding a video. There was lots of talk and drinking and cigarettes. Occasionally I'd catch sight of some food on my internal video but although I'd pushed it around on my plate I hadn't eaten much. I looked further back in the day. I'd forgotten about lunch and, in all probability, about breakfast as well, although I'd got up at five thirty. Had I become some new sort of human being who didn't require sleep or food?

I rummaged in the fridge, and found myself nibbling a slice of pork pie, and then I drank a liquid yoghurt. It all tasted like chalk, and the combination of the different foods made it even worse, different kinds of chalk coating my tongue and the roof of my mouth. What a strange thing, I thought, to take things from the outside world, mash them up in your mouth and push them down into your body so that some of it becomes part of you. It was enough to put anybody off their food, except that I had an unassuageable craving in my stomach. It wasn't so much appetite as the sort of signal a robot might send out when it required charging up.

Charlie was scrutinizing me. 'Here, have some more coffee. I could make you something proper, if you want.'

'It's all right.'

'Bacon and eggs, an omelette, sausages, except we haven't got any sausages. Or bacon, actually. And I'm not sure about eggs. We've got bread, though.'

'No, no,' I said, laughing – trying to laugh, needles of pain in my head. I was in the audience and on stage, all at the same time, watching myself impersonate a normal woman. 'What are your plans last night?'

Charlie looked puzzled. 'Did you say *last* night?' he asked.

'Did I?'

'Last night I was here. Tonight I don't know. Do you know?'

'We could do something. Or nothing. That would be good.' I went and stood beside him, putting my hands in his thick, clean hair, bending forward to smell his warm morning cleanliness, to place a kiss on his warm cheek. 'Charlie?'

'Mmmm?'

'Oh, nothing.'

I reached across for my mug of coffee, but fumbled it and it smashed to the floor, the coffee spreading in a puddle at my feet.

'It's all right,' Charlie said. 'I'll clear it up.' He squatted on the floor, picking up the pieces, mopping at the spillage with kitchen roll.

'It was the one we bought together at that pottery near Brighton.' I felt near to tears.

'I can fix it.'

'No, you can't. I'm so sorry.'

'It's just the handle, Holly. Look. I'll glue it and you won't even know where it was broken. Leave it to me.'

I stared at him, and thought: Now. Tell him now. Don't rush off to work. Instead, take his hand and look into his face. Talk to him honestly, for once in your stupid life. But then there was a sharp knock at the door.

'I'll get it,' I said.

It was Naomi from next door. She had moved in at the beginning of the year and she was our only friend in the street. She looked as unkempt as I felt. Her hair was standing up in wild, dark curls and she was wearing slippers. 'I'm on the scrounge,' she said, stepping into the hallway. 'I'm all out of coffee.'

'We've got plenty, and there's some in the pot. Have a cup.'

She looked nervously from me to Charlie. 'If you're sure . . .'

'I'm on the way out, but Charlie's here.'

I left them together in the kitchen and stepped out gratefully into the street, where no one knew my face or name.

I quite like it when we have projects that are impossible because then people are grateful when you manage anything at all. That was how Meg and I first met, nearly five years ago now, although sometimes it feels we've known each other for ever and it's almost a shock to realize that she wasn't around in my childhood and adolescent years. We were both in our first jobs and we were the dogsbodies in a company that was a total shambles. One day a woman arrived to check the arrangements for the following day and Derek, our boss, had forgotten all about it. As if that wasn't enough, he shut himself away in his office. After about an hour, I went in without knocking and he was crying. Even now I can remember his wretched, crumpled face and his red eyes. He looked desperate, so I told him it would be all right. We'd make sure of it. He held my hand in both of his and told me his wife had run off with her decorator.

We had nothing to lose. We were only twenty-two, and everything seemed possible. We phoned the woman, got some details about the company, then found a hotel and cobbled together some exercises from talking to people around the office. We stayed up the entire night preparing cards and little speeches. The next day, well, it wasn't the greatest office away-day of all time, but Meg and I worked like dogs getting people to cross a carpet with only a plank, a rope, a bucket and a couple of other stupid things, and we flirted and sparkled until our faces hurt – or mine did, at least. Meg is the straight man in our double-act. She doesn't flirt – when she likes a man, she gets clumsy and abrupt, laughs in the wrong places, blushes to the roots of her hair. And she never shows off. I do, and when I do she looks at me with an expression that's a mixture of indulgence and faint anxiety. She has a faint crease between her eyebrows from when she frowns. It makes her look as if she's about to burst into tears.

We did it all day and we did it in the bar all evening. Just after midnight the woman from the company came up and hugged us and said, thank you, thank you, thank you, that we had saved her job, and then Derek the next day, he was so emotional he started crying again. I sat there again and said reassuring things and looked at him. I remember shivering. We were both on a high wire, making it look easy. All it took was a glance down, the realization that there was no safety-net, and you slip and fall.

And yet at the same time it was the biggest high of my life bar nothing. I've heard people say they have a recurring nightmare that they are on a stage and a play is going on and they don't know their lines. That day showed me that it wasn't my ultimate nightmare at all. Quite the opposite: it was something I sought out. My nightmare begins when the show is over.

It wasn't many months later that Meg and I decided to go it alone. I had never met anyone I liked as much as her. I think she was almost the first person in the whole of my adult life I didn't feel the need to put on an act with, didn't need to try to charm or impress. I always knew she was kind-hearted, and in a peculiar way I felt that I was a better, or less bad, person when I was around her. Perhaps, in my twenties, I had at last found my first real friend.

We could have called our company something New Age like Swish or Enthrall or Aspire but we stuck with KS Associates, which is brilliantly derived from Krauss, my surname, and Summers, which is Meg's. We paid an old art-school boyfriend of Meg's five thousand quid to design a logo for us. Imagine the K and then imagine that the sideways V is the top half of the S, which continues below, then curves back and almost touches the bottom of the straight bit of the K. It's rather hard to picture unless you see it. We thought it looked quite classy, but when we had the party in our office to celebrate the launch of the company, someone pointed out, late at night when we were all quite drunk, that it looked like the wheelchair sign you see on disabled toilets. But it was too late to change and, anyway, Meg and I decided it was probably only an effect noticed by the very drunk.

I like the impossible, but there are limits even to impossibility. The previous week one of our staff had gone off on maternity leave and another woman had resigned and we had two away-days coming at us, like something very big and very heavy. As I stood on the Underground platform, for the second time that morning, with my aching head and sore throat and a sense of disaster hanging around me like a toxic miasma, I started to reassign the two absent women's duties in my head and work out a rough timetable and think of what lay ahead in the next seventy-two hours. The train burst out of the tunnel and I suddenly thought: Wouldn't it be nice to let myself tip over like a tree in front of it? I would never have to work out anything ever again. After all, in a hundred years I'd be dead anyway. Everybody on this jam-packed platform would be dead, most of them probably after years of loneliness and illness. I'd just be arriving early. And there are no spreadsheets in the grave. And no greyness. Just blackness, or nothing. Or maybe even as a surprise bonus there would be heaven and I would meet my old budgies and hamsters and my rabbit and my cat from when I was a little girl. And I would see my father again.

But then I saw the face of the driver, homely, jowly, unshaven, shockingly close, and I saw us, the crowd on the platform, from his point of view, all teetering on the edge over the rails. Did he have nightmares that one day someone would jump?

Our office doesn't look like what my father would have called a normal office. Not that he ever worked in a normal office. At least, it's not what normal fathers would call a normal office. We found it on the edge of Soho and took over the lease from a dot com company that had gone bust. It has no walls, no partitions, no doors. There's just a series of parallel tables like a modernist monk's refectory. There's a poky so-called conference room, but usually when we have a meeting with clients, we hold it at another long table on a dais at the end, where the abbot would sit. It has industrial-looking lights hanging from the ceiling and people have lockers but no set desks or terminals – except me, because apparently wherever I sit I make such a mess that no one wants to take my place. We inherited the design from the dot com company and have never got round to changing it. Meg and I have promised each other that one day we'll have it converted into real offices with walls so we won't have to stare at each other all day, but I doubt we'll bother.

I walked through the door at five minutes past eight, which, considering everything, I thought deserved an entry of its own in the *Guinness Book of Records*. The office was empty and silent. Good. I had about half an hour. I made myself a cup of coffee and got to work. I heard a noise and looked round sharply. It was probably something out in the street. I couldn't help smiling nervously at my situation. I was like a burglar in my own office. It took only a moment to locate Deborah's files. It was an easy task because for the most part I knew what I was looking for. Like any skilled thief, I had cased the joint well in advance and I knew where the plunder was to be found. I felt a brief glow of satisfaction at being proved right, but this was quickly replaced by a sour feeling about what had been done. I photocopied some of the papers, then replaced the files in the locker just as I heard footsteps on the stairs.

4

I knew it was Meg, always first in the office. Except today. She was wearing a white cotton shirt and her hair was pulled back from her face. There were little silver studs in her ears but no makeup on her face. I thought how fresh she looked, like an unblemished piece of fruit, an apple or a peach. She started with surprise when she saw me, then came and sat beside me. 'I thought you'd be late,' she said, 'after last night. What did you get up to?'

I gave a sort of shrug that meant: Later. We'll talk about it later.

She stared at me. 'You've done something stupid, haven't you?'

It's important not to underestimate Meg. She sees right through me. She can even see through my shrugs.

'This isn't the time,' I said. 'I came in early because I wanted to check through this. Look.'

I laid out the photocopies in front of her.

She looked at them with a frown of concentration. 'You're going to have to talk me through them,' she said.

'These are Deborah's so-called documents,' I said.

'Invoices, reports, expenses forms, plans, you know. The sort of stuff we do.'

'Yes, I can see that.'

'It's all rubbish,' I said. 'Look at this expenses claim. She wasn't even there for the Sussex job.'

'Yes, but –'

'And the assessment for the weekend after next. The one she's been writing all week, the one she said was finished. This is it.'

Meg picked up an almost blank sheet of paper. 'How do you know?' she said. 'She may have the rest of it at home.'

'I've been through it all. The only question in my mind is whether she's dishonest or a fantasist who believes her chronic lies. By the way, that train she missed last week, back from her friend's funeral. There is no such train. I checked.'

Meg was clearly shocked. 'Are you sure?'

'Yes.'

'We need to talk to her.'

'We need to fire her.'

'Holly, we can't. There are procedures.'

'We're a tiny company, Meg. Someone like Deborah could drag us down. We can deal with it in a decent way. We'll talk to her, explain the situation, say she has to leave. We could even suggest she sees a doctor. We'll do it today. As soon as she walks through the door.'

'She's away today and tomorrow, remember, at that conference.'

'When she comes back, then. No putting it off.'

Meg bit her lip. 'I don't know,' she said. 'We'd better talk to Trish about this.'

'Trish may run the office but this is our company. It's our decision.'

'We're like a family here.'

'Which is why we can't survive with someone like Deborah.'

Meg's cheeks had gone pink as they always did at times of strong emotion. 'How can you do that?' she asked, in a tone of wonder.

'What?'

'Last night you almost get into a fight in a pub. Next thing you're having a drink with the man who could have killed you. That was the moment we left, as soon as we were sure you weren't going to get killed. Where did you go after that? I rang your house when I got in. You weren't there. And now you're in here virtually at dawn pretending to be Sherlock Holmes. How can you compartmentalize your life like that? Don't things ever leak into each other?'

'That's the point of compartments,' I said, tidying the photocopies away. 'That was the problem with the *Titanic*. The hole wouldn't have mattered if the water could have been confined by barriers, but it spread everywhere and the ship sank. If the water had been contained in one area of the ship it would have gone on its merry way and reached New York.'

'The *Titanic*? What on earth are you going on about?'

I sat in the meeting with a look of professional alertness on my face. I was in control of the facts, I jotted down the suggestions of our clients, assured them that the coming weekend was going to answer all their needs. I leaned towards people with a listening smile. I even managed not to be rude to the smug-faced senior executive from the pharmaceutical company.

'Team-building,' he said, and stroked his chin. 'A sense of common purpose, of intellectual adventure, mutuality and shared interests, all pulling in the same direction. That's what we need here.'

Or a pay rise, I thought. And a new boss. 'That's what we're here for,' I said.

'A colleague of mine recommended you. He said you left them all fizzing with excitement at the end of the two days. That's what we'd like.'

'Fizz,' I said. 'We'll do our best.' I heard one of our work-experience girls give a suppressed cough and I stared at her warningly.

I shook his hand firmly when he left, smiled my friendliest smile.

'Right,' said Meg, handing me my coat. 'Coffee.'

'We can have one here. We've got so much to –'

'You don't get let off that easily. Let's go to Luigi's and we can talk properly.'

So we walked into the gusting wind and down the road to the dark little café, whose interior was as warm and snug as a boat's cabin, with its dim lights and hissing espresso machines.

'Was I horrible to that guy last night?' I said. 'What was his name?'

'Todd,' said Meg. 'I think he got a bit of a fright.'

'Seemed nice, though.'

'Quite nice,' said Meg, neutrally. I raised my eyebrows at her. She blushed violently and looked away. 'What did you get up to last night?' she asked, after a pause. 'That's what we're really here for.'

I looked at her soft round face, which always seemed Edwardian to me, with the dimple in her chin, her mop of curly hair. How would she ever understand? 'Oh, you know. It just went on a bit.' I sipped at the coffee, burning my upper lip, relishing the pain. 'Maybe I'd had a bit too much to drink by the end.'

'By the end?'

'You're my friend, not my mother. I was having fun, that's all.'

'Did you go somewhere after?'

'Yes. We went –' I stopped dead. I didn't know who the 'we' was and I didn't know where we'd gone. The evening didn't fit together in my head. It shifted around in queasy fragments. A dark room full of people, a riverbank, splintering glass, a cab, a fever on the bed. Thrashing bodies. I rubbed my temples, trying to ease away the images.

'Well?'

I drained my coffee and put down the mug with a sharp click. 'The truth is, Meg, if you really want to know, I can't remember much about it.'

'Because you were so drunk?'

'It became a bit like a dream. You know.'

'What time did you get home?'

'This is just like being a teenager,' I said. 'A bit before six.' Just five hours ago, I thought. How could five hours crawl by so slowly?

'Six? Christ, Holly, how are you still functioning? What did Charlie say?'

'Not much. He was asleep, and then it was time to go to work.'

'Doesn't he mind?'

I thought of Charlie, squatting on the kitchen floor, carefully picking up the mug I'd broken. 'I think we should get back to the office now.'

'Was there a man involved?' She said it so that it sounded more like a statement of fact than a question.

'What?'

'Last night.'

'Kind of,' I mumbled, then made myself look into Meg's eyes defiantly.

'Kind of. You mean, you had sex with someone else?'

'It didn't mean anything.'

'How can it not mean anything?'

'I was drunk and hyped up. I had sex with a stranger. End of story.'

'Or beginning of story. Holly, can you hear yourself?'

I could. My voice was coming from a long way off and I was listening to it carefully, trying to make sense of the words, which didn't seem to have boundaries but ran together like a dirty river so that I had to concentrate hard to make sense of them.

'What about Charlie?' She said it very softly, and her voice had an ominous gravity about it.

'Charlie's Charlie,' I replied inanely.

'Are you going to tell him?'

'What for? To make him feel terrible too? It happened and it's over and it won't happen again.'

'How do you know?'

'I – I won't let it happen again. It was . . .' In the fog of my brain, I searched for the word. 'An aberration.'

Meg looked at me for a long time. My heart was pounding uncomfortably quickly, but I made myself glare back at her. I wasn't going to drop my eyes or look away. In the end I had to because she looked so sober and thoughtful, as if she was making up her mind about something. She looked, I thought suddenly, as if she pitied me. I couldn't bear that.

It was Meg who had introduced me to Charlie. She'd met him because he had gone to art college with her cousin Luke, and she invited me to go with the three of them to a film. I remember the film, *Lost in Translation*. I remember the weather, warm and windy, with leaves swirling around us when we walked up the road together. I remember what I was wearing: jeans ripped at the knee, canvas boots and my oldest leather jacket. I hadn't thought it was going to be a special day. And I remember what Charlie was wearing. Meg and Luke faded into the background. It was Charlie I was aware of, every gesture he made, every word he spoke, every tiny glance he sent in my direction. I knew, with that delicious, unbeatable feeling of terror, that he was equally aware of me. In the bar our hands brushed, and it sent little jolts of electricity through me. In the cinema, we were separated and I sat next to Meg, who had a bad cold. She kept blowing her reddened nose with a large handkerchief. Her eyes were watering. Did I think, Meg likes Charlie too; you mustn't? Yes. But I also thought, He's looking at me now, I can feel the weight of his glance on me like something tangible. I thought, Something's got to happen.

Afterwards, Luke and Charlie invited us to have a meal with them in the brasserie across the road, but Meg said she needed to get home to bed, and I went with her. We got a taxi, and at first sat in an awkward silence, not looking at each other. Then, as we arrived at her flat, she laid a hand on my knee, and said, 'It's all right, you know, Holly. He likes you, not me.' I muttered something inadequate, and then – this is typical of Meg's generosity – she said, 'Even if he didn't like you, that doesn't mean he'd like me instead. You're not taking him away or anything.' She blew her nose firmly on her handkerchief, kissed my cheek and got out of the taxi.

What would I have done if she hadn't spoken? I like to think I would have done nothing, but who knows? I waited until she'd opened her front door and disappeared inside, then told the cab driver to turn round and go back the way we'd come. Luke and Charlie were still eating when I got there and I sat with them, drank red wine from their glasses, stole their chips and tried not to think about Meg, lying in bed with her watery eyes. I ate a spoonful of lemon sorbet, put my hand on Charlie's thigh and he put his leg across mine. We shifted close to each other and pretended to listen to Luke. Later, he took me home.

Meg had said I'd like him and I did. She had said he was shy at first but when you got to know him he was funny – and he was funny. He made me laugh from the moment we met. She had said he was a talented artist. He could do anything, oil-painting, watercolour, sketching in charcoal. At art school he had written a comic strip about an inadequate super hero that had become a local cult. For his degree show he took the contents of a skip and turned them into an installation. I saw the photos. It was amazing. As soon as I met him, I said to myself, You're the one. I would have married him the day after we met, if the law had permitted it. Instead it took a month.

Since that day in the taxi, Meg has never said anything to me, except nice things, and I've never said anything to her, except nice things, and probably we never will talk about it properly, not even when we're old and the urgent fever of love is all in the past. But it's no use pretending. I always knew she wanted Charlie, and that she didn't stop wanting him because he'd fallen for me. She isn't like that. She has a fuse that takes a long time to light and then it burns slowly, steadily, hard to extinguish. Charlie and I have never talked about it either, but he's especially nice to her – warm and slightly teasing – and she's shy with him, self-conscious and a bit abrupt. Now, confessing my infidelity to her, I felt sharply shamed by how I had trampled on so many precious things.

'The thing is,' I said slowly, honest at last, 'the thing is, Meg, I don't know why I did it. I'm not just dismissing it. I don't want to tell Charlie because then it would have a meaning, when really it was senseless.' That wasn't enough. I was being too easy on myself. 'Horribly, cruelly senseless.'

There was a long silence. I looked at her face and I couldn't tell what she was thinking. She ran a finger round the rim of her coffee cup and frowned. 'Are things going wrong with you and Charlie?' she asked at last.

I shook my head. 'We don't have a marriage like . . . well, I was going to say my parents, but they're not really anyone's model, are they? Like your parents, then. We often lead separate lives. I'm always charging around with work, and he's trying to get his going properly. He can shut himself up in his study for hours and when I go in he looks at me as if I'm a stranger. I know it all happened quickly. I mean our marriage. I wasn't exactly the type to settle down anyway, but I know we were right. Well, I was right. Maybe Charlie wasn't, maybe I'm a bad bet. But you shouldn't stop to think too much about things like marriage, you should just do it. Hold on to what you want. Hold on to love.'

I sat back in my seat, exhausted. I didn't know if I believed what I'd just said, or at least somewhere inside myself believed it, but couldn't reach that part of me so had to mouth the words, mimic the feelings and wait for them to come true again. That's the way to do it: pretend to be yourself and maybe you will be again.

'Do you feel awful?'

'I could do with an early night. But I'll be fine. That's not what you meant, is it?'

She looked at me curiously and put one finger on the side of her mouth, which is something she does when she's thinking. 'You should be more careful, my friend,' she said.

I phoned Charlie at home. 'Day going all right?' I asked.

'Yes,' he said.

'Have you started on the illustration yet?'

'Not yet. I need time.'

'I know, but it would be a shame to lose the commission and you know how much we need the –'

'I've said I'll do it. I'm sorry. We can't all get ten things done before breakfast.'

I felt a hot jet of rage in my chest, followed immediately by a liquid jolt of shame. Who was I to get angry with anybody, let alone Charlie? 'You're right,' I said. I told him I'd be home by six. I'd buy something to eat or we could get a takeaway.

'Great,' he said.

'Love you,' I said, but he'd already put the phone down.

I did leave work at the proper time. I had planned to go to the supermarket and behave like a proper wife, loading the trolley with food for the week, planning ahead rather than living from moment to moment. I could cook a real meal, a chicken; even I could cook a chicken, surely. The thought of food made me want to gag, although at the same time I was hungry.

On my way to the Underground I passed a row of shops. One, a little food store, had a smashed window, covered with a plastic sheet flapping in the wind. An Asian woman in a grey nylon work coat was bent down on the pavement. A queasy memory wormed its way into my consciousness. This was where I had been last night. This was my fault. She looked up at me as I stopped beside her. 'How awful for you,' I said.

She just shrugged. She looked tired and almost accepting, as if it was a part of life to be dealt with, like the wind and the rain. 'It's not the first time.'

I picked up a basket from outside the shop. 'I need to get some stuff, anyway,' I said. 'I can't think why I've never come in here before. It's on my way home.'

It wouldn't be chicken now. I bought a packet of ground coffee and some tea-bags, a couple of pints of milk, which, when I got home, I discovered had been mechanically treated in some way so that it didn't go sour and was impossible to drink. I also chose two shrivelled yellow apples in a Cellophane pack, eight extra-soft pink toilet rolls and some washing-up liquid, four packets of cigarettes, half a bottle of overpriced gin, lime juice, orange-juice concentrate, which I hate and Charlie hates even more. I had to collect a second basket for muesli, sesame-seed bread, a jar of marmalade, a tub of spreadable butter, several packets of chewing-gum, digestive biscuits and beer. When I'd paid, I heaved up the bags, the handles cutting into my fingers, and turned to go.

In the next street I passed a branch of my bank. I stopped at the machine outside and checked my balance. A hundred and forty-two pounds and forty-three pence. I withdrew a hundred and forty in clean, bright, factory-fresh notes. I rummaged in my bag and found an old envelope. I put the money inside and scrawled on it, in what I thought might look like the handwriting of a moronic hooligan, 'FOR THE WINDOW'. I took a deep breath and walked back to the shop. There was a man behind the counter. I supposed him to be the husband of the woman I'd met outside. I put the envelope on the counter.

'I found this outside on the pavement,' I said. 'It must be for you.'

He looked puzzled and I left. As I got outside it started to rain with the plump drops that soak you instantly. I hoped it was a convincing enough story and he wouldn't hand over the money to the police. What would God say, if He existed? He would probably say I ought to have confessed. Instead I just stood still in the rain, letting it drench me thoroughly.

I called out as I came in, but there was no reply. I unpacked the supplies and put my head round Charlie's study door. He wasn't there, although the radio was on, and the room was in a catastrophic mess. Sheets of paper were scattered over the floor, piles of books had toppled, ashtrays were pushed under the chair and the drawing-board, CDs teetered on every spare surface. On the sketch pad on his desk a faint line of pencil ended in an elaborate doodle. There were also five half-finished mugs of tea, two brown apple cores and the skin of a satsuma. And there, on the window-sill, was the mug I'd dropped that morning. I examined it: you could barely see the hairline crack where Charlie had mended it. I closed the door.

If I went to sleep now, I'd never be able to wake up. Instead I pulled on some old jeans and one of Charlie's paint-spattered T-shirts, and forced myself into action. I turned on all the lights downstairs, fake daytime in the darkening evening, then hauled the step-ladder into the middle of the hall so I could scrape off wallpaper. It was a job I'd started several months ago when we'd moved here but hadn't got round to finishing. It's odd how you can get used to living in a house with unlovely shredding walls and bare plaster.

And that was how Charlie found me, three-quarters of an hour later, when he came through the door in his lovely soft suede jacket that I'd bought for him. I stepped off the ladder and kissed his eyelids, and he hugged my dusty, aching, tired, guilty body.

'What I want to know is, where do you get all your energy from? Can I have some?'

Now, at this moment I could have stepped back, looked him in the eye and said, 'Yesterday night, Charlie, I don't know why, I can't say who, I had sex with a stranger.' A little thrill ran through me, like a shiver of pure and infinite cold, like a delicious lick of terror.

I smiled back at him, bright as innocence. 'Big decision. Chinese, Indian or Thai takeaway?'

Later, we had sex, made love, fucked. I don't know what to call it, because I didn't want to do anything but close my eyes and sleep and sleep and sleep, but I couldn't say that. Not after everything. So when he smiled at me in that particular way, I smiled back, although my face felt tight and my eyes raw. And when he put his arms round me, I put mine round him too and pulled him close and murmured into his ear. And he didn't know, he didn't begin to guess, that I wasn't there at all.

5

As I was standing on the Tube, swaying between two large sweaty men, I had a feeling of existential freedom. There was no law of nature, like gravity, forcing me to go to work, to continue on the rails of my old life. I could stay on the train, change at Leicester Square, go to Heathrow, catch any plane and never come back to England for the rest of my life. First, I'd have to go home for my passport. And what about money? Everything was in the house. As an investment that was probably fine, but there was a definite liquidity problem. Abroad was difficult as well. The idea of existential freedom had probably been invented at a time when visas weren't such a big deal, and you didn't get grilled in the arrivals hall of airports about how long you wanted to stay and whether you were planning to get a job. There were limits to freedom, limits to whom you could become.

So I got out of the train, went up the escalators and out into a grey, drizzly morning. I thought of Charlie lying in bed and wondered if he had any work to do. I decided I ought to phone him. I reached into my bag but couldn't find my mobile. I couldn't find it when I got to the office either. I tried to remember when I had last used it and couldn't. On the previous day I'd used the office phone. So either it was at home or I'd dropped it somewhere, most probably on my lost evening. It might have been stolen by now, but perhaps a normal human being had picked it up. I've spent my life breaking and losing things. I don't think I've ever owned an umbrella for longer than a week. Everything – purses, sunglasses, keys, hats, anything that isn't permanently buttoned or fastened to my body – I've left around the world. That's a good thing about a mobile phone. You can't call up sunglasses and ask where they are. I dialled my own number and after a couple of rings a man answered. 'You've got my phone,' I said.

'I didn't steal it,' said the voice, then laughed as if it was a big joke.

'I'll take your word for it,' I said. 'I think I left it in a pub or club in Soho.'

'A pub or club?'

'I'm not very good on names,' I said. 'It might have been a pub on Wardour Street or . . . there's a club round the corner from there, one called the something house . . .'

'The Red House.'

'Exactly,' I said. 'It was there, then. I'm so sorry. I leave it everywhere. I was wondering if there's any way you could get it to me. I could send a messenger.'

'Where do you work?'

'Soho.'

'I'm in the Strand. I'll drop it by at lunchtime.'

'That would be fantastic.'

'It would be my pleasure.'

'Have you got it with you? Sorry. That's a very stupid question. Obviously you have it with you.'

'I was trying to think what to do with it.'

'Well, you can stop now.'

I named a café in Dean Street, one o'clock, and put the phone down, then plunged into my day as if I had held my nose and jumped into a foaming torrent. I'd written a 'to do' list that covered two sheets of paper. It was a mixture of calls to be made, messages to be written, meetings to be held, arrangements to be made, decisions to be taken, ideas to be had. It was like a malignant alien creature in an old science-fiction film. The more you chopped bits off, the larger and more aggressive it became. I didn't have time to think or feel. All I did was respond to the immediate stimulus in front of me, deal with it and push it behind me. Things came in and out of my field of attention. Most notably there was Meg. Together we would talk and make quick decisions. Full cups of coffee were pushed in front of me and empty ones taken away. I ate mouthfuls of food without knowing what they were. Then I looked up and saw it was ten past one. I glanced around me, dazed. I barely knew where I was. My list was obliterated under a series of arrows, scrawled notes and crossings-out. My desk was clear, spiritually, if not in actuality. Everything was in a file or somebody else's problem. I gathered what remained into a pile and pushed it into my locker. I shouted to Meg that I would be back in a minute. Meg called a response, but I couldn't hear it as I clattered down the stairs.

I saw him as soon as I entered the café. He was a big man, solid. His jacket was hung over the back of his chair and he'd rolled up his shirtsleeves. He had thick dark hair combed carefully backwards. A mobile phone lay on the table in front of him. 'My phone, I presume,' I said glibly.

He stood up, smiled and held out his hand, but when I took it he didn't let it go at once, squeezing my fingers between his.

'Hello, Holly,' he said. 'My beautiful Holly.'

The knowledge crawled into my brain like a small insect. I could almost feel it making its way to the front of my consciousness. Oh no, I thought. Not this. Please. I thought of picking up the phone and making a dash for it, but my body felt heavy and leaden. You can run but you can't hide. That was what my father used to shout when he played tag with me in the park near our house. It used to make me feel scared even then. I pulled my hand from his.

'Just as beautiful in the light,' he said.

'I'm sorry,' I said. 'I don't . . . I can't . . .'

'Don't be sorry.'

'I mean, it was a stupid mistake.'

'Oh, I don't think so,' he said with a smile. 'It's Rees, by the way. In case you don't remember.'

'I don't want to remember. I was drunk. That's all.'

'You were wild.'

'I'm going now.'

'No, you're not.'

I put out my hand for the phone but he grasped me tightly by the wrist and wrenched me towards him. 'Let go.'

'Don't tell me you don't want it again. Not after our night together.'

'Let go,' I said, more firmly.

'You wanted it then, just as much as I did. You said –'

'Don't be ridiculous.'

'Married, are you?' he said, twisting my wrist so that my ring showed. 'Who to? Which poor sod? Let me see, is it David, or Connor or Fred or Charlie or Wesley? Ah, Charlie, is it?'

'Take your hand off me, you creep.'

'I've got his number safely on my phone anyway. And some others.'

I made myself look him in the eyes and the thought of him and what we'd done caused a wave of nausea to ripple through me. 'Don't be pathetic,' I said. 'Just let this go.'

'And I've got your knickers. Remember? Lacy black things.'

There was a red mist in front of my eyes. I jerked at my wrist but he held me firmly, fingers digging into my flesh. 'What?' I said. 'If you think you can blackmail me, you're even more stupid than you look.'

'Yeah?' he said. 'If you think you can just walk out of this door and pretend it didn't happen, then . . .'

He didn't finish the sentence. I drew back the hand he wasn't holding and slapped his cheek as hard as I could, leaving the stinging red marks of my fingers to fade slowly.

'You little bitch,' he gasped.

'Excuse me, but if you're going to do that,' said a voice behind us, 'take it outside.'

'I'm going right now,' I said. 'And you'd better stay out of my way.'

'You're asking for trouble,' he shouted, as I left. 'And I swear you'll get it. You're fucked, you are.'

6

I walked around the area for an hour. Lunch was a
nectarine I bought in the market. Even so, when I
got back to the office I was still steaming. I was so
angry with that man and so bitterly, contemptuously
angry with myself and so humiliated and upset that
I was in my own hot emotional fog. I stumbled into
our so-called conference room and found Meg and
Trish having a muttered conversation. Meg looked
round at me and seemed embarrassed, as if I'd caught
her doing something she shouldn't.

'I had a word with Deborah,' she said, 'about the
various problems we've been having.'

'Deborah?' I said. 'I thought she was at the conference.'

'She left early,' said Trish. 'She just got in.'

'And?'

'We raised some of the concerns with her. We
wanted to hear her side of the story. She admitted
that she had got behind. She hadn't wanted to tell us
about it because it was Lola's fault.'

'What?'

Lola had joined us only a couple of months before.
She was young and eager. She was learning fast but

her responsibilities didn't extend much beyond making coffee and carrying files around.

'She was trying to involve her in the Cook account.'

Trish embarked on a complicated story of what was supposed to have gone wrong but I interrupted her.

'No, no, no,' I said. 'That's rubbish. Leave this to me. I'm going to talk to Deborah myself. Ask her to come and see me in five minutes, will you, Trish? I need to make a call first.'

Even now I could see Deborah as Meg and I had seen her when we had first interviewed her a few months earlier. She was tall, immaculately groomed and had an air of complete confidence. It had almost felt as if she was the one conducting the interview. If we hadn't exactly warmed to her, well, that was part of the point. We weren't looking for a new best friend. We wanted someone hard-working, efficient and generally formidable. Deborah looked all of that as soon as she walked though the door. Her reference had been a bit odd. It was clear she had fallen out with her previous employer, but even that didn't worry us. Especially me. I liked the idea of employing someone abrasive. I told Meg we needed a bad cop in the office. We already had enough good ones. The problem was that she was meant to be a bad cop to other people, not to us.

When she came into the conference room, she was looking as impressive as ever.

'How was Roehampton?' I asked.

'It was all right,' she said.

'Anything stand out?'

She gave a shrug. 'Not really,' she said. 'I left early.'

'Oh, stop this,' I said. 'I just rang Jo Palmer, who happens to be running the conference. You never even signed on.'

I have to admit that I was impressed by the aplomb with which Deborah responded to being caught out. She looked puzzled and slightly hurt. 'Have you been spying on me?' she said.

'That's my job,' I said. 'I run this company.'

'I went to the conference,' she said. 'Maybe I forgot to pick up my badge.'

But I had my file with me. I opened it and laid out in front of her the photocopies I had made, like an unbeatable poker hand.

'What's this?' she said.

'You know what it is,' I said. 'We talked about what to do about you and I had a moment of weakness where I thought we could let you off with a warning. But then you tried to put the blame on Lola. What was that about?'

'She's inexperienced,' Deborah said. 'I've been covering for her.'

'Are you insane?' I said. 'Do you never give up? Look at these pieces of paper. You've been lying. You've been defrauding the company.'

She looked at me, unshaken. 'I'm good at my job,' she said. 'You know that.'

'You're fired,' I said. I looked at my watch. I couldn't remember the date. I couldn't even remember the time of year. Leaves were falling, weren't they? 'We'll pay you until the end of the month. But I want you out of the office.'

There was a long pause. I had her attention now.

'You can't do this,' she said. 'I left a good job to come here. I've got a flat. I've got a mortgage.'

'You're right,' I said. 'You're good at your job. I don't know what's gone wrong. You clearly can't carry on here. But I wonder if you need some help . . .'

Deborah pulled a face as if there was suddenly a terrible smell in the room. 'Don't patronize me, you stuck up . . .' She paused as if she was unable to find a word bad enough for what I was. 'They don't like you, you know. You think you're brilliant, dashing around, being crazy and dipsy and winning people over, but you don't fool us. You're pathetic, really. You're a fake.'

I took a deep breath and made myself speak quietly and slowly. 'You'd better leave now,' I said.

She laughed. 'You think you're so fucking clever,' she said. 'One day someone's going to do something to that stuck-up little face of yours.'

I couldn't stop myself smiling. 'Are you threatening me, Deborah?'

She stood up and there was a fierce glow in her eyes. 'You think everybody will just lie down for you, that's what you think. One day someone will get back up and then you'll see. It'll just take one.'

She left like a small hurricane, sweeping through the office. When she was gone, I walked down to Old Compton Street. There's a particular cream cake they make in the patisserie: it's got this very light pastry on top, it's really one of the great creations of the Western world. I bought ten, one for everybody in the office, and ten cappuccinos. I took them back to the office. Trish and Meg looked a bit shellshocked. I walked over to them. 'You think I did the wrong thing?'

They looked at each other.

'I don't know,' said Meg. 'It was complicated.'

'No, it wasn't,' I said.

I called everybody together. I talked very briefly about the problems in the office and how it was important for all of us to talk to each other when things were going wrong, but this inspirational sermon segued into a tribute to the cream cakes and within a couple of minutes everybody's nose was deep into them and it looked like a toddler's birthday party.

Forty-five minutes later, Meg and I were driving out of London. Meg was reading the map with great precision and I was driving too quickly. We were on our way to inspect the venue for the weekend event.

'Venue' makes it sound formal and bland, like a modern hotel with identical bedrooms, well-stocked and over-priced mini-bars, a dinky gym where businessmen sit on rowing machines for fifteen minutes before their nine o'clock meeting, and conference facilities. It wasn't. It was a semi-converted water-mill in Oxfordshire, covered with Virginia creeper. As well as the stream running through it, there was a small duckweedy lake at the end of the tangled stretch of land, a dozen or so higgledy-piggledy bed-rooms with the suspicion of damp under the wall-paper. It was perfect: trees for adults to climb; water for them to fall into; a long, shuttered dining room where they'd have to sit round a single table together in the evenings, no other building for miles and miles. It had been bought recently by friends of friends of Meg, who wanted to get away from their stressed life in London and were now discovering what real stress was, among the cowpats, under the dripping trees.

'This feels good,' I said. 'It reminds me of when it was just you and me.'

'Yes,' said Meg, with a hollow laugh. 'Those were the days.' There was a pause. I thought she was looking at the map. 'I suppose it's all right. About Deborah. I mean, I hope she won't sue us.'

'I hope she will,' I said. 'We'll show her.'

Meg just coughed.

London feels like a different city according to which way you leave it. When you head towards

Oxford, it seems to dribble on and on and then you blink and everything's green. Water sprayed up from the wheels of cars as the rain, which had been threatening all morning, started to fall at last. I turned on the windscreen wipers and, through the arcs swept clear with each stroke, saw a grey, sodden, empty landscape. I turned on the radio, jabbed at buttons, jumping between stations, then gave up and turned it off again.

Corinne and Richard were waiting. They'd lit a fire in the large sitting room, and made a pot of coffee. Corinne handed round a plate of little sponge cakes with raspberries on top and I devoured two, one after the other, my cheeks bulging like a hamster's. I stretched out my legs to feel the warmth of the flames and sighed. The stream gushed and burbled outside, and when the sun came out from the heavy clouds it threw weak beams of light over the wooden floor.

'Maybe I should do it,' I said.

'Do what?'

'Run away from London.'

'I wouldn't call this running away, exactly.'

'Escape,' I said dreamily. 'Begin afflict.'

'What? Afflict?'

'Begin afresh,' I corrected myself. My eyelids were dragging down, so I snapped them open, sat up straighter, gulped my good, strong coffee, listened to the rain on the windowpanes. The garden outside was damp green; on Saturday, seven men and five women would be playing games out there.

'Right,' I said, reaching for the last cake. 'To work.'

We went to the bedrooms first: fine, except that a fire blanket and mini-extinguisher were needed on the top landing. Then we visited the kitchen, which had a blissful half-sized door that opened on to the gushing stream.

'Is this safe?' asked Meg, always the practical one.

'We're not opening a crèche here,' I said.

'We keep it locked,' said Richard. 'It's an architectural feature.'

With some difficulty, I drew back the heavy set of bolts, pushed open the little hatch, and pushed my head out. Flicks of water stung my cheek and the wind whipped my hair across my face. I sighed and closed my eyes.

'Holly?'

'Mmmm. Coming.'

I pulled my head in, shut the door.

'Do you want to discuss the food for Saturday evening?'

'I'm sure it's fine.'

'I've done a menu for lunch, and breakfast on Sunday and made a list of ingredients that are available for them to use in the curry you want them to cook, so if you care to look at it and –'

'I'm sure it's fine,' I repeated.

'Oh.' Corinne looked taken aback, but she rallied brightly. 'Then there's the drink.'

'I trust you completely.'

'But –'

'Just make sure that there's more than you think necessary, then double it. Let's go and have a look outside.'

'Do you want to borrow some boots? The grass is still wet.'

'It doesn't matter.'

Meg and I walked past the stream, through what must once have been a vegetable garden and over the spongy ground towards the lake. It was gorgeously dank and green. I picked up a stone and threw it into the water, watching how the duckweed closed over it immediately, leaving no trace. We looked at each other and giggled.

'I'm looking forward to seeing them fall off their raft into that,' I said.

'We want them to recommend us to their friends,' said Meg.

'We'll give them blankets and we'll sparkle and flutter our eyelashes at them,' I said. 'They'll recommend us.'

Meg pulled a face. 'You make us sound like escort girls,' she said.

'Aren't we?' I said.

'Stop it, Holly,' she said. 'Don't talk like that. You've seen the letters we've had – raised productivity, improved morale.'

I put my arm round her shoulders and she put her hand on mine. 'That's right, my dear,' I said. 'I've read the brochure. Do you notice something?'

'What?'

'There are some birds making an annoying noise and the wind is rustling in the trees, but apart from that it's almost quiet. It's difficult to believe that London's in the same world.'

'We're about to go back there.'

'What I'd really like to do is check into one of the rooms myself, go to sleep and you could wake me up when you come for the weekend.'

'Unfortunately you've got a life you have to deal with. And a husband.'

Meg drove back and I tried to read the map, and talked. 'Since I couldn't book a room, what I'd really like to do is climb into the back and go to sleep.'

'Be my guest,' said Meg.

People always say that that's when they felt safest. Their parents would drive them back from somewhere late at night and they would sleep and feel safe. My main memory of being driven by my father is that we left London to go to some party and we didn't find it, and then my mum and dad started having a row and my dad lost control of the car and drove off the road and we ended up in a ditch. A farmer had to pull us out with his tractor. It was quite fun, actually.

I didn't crawl into the back but I did fall asleep

and I only woke when Meg pulled up outside my house and said cheerfully that we were home.

'You're the best driver in the world,' I said. 'I didn't feel a thing.'

7

And then it was Sunday evening and it was all over. I came back into the house to find Meg in Corinne and Richard's kitchen, her hands cupped round a mug of coffee. 'You can come out now,' I said. 'They've gone.'

Meg gave me a weary grin. 'Are you sure there isn't one hiding somewhere?'

I shook my head. 'I counted them all out,' I said. 'Is there any more of that?' Meg nodded at a cafetière by the sink and I poured black coffee into a mug with a jaunty message written on it. 'I always feel there should be something more,' I said. 'Shouts of "encore" and bouquets of flowers.'

'Just so long as their cheque doesn't bounce,' said Meg. 'How much sleep did you get?'

'I'm not sure. Did I sleep?'

'I did.'

'You always do.'

'It's not a crime, you know. Sleep's not immoral or lazy. You don't have to stay up all night to prove yourself.'

'I know that. Meg?'

'Yes.'

'Do you ever feel squeezed out?'

'Squeezed out?'

'Like one of those old cloths you use for wiping the floor. Then you twist it and lots of horrible dirty water pours out.'

'Let me get this straight,' said Meg. 'In this image, if you're the old cloth, the horrible dirty water must represent the employees of Macadam Associates with whom we've just spent the weekend.'

'And then you put the cloth into a cupboard and when you next find it, it's gone all stiff and nasty and crusty.'

Her tone became more serious. 'It's Sunday evening. It's raining. You've worked solidly for days.'

'I don't know if "solidly" is the right word. "Hollowly", maybe.'

'You're tired,' she continued. 'You need to go home and see Charlie and have a long bath and sleep without the alarm clock.'

'Yeah.'

'We can come into work later than usual tomorrow. I think we owe ourselves that, at least.'

'In lieu of paying ourselves.'

'Maybe we'll be able to take a proper salary before long. We're doing well.'

'Sometimes I think the only grown-up thing about my marriage is that we've started to worry about our mortgage.'

'We'll be fine,' said Meg.

'You're being very reassuring this evening.'

She glanced at me briefly. 'That's my role, isn't it?' she said drily.

'What about you?' I said.

'What do you mean?'

'Are you seeing that guy? Todd? Or was I so horrible to him that I scared him away from you as well as me?'

'I'm not sure,' she said. She stared straight ahead.

'Have you seen —'

'Leave it. I don't want to talk about it.'

'Whenever you do want to . . .' I said. I was going to add something, but I couldn't make the right words come out.

Everyone has their own story, but sometimes they don't know what the story is, or where they fit into it. Say your parents think of you as fickle and irresponsible; say your friends think you're a cheery extrovert; say at work they insist that you're the life and soul of the party: and there you are, you're trapped in a version of yourself, in your narrow margins, and the terrible thing is that mostly you don't even know it. And because we're all a mystery to ourselves and we need other people to explain us and make us come true, you gradually see yourself like that as well. It's the story you think you're in. A comedy. A farce. You lose the other bits of yourself. But every so often you're allowed to see yourself differently, tell yourself differently. You become another story altogether, deeper and stranger and more interesting, with new meanings.

Meg and I earn our money by shaking people up, letting the pattern fall differently for a while. But then they go home, and we go home, and what's really different? Your old world closes round you, your old self returns. People think that they can change their lives and themselves. Build a raft and cross a lake, play a game where you have to relax and fall backwards into the arms of your colleague, sit round in a circle talking about all the things in your life you've ever done wrong and all the choices you regret. And then you'll be able to start again.

When I say 'you' I mean me, of course. Me, Holly Krauss, whom I can't escape however hard I try. I'd tried so hard that weekend, harder than ever before, the most energetic person among the whole crowd of energetic, intoxicated people, so that now my tank was empty, my cupboard was bare.

I was thinking about Stuart, one of the participants. He was about forty, maybe a bit older, gangly, with long, slightly dirty, straw-coloured hair and a faintly decadent air. He smoked foul-smelling roll-ups out of the corner of his mouth and wore a battered leather jacket at all times. He was the cynic of the bunch, and kept a faint sneer on his face during the group activities. He'd been my challenge, the one I was going to disarm. So I'd tracked him down after dinner, and we'd stayed up late, very late, until everyone else had gone to bed and there was only the sound of the wind and the stream outside. After we'd made inroads into the bottle of Scotch that

Richard had left on the table between us, he told me about his two sons.

'They're nearly young men,' he said. 'I left their mother when they were three and two. I was hopelessly in love with this other woman, but that didn't last long. Anyway, they're teenagers now. Fergal's almost nineteen, for God's sake. They have girlfriends and take drugs and I might as well be invisible to them. They look through me. I say things and they don't seem to hear me.'

'It'll change when they're older,' I said.

'Maybe. Probably. But it's the oddest feeling, as if I didn't exist. I'm like a ghost in my own life.'

He rolled another cigarette and put it into the corner of his mouth.

'I bet you never have that feeling,' he said, after he'd lit it and taken a long drag. 'I bet no one ever treats you as if you didn't exist. How could they? Anyway, you wouldn't let them, would you?' He gave a laugh.

'I don't know,' I said. 'I wish they did. I think I'd like it.' I asked him to roll me a cigarette and he did it in a few deft movements. I poured us some more whisky.

'Now, what about you?'

'Me?'

'What's your story?'

My story. I considered the welter of anecdotes that were rehearsed and fairly painless by now: my father's business ventures, which had seemed funny at the time but not so funny when I looked back at them years later. Or was it the other way round? Was it that they became funny when turned into anecdotes? Or my two expulsions from school, for unruly behaviour (the first) and drugs (the second). Or there was the time I ran away from home, aged eleven, taking the beloved family dog with me, all the way to the corner of the road. That was a sweet story. I could tell him that one. I shook my head. 'Another time. Now I need to go to bed.'

'I hate getting older,' he said.

I gave an internal groan. It was the darkest part of the night: early-hours, whisky-sodden confession time. 'Why's that, then?'

'Everything, really. Doors closing. Dreams fading. Kids treating you like you're some old has-been. Everything seemed so easy when I was your age. You'd get drunk and the next morning feel fine. I'm going to feel shitty in the morning, but I bet you'll be as fresh as a daisy.'

'Speaking of morning . . .'

'You think, Is this it, then? The life I wanted. Is this all there is?'

'How old are you?' Forty? Forty-one? Surely it's a bit early to – '

'And then there's sex.'

'Stuart . . .'

'I don't know why I'm telling you this. Somehow I don't think you'll laugh at me. Not like some people. You see, I've always been good at sex.'

As if sex was like high-jump or mental arithmetic, I thought.

'Never any problem,' he continued. He sloshed more whisky into his glass and downed it. 'Until the last couple of years.'

'Ah,' I said neutrally.

'Now, well, I can't – you know – rely on myself any more. If you know what I mean.'

'I think so.'

'It's a vicious circle – the more I lose confidence, the more of a problem it is. Women don't know what it's like.' He went very red. 'I used to be able to control myself. Now it just . . . well, it's over too quickly. Do you know what I mean?'

I made an indeterminate sound.

'Now you think I'm pathetic.'

'Not at all. I bet you'd find lots of your male friends have gone through something similar, only they never talk about it.'

'You think so?'

'I'm sure of it.'

'I keep thinking there must be some woman out there who'd help me through this. I've got a picture in my head, someone outwardly cool and collected.'

At least he wasn't thinking of me.

'But inside she's troubled and passionate.'

'Well . . .' I began.

'I should never have cheated on my wife. I would have been all right then. Perhaps I'm reaping what

I sowed. God's revenge, to make me a laughing-stock. Have you ever cheated on your husband?'

'No.' I managed a tone of outrage that he should even ask, and added, 'We've only been married just over a year.'

'What's his name?'

'Charlie.'

'I hope Charlie realizes what a lucky man he is.'

Meg dropped me at home just after nine. She said she wouldn't stop, she'd seen quite enough of me for one weekend, but wandered in with me anyway. In the house we found Charlie with his old friend Sam watching a DVD in the dark. I kissed Charlie on the top of his head and took a gulp of wine from his glass.

'Hi,' he said, reaching out a hand. 'Hello, Meg.'

'Hello,' she said. I looked at the way her blush spread over her face.

'Good weekend?'

'Knackering.'

'Do either of you want something to drink? Or eat, even? There may be some pizza left.'

'Just a cup of tea. I'll get it.'

'Don't worry. I can't work out what's going on in this anyway.'

He disappeared into the kitchen, followed a few moments later by Meg. I could hear them talking in low voices, and then his burst of laughter. I lowered myself into the sofa next to Sam and looked at the screen. Something blew up.

'What's happening?' I said.

'It's a bit complicated,' said Sam. 'He's an assassin who's agreed to do one last job. And his daughter's been kidnapped. We think the two things might be connected.'

'Did you get your accounts done?' I called through to Charlie.

'I made a start,' he replied.

'I thought they were overdue.'

There was no reply.

I went out into the garden, which was a bit like a wasteland, but Charlie and I had plans for it. We were going to run a winding paved path up the middle, make a lawn on either side, plant an apple tree and a cherry tree at the end and – this was my particular task – make a small gravelled patio by the kitchen door, which I was going to fill with dozens of terracotta pots full of shrubs, fragrant flowers and ornamental trees. I'd already ordered a bay. I leaned back against the wall where I was going to grow jasmine and honeysuckle, and imagined myself sitting out there in the summer, nothing to do, a glass of cold white wine in my hand, watching Charlie at the barbecue he'd said he was going to build.

But it was cold outside, and dark, so after a few minutes I went back in. Meg said she was about to go and for once I didn't try to dissuade her. I had a shower. I was exhausted, yet still buzzing from the weekend and I felt as if I wanted the water to extinguish something in me so I could go to bed and sleep. I put on the pyjamas Charlie had given me and joined the men again, but the film was too jangly, busy, fast-moving and it made me feel even more agitated. I went upstairs and picked up the novel I was reading, but after a couple of pages I hadn't taken any of it in and would have to go back to the beginning. I wasn't in the mood for reading. I needed to do something mindless. I padded down the stairs again and peeked into Charlie's work room. I couldn't help grimacing.

When I first heard that Charlie was an illustrator, I thought I knew what that meant. 'Illustrator' wasn't the same as 'artist', which was a vague, vast and splendid word, full of drift and danger. It was neater and more precise, with clear boundaries and a sense of wit about it. An illustrator had a commission and a deadline, a subject and a portfolio. I imagined that editors would ring Charlie up and ask him to do a newspaper drawing for the following day, a magazine one for the following week, a book-jacket for several months away. Maybe he'd do children's illustrations too. I'd pictured him in a neat, airy room, with a large table and lots of sharp pencils in a mug. And that seemed to fit with what I saw of him: that he was dreamy and interior, but solid and humorous at the same time; absent-minded, yet meticulously clever and focused on the task in front of him. He had delicate, rough hands. He could make things (wooden carvings, shelves and intricate boxes, a go-kart for the autistic boy three doors down) and mend things (windows, bicycles, all the plates and mugs I broke, even the washing-machine).

What I hadn't realized was that being an illustrator is a grubby nasty business just like any other. You need to put your foot in the door, hustle your port-folio round editors and agents. It's about making contacts, then exploiting them. I had come to under-stand that in the back of Charlie's mind, when we were lying in bed together, when we were away, was that every year another flood, another Niagara, of new, hungry, talented illustrators poured out of the art colleges on to the streets with their portfolios, their ambition and their fresh, new ideas.

I was desperate to fight for him like a tiger, to be his muse, his agent, his hit-woman, but he was too laid-back for that. Maybe he was too much of an artist. I loved that about him and I hated it and wanted to claw the walls in frustration. I bit my tongue because he was wonderfully talented and I tried to explain it to people, but the only people who really understood were the ones who knew him, who had seen the drawings or, better still, had seen him at work. There was a look in his eye when he stared at the paper, the wonderful economy and dexterity he had with a line and a blob of colour, the incredible feeling he had for putting them in the right place and doing enough and knowing when to stop. I wasn't going to be the nagging woman who stopped him fulfilling his potential. I'd seen the terrible old movies. I wasn't going to be the harridan who says, 'All right, Leonardo, go and paint that *Last Supper*, if you have to, but don't expect me to be here when you come back.'

He always said he'd do it in his own way and in his own time. Sometimes this meant he wouldn't do it at all. Deadlines passed. I couldn't bear it when that happened. It wasn't just the money, though God knew we needed it badly enough, with the huge mortgage and me and Meg starting the company. It was the waste of it that I hated. I hated it so much that I felt itchy and crackly with rage when it happened. I told myself not to say anything, not to nag: that only made it worse. But more often than not I couldn't keep my mouth shut. I once read a collection of Van Gogh's letters. It was Charlie's favourite book. It was his Bible. I kept thinking that what Van Gogh really needed was a good woman and some medical help. But he painted the pictures. And killed himself.

There were papers all over the floor. There were envelopes, some unopened. There were books face down, spines cracking – one about black holes, one about new evolutionary theories, an anthology of chess games. The Van Gogh letters. I could imagine Charlie's weekend all too clearly: cups of tea, coffee. A run in Highgate Woods. Bits of TV. Flick through a book, a magazine. Start some job around the house. A drink with friends. A few hours online. A takeaway.

At some point he had steeled himself to get going with his accounts. He had taken the large piles of papers on his desk and next to his desk and broken them up into smaller piles which he had arranged around the room. He had given himself a glimpse of the horror, then retreated. That was probably when he had called Sam. It was at moments like that that you needed friends, to keep your mind off what you ought to be doing.

The kitchen looked as if it had been burgled and vandalized, so while they watched the movie I cleaned and scoured and wiped and put things away in cupboards, then got things out of cupboards and looked at them and put some in a bin bag, then replaced the rest. When Charlie came in, I was finishing off and I felt as if I had climbed a mountain and was standing on the summit looking over a beautiful valley in the sunshine.

'I was going to do that,' Charlie said.

'It's not a problem,' I said. 'I was meaning to sort it out.'

'Sort it out?'

'I've done the cupboards as well. I've thrown lots of stuff away. Like the ice-cream maker with the stirrer thing, except the stirrer thing was missing.'

'I was going to replace it.'

'How? Where? This isn't the nineteenth century. There aren't hardware shops any more where you can buy replacements. It's cheaper to buy a new ice-cream maker. If we need one. Which we don't because we've never made ice-cream. Or home-made pasta. I threw that machine away as well. It was rusty. We never make anything, really, except toast and bacon and eggs.'

'How can you do this,' he said, 'after your week-end? I bet you hardly slept. Aren't you exhausted?'

'It's the opposite,' I said. 'It's good. It helps me wind down.'

'You know, I love you in those pyjamas. But some-times I regret buying them for you.'

I knew what he was saying but pretended I didn't. My body felt all wrong. I couldn't bear the thought of someone touching it.

'I looked into your study . . .' I began.

'I know, I know,' he said.

'Your tax form. It was due in last week, wasn't it? Or was it the week before last?'

'I'll do it soon,' he said.

'Let me have a look.'

'Don't be ridiculous. It's half past eleven. You've probably not had any sleep all weekend, if I know you. And you've a company of your own to run.'

'I'm not tired, I just want to have a quick look. Come on.'

I put on slippers and a dressing-gown, and dragged Charlie to his work room. It really was a scary place.

'It's like a diagram of the inside of my brain,' he said, with a smile.

'Don't say that.'

'I'll deal with it tomorrow,' he said. 'I promise.

I'll even open some of the letters. The ones with red bits on.'

I took a deep breath. 'The main bit of advice we got when we started KS was to keep in touch with people. They get worried when they don't hear from you. This,' I gestured at the atrocious scene, 'is like when a child puts his hand over his eyes and thinks nobody can see him.'

He grimaced.

'We don't want to lose the house, Charlie,' I said.

'Things aren't that bad,' he said, in a light tone. 'You could always kill me and collect the insurance.'

I fetched a bin bag, my second of the evening, and a notebook, and got to work. I opened all the letters and started putting them into piles: real, meaningful, consciously arranged piles. Charlie protested at first, but then he lay down on the old sofa and drifted into a half-sleep from which I woke him occasionally with shouted inquiries. Envelopes and bumf and other rubbish went into the bag. Then I read through everything and arranged it first by subject and then in order of scariness. Charlie hadn't been keeping proper accounts, so I created a rough-and-ready account book that could just about be presented to a tax man.

I woke Charlie and he went and made us hot chocolate, into which we dunked digestive biscuits. My feet were chilly and I could feel I was starting to slow down. A great weariness lurked behind my eyes, waiting to pounce. I put the piles of papers that could be forgotten about on the floor. I scribbled in the account book, I took notes, I prodded Charlie and reduced and reordered the papers, boiling it down, boiling it down, until there were just six pieces of paper that absolutely had to be dealt with. Three were unpaid bills; three were invoices he'd never sent off.

As Charlie dozed off again, I came across a letter in the bottom drawer, scrunched-up, as if Charlie had balled it angrily in his fist before chucking it in there. It was three lines long, not counting the signature, from a publishing company, rejecting his proposal for a graphic novel that I hadn't even known he was working on. I shut the drawer quietly, and looked at Charlie, his head tipped to the side, his soft hair falling over one eye, his mouth half open, and a tiny rumble in the back of his throat. He hadn't told me. He'd hidden it and pretended it didn't exist. A violent spasm of tenderness shot through me, leaving me shaky and anxious.

'Some of these are really good,' I said brightly, when he woke, gesturing at the pile of drawings I'd put on the desk, except for the one of Meg and me together in which I looked scrawny and cartoonishly demented, which I'd surreptitiously screwed into a ball and crammed into the bin bag.

'They're nothing,' he said, rubbing his eyes. 'Just stupid doodles.'

I looked at him curiously. 'You don't enjoy it any more, do you?'

'What?'

'Drawing.'

He shrugged. 'It's just work.'

'It's not just work. You're good at it, really gifted. God, if I only had a gift like yours. And you always used to love it.'

'That was before I had to do it. Before it was a job. Like you keep telling me, we have to pay the mortgage.'

'You really feel that it's just a grind?'

'This isn't the time to talk about it, Holly. It's two o'clock in the morning.'

'Then stop doing it,' I said. 'You don't need to.'

'What are you going on about?'

'You know what you really love doing, what makes you contented? Making things, fixing things. I've seen the expression on your face. That's what you should do.'

'I should fix things?'

'Yes. Forget being an artist or an illustrator. Retrain. Retrain as a . . . as a *plumber*. I'm always reading about how plumbers can ask any price they want, they're in such demand. We can remortgage the house and put you through an apprenticeship. You'd love it.'

'So that's what you think of me, is it? I should fix drains and broken pipes and clogged gutters.'

I heard the danger signs and ignored them. 'It'd be better than sitting here day after day failing to work, staring into space, and feeling miserable, with me getting all resentful. Let's just do it.'

'So you're in Soho being a consultant or an enabler or whatever you fucking care to call it. And what does your husband do? Oh, he's a plumber. If you've got a blocked toilet, you know who to call.'

'Why not, Charlie? What's wrong with being a plumber?'

'I thought you believed in me.'

'I do – of course I do.'

'I thought you said I had a great future ahead of me.'

'I just want you to be –'

The phone rang. We looked at each other in puzzlement.

'Who the fuck could possibly ring at this time?'

A shudder of apprehension passed through me and I leaped to it, but Charlie got there first. 'Yes? Oh.' His expression changed and his voice lost some of its aggression. 'No, unbelievably I wasn't asleep. Yes. Yes, OK. I'll be right over.' He put the phone down.

'What's wrong?'

'Naomi in a panic. She needs my help with something.'

'At this time of night?'

'She saw our lights on.'

'What can be so urgent?'

'She can smell something burning. She's worried there might be an electrical fire.'

'Can't she call someone?' I said.

'She did call someone,' he said. 'She called us.'

'It's the middle of the night.'

'I know, I know,' said Charlie, 'and I'm a plumber, not an electrician. But she's a neighbour. If her house burns down, it'll take ours with it.'

'Come back soon, Charlie. We can't leave things like this.'

'I thought you'd sorted it all out,' he said, and he was gone. I heard the front door slam, his footsteps ring out in the silence.

I sat there for a few moments, going over the conversation in my head, seeing his hard, furious face. Then I put each pile of paper into a separate folder. I picked up all his pencils and pens and put them into a glass jar. I pushed rubbish into the bin bag. I returned all the mugs and ashtrays to the kitchen. I wiped every surface with a cloth. At last I sat down at his clear desk in his clean room, put my head on my arms and let myself sink into a shallow, fretful sleep.

When I woke, with a jerk as if I was falling, I felt stiff and unrested. I looked at my watch and saw it was nearly five o'clock. I trudged upstairs, but Charlie still wasn't back so I made a large pot of strong coffee, then phoned Naomi.

'Naomi. It's Holly.'

'Holly! Oh, God, I'm sorry if I've ruined your night. Charlie's been my saviour. It was an electric cable. The wires were exposed and they'd got terribly hot. He's patched it up for the time being, but he had to unscrew this box on the wall and unfasten –'

'That's enough information,' I said blearily. 'I've made us all a pot of coffee. Come over and drink it.'

'I don't have your energy. I need to go to sleep, not drink coffee to wake me up.'

Ten minutes later, Charlie returned. He looked dazed and disconnected, but I took him into his study. He blinked at his room. It was tidy. It was almost bare.

'Here,' I said, handing him my piece of paper. He looked at it blankly. 'I've written it down for you. It's very simple. You've got to make four phone calls, one after another, starting at ten a.m. And you've got to write three letters. I've drafted them for you. It's not as bad as it seemed. And send off the invoices. Then people might send you some money.'

He looked at the paper, then looked at me. 'How can you do this?' he said.

'Once I get going with something I can't leave it until it's done.'

'I don't know what to say.'

'I'm sorry about earlier,' I said.

'No. No, it's me who should be sorry.'

I put my arms round him. 'We're all right, aren't we?'

'I'm going to take a shower,' he said. 'Then we should try and get some sleep.'

'It's way too late to go to bed,' I said, trying not to notice that he hadn't answered my question. 'I thought we could have some breakfast. We could have a walk before I go to work.'

'Aren't you shattered?'

'Sleep's overrated,' I said. 'There are too many interesting other . . .' The words were tripping over themselves and getting caught in my mouth like something too dry to eat. 'Other things. You know what I mean?'

'I don't know if I do,' said Charlie. 'You're way beyond me.'

'Is that a compliment?' I asked, but he didn't reply.

8

It's easier to think when you walk, and easier not to think, as well. You just stride along, your feet hitting the pavement and the cold air rinsing through you. You can see things without seeing them, hear them but take no notice.

I walked all the way to work that morning, Archway to Soho, maybe six miles along big, busy roads. Across the dizzying bridge, trying not to look over this morning. Down the hill, Kentish Town Road, Camden High Street. I had a perfect cup of coffee in a little café, smoked an illicit cigarette that I cadged from a young woman, and eavesdropped on a conversation between two schoolgirls about how difficult it was to snog properly when you wore braces on your teeth. Then along Hampstead Road, on to Tottenham Court Road, and there I was, a stone's throw from our office. I looked at my watch. It seemed to have taken me just over an hour and a half, including the coffee stop, which seemed rather quick. Maybe it wasn't six miles after all, or maybe I'd walked very fast. I noticed that my cheeks were glowing and my hair was stuck to my forehead with sweat.

I bought a poppy-seed muffin in Luigi's and ate it leaning against the wall outside the office, allowing myself to cool down. A woman on roller-blades tacked gracefully towards me and gave me a wide smile as she passed. Perhaps, I thought, I should get some of those. Then I could slide and swoop to work every morning. It didn't look too hard.

'Hi!'

'Meg, I didn't see you. I was in another world.'

'Sleep well?'

'Fine.'

'I went to bed before ten and got up at eight. Bliss.'

'You look different,' I said. 'What have you done to yourself?'

'Nothing!'

'You have. You've done something to your hair.'

She flushed and put a hand up. 'I bought one of those straighteners out of a catalogue, and when I got up this morning I just did it,' she said. 'I looked in the mirror and saw the same face I always see with a frizz on top.' Then, defensively: 'Does it look dreadful?'

'No. But you don't have a frizz, you have curls. They're lovely. I wish I had curly hair like you.'

'No, you bloody don't, Holly,' she said, and for a minute her mouth tightened and her eyes narrowed and she looked like someone else. She looked like Charlie had the night before, when I'd told him he should become a plumber. Then she smiled. 'Oh, well, it makes a change. It'll roll itself up when the wind changes. One other thing . . .' She stopped.

'What?'

'I didn't know if I should tell you.'

'Go on. You've got to tell me now.'

'Someone phoned me. A man. He didn't say who he was, but he said he knew you and you were heading for trouble. He said we all reap what we sow, or something. He sounded rather sinister.'

'Was he carrying a scythe?'

'Holly!' she said reprovingly.

I couldn't think of anything else to say.

There are three lavatories at our office. At nine minutes to twelve, I went into the largest one, rolled my coat into a bolster and put it on top of the closed toilet seat. Then I kicked off my shoes, lowered myself to the floor and laid my cheek gratefully on the rough warmth of the coat. I closed my eyes.

The toilet next to mine flushed. I opened my eyes again and looked at my watch. A quarter past midday. The strange buzzing seemed to have gone from my head, so I stood up, slipped my shoes back on, picked up my coat and walked out of the cubicle. I washed my hands and face, brushed my hair in front of the small mirror and marched back into the office.

'We have a letter from Deborah's lawyer and he's threatening to take action against us for her unfair dismissal,' said Meg, as I took a seat opposite her.

'Is it a problem?'

'I've asked Chris to come round this afternoon to talk about it.'

'Maybe I've brought ruination on the firm,' I said. 'I'm sorry.'

'And there's someone on his way up to see you.'

'Who's that?' I started riffling helplessly through the diary.

'He didn't say. He just said he was here to see Holly Krauss. I assumed –'

'It doesn't matter.'

But it did matter. Rees's smile didn't waver as he approached me across the room. Once more, I felt that sense of queasy revulsion.

'Hello there, Holly.'

I could feel several pairs of eyes watching us curiously.

'I have nothing to say to you,' I said coldly. 'Please leave.'

'Oh, I haven't really come to see you. I was at a loose end and I just wanted a look round where you work. Get a sense of your life, you know the kind of thing. And you must be Meg?'

'That's right. Can I help you?'

'We talked last night on the telephone. Remember?'

'In which case, I think Holly's right and you should leave immediately,' she said splendidly. 'Or shall I call the police?'

'All women here, is it?'

Meg picked up the phone.

'Don't worry,' he said. 'I'm just going.' He looked

at me, then pinched my cheek between his finger and thumb so it hurt. 'I'll wait for your call, Holly. But I won't wait long. And I won't go away.'

Numbers and dates slid mysteriously into the right grids on the screen. How did I do that? I could sense that Meg hadn't gone away.

'What?'

'That man, he's dangerous,' said Meg.

'Oh, I don't think so. He's just a creep.'

'Holly, can you hear yourself?'

'No.'

'Have you told Charlie?'

'You know when a machine's running smoothly and the cogs and wheels are clicking round together and it's all oiled and you feel you could just go on and on working like that for ages? Then along comes Rees, and he's like a spare bolt that's been dropped into your perfectly running machine and you know if you don't get rid of him at once that there'll be this terrible screeching of metal and sparks and things will fly out at you, and with a grinding and a wrenching and a rusty screech it'll all come to a halt. You know that feeling?'

'You haven't told Charlie, then.'

'No. I'm not going to . . . What? You don't really think I should?'

Meg looked at me and I couldn't read her expression. Then she looked away and drummed her fingers on her desk. 'Sometimes,' she said, in a voice so quiet I had to strain to hear it, 'things are better out in the open.'

'Sometimes they are,' I said. 'Sometimes they definitely aren't.'

'Holly . . .' She hesitated.

'Yes?'

'Doesn't matter. You should at least call the police.'

'No.'

'So you're just going to ignore it and hope it goes away all by itself?'

I thought for a moment. 'I think most things go away, if you ignore them enough.'

9

There are times when I feel scared of going to sleep. It's too like dying. That evening I didn't dare sleep, although I knew I was stupid with exhaustion. I picked at a takeaway Charlie had ordered for us and talked incessantly so that he wouldn't ask me any questions. Every time there was a second of terrifying silence, I rushed to fill it. We watched the television news, and after it a quiz show. I kept shouting out the wrong answers. Eventually Charlie turned it off and said he was tired and was going up to bed.

'I'll be up soon,' I said. 'Any minute now.'

I made myself a cup of tea, hoping it would calm me, but it tasted odd, like mouldy straw. I turned on the television again and flicked through the channels, waiting for something to grab my attention. I was unable to settle on anything for longer than a few minutes. Faces leered at me from the screen, words pounded in my ears but didn't make sense. At half past one, I finally crept upstairs, stubbing my toe on the bedroom door and yelping in pain.

Charlie half opened his right eye. 'Holly?' he mumbled.

I waited till he was fully asleep again, then turned on my bedside light. I like reading poems when I can't sleep. Poems and cookbooks. I never cook, but one day I'm going to start, and by then my head will be full of mouthwatering recipes, like this one for smoked haddock and mussel pie.

I realized I was hungry, so I dragged myself back out of bed and padded downstairs to the fridge. We have a huge fridge – far too big for two people – and there's hardly ever anything in it except coffee and beer and butter and the little drinking yoghurts that Charlie insists on buying and which remind me of artificially sweetened blancmange. Tonight there were some marinated anchovies I couldn't remember seeing before, so I ate half of one, but it wasn't right for a midnight feast. Too salty. I thought of waves crashing against limpet-encrusted rocks. Men with grated knuckles hauling nets full of writhing silver.

When I got back into bed I pressed my chilly, tense body against Charlie's warm, sleeping one and tried to work out how many hours of sleep I'd had in the last week, but the arithmetic seemed enormously difficult. I kept losing count. I put my arms round Charlie – my lovely, warm, solid, kind, trusting husband – and my lips against the nape of his neck.

'I'm going to be so very good now,' I said, into the tightness of his skin. 'I'm going to be quite extraordinarily good. You won't recognize me. Another woman entirely.'

Dawn came softly. My eyes snapped open. I remembered I hadn't dug out the information on training days I'd promised Trish, and some time during the night I'd remembered that I'd promised to drop off a blanket to a homeless woman who always sat outside the Underground station on my way into the office. I put my clothes on quickly – my leather trousers, because I was giving a talk to a group of men in suits – and took the stairs two at a time. I put the kettle on, pinged my computer into life.

At seven I woke Charlie with coffee, then poked around in the cupboard for cereal. I hate cereal, with its texture of sweet, mushy cardboard. I prodded the flakes with my spoon then tipped the bowl into the bin. Charlie stared at the paper, never turning the pages. He hadn't shaved this morning.

'Did you sleep well?' I asked.

He muttered something.

'I didn't. Insomnia again.'

I squinted at the back of his paper. '"Is afraid of disturbing adders", six letters. Dreads. Yes! How about that for brilliance? Or what about "Big name that appears nightly"? VIP. No. Star. *Star!* OK, thirteen letters, "Vigilant chap who never does a day's work . . ,"'

Charlie folded the paper and the crossword disappeared.

Meg rang me as soon as I arrived in the office, her voice thick. 'Holly, is it all right if I take the day off? I feel lousy.'

'Of course,' I said. 'Snuggle up with a hot-water bottle. Can I do anything for you?'

'It's probably just a cold coming, plus exhaustion. I can't keep going like you. I'll be in tomorrow. The only thing is, I was going to drive to that place near Bedford to have a look at it this afternoon. We can put it off till later. I don't think it'd matter.'

I did frantic calculations in my head. I was talking to a group of management consultants later in the morning, but that wouldn't clash. I could move back my meeting with the computer people. 'I can do it.'

'Are you sure? I don't want to pile things on you. You've been working so hard.'

'No, honestly. It'll all be fine. No problem. Leave it to me.'

There was a time a couple of years ago when I was single and, although I wasn't exactly an old maid – I was twenty-four – friends used to invite me round because they had found someone they thought I'd like. These events weren't generally very successful. I'm not good at following plans. You can't go looking for the important things in life. They happen on the edges of your vision when you think you're doing something else. So when I was told that X was exactly my type, I would be mildly insulted by the idea that somebody could ever really understand what my type was. I would spend a whole evening talking with great intensity to a married woman sitting on the other side of the dinner-table, ignoring the probably very nice young man who had been carefully placed next to me. Worse still, there were occasions where friends tried to be more subtle about it and I didn't cotton on, or at least not until weeks later. I was like a fish that hadn't bitten the bait because I hadn't known there was any to bite. I would be lifting a coffee cup to my mouth and would stop and say to myself: 'So that's what the evening was for.'

Sometimes it would all happen in reverse. I was once having supper with a friend I knew vaguely and three or four other people I didn't know at all. It was one of those evenings when everything seemed in tune with everything else, the colours a little brighter, the focus sharper. There was a gorgeous man sitting next to me. He was so perfect in every way that he was almost like a character in a porn movie. He had some over-the-top job like organizing round-the-world yachting races and he was tanned and tall and I even remember his name: Glenn. I decided that I was going to make him fall in love with me that very evening and I was dazzling. I seemed to be thinking twice as quickly as everybody else. I was always a step ahead of them. I had the sensation of what it must be like to be an actor on a great night in the theatre when you know, you just *know* – because of the quality of the silence as much as the laughter or the applause – that you have a complete grip on the audience. When I left, I felt it was the best evening I had spent in my entire life. I was happy and I knew I was happy, which made me even happier.

On the way home I realized I didn't have Glenn's phone number and he didn't have mine, but it didn't matter. He wouldn't have to wander through London with a glass slipper to find me. He'd get my number from my friend, and in future years we'd look back on that evening and laugh about the way we'd met, the way people meet in the movies. In any case it had been such an extraordinary evening that we'd probably all get together soon, although I was aware that you should always beware of trying to recapture a brilliant experience. I dropped Annie a cheerful postcard saying what fun it had been, with a flirtatious reference to Glenn. And then nothing. I didn't hear back from her. Or him. About a year later I bumped into her at a party. I mentioned the dinner and she just mumbled something. I asked about Glenn and she turned vague, said she wasn't sure. She was blatantly unfriendly, looking over my shoulder at the room, getting away from me with a brusque excuse.

I went over the evening again and again in my mind and tried to see it from other perspectives. Had I been kidding myself? Had I just been loud and brash when I thought I was being charming? I tried to remember other people's responses but I couldn't. That might have been the problem. Maybe I hadn't let anyone else get a word in.

I wasn't sure if it was me or if everybody experienced this disconnection between their own feelings and those of the people around them. I thought I was making Glenn fall hopelessly in love with me and he had disappeared in a cloud of dust. And then there was the wretched Rees. A casual, meaningless, repulsive one-night stand and he felt we were bound together. I didn't know if he loved me or hated me, or which of the two was worse. All these discrepancies. If only the world matched the insides of our brains; if only the insides of our brains matched the insides of other people's brains.

Nothing fitted together. You're wearing head-phones and you think you're talking normally and people are flinching because you're shouting. It was all like that. I knew that things had got out of control, in my life and inside my head. There was a storm in my head and what I needed to do was batten down the hatches and ride it out, like Glenn with his round-the-world yachts. At the now-legendary dinner, I'd asked him what was the biggest storm he'd ever been in but, now that I thought about it, I couldn't remember his answer. I probably hadn't given him a chance to utter one.

That's one of the things about life. The times you really want it to go well, it's a disaster. When you don't care, everybody loves you. And so, when I gave this talk to a collection of businesspeople – at a time when I had too much else on my mind – it went fine. I didn't look at my notes. I just climbed up on the platform, opened my mouth and did my party piece. The man who had introduced me wouldn't let me go. He talked about what I'd said, asked me about strategy and whether I could visit their office and see them at work. It sounded like a result. I raced back to the office, had a quick meeting with Trish while

Lola organized the hire car for me, drank a double espresso, then jumped into the car, which smelt of leather and pine and cleanness. It was slow getting out of London, as always. I was starting to live like a commuter, but without the country house. I shifted between crawling queues, revved up at traffic-lights, looking anxiously at the clock on the dashboard. It seemed urgent that I should get there on time, though I knew it didn't matter that much.

I sped off from a light with a screech of tyres. The car I left behind blared its horn furiously and I looked up as it drew level with me at the next lights. A man was shouting soundlessly through the window and then, as if I couldn't imagine what he was saying, he jabbed his middle finger in the air. There was a woman next to him who was also shouting something. I looked at her face, twisted, a gargoyle. I put my index finger against my forehead and mouthed, 'CRAZY,' out of the window. Their faces contorted even more furiously. The lights changed and I drove off, out into the clearing road ahead.

The next thing I knew, the red Escort had shot past and braked in front of me, forcing me to stop. The man got out of the car and strutted over like a big fat cockerel. I opened my door and got out too.

'Yes?' I said.

'Cunt,' he said. 'What the fuck are you playing at?'

He stepped towards me. I looked down at my left hand, which was coming up towards me. My nails were getting a bit too long, I thought. I must remember to cut them this evening. My fingers curled round themselves. I saw my wedding ring, my knuckles. I saw his shouting mouth. That's where I punched him, smack on his lips, with all the weight of my shoulder behind the blow, shoving his words back down his throat.

He folded up neatly, his knees collapsing on to the ground. He looked as if he was praying or abasing himself.

'Nightwatchman,' I said. 'That's the answer to that crossword clue. Yes!'

I stood back a few feet. There was a racket going on behind me. The woman got out of the car and wobbled hysterically towards him and he lifted his head, his face wiped clean of any expression, his mouth open in mute astonishment, blood on his teeth. I edged back towards my car and watched him unconcertina himself and stand up. Quite calmly, I got into the car and drove away. I wasn't even late.

Charlie and I went to see a film with Sam and Luke, Meg's cousin. I invited Meg, who said she was feeling better and maybe she'd join us but cancelled at the last minute and wouldn't tell me why. After the film, we all went out for an Indian meal together, though I only pretended to eat, pushing the red, oily chunks of meat round the plate, making little heaps of rice. I assumed I was losing weight. I had stood on the scales that morning, but the figures were in kilos. I'd made an attempt to convert it to something I understood by multiplying it by two and a bit, then trying to divide it by fourteen in my head but the figure I got was something meaningless like three stone or twenty-seven stone, so I must have made a mistake somewhere. Or maybe I was disappearing, becoming invisible at last, or even filling the entire world so that soon there would be no room for anyone else.

At one point Charlie leaned across the messy plates and took my hand. I flinched, and saw for the first time, with a mild, dispassionate interest, that there was a dark bruise across my knuckles. I was puzzled, then remembered the man I'd hit. Only when I noticed the bruise did it start hurting.

'You should see the other guy,' I said, and they all laughed and I laughed too, louder than the rest of them.

We got back at half past ten. Sam and Luke came in for coffee, and then the doorbell rang. Naomi stood on the doorstep, clutching something. 'A parcel came for you a couple of hours ago,' she said. 'Courier service. I had to sign for it, and then it was too wide to fit through your box. I thought it might be important.'

'Thanks.' I took it from her.

'Are you OK? You don't look yourself, Holly.'

'I'm just a bit washed up. Done in, I mean. Why don't you come in for a bit?'

'Are you sure?'

'The more the merrier,' I said, and she followed me into the living room and took her place between Sam and Charlie, looking as plump and pretty as a cat.

'Open your parcel, then,' said Luke.

I tried to pull open the padded envelope, which turned out to be full of the horrible grey fluff that gets everywhere, and in the process I jabbed myself on a staple, cutting my finger. 'I hate these bloody things. They ought to be banned, along with clingfilm.'

'Here. Let me,' said Charlie. He took the envelope and pulled it open, then thrust his hand inside. 'What's wrong with clingfilm?'

'It's –' I began, then stopped dead.

'What's this?' said Charlie.

I looked at the flimsy black object dangling from his fingers. Suddenly I felt feverish. I could feel the dots of sweat on my forehead.

'Some dumb publicity stunt,' I said, in a high, merry voice, and grabbed at them. 'Who thought this was a smart idea? Imagine lots of middle-aged men in suits sitting round a shiny table and one of them saying, "We should send sexy underwear out to all our clients."'

Naomi turned the envelope upside down. 'Publicity for what, Holly?'

'That's the stunt,' I said desperately. I put the knickers against my hot cheek and realized they hadn't been washed. They smelt of me. My face burned with shame. 'It's meant to get you wondering.'

'Well, it certainly does that,' said Luke, and snickered.

'Then later,' I prattled on, 'something else will arrive and you'll understand what it's all about. They do it all the time. The latest thing. Drives me mad. Anyway, I wish they wouldn't send me stuff at home like this. Look, they're quite the wrong size. I'd never wear these, would I? I'll just chuck them in the bin, shall I?'

Charlie didn't say anything. He looked at the knickers clutched in my sweating hand, and he looked at me.

IO

I ordered a spicy tomato juice at the bar. Twenty past five and it was already getting dark outside. Soon it wouldn't be autumn any more but proper winter, pinched grey days and long black nights. In certain moods I love the dark. It's like velvet around me, not scary but protective.

'I thought I'd find you here!'

I turned and saw a face I recognized, but out of context I couldn't place it. White smooth face, dark hair pulled back. Attractive face, though now it was filled with hostility and the red mouth was open and words were streaming out.

'Holly Krauss. Swilling your drink as if you didn't have a care in the world.'

'Deborah,' I said, startled. 'What are you –'

'You didn't think you'd not see me again, did you? I told you I wouldn't go that easily.'

'What do you want?'

'What do I want? What do I *want*? I want my job. I want to keep my flat. I want my self-respect back. I want an apology. I want you to grovel. Or, failing that, I want to take you to the cleaners. And I will, you'll see.'

I managed a shrug that I thought might look as if

I wasn't bothered. 'If you've anything to say, you need to talk to our lawyer.'

'Yeah, yeah, we're dealing with Mr Graham. But I wanted to deal with you too. In person. You can't just wreck someone's life and expect to hand it all over to a solicitor.'

I looked at her, the creamy face and thick brows and red lips. 'Look, Deborah, I don't want to discuss this here –'

'You don't want to discuss it,' said Deborah. 'Don't *want* to? Poor Holly.'

She took a step forward, and I backed away so I was wedged against the bar.

'I think you need help,' I said. 'Medical help.'

Her whole face seemed to shiver with rage. It was like seeing a mask crack open, and I couldn't take my eyes off her.

'How dare you suggest there's anything wrong with me?' she hissed. 'How dare you? First you fire me, then you say I'm sick. The only thing I'm sick of is you.'

And she raised her hand and took a wild swipe at me, knocking the glass from my hand. Tomato juice flew in an arc, splattering both of us. I looked at her, with a red stain down her white shirt and her face trickling with thick juice. 'Oops! You look like a Jackson Pollock painting,' I said cheerfully.

'Holly, are you all right? Can I be of any help?'

A tall, gangly man with a hooked nose, slightly close-together eyes and a flop of fair, greying hair.

White shirt, black-leather jacket, grey cords, laced, high-ankled suede shoes. Stuart from the weekend. The premature-ejaculation man, who felt invisible with his sons. I smiled at him. For once I was pleased to meet a client out of office hours. 'I bet I know where all your items of furniture come from,' I said, and gave a giggle that even I recognized as a bit mad.

'*Furniture?*'

'Gap. That's definitely a classic Gap shirt, anyway. And, yes, since you asked, you can help. You can ask Deborah – this is Deborah, by the way – to buy me another tomato juice. I'll waive the cleaning bill.'

'Is this another of your lovers?' asked Deborah. 'Another of the men you string along? Watch it,' she said, turning to Stuart. 'She'll kick you out as soon as she has no more use for you.'

'We're late for the exhibition,' said Stuart to me, though he was staring at Deborah with fascination. 'Put your coat on and we'll go.'

'I'm not done with you,' said Deborah, as I slid into my coat. 'You wait and see. You don't go wrecking people's lives on a whim and then just walk away.'

I took Stuart's arm. 'Let's go.'

'Goodbye,' he said to Deborah, with curiously chivalric formality. 'I'm sorry we met in these circumstances.'

'Oh, come on.'

He hesitated, gazing into Deborah's furious, beautiful face, then turned away.

'I'll ruin you,' she called after us. 'Don't think I won't. Bitch.'

'Thanks so much for that,' I said, dropping Stuart's arm as we reached the street. 'I dread to think what you made of it.'

'It was fun. I felt like your knight in shining armour. What did you do to her?'

'Just a problem in the office.'

'Hmm. It looks like a problem that's got out of hand.'

'Yeah,' I said. My legs were shaking. 'You're probably right. Maybe she was right to call me a bitch. I don't know.'

'What did you do?'

'Fired her, basically. I had to. We're only a little company, a bit like a family. We've all got to trust each other or the whole thing collapses. But I know I can be confrontational. Compromise isn't my strong suit. Charlie always says that in an argument I miss out all the build-up part and go nuclear at once. But I guess we should try to come to some agreement. We'll all lose out if we spend months with solicitors involved. I know that's what Meg and Trish think, anyway.'

'Can I do anything for you? I could be your middle man, no legal fee involved.'

'No, don't be daft. It's sweet of you but it's my fault and my problem, and if anyone's going to sort it out it's me.'

'You're the one person who can't, I'd say. Anyway,

this is what I do in my job. I sort out personnel problems. Let me do it as a favour.'

'It wouldn't work. You saw what she was like.'

'Very fiery,' agreed Stuart. 'Let me give it a go at least. What's her phone number?'

'I don't know. Trish would have it.'

'Trish?'

'In the office. You could ask her. Or look her up in the directory – her name's Deborah Trickett and she lives in Kennington, I know that. Willow Lane, I think.'

'Deborah Trickett, Willow Lane,' he repeated.

'I don't think it's a good idea.'

'It's a challenge.'

'Listen, Stuart, I ought to be getting home.'

'But you're coming to the exhibition. That wasn't a brilliant improvisation. I really am going to a friend's opening, just down the road from here. Come along. It might be fun.'

'That's very kind of you, and on another day maybe, but it's been a busy time and I don't think I'm up to it this evening. I've kind of run out of energy.'

'That doesn't sound like you.'

'What do you mean?'

'Running out of energy. That was one of the reasons I wanted to talk to you. That weekend, there was something extraordinary about it. It wasn't what we did. I guess everybody does that stupid raft stuff. But the people in the office, they're really excited. You did that.'

'All right,' I said. 'I'll come for a bit.' I stood up straight and hitched my shoulder-bag higher. My knuckles had started to throb, and I had blisters on my heels. My face was tingling a bit, as if it had pins and needles, but I don't think you can get pins and needles in your face. I put up a hand to rub my cheek but missed and jabbed my nose.

'What kind of friend is it?'

'What kind of friend? Well, he's . . .'

'No, I mean, what kind of exhibition?'

'Oh, sort of art. Objects made out of, you know, things. It's a bit difficult to describe. Some of it's beautiful, in a weird kind of way.'

'Great,' I said. 'Let's go, then.'

I stumbled on the pavement. He put out an arm to steady me and looked at me intently. 'Maybe you are a bit tired.'

'I'm fine. I've decided.' My enthusiasm felt forced, obviously fake.

'It's this way, to the left. The Oryx Gallery.'

'I know the one. It had shoes made of food in it a few weeks ago.'

'Do you always walk this fast?'

'Is this fast?'

'We're not in a race, Holly.'

'A race against time. We can win. Here we are, do we need an invitation to get in?'

'I've got one, admits two.'

'Two. So, did someone let you down?'

'I let someone down.'

'Ah.'

He pushed open the door, and all at once the crowd and the wind and the rain and the vague, pulsing stars were gone, and we had stepped into a bright cocoon of space, glowing white walls, polished floorboards, lights strung along the ceiling and shining off the puddles of wood below, a soft babble of voices. I took a fluted glass, full to the brim with cool yellow wine, from a tray that was held out to me and edged into the crowd.

'Cheers,' said Stuart, in an ironic tone that seemed habitual to him.

'Cheers,' I said. I raised it so it glinted under the spotlights then took a deep swallow. 'Let's look at your friend's work, then. Is he here? Which one is he? What's his name?'

'Laurie. He's probably in the next room, or in the pub down the road, hiding.'

'I like it,' I said. 'I do. I'd like to have that on my mantelpiece. I'm not going to sleep with you, you know.'

Stuart's drink seemed to go down the wrong way and he coughed helplessly so that I had to pat him on his back.

'I'm married to someone called Charlie Carter,' I continued, when he'd stopped spluttering. 'I think I told you that before. He's an artist, though I think he should be a plumber. Look, I'm wearing a ring.'

'So I see.'

'Though sometimes I take it off. Perhaps I shouldn't do that.'

'You don't seem like a married woman.'

'What does that mean? A married woman. There are probably lots of Victorian novels with titles like that. I don't know what it means, anyway. Does it mean I should bake sponges with – with jam and cream in the middle? And wear an apron in the kitchen? And go around saying, "I'm Holly-and-Charlie"? And ring him up to ask permission, like right now?' I pulled my mobile phone out of my pocket and brandished it. Little splashes of wine jolted out of my glass. 'I should ring him and ask if he will kindly allow his wife to go to an art gallery with a middle-aged man from Gap called Stuart. Look, I like that one there, with the burnished metal. Kind of soft and dazzling all at once. It makes you want to touch it, doesn't it?'

Stuart glared at me, emptied his glass in a single gulp and set it down with a sharp clink on a passing tray. 'Are you always so rude?'

'Am I being rude?' I put my phone back into my pocket, where it immediately started to vibrate, but I ignored it. 'I'm sorry. I really, really don't want to be rude to you. I told you I was a bit tired, that's all it is. I'm just an idiot, a fool. I like you. Don't you think you meet some people and know at once whether or not you could be friends? It's like a click between you. Or maybe it's more a gulp, if you know what I mean. They say the most important time in any relationship is the first second or something – or maybe that's just with lovers. I don't even know if that's a glorious thought or a completely terrifying one. It doesn't make you feel you're in control, though, does it? Probably not. Is that your artist, waving at us? God, he's tall. He's nearly a giant. Does he look ridiculous, or does he make everyone else look ridiculous?'

'Yes, that's Laurie.'

As we made our way towards him, we edged past a tall woman with a magnificent mane of red hair who was contemplating one of the sculptures. She was speaking to her companion in a loud, clear voice: 'Rather trashy, don't you think?'

I saw Laurie's smiling, benign face become blank, as if someone had taken a sponge and wiped away the last traces of expression. Even his eyes seemed to become deep, meaningless holes. I stepped forward and stared up at him. 'I love your things,' I said, even more loudly. 'Really love them. Probably some people don't get them, but I love them so much I've got to buy one. That one there.' I waved a hand towards it.

'I'm so glad,' he said, the warmth returning to his features. 'You should meet my agent. She's coming our way now.'

Behind me, Stuart was saying something in an urgent hiss about how expensive his things were, but I ignored him.

'I can write a cheque,' I said. My phone was buzzing in my pocket again, like a huge bluebottle. 'A deposit. Whatever. Shall I settle things with your agent, then?'

'Holly?' said Stuart again. He'd managed to acquire two more glasses of wine, one red and one white, and took a huge gulp from each in turn. 'Are you sure –'

'Absolutely. What's the point of earning money if you can't spend it?'

Half an hour later, I made my way to the ladies'. My head felt oddly hollow and an annoying little tic was bouncing in my left cheek. Someone was in the toilet already and they had left their brocaded shawl and their expensive leather gloves on the side. I recognized them as belonging to the red-haired, loud-voiced monster who'd insulted Laurie. My heart started to beat erratically; my throat closed. Beads of sweat stood out on my forehead. I gave a little snort of mirth, then another, picked up the shawl and gloves and slid them into my bag, leaving hurriedly as the lavatory flushed in the cubicle.

'I've got to go,' I said, as soon as I had rejoined Stuart.

'But we –'

'Sorry, an emergency. I'll call you, or you can call me at work. Tomorrow or the next day. It'd be nice to see you again. 'Bye.'

I barged out of the art gallery and ran down the

road, clutching my bulging bag to me, little laughs shaking me. I darted down the narrow streets, avoiding bikes and taxis. Horns blared at me. My phone buzzed once more and this time I snatched it out. It was Charlie. He was furious. 'Holly, I've been calling and calling. Where the fuck are you?'

'I'm in Soho somewhere. Why?'

'We had a date. Remember?'

'Oh, God.' Wretchedness grabbed me by the throat and shook. I stopped dead and stared around me at the dark, littered road, the puddles of sulphurous light where strange men loitered. 'Oh, no.'

'You forgot.'

'No! Yes. Oh, shit, I'm sorry. I'm on my way now. What time is it?'

'Nearly nine. I've been sitting here for forty-five minutes.'

I stayed on the phone all the way there, apologizing and apologizing.

11

'What we need to do,' said Charlie, 'is make a plan.'

'A plan?'

'This hasn't exactly been a productive day.'

My first thought was that if we had got to the stage where I was relying on Charlie to make plans, I must really be in trouble. My second thought was that he was probably right. It was Saturday, the day after I had met Stuart, gone to that awful exhibition and forgotten to meet Charlie. Another evening of fun. Now it was ten past four in the afternoon. When I was nine years old my school used to finish at quarter past four so by this time I would have sung a couple of hymns, had two playtimes, learned maths, written a story, drunk a carton of milk, eaten lunch, made a clay model. What did I, aged twenty-seven, have to show for the day?

Not very much. I'd had a dream where I was meant to be going away. I don't know if I was emigrating or just going on holiday, but it didn't matter. I couldn't find my ticket or my passport and I couldn't remember where I was meant to be going. And then I realized I hadn't packed, although I thought I had, so I started again. I couldn't find a bag to put my things in and there was a further problem in that the floor was covered with porridge, which slowed me down. I kept looking at my watch to see if I was late but couldn't read the time on the dial. Then I woke up and the failed packing in my dreams was about as constructively busy as I got all day.

There was cold tea by the side of the bed. I had a distant memory of Charlie bringing it to me hours before. I'd meant to get up and get busy but hadn't. I didn't feel as bad as I had expected. I wasn't exactly ill. There was a nasty taste in my mouth and a slightly hot feeling on my skin, which usually signals that I'm about to get flu. I couldn't get out of bed. I needed a bit more time. As I lay there I discovered more symptoms. The inside of my chest was aching and I found it difficult to breathe, as if the oxygen had been sucked from the room. In a panic I fought for breath and then my lungs felt too small for the air I needed. Suddenly I knew what it must be like to drown, resisting and resisting and resisting, flexing in spasms, then, almost with relief, breathing the water into your lungs. I choked and coughed and felt myself breathe.

I took a gulp of the cold tea, then pulled the duvet over my head. Wasn't this what I had been dreaming of for days? Retreating to bed and safety? My skin felt clammy and I was shivering. I reached out and pulled the cover more securely over me but I couldn't get it straight. We'd always had this problem. Always. I mean for months and months. We'd made a mistake when we bought our duvet and the cover was bigger than the duvet itself. That may be better than the cover being smaller than the duvet, but in that case it wouldn't work at all and you'd have to do something about it. The problem, as it stood, was that the duvet rattled around in the cover like a pea in an oversize pod, leaving flapping bits that looked like duvet but didn't provide warmth. Worse, it kept getting twisted out of shape inside the cover. At that moment it was particularly fucked up and my efforts to sort it out just made it worse. I felt as if someone was dragging me through dog shit while I was scraping my fingernails down a blackboard and being fed marzipan. I found myself ripping the seam of the duvet in frustration. What I would really have liked to do was rip it into small pieces and set fire to them so that it could never again cause me suffering, but I just wrapped it tight round myself. It felt unsatisfactory because I could feel the hard bits where it had folded in on itself.

What I normally do when I'm lying in bed and not sleeping is make plans, but this Saturday morning my brain wouldn't work. I kept going over and over things in a way that felt unproductive. When I was about twelve I ate artichoke for the one and only time in my life. As it happens, most of my memories of family meals when I was a child are pretty farcical. Frequently my father would be lying in a dark room somewhere, reeking of something mysteriously medicinal, being 'ill'. Then, later, he wasn't there at all. That particular time he wasn't there and we had this strange vegetable my mother had brought back from the market. I was so excited by my artichoke, by the whole ritual of peeling it and dipping it in melted butter, that I gorged myself. I scraped the flesh off the leaves with my front teeth. I even have a blurred memory of myself at the end of it, with a shiny, greasy face, but I see it through the lens of what happened next. I woke in the night and threw up and threw up as if I wanted to turn myself inside out. My mother lay with me, her cool hand on my hot forehead and I asked her if I was going to die. The funny thing is that I remember what she said. She didn't say, 'No,' as any normal mother would. She said, 'Of course, Holly, we're all going to die. But not for a very, very long time.' That's always made me laugh as a hilariously rubbish bit of parenting.

Ever since that awful meal, which was so wonderful while I was eating it, even the thought of artichoke makes me feel queasy. If I see one in a shop, a wave of nausea ripples through me. I went through the events of the previous weeks and felt as if I was plunging my arms into something disgusting, something reeking, maggoty, going off. Lying in bed, shivering in a useless duvet, it felt like that artichoke all over again. I had been running around gorging on everything as if I couldn't get enough, and now I felt it had made me sick and squeezed me out. Everything seemed bad, from every angle. My seedy encounter with . . . him. I tried not to think of his name or his face and then I made myself do it, as a form of punishment. I couldn't think how I had let someone do that to me. The knowledge that this man was in my life, stalking me, sending me my knickers filled me with a ghastly apprehension. I knew it would get worse.

The rest of my recent past wasn't on that level but maybe it had been contaminated by it. I seemed to have rushed through the days without thinking, like someone running along the edge of a precipice and now, finally, I was looking down. Everything seemed different from the way it had at the time. There were the obviously awful bits: the brick through the window, hitting that man. I seemed to have spent about half my time shouting at people or getting into arguments or just talking too loudly, like the scary people you see in the street and feel grateful you don't know. Or what about firing the wretched Deborah? What was that about? I hadn't investigated the situation properly. I just wanted to put on an act for Meg to show that I could do something she couldn't. Basically I had sacked an employee as a way of showing off and now I was being punished for it.

I tried an experiment. I tried to find any bit of my recent behaviour that didn't make me feel just a bit queasy. There was, for example, my treatment of Charlie, which was a huge issue in itself. I'd lied to him, betrayed him, let him down, even my attempt at helping him, with his bloody accounts, had it been just a way of showing that – apart from everything else – I was better at doing his job than he was?

As for my work, as soon as I thought of KS a sour, sharp liquid rose into the back of my mouth, and for a moment I felt I was about to throw up. I was like a lap-dancer. I knew how to give the punters a good time and get them to do the equivalent of pushing ten-pound notes into my costume. That wasn't something to be proud of. Precisely the opposite. I thought for a moment of this bed in Archway as my deathbed. If I were lying at the end of my life, about to enter an eternity of nothingness, how would I look back on my career? I'd entertained fatigued businessmen and sent them back to their crappy companies feeling a bit better about themselves. I would have been better occupied planting bombs in their offices. Almost anything would be better than what I was doing. It would be better if I gave up everything, gave the house back to the building society and learned an honest trade, learned how to make something real.

I almost made myself laugh with that one. I thought about that line in 'Goodbye Yellow Brick Road', about going back to my plough. Yeah, right. If there was anything more ludicrous than my life, it was my solution for dealing with it: Charlie could be a plumber and I could be a carpenter.

I got out of bed because I was starting to bore myself with my own thoughts. I had a shower and washed my hair, felt my nails scratching my scalp. When I got out I rummaged around on the bathroom shelf and in the cupboard, among all my ridiculous creams and lotions, for the nail-clippers and didn't find them. I shouted down to Charlie asking where they were and he shouted something back and I shouted something rude in return. About number fourteen in Charlie's top twenty irritating habits is using the nail-clippers anywhere but in the bathroom. One result is that I keep finding little crescent moons of nail-clippings sticking into my flesh in bed and another is that I can't find the nail-clippers when I want them. I yelled down to Charlie that I was going to buy a pair of nail-clippers that I was going to keep entirely to myself. He didn't reply. There was a particularly long jagged nail on my ring finger that kept catching on my clothing. I bit it until it split, then tore away the nail. Of course I got the angle wrong and it broke off far too low down and came away with a rip of pain, leaving exposed flesh beneath, which started to bleed. It looked insane as well. I had to bite off more of the nail just to make it even. Now it would need to grow for about two weeks before I could cut it again and make it look normal.

Charlie, or God, had hidden the nail-clippers somewhere, and then things got worse. I didn't want to put real clothes on. I had no intention of going outside today. I pulled on an old pair of tracksuit trousers, the sort with a cord round the waist. I tugged at one end and saw the other disappear into the hole of the waistband. I howled at it. I tried to extract the fuzzy end of the cord from the hole but it was too far in. I tried to concertina the waistband to bring it closer but it didn't work. I could feel the cord but I couldn't get at it. I was once taught how to deal with this crisis. It involved a needle, a steady hand and patience, and I didn't have any of them. I could feel arteries throbbing in my head. I was probably about to have a stroke and I would almost have welcomed it. The inanimate world was turning on me. The duvet, the nail-clippers, the tracksuit trousers. I pulled the trousers off, ripped at them, then threw them into the corner and squatted on the floor, holding my head.

There was a hand on my shoulder.

'Charlie?' I mumbled.

'What's going on? What is it?'

'Bad night,' I said.

'I know,' he said. 'You were talking in your sleep.'

That gave me a jolt. 'What did I say?'

'It was just babble,' he said. 'Do you want something to eat?'

'I'm not hungry.'

'What happened to your finger?'

I looked at my ring finger. The tip was dark with dried blood. 'I cut the nail too short,' I said.

'Get dressed anyway. We could go for a walk.'

'I want to have a bath first.'

'Didn't you have a shower?'

'I'm cold. I need to warm up.'

Charlie looked at me suspiciously. It reminded me of the look you give people when you suddenly realize that their puzzling behaviour is explained by the fact that they're drunk. 'Can I bring you anything in the bath?' he said. 'Coffee? A biscuit?'

'I'll be fine in a minute.'

In the bath I chewed all my nails down to an acceptable shortness. I was more skilful this time and they didn't bleed. I don't know how long I was in the bath, but I refilled it several times until at last there was no more hot water and I got out. I took a long time to get dressed. Deciding what to wear and then putting it on seemed the most enormous effort. Even the idea of pulling dry jeans over my damp skin made me feel dizzy. I lay on the bed and fell asleep briefly. Every time I slept I felt more tired when I woke up. I put my arm over my eyes to block out the wintry light.

Later, I don't know how much later, I heard a voice. Meg's voice.

'Why are you crying like this?' she said.

I opened my eyes and saw that Meg and Charlie were sitting on either side of the bed, looking down at me.

'What's happening? Am I ill? Maybe I'm dying? Maybe I'm already dead and this is my corpse and you're both sitting here and soon one of you will sigh deeply and say, "Well, it's probably for the best."'

'What are you on about?' said Meg.

'Meg and I are worried about you,' explained Charlie.

'Can't think why.'

'Do you want to get up now?'

'Not with both of you sitting there looking at me as if I've got some fatal disease that might carry me off any minute. I'll get up soon.'

'I'll put the kettle on,' said Charlie, with a reassuring, sympathetic expression.

I had an impulse to punch him in the face as a way of removing that smile and at the same time I was aware, in a distant way, that he was behaving extremely kindly and patiently in the face of intolerable behaviour from me. A little voice deep in my brain was telling me that at some point I was going to have to start behaving like a human being again.

'I'll count to ten and then get out of bed,' I said. 'One, two, three . . .'

Meg left when I reached nine and three-quarters. I lay there a while longer, then gritted my teeth, made the most enormous effort and got dressed. I opened the curtains of the smaller window that looks out on to the street: the pavements were wet and the sky overcast. I opened the curtains of the larger window and pressed my forehead to the cool glass. Charlie was in the garden, then Meg came out and stood beside him. She touched his shoulder and he turned towards her. They stood very close together, talking. Then he took her hand and laid it against his cheek and she smiled up at him. Together they returned to the house.

I clomped down the stairs, feeling as if there were lead weights attached to my feet. At least they could hear me coming.

Charlie made yet another pot of tea and pushed a steaming mug in front of me, telling me to drink. Meg toasted some bread and spread honey on it. Then Naomi appeared, carrying a tin.

'Charlie said you weren't feeling too good,' she said. 'I've made some ginger biscuits. Ginger's very good when you're feeling sick. Hi there, Meg.'

'Hello, Naomi.'

'I'm not feeling sick,' I said mutinously.

'Oh, well, they're nice anyway. Here, try one.'

She smiled at me, and I saw her even white teeth with a gap between the two front ones. She wasn't wearing a jacket or even a sweater, just a bright yellow T-shirt. She looked so tangy and clean, like a spring day.

'Holly's been overworking,' Meg said.

'And not sleeping properly,' added Charlie.

'You poor thing,' said Naomi. 'No wonder you feel grotty. There's this herbal tea I give to my patients with insomnia. It's a mixture of Chinese herbs. It looks a bit like grey dust, but it's very soothing and seems to do the trick. Do you want some?'

'No.'

'Yes,' said Charlie. 'Yes, she does.'

'I can't stand herbal tea.' I looked at the three of them, standing over me. 'Or sympathy.'

There was a ring at our front door and Charlie went to answer it. I heard a murmur of voices, then Charlie called me. I joined him at the front door and looked out. Two men were unloading something from the back of a van. It was a bulky object wrapped in a green tarpaulin.

'What's this?' I said.

A fourth man handed me a clipboard. 'Holly Krauss?' he said.

'That's right.'

'Print and sign,' he said.

I looked at the receipt. ORYX GALLERY was written at the top, with a picture of something with horns that was in all probability an oryx.

'Oh,' I said, as the horrible truth dawned. 'Can you take it back?'

The man shook his head. 'We're heading straight up to Leicester, love. Anyway, I don't think it works like that. You've paid for it. It's yours now. Where do you want it?'

It took three of them to get it into our living room; it wasn't that big but it was enormously heavy. Charlie said nothing as they removed the tarpaulin with a flourish.

'Gracious!' said Naomi. 'What on earth is it?'

I couldn't even remember which object I'd bought. It was several pieces of defunct machinery welded together at strange angles, then balanced on a plinth. It looked extremely ugly and far too big for the narrow room. Charlie still said nothing until the door closed and the men were gone. 'What's this?' he said. His fists were clenched by his side.

'I had a rush of blood to the head,' I said brightly. 'Whoosh!'

He picked up my copy of the receipt I'd signed. 'Jesus Christ, Holly,' he said.

'How much?' I asked.

'You mean you don't know?'

'I'm going to return it.'

'Of course you're going to fucking return it. Or try to. How do you know they'll take it back? I wouldn't. Why did you go and buy it in the first place? What did you think you were doing?'

'It seemed like fun at the time.' I gave a little chuckle to prove my point. 'And it might be an investment. Who knows?'

Charlie had gone white with anger. The receipt was trembling in his hand as if a wind were blowing. He could barely speak. 'We have a ninety per cent mortgage,' he said. 'We lied about our salaries to get it. I don't understand.'

We all looked at the dreadful object in our living room.

'I think we should go now,' said Meg, but she and Naomi stood as though rooted to the spot.

'What are you up to, Holly? What the fuck is going on with you? Tell me! *Tell me!*'

I was looking at the sculpture and for the first time that day something seemed funny. To my horror and shame, I started to laugh. And once I'd started, I couldn't stop.

12

Meg hates November. She says it's the year's corridor: a grim, narrow time that you have to go along to get somewhere else. She hates February as well. The greyness, the cold, the hard earth, the bare trees, the brief, pale, pinched days. None of this has ever made much sense for me. Seasons are for farmers and gardeners. I think it's the weather in your head that matters and suddenly, in the third week of November, when the streets were wet and the air grainy with drizzle, the weather in my head was blazing yellow sunshine, high blue skies. It happens like that. There had been weeks of pushing along through the tunnel of days like a blind, slow, grimy old mole, and then, without warning, I surfaced, half dazed, into the beautiful light.

I pulled apart the curtains and let in the morning. The fog outside blurred the shapes of the houses and trees and muffled the sound of the traffic. Familiar objects had become mysterious. Anything could happen on a day like today.

'Wake up, Charlie, here's some coffee.' I sat on the side of the bed and put a hand on his warm shoulder. He didn't stir and I gave him a shake. 'It's half past seven. You said you wanted to be gone by eight.'

He muttered something and retreated down the bed, gathering the duvet around him like a soft, billowy cave.

'Shall we meet for lunch today? I'll treat you.'

'I'm seeing someone,' he said, from under the duvet. 'The accountant and then the design editor of the *Correspondent*.'

The accountant. It sounded grand but it was actually Tina, who had helped Meg set up the KS accounting system.

'I'll take you out afterwards,' I said.

He half sat up and took the coffee, cupping both hands round it and letting the steam rise into his face. 'I said I'd go out with Sam and that lot for a drink.'

'Pity,' I said. 'I wanted to celebrate.'

'Celebrate what? It's not my birthday, is it?'

'Just celebrate. What colour shall we paint this room?'

'What?'

'I was thinking about it in the night. I thought yellow for the kitchen, not a horrible, stinging yellow, of course, something soft and buttery and alluring, and then a terracotta colour in here, maybe. Like the roof tiles of an Italian house. Or greeny-grey. What do you think? Something sexy or something restful? I'll buy the paint and get started on Saturday. Or even before. I'm owed about a hundred days off. I could do it really quickly once I get started. You don't need to do a thing. I've been letting things slide a bit and I want to look after you now. What I hate are all the preparations you're supposed to do first. You know, cleaning the skirting-boards and putting paper down and clearing shelves. Or cleaning the brushes afterwards. It's as bad as reading instruction manuals. One promise I've made to myself is that I will never, ever again read an instruction manual. Trish was saying yesterday that when you decorate you should put masking tape all the way along the wood where it adjoins the walls, so you get clean lines. That sounds excessive to me. Sometimes I think Trish should have been in the army. I've always had steady hands.'

I held my left hand straight out in front of me. 'Look at that!' There was a tremor in my fingers, a visible vibration.

'They've never done that before,' I said. 'Just as well I'm not a brain surgeon. I could wipe out entire areas of activity with one little wobble. Maybe I'm drinking too much caffeine. Or not enough. Caffeine withdrawal?'

Charlie waited a long time before answering. 'Yellow?' he said at last.

'What?'

'I was trying to follow your train of thought and I got stuck somewhere near the beginning. How long do you think you could go on talking without receiving a reply?'

'What? Oh, sorry. Shall I make you some toast? Toast and marmalade? I could even iron a shirt for you.'

'Liar,' he said, and I giggled. Then the giggle turned

into a strange, snorting laugh that I couldn't control.

He swung his feet to the floor and stood up, strong and naked in front of me. I reached up and put a hand on the small of his warm, golden back. 'All that running,' I said. 'You could be a bit late.'

'I can't today.'

'Another time.'

As he pulled on his jacket, his mobile phone played its daft tune in the pocket. 'Hello?' he said. 'Yes? No, eight's fine. Of course I'll be there.' His face relaxed into an intimate little smile and I knew he was talking to a woman. He changed the phone to the other hand and half turned away from me. 'I won't be late.'

Suddenly it was like watching a stranger, a handsome stranger with crow's feet round his eyes.

'Who won't you be late for?' I asked, as he slid the phone back into his pocket and fiddled with the knot of his tie in front of the mirror.

'Nobody. Sam and that lot.'

'You can flirt but you're not allowed to fall in love with someone else.' The words were out of my mouth before I had time to stop them. A lightning bolt of panic slashed through me as I heard myself speak. How could I say things like that, and mean them too, after my behaviour? How could I mind if Charlie was going to lean across a restaurant table this evening, staring into some woman's face, when I'd spent a night being kissed, touched, scratched, fucked, turned inside out by a stranger?

'Don't worry,' said Charlie. 'I'm a married man, remember?'

'I remember.' I reached out and adjusted his shirt unnecessarily with my quivering fingers. 'Have a good day.'

I was too jumpy to work properly. I spent a couple of hours at lunch trying to choose paints in a warehouse-sized shop just up from the office. They had such distractingly evocative names: celandine yellow, silver flax and Thames mud; ice grey, liquorice, spice. I ended up buying five litres of a deep, orangey-red paint called fox brown, and five of a mustardy yellow, plus three sleek black brushes – thick, medium and thin – a paint tray, six sheets of coarse-grained sandpaper and a bottle of methylated spirits. In the afternoon, through a meeting and then the fortnightly office discussion about new ideas, I kept thinking about standing in front of a smoothly plastered wall, with a full brush of yellow paint in my hand. That first lick of colour; a vivid streak across blankness.

Just after six, Stuart rang me on my mobile. I heard voices in the background. Did he spend his entire life in bars? I hadn't seen him since that evening, another of those evenings that I was trying to forget. The Oryx Gallery were proving resistant to my idea – more like a plea – of returning the sculpture and it was now standing in our bedroom, where no one else had to see it, a monument to something. Charlie had already stubbed his toe on the base and I had torn a skirt quite badly on one of its many jagged edges.

Stuart had left two messages – one sober, one drunk – and although I'd promised myself I'd call him back, I hadn't got round to it. He was that kind of man: the one you quite like, the one who's quite interesting, quite good-looking, yet oddly diffuse. He talked a lot and I could never remember precisely what he'd said. He drank a lot, and then all his words ran together in a stream that trickled over me.

'Holly!' he said now. 'It's Stuart, the one you ran away from and the one whose calls you haven't been returning. I haven't taken it personally.'

Drunk, I thought. 'Hi, Stuart.'

'What are you up to?'

'In general?'

'In the next hour or so.'

I opened my mouth to say I was busy. In reality I was tired, but I wasn't busy. Charlie was out for the evening. With a woman, for all I knew. I had no plans. I wasn't tired. I was restlessly agitated. A woman in search of adventure.

'Why?'

'I'm going to a poker game at a friend's house, just six of us or so, and I thought it might be fun if you came as well.'

'I haven't played poker since I was at college. I can play animal snap and racing demon and patience, and that's about it.'

'I don't think the others would like that much.

You don't have to play, though. You can watch us and drink whisky and blow smoke-rings.'

'That sounds fantastic fun,' I said. 'Watching six people play cards all evening.'

'You'll come, then?' he said enthusiastically. 'Great. I'll pick you up in an hour from your office.' And he was gone.

'Why not?' I said aloud.

I saw Meg watching me from across the desk and I looked away. After all, she wasn't my mother and I was only going to watch a card game for a bit. What was the harm in that? I got up from my chair and went into the ladies', where I stood in front of the mirror and painted my lips red. I pinned back my hair in an elegant bun and raised my eyebrows at myself. I wanted to look like a *femme fatale* in a *noir* film of the forties, standing in a stairwell with slabbed shadows falling across my face. I wanted to wear stiletto heels and a tight skirt and shrug nonchalantly at pain and danger.

13

I heaved my tins of paint into the back of the cab and clambered in after them. When I looked back on this evening in the days that followed, this was the last part I remembered as a coherent whole. I sat in the cab with Stuart and his friend, Fergus. Stuart was cheerful but wary. I think he was surprised I had come but he must have remembered that our visit to the exhibition had taken an unexpected turn. I couldn't make out Fergus's face clearly in the gloom, but I could see he was thin, loose-skinned, sharp-boned.

He held out a cigarette and I took it and, in the sudden flare of the lighter, saw his cadaverous face. For a moment I thought of telling the driver to stop and let me out, but the moment passed away – or, at least, it passed into me. I almost felt it fall through my mind to lodge deep inside me.

'Where are we going, then?' I asked.

'Wandsworth.'

'I don't know Wandsworth.'

From then on the evening was like an old and damaged piece of film footage. The sound comes and goes, sequences are in black-and-white or projected at the wrong speed, images are blurred, entire scenes are missing. Of the house, I only remember details: an enormous plasma TV screen, a leather sofa, a trashy 'tastefully erotic' picture on the wall – a woman peels a stocking from a long white leg, a man watches from the shadows. In the kitchen there is a fridge of gleaming stainless steel.

A group of men is already there, five of them, drinking Scotch. All are in suits without ties, except one. He is a fat, florid-faced man in a suit with a tie. It's his house and his poker game. Two younger men are talking loudly. One is Fergus. The other is Tony. Stuart told me about Tony in the taxi on the way over. He runs a building company but Stuart gave me a wink and said he had other interests as well.

'You mean criminal?' I said.

Stuart laughed. 'Tony doesn't exactly operate through normal channels,' he said.

Stuart is evidently eager that I'm aware he knows someone like Tony. When Stuart introduces me boisterously to him, he hardly speaks. He is tall, broad-shouldered. I shake his hand. It is large and rough. He looks at me curiously for a moment. I am the only woman there. I feel the exhilaration of escaping into another world, where different things are done.

They are playing poker. There is no money on the table, just brightly coloured discs in stacks. I stand behind Tony's shoulder. I have a drink in my hand, ice clinking. I walk round the table looking at the cards. I like this. The murmur of bidding, frowns of concentration, technical talk. It's coming back to me. I know this game. I used to be good at it.

Stuart is sitting on the other side of the table. He tells me to come over and give him luck. I say that I can see fine from where I am. Stuart is talking about me possessively. If any of the men think that I am his girlfriend, he is saying nothing to correct them. He tells me I look like a gangster's moll. I have been thinking the same myself and the idea amused me but when it's spoken aloud it doesn't seem funny any more.

A mobile phone rings. Tony leaves. Something requires his attention.

There is an empty chair at the table. Now it's not empty because I'm sitting at the table. I'm playing. Stuart gives me a puzzled look. He says he thought I didn't play poker and wouldn't it be better if I stuck to looking decorative? He's very much one of the lads now, nothing like the sensitive soul I sat up with late into the Oxfordshire night. I take a long time at first, staring at the two queens in my hand. Do I dare to stay in? What should I bet? Stuart says something I can't quite hear and the men all laugh. Then he tells the story about my buying the sculpture and somehow connects it to getting me to make up my mind, urging me to hurry. The men laugh again. I feel my cheeks burning.

At least it's better than coming too quickly, I say, looking over at Stuart. At least, that's what you tell me. The other men find this very funny indeed. They're laughing loudly and joshing Stuart, jabbing at him. He doesn't speak.

I feel a lurch in my stomach. I've got back at Stuart all right, but I may have got back at him too much. I take someone's glass and finish their drink in one gulp. I feel a jolt like an electric shock. I feel better. I feel number.

It's all so easy. I have my own colourful heap of chips. I arrange them in order. It all goes perfectly. I throw away three cards and get another queen. It beats everybody. My heap is bigger now, overflowing. Later, I don't know how much later, I get three of something again. But I don't win. Somebody has something better. My pile of chips is gone.

I'm playing and then I'm not playing. Stuart is gone now. He's nowhere to be seen. I'm sitting on the leather sofa. It's all seemed like the biggest joke. I've been the gangster's moll, flirting and smoking and drinking and dangling on men's shoulders while they play cards. Then I was something else. I was the naughty little sister joining in with the big boys, playing with their toys. It was the biggest joke, funnier and funnier, like those times when you were a girl with your best girlfriend and you got the giggles and you giggled and everything that happened made you giggle more and you thought you would laugh for the rest of your life until you died. Then the laughter started to hurt, yet you were afraid to stop laughing. Now I'm sitting on the leather sofa, which stings my thighs, drinking another drink and I have a feeling that there are things about this that are not funny at all. I don't know the people here and I don't know how to get home and I don't think I've got any money left. Money. Yes, there's that. There's something that somebody said after a few hands didn't go so well. Somebody said a figure: nine thousand pounds. That's what I owe. That can't be right. I was just playing. I just came with Stuart.

I'm drinking so I won't be able to feel any more. Someone next to me passes me a cigarette and lights it for me. I draw the smoke deep into my lungs. I feel blurrier and blurrier. I think of my tins of paint. Where are they?

I'm accident-prone, always have been. I break glasses, bump into things. If I'm cutting up vegetables, which I hardly ever am, then I'm as likely as not to push the blade into my thumb. So I'm well used to anaesthetics in casualty departments as well as dentists' chairs. The thing about an anaesthetic is that it doesn't abolish pain. It just picks it up and puts it away in the corner where it doesn't bother you. You can even feel that hurting is going on somewhere. I knew somewhere there was a bit of me that wasn't having such a good time and that when everything wore off none of me would be having a good time.

Tony leans over me. 'All right?'

I just stare at him.

'We should go,' he says. 'Game's over.' He helps me up and leads me out of the room.

'I'll drive you,' he says.

'My paint,' I say. 'I need my cans of paint.'

'Forget about your paint.'

14

'Where to?'

I stared at him. Where to? Where could I go now? I gazed out of the window. It was still dark, although there was a smudgy grey on the horizon, and I saw both the empty, lonely streets outside, and my own face staring back at me. I pushed my hair back behind my ears and pulled my skirt down over my knees.

'Where do you live?'

'I don't want to go there,' I said dully. 'Meg's. That's it. Meg.'

'So where does Meg live?' he asked patiently.

'Oh. Sorry, yes. Ventura Street. Near Marylebone Road. You have to go . . .'

'I know the area. I used to work there.'

'Where do you work now?'

'Building site near Tate Modern. You don't want to know that, do you?'

'Not really.'

'There's a blanket under the back seat.'

'A blanket?'

'You're shivering. Wrap yourself in it.'

We drove in silence and, after a few minutes, crossed the river. Tony's Mercedes nosed its way smoothly along the streets, its headlights picking out black bin bags in piles on pavements, ready for collection, the skeletal plane trees waving their branches, the low slink of a cat into the shadows, a man in a trench-coat walking slowly. There was traffic as well, more than I expected. Sometimes I closed my eyes, but when I did that I felt as if I was dying and my whole garish life was unrolling, and sometimes I stared out of the windows at the ghostly city moving towards me, rushing past me, and every so often I glanced across at Tony as he drove, a cigarette hanging from his lip.

'You've got to direct me from here.'

When he pulled up outside Meg's flat, I wanted to get out of the car and leave without speaking. But there was something I had to say.

'When you were gone, I – I shouldn't have, I joined the game. I don't really remember it properly. But I lost some money. Quite a lot.'

Tony lit another cigarette. 'Yeah. I heard.'

'It was all a mistake.' I waited but he didn't speak. 'What do I do?'

He took a deep drag on the cigarette and let the smoke spill out of his mouth. 'Pay it,' he said.

'I'm not sure if I've got the money.'

'You can always find money.'

'I don't know who to give it to.'

'Contact Vic. Or he'll contact you. Doesn't matter which.'

I'd thought Tony would rescue me from that. I got

out of the car. I could almost feel the damp of the pavement through my shoes. Tony waited while I rang the bell. A minute later, after I had rung a second time, I could hear a shuffling and then the chain slid back. Her face peered out of the gap, puffy with sleep.

'Meg,' I said.

'Holly? What on earth . . .'

'Can I come in?'

'Sure, sure.'

A rattle of chain, the slide of metal on metal, then the door opened and Meg was there, clutching at the neck of her thick grey dressing-gown.

'What the fuck?' she said. She peered at my face. 'Are you all right? What's going on?'

I turned and waved at Tony. He gave a nod and his Mercedes purred away.

'I see,' said Meg. Her face had become expressionless.

'Let's go up,' I said, and as we mounted the stairs I addressed her stiff, disapproving back. 'I'm sorry to wake you. I didn't want to go home right away.'

'I can understand that,' said Meg, in a cool voice that made me want to sit on the stairs and put my head in my hands.

'Things have gone a bit wrong,' I said, as we reached her warm, familiar flat.

'I'll make coffee,' she said. 'Then we can talk about it.'

'I can't talk about it. I'm too tired.'

Meg rubbed her eyes, ran her fingers through her hair. 'Have a shower,' she said.

'I'm in trouble, Meg.'

'I know.'

Dread filled me, top to toe. What did she mean, she knew? How could she know? I didn't want her to be looking at me with her shrewd eyes. I didn't want anyone to look at me. But eyes are everywhere, wherever you go, and you can't hide yourself, or your dirty secrets and your shame.

'I'll have a bath,' I said weakly, and shuffled into her bathroom, where the radiator was humming.

I had a hot, deep soak, then got dressed in a pair of black cords and a soft pink shirt that I'd given her for her last birthday. Meg even gave me a little toothbrush she'd saved from her last long plane journey so I could clean my teeth. I avoided looking in the mirror. I was scared of my own face, and the eyes that would stare back. I had to stand quite still, holding the wash-basin and waiting for the horror to slide back inside myself, where it could grow and flourish in my private darkness.

'Here, coffee,' said Meg.

I tried to pick it up but my hands were shaking so much that hot liquid splashed on to my skin and I had to lower it again and, leaning forward, sip from it like a dog.

'Something to eat?'

'No, I couldn't.'

At that moment I couldn't believe I'd ever eat again. I would starve and purify myself until at last I was empty and clean, like a child just starting out, not grubby and defiled by life.

'So,' said Meg, putting her chin on her hand and gazing at me.

'I've been stupid.'

'That man?'

'No, he just gave me a lift back.'

Meg raised her eyebrows but didn't say anything. She was waiting for me to speak, to tell her everything.

'I can't,' I said. 'Sorry. I need to talk to Charlie. I should say it all to him first. I'll call a cab and arrange to meet him.'

Meg nodded.

'That sounds like a good idea.'

I wanted to say, babyishly, *Please be my friend still.* I nearly did, but Meg, sitting opposite me with her tired, grave face, seemed so grown-up, so sorted-out, so remote from me and my messy, ugly problems that I could scarcely bring myself to believe we were friends and partners, two women who understood each other's language and who could read each other's faces. Far, far away.

'I'm sorry,' I said lamely. 'Meg? I'm sorry.'

There was a long silence, in which I could hear myself breathing hoarsely. I picked at the fabric of the pink shirt and saw that I'd bitten my nails further down, though I couldn't remember doing that.

I waited. 'There is no light at the end of this tunnel,' I said to myself. 'This tunnel goes on and on and things are roaring towards me in the darkness.'

At last Meg looked at me, as if she'd made up her mind about something. Then she spoke. 'I can't do this any more.' Her voice was hard, with nails in it. Her face was hard as well.

'What do you mean, can't do this? Can't do what?' My own voice was a croak, like a crow up in a high tree.

'Go on taking your behaviour. Do you think it's all I've got to do with my life, clear up your messes?'

'I don't know what you —'

'Do you ever think about me? Or Charlie? Or anyone except yourself? Don't bother to answer that. Of course you don't. The world revolves around you and your stupid desires. You think you're wonderful, don't you?'

'Not at this moment, really —' I began.

'With your long hair and your big eyes, fluttering your thick lashes, you think everyone will just fall over backwards to help you, don't you? Help you when you're in trouble, and forgive you when you let them down. Because you never *mean* to. You're so *impulsive*, aren't you? So *spontaneous* and *reckless*, that's what you say to yourself.'

'I'm sorry.'

'What do you think it's like for me? There you are, centre stage, showing off, and it's good old Meg, always there, behind the scenes, unnoticed, picking up the pieces, making sure everything's smoothed over.'

All the resentment she'd been storing up was spilling out now. I knew there were things to be said in reply. I'd been working seven days a week up to twenty hours a day for almost a year. I'd done so much of the hard stuff, getting the clients, working with them, but it all felt too tiring. It didn't matter. Meg was in full flow.

'Holly, you should look at yourself. You sacked a woman just because you felt like it, and now we're having to deal with the fall-out. You slept with a man who's now ringing the office and hassling people. You charm clients or you insult them. You fall asleep at your desk or in the toilets – don't think we don't notice – and then go out all night. You're like a baby, picking things up that catch your eye and dropping them when you get bored. You're being foul to Charlie as well.'

'Charlie's my business,' I said wearily. 'Just because you –' I stopped abruptly and actually put a hand across my mouth to hold back the words.

'What? Just because what? Say it! I know what you were going to say. Just because I fancied him once. I did. It's true, and you knew it. But he fancied you, because men always do, don't they?'

'I wasn't going to say that,' I said weakly. Every spark of anger faded. I stared at Meg in dismay, with her puffy pale face and her frizzy morning hair and her creased brow.

'Have you ever thought about me, Holly?'

'You?'

'Yes. Me. Have you noticed I've been a bit down recently? That my life's not going according to plan? That I've been a bit anxious? No, of course you haven't, because you're so up and down that there's no room to notice other people's ordinary, less dramatic moods.'

'That's not true.'

She stood up and pulled the belt tight on her grey dressing-gown. 'I'm going to have a bath, if you haven't used up all the hot water, and then I'm going to get on with my day. Call your cab and let yourself out.'

I arrived early so I saw him walking towards me. We'd arranged to meet in the park near our house. At first he didn't see me so I could watch him as he came along the road. He was wearing a thick coat we'd chosen together, and his head was slightly down, but I could still see the expression on his face, serious, almost grim. On another day I would have asked him what he was thinking about so hard. But I knew. I knew what made his face so tight and frowning, and his mouth narrow. Me.

When he saw me his face went blank and he pushed his hands deeper into his coat pockets.

'Thanks for coming out to meet me,' I said.

'It's all right.'

We walked together into the unsatisfactory small park. I cleared my throat, but couldn't speak.

'Good night?' he asked quietly.

'No,' I said.

'Have you spent the night with someone?'

'No.' I took a deep, stinging breath. I felt a few cold drops of rain on my face. 'You were out last night, so I went out as well, with a guy called Stuart, a client. It wasn't a date or anything like that. He's the one I went to the art show with, but he's not important. It's stupid. I ought to like being alone sometimes. When I'm with a crowd of people, I often feel I'll go mad, explode, unless I can get away from them and be solitary, but when I'm on my own I can't bear that either. I can't explain it, I don't know where to begin, I –'

'How about beginning with Rees? I think I've got his name right, haven't I?'

I felt cold through to my bones. 'Rees?' I said. 'What about him?'

'That's what I'm asking you.'

'He's not important.'

'You mean, not important like this Stuart's not important?'

'No, I mean, it's not anything to do with him, what happened, not in a way, though of course he was there, but it could have been anyone. I mean . . .' I rubbed my eyes frantically. I didn't know what I meant. I wanted to speak clearly, authentically, lay out my sins and failures, but it was all tangled up in my head, like a knotted coil of wires, and the words came out wrong. 'How do you know about him?' I said instead.

'He called me,' said Charlie. For the first time, there was a crack in his voice. Grief? Anger? Hatred? I couldn't tell.

'Oh, God, Charlie, I'm sorry. I'm so sorry. What did he say?'

'The first time he called my mobile. How did he get the number?' I just mumbled something miserably, but he continued without paying attention. 'He asked if I knew what you were up to. I thought it was a madman, someone you'd offended. There seem to be a few around at the moment. The second time, two days ago, he called me at home and asked to speak to you, and one thing led to another and he told me who he was.'

'What did he say?'

'The third time, yesterday evening, he said you were a wildcat in bed. And he asked if I knew what you were doing at that precise moment.'

'How horrible for you. How disgusting. You should have told me.'

'What? Then you would have comforted me?'

I started to say something incoherent but Charlie interrupted me: 'Just tell me. Have you had sex with this person?'

'Yes,' I said. 'About a month ago. I was very drunk.'

'Again.'

'Yes. Again. And everything got out of hand.

I couldn't believe I'd done it. It was like a dream, a nightmare, like someone else had climbed into my body. I couldn't even remember what he looked like. It was like I'd had an illness. I wanted to pretend it hadn't happened.'

A grimace of intense disgust flashed across Charlie's face. I put out a hand but he pulled himself away, as if he couldn't bear to be touched by me. I understood that. I didn't want to be anywhere near me either. 'I know,' I said. 'What I'm saying is that it was a stupid, stupid, senseless one-night stand. I didn't tell you because . . . well, I knew it would hurt you and it didn't mean anything. It didn't mean anything,' I repeated. 'Or it didn't mean that I don't love you and want you. Only you. Charlie?'

He looked at me almost in wonder. 'Are you listening to yourself?' he said.

'What do you mean?'

'How am I meant to react to that – that fucking crap?'

'I'll change,' I said desperately, 'if you give me the chance. I will be good. If you forgive me.'

'You know what, Holly? I can't talk about this right now.'

'Charlie –'

'I used to be so proud of you . . . Proud of being the one who was married to you.'

'Please, I'll make you proud again. Please.'

'I feel like such an idiot. I don't know what to do. I need to think. I need to be on my own for a bit.'

'Yes, yes, of course. Of course you do. I'll just . . . well, I'll be ready whenever you want to talk again. I'll be at home today. I won't work. I'll just . . . I'll be at home. I'll wait for you, shall I?'

'Whatever.'

He left the park. I watched him, his long coat flapping and his head down against the gusting wind, until he was out of sight. Then I went and sat on a bench.

When I was a little girl I used to go on long walks with my father. Whenever we got to a fence or a wall, I would clamber up to the top, and he would tell me to jump down into his outstretched arms. I never hesitated. Even when it was high up I would throw myself forward and know he would catch me. He called me his wild child. He called me his heroine. I flew through the air towards his safe embrace. Then he left and I was flying through the air but there was nobody who could save me any more, nobody to catch me when I fell.

I stood up at last. I had no idea how long I'd been sitting on the bench, but my hands were white with cold.

As I reached home, I met Naomi and she asked if we could have coffee together. I opened my mouth to send her away, then thought, Why not?

But when I took out my keys, I found the house-key was missing. I scrabbled in the bottom of my bag in case it had fallen there, but couldn't find it.

'I hate this,' I said, almost crying. 'I always lose

my keys. Keys, wallet, sunglasses, phone, umbrella. Anything. I lose everything.'

'How could you lose it when all the others are on the key-ring?' she asked patiently.

'It's a stupid key-ring,' I said. 'Stupid. Look at it. I only keep it because it belonged to my fucking father. Huh.'

'It doesn't matter, anyway. I've got a spare key, remember? You gave it to me a few months ago in case of emergencies. I'll go and fetch it.'

I sat on the doorstep until she returned a few minutes later.

'Here. Keep it until you find the other.'

'Thanks.'

'Unless you think someone might have stolen it.'

'Stolen it?' I tried to keep the sudden fear out of my voice. 'What makes you say that?'

She shrugged, then let me into my house and handed over the key.

In the end it was she who made the coffee and found a packet of biscuits hidden at the back of the cupboard. She told me I looked peaky and made me eat two chocolate digestives, and she asked me what was wrong. I opened my mouth to say nothing, I was fine, but there were tears running down my cheeks. When she hugged me she smelt of vanilla and something spicy, like nutmeg. For a few seconds, I let myself be held in the motherly warmth of her embrace.

'You've been baking,' I said, through my tears.

She wiped my cheeks and held my hand. She told me that everything would be all right.

Then she left. And I just went on sitting at the kitchen table. I waited for Charlie to come home without much hope that he would. After what seemed like hours I put my cheek on the grainy wood and closed my eyes. I could fall asleep. Fall asleep and never wake up.

15

I'd always had the idea that I was the indispensable one who did all the work, who carried the company, who helped Charlie fulfil his artistic destiny, who was the life and soul of the party. Not any more. I had become the one member of the expedition who was injured and holding everybody back, endangering everybody's lives. I was the girl in the old black-and-white science-fiction movie whose stiletto heel broke when they were running away from the monster.

I stood on Regent Street and took a deep breath. It was a matter of what was in my head. All I needed to do was change my attitude, which would then change my behaviour, which would then make everything all right again.

I wandered through some shops. First, in a bookshop, I found a collection of poems specifically designed to make you happy. The introduction said so and I read one short poem, which made me smile. So I bought thirty copies of the book. There were only four copies on the shelf. An assistant had to go to a back room and get a box for me.

Then I went, staggering under the weight of the box, to a stationery shop and found a postcard of a still-life showing just a glass of water and a head of garlic. Again I bought thirty. On the way back to work I went into a kitchen-supply shop. I was looking for something but I couldn't quite picture it. I wanted something made of wood. Suddenly I found the perfect thing. It was a wooden rod and at the end of it were two discs, a small disc and a smaller disc. It looked a bit like a model of one of those pointless towers you see in some cities that have a revolving restaurant at the top and nothing else. I asked an assistant what it was for and she told me it was for runny honey, which was great. It even rhymed. I bought the whole little wicker basketload of them.

When I got back to the office I distributed them to the girls. There were quite a lot left over, so I put them into a package. I wrote a note to go with them addressed to the head of eYe1, the design company for which I was supposed to be running an event: 'Dear Craig. I couldn't be bothered to write a proposal. Have these instead. Love, Holly.' And I got Lola to messenger it round to them.

I looked round the office and thought again about how we needed areas of privacy. On the spur of the moment I rang an architect that Lola's mother's neighbour knew. He said he'd come and have a look soon and draw up some rough plans.

After that I got tired again. I needed to get home and get to bed, the way a drowning person needs to get to the shore. Sleep. If I could just cram some more sleep into me, stuff myself with it until it was coming out of my ears, I could get my mood sorted out and things would be fine again. I left an hour early. I went home and got into bed. I felt cold. What I wanted was a hot-water bottle but there wasn't one in the house so I got up and put on a tracksuit and a sweatshirt, then spread a rug on top of the duvet and got back under it. At some point in the evening I was dimly aware of Charlie coming into the room and saying something – I didn't know if it was to me – and leaving.

When the alarm went at eight the next morning I knew I felt better. I had slept for fourteen hours and when I emerged from unconsciousness it was almost as if I was newly born, blinking and a bit confused. The world's edges were hard and straight and clearly defined again. My panic had receded as well. I knew that there were big problems in my life but I felt finally that I could deal with them. I showered and washed my hair and dressed myself in a dark suit. Charlie was fast asleep. I felt an ache in my chest at the sight of his untidy hair and his face pushed under the pillow. I left a message on the table to say that I loved him very, very much and we must talk.

I was at the office before anyone else. I drank a mug of strong coffee and began to tackle the pile of work I hadn't done and, worse still, the smaller pile I *had* done but that now needed undoing. But it felt good, like spring-cleaning, and I knew I could manage it. I set myself the task of disposing of the whole pile by lunchtime, which I would spend in the office. By the end of the day I would be up to date and moving forward. I worked solidly, head down, virtually unaware of what was going on around me. When Meg tapped my shoulder, I was startled. I didn't even know what time it was. I looked at my watch: ten past twelve.

'Can I have a moment?' she said.

'Sure.'

'In the conference room.'

'What for?'

'It'll just take a moment.'

I followed Meg in and felt a jolt like an electric shock. Trish was already sitting at the table with a woman I didn't know. Between them was Charlie. Weirdly, my first thought wasn't about what he was doing there, but how he had got into the building without my noticing. I realized he must have come up the back stairs. Meg walked round and joined them on their side of the table. She gestured to me to sit on the other side, facing them, like in a job interview.

'What's going on?' I asked. '*This Is Your Life*?'

'This is Dr Jean Difford,' said Meg. 'She gives advice on issues in the workplace.'

'What kind of advice?'

'Medical advice.'

'I'm sorry,' I said. 'What is all this?'

Jean Difford smiled an irritatingly reassuring smile at me. 'I'm glad to meet you, Holly,' she said. 'I've heard a lot about you.'

'What have you heard?'

'Do you know of a place called Glenstone Manor?'

'No, I don't.'

'I've booked you in there today.'

There was a long silence. I looked at Meg, Trish and Charlie in turn. Meg and Trish were staring at the table but Charlie looked at me with concern. For the first time in days, I saw love in his eyes. Or pity.

'This feels like a conspiracy,' I said.

'It is a sort of conspiracy,' he said. 'We all care about you. Something's going wrong with you and we think you need help.'

'You can't go on like this,' said Meg.

'That's for me to decide, I'd say.'

'No,' said Charlie. 'At a certain point, one has to intervene.'

'You've all been talking about me to each other. Discussing me.' I turned on Meg. 'This is your revenge, isn't it?'

'No.'

'You weren't at the dentist yesterday. You were setting up this – this ambush.'

'It's not an ambush. It's a plan of action,' said Trish.

'OK – what's this plan of action?'

'You go to Glenstone Manor,' said Dr Difford. 'You'll be assessed and receive treatment. You will stay there for a week or two.'

'I don't understand,' I said. 'You're a doctor.'

'Yes.'

'This is what puzzles me. You're saying that I need to go into an institution and you've never even met me.'

'I've talked to your colleagues and I've talked to your husband.' At this I flashed a look at Charlie, who had the decency to appear a little shamefaced. 'They want to help you.'

I took a deep breath and then I forced myself to smile. 'Obviously this has taken me a bit by surprise,' I said. 'Am I allowed to ask any questions before they come to take me away?'

'Ask anything you like,' said Dr Difford, with her infuriating tone of patience and calm as if she were talking me down off a window-ledge.

'Does anybody here think I have a drug problem?' I asked.

'No,' said Meg.

'Drink?'

'Not in particular.'

'Then what are you saying about me?'

There was a pause. Nobody looked at me.

'That's for us to discuss at Glenstone Manor,' said Dr Difford.

'You all think I'm going off the rails.'

Nobody said anything.

'All right, I had a wobbly few weeks,' I said. 'I admit that. I've had a night or two out where things got out of control. I'm not proud of my behaviour but I'm sorting it out. The last few days in the office weren't my finest moments but that's all sorted. You should have come to talk to me about this, Meg, Trish' – I gave them fierce looks – 'before going behind my back to some smooth-talking doctor who thinks she can diagnose me before she's even set eyes on me. Especially you, Meg, because you are – used to be, anyway – my friend. As for things with Charlie, I'm aware of my lapses. I know I've got issues to sort out, apologies to make, but that's nobody's business but ours. I'm sorry, but this is a waste of time.'

'We've discussed it,' said Trish. 'We think it's the right thing to do.'

'You should have discussed it with me.'

'We are discussing it with you.'

'You're not. You're –' I could hardly speak. I was becoming hot with the anger bubbling up inside me. 'Look, it's time to take the gloves off, if that's what you want. I've admitted it. This week I've had a couple of bad days –'

'It's not about this week,' said Meg. 'You know that quite well.'

'Meg and I created this company and in the last year I've been running it almost fucking single-handed. Who has found about nine-tenths of our clients? Me. Who schmoozes them in the evening? Me. Who leads the presentations? Who creates the events? Who dreams up the ideas? Who sells them?'

'Some of us work here as well,' said Meg. 'Boring things, like the accounts. Like clearing up your mess.'

'When you were all pissing around not daring to deal with that bully Deborah Trickett, who was it who bit the bullet and fired her? And ever since she's been bad-mouthing me all over London. That was your job, Trish. I've spent a year working seven days a week, and when I wasn't working, I was doing so-called entertaining of clients. Things got a bit out of control and now I'm sorting them out. Because that's what I do. Go out and look at my desk,' I said. 'If you can find a single mistake, any task that hasn't been sorted out, you can haul me into the bin and inject me with anything you want.'

Trish gave a little cough and I saw she had in front of her some printouts. 'In the last few days,' she said, in a businesslike voice, 'you've made some very strange errors. There've been inquiries from clients.'

'Give me that!' I snatched the papers from her and glanced down at them. My cheeks burned with humiliation.

There was a knock. Meg and Trish looked round irritably. The door opened and Lola's face appeared.

'Call for Holly,' she said.

'Tell them we're in a meeting,' said Trish. 'We'll call back.'

'It's Craig from the people we're doing the event with, eYe1,' she said. 'He wants to talk to Holly straight away.'

Meg and Trish exchanged glances. Meg stood up. 'I'll go and take it in the office,' she said.

'Holly,' said Charlie, his voice dripping with pity, 'we're only thinking about what's good for you.'

'This is the question,' I said. 'Are you going to

drag me forcibly, against my will? I don't think you'll stoop to that. Anyway, it's probably illegal. Trish won't let you do something that isn't in the rule book. I'm not going to this Glenstone Manor. I'm going to stay put, and I'm going to come to work every day at nine o'clock and leave at six o'clock and show you how calm and rational and well-behaved I can be. If I do things you don't approve of, or if I make mistakes, come and tell me about them.'

There was a long, exceedingly awkward silence until Meg came back into the room. She sat down looking flustered. 'Well?' said Trish.

Meg ignored her and looked at me. 'If you're going to do off-the-wall things like sending packages of kitchen implements and books of poetry to important clients with whom we haven't yet signed a contract, I think it might be a good idea if we all talked it over first.'

'Sorry,' I said. I should have the word tattooed on my forehead to save time.

'What were you thinking?' said Trish. 'We needed that job.'

'He wants to see you tomorrow,' said Meg.

'So they didn't walk away?'

Meg looked embarrassed. 'He wants to talk about it tomorrow.'

'With all of us?'

'He said he wanted to meet Holly.'

'You still should have talked about this with us,' said Trish. 'And we haven't come to a decision.'

I could see that their resolve had crumbled and I stood up. 'I'm sorry you had to go to all this bother,' I said, very politely. 'And I'm sorry you've been worrying needlessly.'

I turned to Charlie. 'We should talk,' I said. 'Can I take you out to dinner tonight? I've got a lot to say. A lot of apologies to make.'

He looked at me for a long moment. 'All right, Holly,' he said.

'That's the only kind of therapy I need.'

It was like a play having to be abandoned before the final scene. I saw Meg and Dr Difford sharing a muttered exchange on the way out. I didn't care, I had other priorities. I had a life and a marriage to sort out.

We found a quiet Italian restaurant round the corner with a table in the window. Charlie drank a beer and I sipped mineral water while we watched people walking past, hurrying to get out of the rain. I reminded Charlie that when we first met, we would sit in restaurants and look at the people at other tables and try to guess what their stories were. He forced a smile. He was making an effort but he was clearly angry and hurt as well. He leaned over the table, close to me so that nobody else could hear what he was saying. 'I thought about just walking away and never seeing you again. But then . . .' He stopped and stared at me, as if he was struggling with something in his mind.

'Yes?'

'I don't know. It's all such a mess. But you're not yourself.'

'Oh, please, don't you start. What? What are you thinking?'

He took my trembling, cold hands between his and told me that we were going to sort things out, whatever it took. He said this was our anniversary dinner, and if we weren't celebrating exactly, we were making resolutions. The next year of our marriage was going to be better. It was going to be a real marriage. We were going to look after each other and he was going to help me.

I had wanted to talk. I tried to say that I didn't need any help because I really was going to change, had indeed already started to change, he would see, but he hushed me and said we would discuss all of that later. First I had to rest and recover. I started to say, indignantly, that I wasn't ill, but he said I should let it all be. 'Sometimes you don't need to articulate everything,' he said. I opened my mouth to argue, but all of a sudden the fight went out of me. It was as if my mind had been cut into segments. I was neatly sliced into anger and defiance, humiliation and shame, grim irony, rampant irritation and a sluggish indifference. None of the slices seemed to connect with each other, and I didn't know which bit of myself to speak with. I asked him, pathetically, if he still loved me but he didn't seem to hear. So I said, out of the blue and surprising myself as well, 'I've lost my key.'

'What?'

'I've lost my key,' I repeated. 'It's not on my key-ring.'

'You're always losing keys,' he said, stopped in his tracks. 'What's this got to do with anything?'

'I don't know. I just wanted to tell you.'

'All right, you've told me,' he said. 'I'll get another one cut – and you get yourself a key-ring that doesn't come apart all the time.'

We ordered a simple meal, just risotto and salad. Charlie had a glass of wine while I stuck to water. We ate warily, almost in silence, as if we were unfamiliar to each other, circling cautiously.

Charlie seemed different. Over the previous weeks he had been evasive, tetchy, ill-at-ease, resentful. Some of this was his own fault and had made me angry, which had made him worse, which had made me angrier. And, God knows, some of it had also been an understandable reaction to my behaviour. Sometimes I had thought that what had started out as a marriage had become a psychological experiment in which two people were confined in a small space to torment each other to death.

Now he seemed calmer, almost contented, as if he was in control, as if he could protect me. He'd made his decision about us. It was a face I had never seen before, and it made me want to crawl into his arms. It also made me want to drag myself into a deep, dark hole and sleep until spring came again. I did the next best thing. I ate a few forkfuls of warm, comforting risotto, took a sip of his wine, then let him take me home in a cab. He ran me a bath and after I had soaked for a long time I climbed into bed. I lay there and stared at that fucking horrible sculpture and it stared back at me, accusing me of terrible things, until Charlie came in with a mug of tea and a digestive biscuit. It was like being a child again. He turned the light off and stood in the doorway watching me, watching over me. I wrapped my arms round my pillow and pretended to sleep and at some point I was no longer pretending and the long day ended at last.

The next morning I arrived to find a message from eYe1. It was just the name of the bar round the corner from our office where Craig wanted to meet me after work. With a spasm of embarrassment I thought about the package I'd sent them. What must they have thought? I had a sudden vision of a life spent clearing up after myself. I could explain it away as a joke or a moment of madness or lovable eccentricity or . . . I asked Lola to go over the road and fetch me two double espressos. When she returned, I took them to a grim-faced Meg.

'Maybe you should come as well,' I said.

'You don't need me,' she said.

'I think I need you too much.'

'He specifically asked to see you,' said Meg.

I gulped at my coffee, grateful for the scalding sensation on my tongue. Meg's stood untouched on her desk.

'I don't know,' she said.

'What?'

'Do you have to bet the company every day? We're not like you. We don't need all that excitement.'

The moment I saw Craig at the bar, I realized it was going to be all right. He was half-way through a dry martini and when he saw me he smiled broadly. He started to order me a drink but I shook my head. It was going to be water for the moment. I was already a couple of martinis ahead of the rest of humanity.

'You're crazy,' he said, draining his glass and signalling to the woman behind the bar for another. 'It was just what we needed. Thinking outside the box. Here, listen to this.'

The poetry book was lying on the bar beside his martini. He picked it up and read a poem aloud. I found it hard to follow.

'Isn't that great? I haven't read a poem since I left Oxford. And this thing . . .' He took the runny honey device out of his pocket. 'It's a functional object,' he said, 'and yet there's something comic about it. I've shown it to people and it makes them smile.'

'I just thought it was funny,' I said, and indeed, that was about all I said. My brain was too fuzzed up to speak so Craig told me about the design business and I nodded at the right places, to give the impression of deep thought, and sometimes smiled, to give the impression of sympathy.

After an hour, he stood up and held out his hand. 'This has been great,' he said. 'I feel we've really clarified our ideas.'

I shook his hand.

'Can I drop you somewhere?' he said.

'No. I'm going back to the office,' I said falsely.

'You people,' he said, with a smile. 'I'll call you tomorrow. We're going to make money together.'

When I was alone, I ordered another mineral

water. What I really needed was paper and a pencil but I started to make the list in my head. It was a matter of sorting things out one by one. First, Charlie. Second, work. Then there was the other stuff. I had to make that go away. There was that gambling mess. Surely they understood that that was all a mistake. That would be number three on my list. I would deal with it. Somehow. I paid for my drink and asked where the toilet was. The barwoman directed me to the basement. After I had washed my hands I stood and looked at myself in the mirror and smoothed my hair with my hands. 'One step at a time,' I said to myself.

As I came out into the bare stone corridor, I brushed against a man in a suit and muttered an apology. I felt a hand on my shoulder and I was pushed back hard against the brick wall. I felt it cold through the silk of my dress. Rees's face was looking down at me with an expression almost of curiosity. 'You haven't been in touch,' he said.

I tried to move out of his grip. His hand came up. I didn't feel the blow. I saw it, an explosion of white light, and I heard the slap of his hand on my face. All of my breath was gone.

'You're fucking me around,' he said. 'I don't like that.'

His left hand was now tight on my neck so I couldn't cry out. His right hand stroked my cheek where he had hit me, then it moved down my body, down my breast, my stomach, pushing between my legs thi ██████████ leaned against me. I could still hear the sound of clinking glasses and chatter from upstairs. He whispered into my ear, 'You've played with me. You've made me do this. I'm not like this. I was just a normal man with a girlfriend . . .'

It was crazy. I was so frightened that my insides felt liquid. I knew he could do anything he wanted to me and I couldn't stop him, but even so, even with his hand on my throat, when he started talking self-pityingly about being an ordinary man, I couldn't stop myself laughing.

His face turned almost black with anger. 'You fucking . . . you fucking –' he gasped at me. 'How do you like it now?' he said. He shoved a knee in my groin making me cry out in agony, then ripped at my dress. His face came down towards me, really close so I could feel his breath on my face, see the wetness on his lips.

'You fucked me,' he whispered. 'I can do anything I want to you now.'

With all my energy, I spat at him, and saw with satisfaction the gob of phlegm on his neck. He lifted his hand and hit me again. I jerked back, hearing but not feeling the sharp rap of my head against the wall. He put a hand on the neck of my dress and ripped it, then brought his lips down on mine. I bit hard and tasted blood. I heard him cry out and once again there was an explosion of pain as he hit me.

There was the sound of footsteps on the stairs. Rees pulled away from me and was gone. As he ran up the steps, two women came down and passed me without speaking to me. They didn't even seem to see me cowering there.

My legs were trembling and my heart thumping so much that for a few minutes I couldn't bring myself to move. I just leaned against the wall and listened to the sound of my breathing. Then the toilet flushed in the cloakroom, so I made myself walk up the stairs, back into the bright lights and laughter of the bar, out into the dark streets again.

17

I stared around. A bulky figure stumbled out of the alleyway and I felt a tightness in my chest but it wasn't him, just another man in a suit. I looked at my watch and it was only just past seven. In June, there would be hours more of daylight left.

Where to? I should go home, but the taxis that sped past were occupied and I couldn't go on the Underground. I pulled out my mobile, but who did I want to call? I put a hand to my cheek, under my eye, and gently touched the puffy skin, wincing as I did so. I pulled my coat round me more firmly, trying not to think about his hand on my body. All of a sudden, I felt clammy and sick.

The office was a minute's walk away, so that was where I went, slowly on my shaky legs, looking around me all the time in case he was still near. I went straight to the cloakroom, turned on the light and stood in front of the mirror, gazing at the stranger in front of me, with bloodshot eyes, puffy skin, torn dress and a blue bruise flowering on her cheek. I slid out of my coat and inspected the damage, then ran some cold water and dabbed it on the swollen skin. I touched the back of my head, where I'd bumped it against the wall, and came away with a smear of blood on my fingers. The pain I hadn't felt at the time I felt now, and I was also assailed by a sense of despair, which left me dizzy so that I had to hold on to the wash-basin to stay upright.

I closed my eyes. Then I heard a faint sound outside and opened them again. Footsteps coming through the office. A light turned on. I couldn't move, just stayed staring at the damaged, helpless woman in the mirror. The footsteps tapped towards me, stopped, continued. The door creaked open.

Then Meg was standing behind me. I didn't turn round, but our eyes met in the mirror and we gazed at each other wordlessly. It was as if she could see right into me, into all the ghastly parts of me that even I didn't know about, and I felt so frightened and alone that I barely managed to stay upright, keep meeting her eyes. Was this friendship, I wondered, beyond affection or even love, a kind of terrible intimacy of knowledge? Or was it something else?

'Meg,' I said at last. 'What?'

'This can't go on.' She stepped forward and put a hand on my shoulder. I felt her warm fingers through my thin dress. Her hand felt very heavy. Was she comforting me, or was she like a warder leading the prisoner away? I turned at last; she put an arm round my shoulders and guided me into the office.

'You have to tell the police – I wanted you to before, but now you must.'

'But –'

'No buts. He's dangerous – I knew it as soon as I saw him. He won't stop there.'

'Meg?'

'I'm going to take you round to the station now. My car's outside in the loading bay. I just came back to collect a couple of files. I'll go and get your coat for you.'

She came back with it, wrapped it round me, then helped me downstairs to her car. She pressed me into the passenger seat, and fastened the seat-belt.

'Meg,' I said, as she got in on the driver's side and turned on the ignition.

'Yes?'

'What's going on with me?'

'I don't know.'

'I keep thinking there's something you haven't told me.'

'We'll talk about that later.'

'We never used to have secrets from each other. We used to tell each other everything.'

'You're going to report this Rees to the police. Everything else can wait.'

'I hate waiting.'

'I know,' she said drily.

'Is Charlie having an affair?'

'Later, Holly.'

'He is, isn't he? I wouldn't blame him. The question is, who with? Meg, who with?'

'Here we are.'

*

When, after forty minutes of waiting, I found myself sitting opposite a policewoman called Gill Corcoran, I found I didn't know how to tell the story. It seemed so hard to grasp, vivid and yet blurred, a nightmare that makes you wake up with sweat pouring off you in the small hours. It was Meg, sitting to one side of the desk, who prompted me so that in the end I managed to stumble through the squalid tale.

Gill Corcoran had a pleasant face, shrewd eyes, a sympathetic way of listening. She kept pouring water into a polystyrene cup for me, and I kept gulping it back, as if I could swill everything through me, out of me. She made me go over in detail how Rees had hit me. She looked at my cheek and the gash on my head, which was still bleeding. She told me to show her exactly where he'd touched me, what he'd done.

Without looking at Meg but feeling her eyes on me, I told her how I'd met him. I told her about the night we'd spent together. I told her about the phone calls he'd made to Charlie, about the knickers he'd sent. Meg looked down at her hands, which were resting on her knees. At one point I sensed, rather than saw, her flinch, but I kept going. Now she was going to see what kind of person I really was. Gill Corcoran didn't look shocked or judgemental and I was grateful to her.

'I'm going to be honest with you, Ms Krauss.'
'Holly.'
'Holly. We can interview him. There are various potential charges. But it won't be easy.'

'Look at that bruise,' said Meg.

'You have had a relationship with this man.'

'Not a relationship, a pointless, ugly one-night –'

'That's none of my business. I just know how it would look – how it would be *made* to look – if it ever came to court.'

'I was drunk,' I said. 'Drunk, stupid, treacherous, mad. Are you saying that because I had sex with him once, he can attack me and threaten me and get away with it?'

'No. Not at all. I just want you to know what it will involve. You would have to describe to a jury everything you've described to me. You'd have to let your private life and your behaviour be scrutinized. Do you know how many rape cases result in a sentence?'

'No.'

'In some areas of the country it's fewer than one in five. And that includes stranger-rape cases. And these are the cases that reach court, where the police and the CPS think there's a chance of conviction. In the case of date-rapes –'

'He didn't rape me. And he was never a date,' I said bleakly.

'You don't need to convince me, Holly. You need to know this before you go any further. In your own interests.'

'I see.'

'You're a married woman.'

'Yes.'

There was a pause. Then Meg said angrily, 'But he may try again.'

Gill Corcoran didn't speak. She just looked at me. She was clearly right.

'They'd eat me alive,' I said. I turned to Meg. 'I had this dream recently. Nightmare. There were all these people pointing at me and screaming, and their faces were coming in and out of focus. Rees was there, and Deborah. And the guy who had the poker game, and that man I knocked to the ground.' I saw Meg blink in surprise but I ploughed on, 'And Charlie was there, I think. You too. You were all accusing me. If I went to court, I'd be making my nightmare come true. I'd bring it all about.'

I stood up and found my legs were no longer so shaky. 'Thank you,' I said to Gill Corcoran. 'You've been very helpful.'

We shook hands and I thought, She could have been my friend. A careworn police officer on the night shift. It was a little shaft of light in the grim dark.

Meg drove me home, and although she wanted to come in, I insisted she left. I wanted to see Charlie alone.

18

But Charlie wasn't at home. The house was dark, silent, empty.

I went upstairs, took off my dress and threw it in the corner, then put on a dressing-gown. I brushed my hair, without looking at myself in the mirror again, tied it back in a severe ponytail, put my feet into warm slippers. Then I went into the kitchen, where I took ice cubes from the freezer compartment, tied them up in a cloth and pressed them to my throbbing cheek.

I called his mobile. But it rang from its hiding-place behind the toaster. A small part of me was relieved that I didn't have to talk to him about what had happened, but I also knew that every time we didn't talk, putting off the hour of reckoning, delaying the explanations and the confessions, our relationship unravelled a little bit more, until there would be nothing left to knit up again, just a string of memories. Ah, yes, I was that woman once and he was that man. There had been a time when we knew every detail of each other's days, and also the thoughts that passed through the other's head. You share the little things – the mild sore throat, the sandwich he had at lunch, the words someone said to you on the bus, the sunset you saw, the socks he bought – as well as the big, and they are almost more important.

I didn't know where he was now. I didn't know who he was with or what he would be doing with them. I didn't know what he would be thinking about. I didn't know, when he came in, what I was going to say to him and I didn't know how he would reply. Would his face be kind, or would it be hard? Would I smell another woman on him? A woman who was kind, calm, tolerant, easy on the nerves.

I made myself scrambled egg on toast and forced myself to eat it, then drank two cups of green tea. I pressed my forehead against the kitchen window, looking out into the dark, unkempt garden where a gusting wind was swishing up the long grass and plucking at the branches of the trees. A shudder passed through me.

The doorbell rang. I moved into the centre of the kitchen and stood there uncertainly. It wouldn't be Charlie, and I didn't want to see anyone else. The thought of making any kind of effort to curve my lips into a smile, form shapes with my mouth so that the right words came out, 'Yes, no, I'm fine, come in . . .' Unbearable.

Then the bell rang again. Two quick jabs and a longer one. Maybe Charlie had forgotten his keys. I pulled the belt tight on my dressing-gown, walked down the hall and opened the front door a fraction, peering out through the crack.

'You must have the wrong –'

His hefty boot was in the door before I could slam it shut, and at the same time he gave a funny little scream of laughter, as if I'd said something hilarious.

'Wotcha,' he said, and pushed the door violently so that I staggered backwards into the hall. 'You must be Holly.'

He was young, maybe still in his teens, with the acne of youth across his face and a thin neck. His hair was shaved to bristle. He had a ring in his left eyebrow, several more in his left ear but none in the right because only the remains of an ear was there. It was as if someone had taken a giant bite out of it. He was wearing baggy combat trousers and a grubby grey singlet in spite of the cold. There were swirling tattoos on both arms and I saw the beginnings of another on his chest.

'I don't know you,' I said. 'Please leave now.'

'Nice place you have,' he said, with another screech of laughter, then sniffed violently and wiped his arm against his nose.

'I'm going to call the police.'

He took an object from his pocket – I couldn't see what it was – and tossed it from one hand to the other. Then, suddenly, there was a click and a blade shone in the dim light. We both stared at it. He gave a smile as if he'd just performed a conjuring trick.

'Don't,' he said, closing the blade and pushing it back into his pocket. He sniffed again and scratched one arm ferociously. There was a powerful smell of wet dog, armpits and solvents on him. This man is off the wall, I thought. He could do anything, anything at all. I clenched my fists.

'What do you want?'

'A beer for a start.'

He grabbed me by my wrist and yanked me after him into the kitchen, opened the fridge and peered inside.

'This'll do.' He snapped it open, took a swig and belched loudly. 'All neat and dandy. Sheets turned down.' That curdled laughter again. 'You know Vic Norris.'

'No, I don't.'

'You owe him eleven thousand pounds. Or, specifically,' he drew out the words as if he was proud of knowing them, 'you owe it to a company called Cowden Brothers.'

'It was all a mistake,' I said. 'I've not been well. I can't really play poker. I didn't know what I was doing.'

He was looking at me, still smiling broadly. 'Nasty bruise on your cheek,' he said.

'I lost nine thousand, not eleven,' I said. 'And I don't have it. I don't have anything.'

He drank a few more gulps of beer and sighed heavily. 'I don't care,' he said. 'I'm just telling you what he told me. Pay up. Geddit?'

'Yes,' I said. I just wanted him out of the house.

But he sat down on a kitchen chair as if he had all the time in the world, spread his legs. He had scabs on his head and on his arms, which he kept scratching with his chewed fingernails.

'Let's have a look in here, then,' he said, pulling my bag towards him and rummaging around in it for my purse, which he opened. There was twenty-five pounds in it and some change. He took it all and put it into his trouser pocket. 'What's your old man say about all of this?'

I didn't answer.

'I bet you haven't told him.' He stood up and came up to me, his beery breath in my face. 'Right, what haven't I told you? Oh, yeah. Vic says it's eleven at the moment, in a week's time it'll be twelve. The next, thirteen. And so on. Geddit? I'll come again and get it. Cash.'

I nodded.

'My name's Dean. See you, then, Holly.'

He ambled out of the kitchen, into the hall, out of the door. I went to the door and watched him as he walked on to the pavement, then down the road, with his lopsided, addled gait. Watched as he passed Charlie coming in the other direction. Then I closed the door and leaned, whimpering, against it until a few moments later I heard the key in the lock.

I stood up, straightened my shoulders, put a welcoming smile on my face. 'Hello, Charlie,' I said, as he came in from the cold, his cheeks glowing and his eyes bright, a spring in his step. 'I've just got in too. I had a fall and hurt my cheek, but don't worry, it looks worse than it is. Good day?'

Oh, help me, help me, help me, darling Charlie. Help me, someone. Anyone. Help me before I fall apart, is what I didn't say.

19

Charlie woke me the next day. He helped me to sit up and gave me a flannel wrapped around several cubes of ice for my cheek, and a mug of coffee, very hot and very strong. He sat by me on the bed and watched me drink it. It brought me round a bit. The layer of glass that seemed to separate me from everything that wasn't me grew a bit thinner.

'I'm sorry,' I said. 'About ... about, well, everything, really.'

'That's all right,' he said, stroking my hair.

'I think I'm not completely well.'

'We're going to get you better,' he said.

'Oh, Charlie,' I said. 'I know you're good at fixing things, but ...'

'It'll be my hobby.' He had shining eyes.

I wanted to say, Who are you sleeping with? I knew there was someone: he was being so attentive and yet at the same time so remote. All of a sudden, he looked younger, smoother, more like the eager young man I'd met and fallen for a year ago. I wanted to say: 'Why don't we stop lying to each other? Why don't we spill out the dirty, toxic truth and look at it and call it by its name?' Instead I touched his cheek and rolled away so he wouldn't see my face.

It was almost eight o'clock. I would leave work at six. I would have to play the part of Holly Krauss for ten hours until I could get off the stage, lock the door and go to bed. If I could get through the day without making anything worse, tomorrow would be a little better and so on and so on.

At first it went all right. I got through all the early-morning rituals and I even managed to pick at something that Charlie pushed in front of me, saying it was important to eat, which sounded right. My skin felt prickly as if I had just been ill or was just about to become ill. A light fog hung over everything, indoors as well as outside. I took great care dressing and applying makeup, my disguise, my armour against the world, although nothing could cover up my puffy discoloured cheek. I pulled on my coat under Charlie's careful gaze.

Before leaving for work, I took my mobile out into the garden, where there was no chance of Charlie overhearing, and phoned Stuart.

'Holly? Well, well, well. I didn't think I'd be hearing from you for a bit.'

'Oh?' I said weakly.

'Great evening, wasn't it?' he said, too loudly.

'Which one?'

'I guess you have lots to choose from. I was thinking of your card-playing exploits and everything that went with them.'

'That's what I wanted to talk to you about.'

'Where shall we meet, then?' he asked, strangely quick to agree.

I took a deep breath. I didn't want to meet him at all but I couldn't think of a way of saying, 'I need a big favour but could we handle it quickly?' over the phone. So we made an arrangement for mid-morning.

I met him in a coffee bar. I tried not to feel guilty about slipping out of the office, telling myself they were probably glad to have me out of their sight. Stuart arrived looking smart and assured in a dark suit and a white shirt with no tie. He bought us coffee in vast, brightly coloured mugs that looked as if they had been designed for giant toddlers.

He looked at me with an appraising air. 'Someone finally showed you exactly what they thought of you?'

I put my hand to my cheek. 'I fell over.'

'Oh, yeah?' He grinned sarcastically. 'And you're looking wiped out as well.'

'I'll sleep when I'm dead,' I said. 'As the saying goes. Or at least when I've got everything sorted out. You saw what happened with the poker game?'

Stuart's smile became even more fixed. 'Yes, I saw.'

'I'm sorry,' I said. 'My memory of the evening is a bit patchy. But I remember being a bit rude. If I was rude to you, I'm sorry.'

'You *were* rude to me.'

'I'm sorry.'

'Afterwards I was wondering what I'd done to you to make you want to humiliate me like that.'

'I'm sorry, Stuart. I think I must have felt that you were getting at me and I hit back. But it was unforgivable.'

'What did you want to see me about?'

'I lost a lot of money.'

'I know. I was there.'

'They must have seen that I wasn't experienced at all that. I can't believe they want to take my money. But this guy came round to the house. He threatened me. I don't even know how he got my address.'

Stuart looked at me evenly but he didn't speak.

'Do you think I could talk to someone?'

Stuart pulled a face as if none of it really mattered very much. 'You could talk to Tony, if you want. Or Vic. But I don't know what you expect them to say. It was a serious poker game. You saw that they were playing for money. It's a bit like going to a supermarket, filling your trolley, then asking if you can take it all away without paying.'

'It's eleven thousand pounds.'

'As I said, you could talk to Tony.'

This was the really awful bit. I swallowed hard.

'Actually, Stuart, what I was hoping was that maybe you could, you know, say something to them.'

There was a long pause now. I got the impression that in some way he was savouring the moment.

'You want me to deal with that?' he said. 'As well?'

'What do you mean, "as well"?'

'You asked me to deal with Debbie Trickett, remember?'

'I didn't actually ask you. You offered. Anyway, I haven't heard anything from her for days.'

'And why do you think that is?'

'Because she knows she hasn't got a case.'

'I hope you're sure about that,' said Stuart.

'What do you mean?'

'I've seen her. I've talked to her. Her flat is on the market. She's going to be homeless. She's got to look for work without any references. She left a good job to come to KS Associates and now she's lost everything. So it would be good to know that she was treated justly.'

'Whose side are you on?'

'I'm not on anybody's side. I'm a mediator. I want to find common ground. I thought it was important for you to realize that she's been hurt by this. She's vulnerable. You may not have fully understood that.'

'Oh, I understood . . .' I began, and then I stopped and looked at him hard. He reddened slightly. 'I can't believe it. You're fucking her.'

Stuart's face flushed terribly red and he glanced around.

'Keep your voice down,' he said. 'What's wrong with you?'

'Well, are you?'

He jabbed at me with a trembling finger. I thought he was going to poke me in the eye. 'I'm not, as it happens,' he said. He could barely speak. He was gasping for breath. 'What is it with you? You do it to everybody. You look for their weak spot. We've all

198

got one. You find it and then you destroy them. That's what you did with Debbie. You caught her out making a mistake. Clever you. And you used it to destroy her. You did it to me. And you think you can get away with it all. Is it to do with power? Or do you enjoy it? Just seeing how far you can go. For a start, you can't sweet-talk your way out of what you owe to Vic Norris. You try fluttering your eyelashes at him and see where it gets you. He does not forgive and he does not forget, and if you hang around hoping for the best, you'll discover what I mean.'

He stopped, as if he had run out of breath.

'Have you finished?' I said.

'No,' he said. 'I came here to talk to you about Debbie.'

'And?'

'Show how you can make at least one disaster go away. Give her another chance. She promises it'll be different. And she says she'll put it all behind her.'

'She'll put it all behind her?'

'That's right. So, what can I tell her?'

I had to take a moment. My heart was beating so hard I could barely hear what Stuart was saying. I couldn't think properly.

'I've got a message for Deborah,' I said. Stuart leaned forward. 'You can tell her to fuck off. We were lucky we caught her when we did. I wouldn't trust her to carry out the garbage.'

I got up and left.

*

I came back to the office, lurching like a drunk woman, and fumbled my way into my chair. My legs shook under me and when I tried to access my computer my fingers were trembling so violently that I kept pressing the wrong keys, bringing up forests of nonsense words. I don't know how much time passed: everything seemed to run together. There was a cup of coffee that Lola put down in front of me but I spilled it all over the desk and I remember lots of fuss with files being whisked out of the way and sodden tissues and people saying it didn't matter really. There was a sandwich that I took one mouthful of but it made me feel sick so I dropped it into the bin.

I do remember a conversation I had with Meg and Trish, because it was about Deborah. I heard myself saying, in a voice that didn't seem to belong to me, that maybe I'd been too hasty and did they think she needed a second chance, and Trish replying firmly that our solicitor had now been through all the documents and seemed satisfied that we had behaved perfectly correctly in the circumstances. It was an open-and-shut case, and there were no second chances.

'So that's that,' said Meg. 'Don't think about Deborah any more.'

'Don't think about her,' I repeated bleakly.

Later, I remember that Meg put her hand on my shoulder and said my name over and over again, asking me if I was all right. I told her I was fine, but it was hard to concentrate on anything. I kept picturing the youth last night, Dean, smelling of glue and sweat, giggling as he told me to pay up, sauntering out of the house as Charlie came in. And recalling Stuart's face, which I'd thought of as pleasant and amiable but this morning had been wrenched with hostility and disgust. And then there was Rees. Was it only yesterday that he'd ripped my dress, slapped my face? I heard the rap of my head against the stone wall. It was all like a dream, a horrible dream where all bad things come at you at once, all the terrible things you've done return to haunt you and you know you can't escape. Everything you do, fighting or fleeing or crying out for help, is futile. Risible.

'You're crying,' said a voice by my side. Meg, who seemed to have come out of nowhere. 'Why are you crying?'

'I can't stop.'

I sat there for a while, staring at the blank screen and hearing phones ringing, and she returned with Lola. She said there was a cab outside and that Lola would go back with me to see me to my house. That sounded an odd idea but sensible as well. I wasn't sure I'd be able to remember the way if the cab driver needed instructions. I told Meg I just needed to batten down the hatches to survive the storm and then I'd be back to normal. She told me to take as long as I needed. I said that was all I'd been asking for. She said that tomorrow we had to talk about how I should take precautions against Rees. And against Deborah, I didn't say. And the debt collector's off-the-wall messenger. And me. How was I going to take precautions against myself?

We seemed to arrive home in just a couple of minutes. Lola let me inside with my own key. As she undressed me, I told her it was the first time I had been undressed by a woman since my mother. A few men, I said, but no women. I apologized to Lola. I should be helping *her*. That was my job. She tucked me into bed, the cover pulled right up to my chin. I wriggled inside, warming myself. I heard the door close. The house was quiet. I was alone. A few noises leaked in, hisses and squeals and toots from the traffic. Outside there were people who hated me, for good reasons and bad reasons and no reasons at all. They were everywhere. I pulled my head under the cover. I pulled my knees up under my chin; I pressed them against my weeping, scalding eyes.

20

It was afternoon, then it was evening, and then it was an early winter night. The sky darkened outside the window; the air chilled; the green numbers on the clock clicked round, from five, to six, to six thirty . . . Charlie didn't come home. Where was he? He always used to be at home, waiting for me.

At last I made myself get out of bed and, wrapped in my dressing-gown, I went downstairs and phoned Charlie's mobile.

'Yes?'

'Charlie, are you coming back soon? I feel a bit odd.'

'Do you? Do you want me to come back now?'

'Where are you?'

'With friends.'

I strained to make out sounds in the background. 'Don't worry,' I said at last. 'I'm being ridiculous. Don't rush back. I'll be fine.'

'I won't be long,' he promised. 'Back by eight or so, all right?'

'Yes,' I said finally. 'That's fine.'

I called Meg.

'It's me,' I said, when she answered.

'Holly.' She sounded flustered. 'Are you feeling any better?'

'Sorry about earlier.'

'Don't worry about that. But listen, can I phone you back later? It's not such a good time . . .'

I heard a man's voice calling her name.

'Who are you with?' I asked. 'Meg, who are you with?'

'Listen, we'll talk tomorrow, if you're in. Not now, not on the phone. Get some rest, take care of yourself, get well.'

'Meg,' I said. But she'd gone. There was no one there, and all I could hear as I pressed the receiver to my ear was the sound of my own frantic breathing.

I trudged back up the stairs and climbed into bed once more. I watched the clock tick.

When I heard the sound of someone ringing, then banging at the door, banging so hard it sounded as if the door would break, I thought it was part of a dream in which someone was coming for me. But then I woke and sat up and the noise continued, and then I heard the sound of glass breaking. I didn't do anything at all. I just lay down again on my bed. A weariness came over me, so profound it felt as if I was rolled up in a fire blanket and didn't have the strength to throw it off. I knew something bad was going to happen, but I didn't have the energy to feel frightened. My legs were logs, my chest a boulder. I lay still, hugging the pillow to my breast. I heard the sound of a door banging, a chair being violently scraped along the kitchen floor.

I heard footsteps and at last hot terror swept through me, pumping round my body, leaving me breathless, prickling my skin, a thick snake in my throat.

The footsteps reached the stairs, paused, then began a heavy ascent.

'Get up, Holly,' I said to myself. 'Get the fuck up.'

I lurched out of bed, half falling as my feet hit the floor. A small part of me was aware of my throbbing cheek, my hurting head, the grain of the floorboards beneath my soles, the glittering darkness of the clear night sky, the sounds of the world going on out there.

Phone, I thought. That was it – call the police. I crouched on the floor, grabbed the phone from the bedside table, and tried to jab 999, but the room was dark and my fingers were thick as sausages and I got it wrong. I heard the beep of a misdialled number, then footsteps outside the bedroom door. It was kicked open, banging against the wall. From my position on the floor I could just see black shoes and grey trousers.

In the light spilling in from the hallway, I made out the numbers on the phone and jabbed again, whimpering as I did so.

'There you are. Hiding, are you?'

At his voice, fear ebbed away and I was suddenly gloriously calm and steady, as if a gritty wind had died away and I could see clearly again. I stood up, still holding the phone.

'Stuart? What are you doing?'

'What d'ya think I'm doing? I've come to have a talk, that's all.'

His words slurred together, and he swayed as he spoke.

'You're drunk. Hello? Hello? Yes? Is that the emergency service? Yes. My name's Holly Krauss and there's an intruder in my –'

He surged across the bed, and smashed the receiver from my hand. It bounced on the floor and he kicked it away from both of us, then wrenched the cord from the wall. 'There,' he panted. His face was a mottled red.

'Get out of here at once.'

'Not till we've talked.'

'There's nothing left to say.'

'Holly Krauss. Think you're so clever, don't you? Think you're so gorgeous.'

'I'm going downstairs. Stand aside.'

'We spoke to your fucking lawyer this afternoon, after you and I'd talked. You didn't listen to what I said, did you? You never listen.'

'It was our lawyer's recommen –'

'Shut the fuck up and listen for once. She's not even going to get a reference, is she?' His voice was getting louder as he spoke, his face redder. 'You're just kicking her when she's down. Enjoy it, do you?

Last bit of power. Like you enjoyed humiliating me, sneering at me in front of everyone. How do you think it felt? Get off on it, do you?'

'Just because you're having some kind of thing with Deborah doesn't mean that –'

'Are you fucking insane?' he said. 'Can't you get it into your fucked-up head that there is nothing between me and Deborah? I'm just – I'm just trying . . . and you're sitting there making fun of me.'

'I'll make us coffee,' I said. 'I never meant to make fun of anyone.'

I made for the bedroom door but his hand was on my shoulder, spinning me round to face him. There was spittle on his chin and the sour-sweet reek of alcohol on his breath as he brought his face towards me. 'You're going nowhere.'

'Get your hand off me.'

'You're going nowhere until I say so.'

He pushed me up against the wall. I shoved him hard and he stumbled backwards. From the chest of drawers, I picked up a mirror that my grandmother had given me and, holding it by its handle like a tennis racquet, whacked it into his face, hearing him howl in pain and fury. I was through the door and thought I was free, but he caught me by my dressing-gown and held me back, then hit me a glancing blow across my face, jerking back my head, sending shooting pains down my neck.

He still had his hands on my shoulders but his

face took on an expression of horror and puzzlement. 'Holly, I didn't mean it,' he said, 'but you just went on and on. I had to stop you.'

'No,' I said. 'No.'

He tightened his grip. I brought up my hand and hit out blindly at him, and as he reeled back, I ran for it, out of the room and to the top of the stairs. I thought I could hear him behind me when all of a sudden I was falling, feet catching on the steps, arms reaching out to save myself, and scraping futilely against the wall, head bumping against the banisters, the floor below coming up towards me in slow motion, so that everything was very clear: the plaster on the walls that I'd never got round to painting; the threadbare carpet under my shins; the heavy breathing behind me; the shoes in the hall, laces trailing.

And then my head was bouncing on the hard floor. Lights fizzing inside my skull. Pain exploding round my body. I heard someone whimpering and knew it must be me. I opened my eyes and saw both hands spread in front of me, as if I was a diver entering water. One leg was still half-way up the stairs. I couldn't feel the other, until I tried to move and realized it was bent under me, the ankle twisted and sending out little pulses of agony.

'Holly,' a voice said. 'Oh, God, Holly.'

There was the sound of wailing inside my head. No, not inside my head, outside. Someone banging on the door, the door swinging open, and once more I saw shoes in front of my face, blunt black shoes.

I raised my head and saw a man, two men in uniform, and behind me Stuart was saying, 'It was an accident, I didn't push her, it was an accident, I didn't mean, I never meant . . .'

'Hello,' I said, and laid my face on the cool, dusty floor, closed my eyes. I felt very peaceful, almost happy. 'I'm glad you came.'

They took Stuart away in handcuffs although I kept saying it wasn't his fault, really. I didn't blame him. I didn't blame anyone. I felt far off now from all the ugly, roiling passions of the day. What a day. A day full of hatred and nastiness and spasms of violence; of gargoyle faces and foul words and groping hands.

Now I lay on a stretcher and a soft blanket was put over me and a woman held my hand as I was slid into the ambulance. They all knew what they were doing and I didn't have to think any more; didn't have to feel or fear. There were people gathered on the street, watching, nudging each other, pointing, a rising chatter of excitement. I heard someone say my name and it was repeated like a rustle of wind in rushes. Holly Krauss, Holly Krauss, Holly Krauss . . . But nothing really mattered.

Then someone else was beside me, a figure pushing its way through the open doors of the ambulance, kneeling down beside me.

'Holly?'

'Hi, Charlie. You came home, then.'

'What have you gone and done?'

'More like what was done to her,' said the woman who had held my hand. 'She's lucky.'

'You smell nice,' I said sleepily. 'Vanilla.'

'Who did it?'

'Stuart. But he didn't mean to hurt me. He was drunk, that's all.'

'Your face . . .'

'I'm all right, really.'

'It's all . . .'

'Do I look awful? Never mind.'

There had been a hurricane, I thought, but it had only lashed us with its tail. 'The weather's inside me,' I murmured.

'What?'

'Never mind. Will you hold my hand?'

He took it, but almost absentmindedly, patting it gently, like a man in a daze.

'We have to talk,' I said. I seemed to have been saying the same four syllables for weeks now. Charlie didn't reply. The doors closed and the ambulance moved forward into the darkness.

There wasn't much wrong with me, although they kept me in overnight just to make sure. A bruised face from earlier, a new gash on the back of my head, which needed a couple of stitches; an ankle that had swollen; a sore neck; scuffed shins from my slither down the carpeted stairs. The police officer who came to talk to me the next morning said that Stuart's face looked worse than mine. Poor Stuart. I told her what had happened and she wrote it all down, and read it back to me before I signed the sheet of paper. I asked what would happen to him now and she shrugged. I turned my face to the wall and waited for her to leave.

The peace of the previous night had turned into something more like sadness. I thought about Charlie and me. I thought about Meg and me. And I thought about Charlie and Meg. They were the two people I loved most in the world. Perhaps they were the only people I really loved at all – except my mother maybe, whom I loved only because she was my mother. If you took away Meg and Charlie, who would I have left? A great crowd of bright acquaintances who knew nothing about me except that I was a party animal: fun to have around but could get a bit out of hand. I limped to the bathroom and stood in front of the mirror. Greasy hair and one side of my face a dirty yellow, chapped lips, great rings beneath my eyes. If they could only see me now, perhaps they'd think again.

21

On the way home I felt like a hideous messy parody of a new mother being collected from hospital by her loving husband. Except there was no baby. And no rapture. On my lap I clutched a carrier-bag stuffed with my torn, stained clothes. We hardly spoke until Charlie pulled up outside our house. 'I'm sorry,' he said. 'I should have been there. I should have protected you.'

'The forces of law and order arrived just in time,' I said. 'Who told them?'

'You did, apparently.'

'I didn't have time to give them our address.'

'You don't need to.'

'How clever,' I said.

'I thought he was a friend,' said Charlie.

'He was,' I said. 'Now my friends hate me even more than my enemies do.'

We got out of the car and walked up the steps to the front door.

'Don't say that,' said Charlie.

We stepped inside. I started to say I was sorry at the same time that Charlie started to say something and then we both apologized and both said that the other should go first. I insisted that Charlie go first.

'Are you feeling all right?' he said.

'Is that what you wanted to say?'

'No. I wanted to apologize. I ought to stay and look after you, but I've got a meeting. It's about a job.'

'That's great,' I said. 'Who with?'

'It's on a design magazine. You wouldn't know them.'

'I'm so pleased. When is it?'

'Now, I'm afraid. You don't mind?'

I touched his arm. 'Go. I'm just going to have a rest.'

'It feels wrong to be leaving you.'

'No,' I said. 'It's no problem. This was the crisis everything was building up to. Now the boil has been lanced. The nettle has been grasped. And I'm going to collapse.'

He smiled, then looked quizzical. 'I interrupted you,' he said. 'What were you going to say?'

'I was going to say sorry. Again.'

'What for?' said Charlie. 'You were the one who was attacked.'

'The repetition,' I said.

'What?'

'It happens over and over again. But each time it's worse. It's like a ratchet. Do I mean that? What's a ratchet?'

'Are you serious?' Charlie said. 'It's the bar that goes through the notches on a wheel, so that it can move forward but not back. Like the wheels in a clock.'

'See?' I said. 'You know these things. That's exactly what I meant. When this is over, when we're through this, we'll talk.'

'Yes,' he said shortly. 'But meanwhile . . .' He ran upstairs and came back down in a smarter jacket.

'You look great,' I said. '*I*'d hire you.'

His expression darkened. 'You know I'd never ask you for work.'

'I didn't mean that,' I said, stammering.

'I'd better go.'

'You've forgotten your portfolio.'

Charlie looked at me and paused for just a beat too long. 'He knows my work,' he said. 'I don't need it.'

'Good luck, then,' I said.

He nodded. 'Oh, by the way,' he said. 'I had a key cut for you.' He chucked it on to the table.

'Thanks. But I was thinking, what if someone took the other one?'

'Who?'

'Never mind.'

He left. I just stood where I was. I was trying to remember a poem I'd read at school. 'I lie to her and she lies to me and by these lies de dum de dum de dum.' And possibly 'de dum'. There was a knock at the door and I smiled in anticipation. Charlie. He'd changed his mind. I prepared myself to hug him and have the talk now that we had been putting off for too long.

'That was quick –' I said, and broke off because it wasn't Charlie but Dean, clutching a beer can.

'I waited for your old man to go,' he said, stepping past me into the house. 'I'm being considerate, see?'

He took a sip from his can.

'I brought my own this time,' he said. He looked at me curiously. 'Been in another fight?'

'Sort of,' I said.

He rubbed his nose as if it itched. He muttered something I couldn't make out.

'So?' I said.

'Yeah?'

'What are you here for?'

'You know what I'm here for.'

'I've just been in hospital,' I said. 'I only got back a few minutes ago. Anyway, I told you, I don't have any money. I can't pay Vic Norris.'

'What do you mean you can't pay?' Dean said, in a jeering tone. 'This is your fucking house, isn't it?'

'It's all mortgaged. I don't have any money.'

He took a gulp of beer. 'It don't bother me,' he said. 'I'm just the person he sends to get things. I'm not the person he sends to *do* things. I'll be in the shit when I tell him that you've done nothing but you'll be in worse shit.'

'I can't . . .'

He walked over to the mantelpiece and picked up an ornamental green glass decanter that we'd been given as a wedding present.

'That's worth about a hundred pounds,' I said. 'You can have it.'

He dropped it on to the floor and it shattered into a thousand green fragments. 'It's not enough,' he said. He drained the last of his beer. 'You can get the money. Anybody can get money if they really have to. And you fucking really have to.'

'If you threaten me, I'll call the police.'

Dean placed the can on the coffee-table. Then, almost absent-mindedly, as if he were alone, he unzipped his flies, took out his little pink penis and pissed in a heavy pungent splashing yellow stream that formed a pool on the floorboards. With an awkward twist of his hips he pushed it back inside his trousers and zipped himself up.

'What you'll do,' he said, 'is get the money. If you don't have it next time, you won't see me again. I just do the messenger stuff. I'm the nice one.' He walked to the door. 'We'll discuss it with your old man as well.' He grinned. 'Thanks for the use of your toilet.'

I walked to the lavatory calmly enough, leaned over the bowl and vomited and vomited until my stomach was empty. Then I fetched a bucket, a cloth and a toilet roll and cleaned up the living room, the broken glass and the piss. When it was all gone, I wiped the floor with bleach and then I wiped it with bleach again. When I was done, I looked at my palms. They were like those of a corpse that had been under water for a week.

22

I had a night of jagged dreams and woke to thoughts that were themselves like nightmares.

'You're ill,' Charlie said, standing over me as I tried to get dressed. He even took me by the arm and tried to pull me back to bed but I was stronger.

I tore myself away and plucked a garment from the wardrobe. It had a creamy ruff at the neck and sleeves. I was Elizabeth I. I was a Tudor gentleman. I wrapped a scarf round my gashed head. 'Peasant woman instead,' I said. 'Potato-picker. Northern Spain and donkeys, and the men just sit and drink in the shade.'

'Listen to me, Holly,' said Charlie. His face was very near mine, and his mouth was opening and shutting like that of a fish. I could see the veins on his skin and the individual tiny stubble hairs on his chin. I could smell his breath. I drew back. 'You have to go back to bed now,' he continued. 'You have to let me look after you.'

'Don't shout,' I said. 'It's like a rubber ball inside my head, bouncing all over the place. I could draw a diagram of the surprising angles. Arrows and dotted lines. Cut here.'

'Holly, darling Holly, it's not even seven.'

'I need to work. I need to pay the mortgage. If I stop, everything will just go off the rails,' I said. 'Crash. Shriek of tearing metal. No one else can pick up the pieces. Just me.'

I pulled out a pair of shoes. One seemed higher than the other. Never mind. I pushed my bandaged foot into it.

'You need to work,' I said. 'You need to get going, Charlie. Your life's running away and it's leaving you behind.'

'Look, give me a moment and I'll come with you. All right? You can't go alone. I'll put some clothes on, we'll have breakfast, and then we'll get the Underground together.'

'Never again,' I said.

'What?'

'Never the Underground again. Never. All together like ants in an antheap, bugs under a slimy great boulder. Stone and earth above and beneath and to each side. We're buried alive down there, Charlie, don't you see? Stuck in this little capsule of oxygen and everyone breathing in everyone else's stale, dirty, morning-after breath.'

'We'll get a bus.'

'We can walk together, over the rickety bridge. You have to hold me tight – you never know what I may go and do.'

'Holly, sit on the bed and wait. I'll have a shower. You should put on some proper clothes.'

'Never mind that,' I said. 'Never mind me.'

'Do you promise you'll wait?'

'Promise,' I said. 'Cross my heart and hope to die.'

What a darling idiot to trust me. He went into the bathroom and I heard the water start. I wobbled lopsidedly down the stairs and out of the house.

I was walking but it felt oddly like being in a speeding car. Things loomed up at me unexpectedly, trees and people and walls. My feet hit the kerb and I skidded out on to the road. A horn blared and brakes shrieked. I turned and saw a face twisted up in a car window just behind me. Someone who really hated me, I could tell by their glaring, maddened eyes. I made it across the road, limping, one shoulder higher than the other.

'Look where you're going!'

A woman with a buggy. I could see the dark roots in her dyed blonde hair. I wanted to tell her that everything shows up. You can't get away with tricks. You can't fool anyone for long. We're all ridiculous, thinking we're pulling the wool over people's eyes when all the time we know. Everyone's involved in the same mad charade. I remember charades when I was a child. Film (wind your fist round and round to imitate the reel on a loop). Four words (four fingers held up). First word, two syllables, it's Christmassy – oh, God, Christmas is coming – where was I? Yes, Christmassy, and in a carol it goes with 'ivy'. Right, Holly. Second word, one syllable. You've got it at once, haven't you? Krauss. Holly Krauss. Holly Krauss is crap. Yes, yes, yes.

I walked over the bridge. There were wisps of mist left hanging over the river. It must have been cold because I breathed out plumes of air. I could feel the bridge move beneath me. I swear it was swaying like one of those flimsy suspension bridges with half the wooden slats missing in adventure movies. I kept nearly tripping. And it looked very long, stretching out above the great drop. How would it be possible to get to the other side? I'd done it before. If I'd done it before, did it mean I could do it again? I'd done everything before, lied and laughed and got through the fucking, fucking days, so did that mean I could do it now? Is that what life was? Is that all it was?

The end of the bridge was getting nearer. I glanced around and thought I saw a familiar figure, but the wind was making my eyes water so badly that I couldn't make out anything clearly. Cars sliced past me. People walked in wide circles round me, avoiding me like the plague. Very wise. My shoes slid on the tipping, icy surface. I put one hand on the barrier and it felt sticky with cold. If I left it there, maybe my fingers would glue to the metal and I'd have to pull off the delicate skin at the tips to get free. Left, right, left, right. What was that rhyme my father used to chant? 'Left, left, you had a good home and you left. Right, right, it serves you jolly well right.'

'It serves you right,' I said aloud.

I stepped off the end of the bridge and turned right

and down the hill, the wind in my face, stumbling. A strange little noise was jerked out of my throat, then another.

'Are you all right, love?'

I stared into the face of a woman with spiky brown hair and a pointy chin, looking at me. I could see a dot of condensation on her lip, and a chipped tooth. Nice face. Brown eyes, brows slightly raised.

'Are you all right?' she repeated.

'Why do you want to know?' I said.

'You seem in difficulty. I just wondered if I could do anything to help.'

'Yeah, right.' I started to laugh.

'Who can I call?' she persisted.

'You've no idea.'

Her gloved hand was under my elbow. Someone was making a strange noise, a berserk whining moan. There were people in a circle and all I could see were faces staring down at me. I was sitting on the pavement. That must be cold, I thought. I didn't seem to be wearing tights and there was blood on my knee. It must look very odd. Maybe they'll think I've just slipped and fallen.

'I've slipped and fallen,' I said. 'Slipped and fallen over. Got to get up.'

'Look at the way she's dressed,' said a voice. 'She's drunk.'

'Just disorderly,' I said.

'What's she saying?'

'Disorderly!' I said louder.

'She's shouting something now. She's on something. Call for help.'

It was true that somebody was shouting. Matters were definitely getting out of control. It was like at a party where there's a fight going on in another room and you hear glasses breaking, but by the time you go out to have a look, it's all over. You just see the aftermath: chairs pushed over, people getting up, shouts. It seemed to be all aftermath. I noticed out of the corner of my eye that there had been a scuffle. A couple of figures were sprawled on the ground, making strange noises. I felt a burning sensation on my knees and palms. I examined my hands and saw pink grazes speckled with dots of gravel. Some people were gathering round, as if there had been a car crash. Others were walking quickly past. There was evidently an emergency but as I looked around I couldn't see it. It always seemed to have moved just out of my line of sight. 'It's behind you,' a voice said to me quietly, so nobody could hear. I tried to catch it by looking around quickly but it was too quick for me. I started to ask people what was going on but nobody was able to explain it to me coherently. Some teenage girls simply laughed at me when I asked, so I went for them to teach them a lesson but they were too quick for me, three little matadors with me as the bull.

A car pulled up and a policeman and a policewoman got out. I asked them if we'd met last night. My memory was fuzzy. I expected them to start arresting people and conducting interviews, but the policewoman approached me and looked deep into my eyes. I felt as if my face was a window and she was looking through it at something far away. The two of them took me by each arm. I tried to pull away from them but my arms wouldn't come free. I was pushed into the back of the police car as I attempted to explain that there must be a mistake. They had the wrong person. They didn't seem to hear, so I had to shout and scream at them and still they paid no attention. The policewoman sat firmly beside me and the car drove away.

'I'm late for work,' I said. 'I'll direct you. Unless you're taking me home. That's just up the road. You'll need to do a U-turn.' The car did not make a U-turn. 'Are we going to the police station? I'm sorry, I've got nothing to add to my statements.'

But they didn't drive me to the police station, or to work, or home.

23

'Do you know where you are?'

'Yes,' I said.

There was a pause.

'Well?'

'Well what?'

'Where are you?'

'You didn't ask that,' I said. 'You asked if I knew where I was. And I said yes. Because I do.'

Deep breath.

'All right. Could you tell me where you are?'

'Yes, I could. Do you mean you want me to tell you where I am?'

'Yes, please.'

'Don't you know? You should do. You work here.'

'I want to know if *you* do.'

'I don't work here.'

I couldn't stop myself laughing. The day had started badly but now it seemed comic. I felt as if a migraine had passed away, leaving me a bit light-headed but thinking more quickly and clearly than anybody else in the room. I looked at the young woman: DR CLEEVELY, her name-tag said, in square capital letters. She had a gleaming white coat and a gleaming white smile.

'You're thinking hard,' I said. 'You're trying to come up with a form of question that will get me to say that I'm in the casualty department of a hospital. There, I said it. Unprompted.'

'Do you know why you're here?' she said.

'Oh, no, we're not starting this again, are we? Ever since I was brought here by a man and a woman in uniform – don't you think there's something about people in uniform? When I first saw them I thought they were a pair of strippergrams. I mean, admittedly, it's unusual for strippergrams to appear when you're walking across Suicide Bridge. Suicide Bridge isn't its real name, of course. It would be a terrible name for a bridge. Nobody would ever want to cross it. Or go under it. It's actually called . . .' I couldn't remember the name. 'But it is locally known, affectionately known, as Suicide Bridge. And the reason it's called Suicide Bridge is, one, because people keep commit-ting suicide on it. Well, not on it. Off it. And the reason they do is, one, because it is very high off the ground. The ground underneath. And, two, because, allegedly, I haven't checked this, but allegedly it is the only place in London where you can kill yourself by jumping from one postal district, namely N19, and landing in another, namely N something else. What was the question again?'

'Holly –'

'That's Miss Holly to you.'

'I'm going to fetch someone who will examine you.'

'What was it *you* were doing?'

'I'm just the casualty officer.'

'Don't apologize.'

'I won't be a minute.'

'It doesn't matter,' I said. 'I've got to get to work anyway.'

Dr Cleevely disappeared through the curtain that was pulled round the couch but unfortunately she left me with a very large nurse who said that if I tried to get up I would be made fast. I engaged her in conversation to relax her. We had only just started talking about Zimbabwe, where she came from, when Dr Cleevely came back with another doctor, an Asian woman called Dr Mehta. She said hello and told me she was the duty psychiatrist.

'This is the point where I say, "Psychiatrist? I don't need a psychiatrist. I'm perfectly sane."'

Dr Mehta didn't smile. She was a serious young lady with a clipboard and she began by asking for my name, date of birth and address. 'Do you know why you're here?'

'I can't do this again,' I said. 'I'm really too busy. If you must know, the police brought me.'

'Why?'

'I think they were probably tired of me. I've had some dealings with them lately. It's a long story.'

'Yes?' said Dr Mehta.

'All right, you asked for it. Someone threatened me and – as a matter of fact, lots of people threatened me recently and the one I'm talking about right now, well, he's probably in this hospital at the moment because I hit him with a mirror that used to belong to my grandmother. Anyway, I'm sure it was this hospital and I was here the other day, I can't remember which day – it's hard to tell days apart, isn't it? – but he only tried to hurt me because of this woman I fired, plus there's this man who's fixated with me. We did actually have sex, but it was nothing. I know, I'm married. I know, I know, but I've talked about it to Charlie, it was awful, but we're working at it. Then there's this other youth who came to the house and pissed all over my floor – but I'm not allowed to talk about that. No one must know.' I stopped. 'I'm listening to myself as I'm talking and I realize that, from your point of view, it sounds crazy. But honestly it's true. Ask the police about the man who attacked me. Not the ones who brought me. They probably don't know about it. Or ask Charlie, my husband. I know I sound paranoid but it's completely true. Just check it up.' I stopped. 'No, don't check it, none of it really matters any more. It's not relevant, is it?' I tried to make eye-contact with her but she was scribbling on her clipboard.

She looked up. 'Tell me what was happening when the police picked you up.'

'I didn't see much,' I said. 'I was on my way to work. There was some kind of brawl. The police got the wrong end of the stick. They should have let things take their course.'

'Was your behaviour unusual?'

'I don't know what that means. What are you writing on your clipboard?'

'I'm taking notes.'

'Have I passed?'

'It's not like that.'

'You're trying to fit me into your little boxes. You're trying to assess me, aren't you?'

'Provisionally, yes.'

'It won't work now,' I said, 'because I know what you're doing. You won't be able to work out whether I'm telling the truth or whether I'm saying something I think you'll want to hear or whether I'm saying something that I happen to know a sane person would say or that I'm just a sane person saying sane things or alternatively whether I'm a sane person saying insane things because she's nervous and so is trying to imitate a sane person and failing.'

'You're wearing your nightclothes,' said Dr Mehta.

'Brilliant,' I said. 'You've caught me out. Brilliant. Is this some sort of game?'

'It was just an observation.'

There was a bustle behind the curtain. Someone was trying to get through and failing comically. It made me think of the theatre, curtain down. A face appeared. A familiar face. Charlie's.

'Holly,' he said, 'what's going on? Where did you get to? I tried to find you. I've been running around all over the place trying to find you. One minute you were sitting on the bed in your nightclothes and the next minute – oh, you're still in your nightclothes, aren't you? What's going on? What have you done? There was this call – they said you'd attacked a young –'

'It's nothing,' I said. 'I had a stupid accident.' I held up my hands, which had been bandaged by a nurse when I arrived. 'I fell over and scraped my hands and knees. They brought me in here and now they're asking me a whole lot of questions. It doesn't make any sense.'

'Is this your husband?' asked Dr Mehta.

'Nice, isn't he? Everyone loves Charlie.'

She turned to Charlie. 'Can I have a word?'

The two of them moved back behind the curtain, leaving me alone on the stage without an audience, except God. After a few minutes Dr Mehta returned alone. 'Charlie's just outside,' she said. 'You can see him in a minute.'

'Is he taking me home?'

'I need to ask a few more questions. Tell me about things. How are you sleeping?'

'You're too late,' I said. 'A few weeks ago I was too busy to sleep. I went days and days without it. You know the research that says if you deprive some-one of sleep they go mad? It's true. But I'm over that. I've been sleeping and sleeping like . . . like a whale? Do whales sleep? Like a beach whale.' I laughed. 'It sounds like a whale on holiday. I mean a beached whale. Like a bear. Bears sleep all winter. Lucky them.'

'How's your general health? Are you fit and well?'

'Don't I look it? The picture of health. I'm probably the healthiest person in the building.'

'What about, well, for example, your sex life?'

'What do you mean "well, for example"? Are you embarrassed? Go on, admit it. Are you new to this? Do you think you're competent to assess the state of my sex life?'

'I'm interested in how *you* see it.'

'Things have not been obviously brilliant. Just to show you that I'm brazenly unembarrassable and not a violet blushing unseen wherever it is, I did a few weeks ago have sex with somebody I'd never met before while under the influence of something or other and, yes, I am married, and, yes, I am *happily* married, and do I regret it? Oh, my God, yes – which sounds like a fairly sane response to me.' I paused and tried to concentrate. 'I've told you all this, haven't I? Or did I tell the other one? The other female doctor? You're all women. Don't you allow men to work here? Not that I'm complaining. I'd find it hard to talk like this to a man. Not that you're being much help. I thought you were a psychiatrist. Couldn't you give me some words of comfort? Because I do need comfort. I know I'm gabbling on, but underneath that, I know I'm sad.' I looked at her. Scribble, scribble, scribble. 'Nothing? Just another black mark? Another F? You know, Doctor, I think I've put enough effort into entertaining you. I'm starting to feel tired. My head aches, and my ankle throbs, and my hands and knees hurt and I just want to go off somewhere and lie down. If you want to write me a prescription for something, that's fine. Otherwise I'll be on my way.'

Scribble, scribble, scribble. She looked up. 'What about food?' she asked.

'No, thanks. I'm not hungry.'

No smile.

'I meant appetite. In general.'

'I don't know.'

'Eating heartily?'

'I'm going to maintain a dignified "No comment". No person shall be compelled to give evidence against herself.'

'Are you having problems at work?'

I pulled a face. This was an uncomfortable area. I was going to have to tread carefully here. 'I don't know how much time you've got. They were being completely – which they would admit themselves if they . . . well, they will admit it one day – unreasonable. Oh, this is all pointless anyway. What can you possibly know about my life? I'm brought in here like a dead bird dragged in by a cat and dumped at your feet. I don't even understand my life and I've been stuck with it for twenty-seven years.'

I looked up at Dr Mehta.

She wasn't scribbling, just staring into space. 'Let me have a word with your husband,' she said.

'Haven't we already done this?' I asked. 'I feel we're trapped in a pattern.'

While they were away I worked out a list of things

I was going to say to her. I tried to arrange them in order of priority but they slipped away from me and I had to start again, and then they were back.

'I didn't see you there,' I said.

'Miss Krauss,' said Dr Mehta. 'I'm going to talk to my consultant. No doubt he'll come and talk to you . . .'

'So there is a man on the premises,' I said. 'Do you keep him hidden somewhere? Bring him out on special occasions?'

'However, I'm very clear that I want you to be admitted to a psychiatric ward as a voluntary patient.'

'It was the dead bird, wasn't it? And the cat. It was only a comparison.'

Dr Mehta spoke as if she hadn't heard what I'd said, as if I wasn't even in the room. 'As I said, I would like you to be admitted as a voluntary patient. If you aren't willing to accept that, we're going to consider assessing you under a section of the Mental Health Act for compulsory admission.'

'Sectioning me? Are you serious? That's what they do to lunatics running around in the street with knives threatening people. Look at me. I'm sitting here with you calming, I mean calmly, having this fucking stupid conversation.'

'Compulsory admission is a more cumbersome process. You need two separate doctors and a social worker and we have to fill out a lot of forms, but we'll do it if necessary. And now you might want a word with your husband.'

'To say goodbye? But I don't want to say goodbye, I want to go home. That's all I need. Everything will be all right if I can go home.'

Dr Mehta didn't seem to be paying much attention. I was like a radio that had been left on while she was getting on with her work. She went and Charlie came back and he looked as if he was the one who needed help.

'Holly,' he said, in a dead voice. 'I'm sorry.'

'Did she talk to you? They want me to stay. I'm tempted to make a break for it if you can find me my clothes. I can't go out looking like this.'

Then I saw his face, furrowed and tired and blotchy in the bright hospital light, and all the fight went out of me. I was left feeling drained, humiliated and bitterly ashamed of myself. I put out a hand and touched his arm gently. I saw him wince. 'If you think it's the right thing. I'll do whatever you want. Just tell me.'

'I don't know,' he said. 'I just don't know.'

'It's all right,' I said. 'I'll sign on the dotted line, Charlie. You don't need to worry.'

I wanted him to protest, but he didn't, just nodded slowly.

'They'll make you better,' he said.

24

They didn't make me better. They made me worse.

I was like a car that needed basic repairs but, instead of being taken to the body shop, was taken to the dump where the vehicles are piled on top of each other, stripped of their doors and their radios and anything that's of any value, then left to rust.

The Zimbabwean nurse gave me tablets, which she said would settle me, but I don't think I took them. I remember I had to be held by both arms and something was broken, fragments of jagged glass on the floor.

I behaved like a flailing, frightened toddler. I spat the tablets out as hard as I could. Dr Mehta showed me a syringe, I saw the droplet at the end, glistening. She pushed it into my arm as I tried to wriggle out of the way and almost immediately a wave of warmth spread out from the needle up my arm and across my body. It was safe to let go now. I could let myself fall into sleep and nothing mattered and a little bit of me hoped I would never have to wake and fight and strive again.

The days were like a dream of which I retain only a few fragments. I look back at them and see a woman who must be me. I think she was me, she must have been me, whatever that means. It was as if inner and outside worlds had run into each other so that I could no longer tell the difference between the two. So I watched myself, and then I lost sight of myself, jerking back into consciousness with a start, then once more sliding helplessly away.

I had thought they were going to take me somewhere safe and quiet, where I could get well. It wasn't like that at all. I know, because I was told later, that I was in a psychiatric ward under sedation and then I was assessed and then a few days later I was released into the care of my husband because the consultant judged me not to be an imminent threat either to others or to myself. How could I be? I was in such a vegetative state I couldn't even feed myself. Nobody had been seriously hurt in the rumpus on the bridge. No charges were to be brought.

That's what I was told, but I didn't experience it. I remember images: light on the lino, bandages on a young girl's wrists, an old woman chewing her lip, food served from a trolley, plastic forks, pills. I remember sounds: screams in the middle of the night, a woman holding whispered conversations with herself, the chatter of nurses on their break, the TV. And smells: disinfectant and cooking and piss. I remember the consultant's sparse grey hair, baggy sweater, kind eyes. I think I called him 'Daddy'. I think he held my hand. Or perhaps that was Charlie. Or perhaps that was a dream.

*

I remember Charlie told me one day that a strange youth with a shaved head had thrown a brick through our front window and giggled as he ran away. I moaned something that was going to be the beginning of a confession, but he patted my hand and told me not to worry.

I remember flowers in a jug, blowsy, over-coloured, hothouse things that I could smell in my sleep. Charlie didn't know who they had come from, and I didn't want to imagine, so I tried to get rid of them. I knocked the jug to the floor, but it was plastic, and bounced across the lino. A nurse tutted and mopped up the water and pushed the flowers back into another jug which she stood on the table at the bottom of my bed, out of reach. Every time I looked up, I saw them there.

And I remember a meeting with the consultant psychiatrist Dr Thorne, although even remembering it is like watching a film in a language of which I don't know a single word, a culture in which I can't read the gestures or the facial expressions. I was propped up in bed and my whole body felt heavy and inert. I looked at my arms lying across the blanket. Charlie was on one side of me and Dr Thorne on the other, and there was a cluster of students, younger than me, eager children.

'What's your decision?' I said. Then I surprised

myself, and Dr Thorne, I think, by reaching over and clutching his arm. 'What's happening to me?'

'You're suffering from a bipolar affective disorder,' he said.

'Manic-depressive?' said Charlie. 'Yes. I thought so.'

'No,' I said. 'Not me.' Or maybe I didn't say that, just thought it.

I heard words — 'rapid-cycling bipolar disorder', 'drugs', 'episodes', 'chemical imbalance', 'florid', 'regime'. I heard my name repeated, but I heard it as if it belonged to someone else. I looked down at my hands with their torn nails, the wedding ring on my finger. A tear splashed on to the rough brown blanket and disappeared.

'I'm a manic-depressive?' I said, through the buzz of hard-edged, ugly words.

'Yes, Holly,' said Dr Thorne. 'You're suffering from an illness.'

'No. I'm suffering from me,' I wanted to say. Maybe I did say it.

'We can help you,' he said. 'We can make the pain go away. Lithium,' he said.

I knew that word. It's a word for other people.

'Side-effects,' he was saying now. 'Nausea, diarrhoea, weight gain, thirst, skin problems.'

'Clozapine,' he said. 'Until the lithium kicks in.'

Kicks, I thought. Iron hoofs smashing against my head.

'I'll lose myself,' I said.

'It's not like that,' he said.

I remember going home. Days after I had arrived at St Jude's in a police car, Charlie led me out, clutching my nightie and my own private pharmacy in a paper bag. I felt the cold rain on my face, the ground beneath my feet.

'One step at a time,' said Charlie.

So I began my journey.

There was a taste on my tongue I couldn't get rid of. Headaches came and went. My skin felt twitchy. But above all there was tiredness. I lay in bed. Charlie brought me tea and food and kept track of the pills. He watched me as I swallowed them. Sometimes he even pushed them to the back of my tongue for me and held the beaker of water to my lips to wash them down. Once each day he ran a bath, led me to it and washed me, sponging my shoulders and my breasts and between my legs. He might as well have been washing a piece of dead meat. In fact, once I'd got that image into my mind, I couldn't get rid of it. It explained everything over the previous months. I thought of myself as a hunk of meat, hanging in a forest somewhere. It would attract flies. It would become infested with maggots. It would attract scavenging animals who would bicker and fight among themselves as they each tried to rip away a piece of the dead flesh.

*

I tried to read a novel but I couldn't make sense of the words. I couldn't remember who the people were. Always there was that taste on my tongue, which seemed to underlie everything, what I looked at or heard, so that even music seemed to have a nasty tang. I preferred to lie in silence with the curtains drawn. When I slept, I dreamed about Rees, Stuart and Deborah, about the skinhead pissing at my feet, about hands groping me and faces leering, and the dreams leaked into my waking days. I couldn't stop thinking about all the people who hated me. I'd made them hate me, begged them to hate me. Images from my past clustered around the bed like inquisitive visitors. I saw their faces in my mind, their hostile, watching eyes; I thought of them out there, in the real world beyond my head, waiting to get me when at last I ventured out. I pulled the covers over me. Sleep was better than waking and darkness was better than light.

Every day Naomi came round. I would hear her low, clear voice in the kitchen and it comforted me. She left cakes, bread she'd baked, soup, casseroles that I couldn't eat because I felt so queasy. Sometimes she came upstairs and put a hand on my forehead, or even took my pulse. She said I'd be all right. I mustn't worry. I just closed my eyes and heard her feet tap-tapping their way out of my room again, down the stairs to the kitchen where Charlie sat, not even pretending to work any more, letting everything slip through his fingers, waiting for me to be better again. I heard them talking together, although I couldn't hear what they were saying. My life was going on without me in it.

Meg came: she sat on a chair by my bed and said things that didn't need an answer from me, and I think she even read to me from the book of happy poems that I'd given her all those eternities ago, but maybe that was all a dream. Another dream.

I tried to say that I knew about everything but the words came out wrong; they made no sense. She leaned forward and wiped my cheeks with a tissue, so I knew I must be crying but I was too far away from myself to feel the misery. In my secret life.

Out of nowhere came an image from my childhood: my father, sitting at the kitchen table with his face in his hands and tears dripping through his fingers. I had always thought of him as exuberantly cheery, so where had this picture of wretchedness come from?

'My father,' I said to Charlie, as he pushed pills into my mouth.

'Yes?'

'He was like me.'

'You mean . . . ?'

'He was a manic-depressive. Of course he was. Why on earth didn't I realize it before? It explains everything and —' I put a hand over my mouth.

'What's wrong?'

'He killed himself, didn't he? It's obvious. He was like me and then he killed himself. It's in my blood, hard-wired.'

'Stop it.'

I hated the pills I pushed down my gullet several times a day. They looked modern. They were small and glossy and came in plastic bottles with proprietary names on them. But lithium wasn't a brilliant bit of chemical manufacture like aspirin or penicillin. It was an element, a clayey metal I'd seen in chemistry class at school. It felt geological, and it was in me now, like veins of metal in rock. I could taste it on my tongue and I was sure I could see and feel changes in my body, which no longer felt as though it belonged to me.

'I'm manic-depressive. The bits of me that make me special – made me special – are just part of my illness. Who am I now? I've always thought that I am what I do. I am all my memories of myself. But now that's been taken away from me, the good times and the bad times. The times of feeling so low I wanted everything to end, and the times of feeling I could do anything, fly high, all the wonderful times I've had. Now I think that wasn't me, not the real me. They were all just symptoms. When I've behaved badly, when I've behaved well, it was just because of a chemical imbalance in my body. It's a great excuse but I don't want it. I want to be *me*. Me being bad, me being good, me being me.'

Who was I talking to, shouting at? Me, of course – another me, the old Holly Krauss, that distant figure from a lost world whose colours and vivid sensations I barely recalled. Just me.

I wanted to be hugged tenderly, to be held carefully, so that I didn't break again. I lay in my bed, which felt like a fragile boat tossed on towering waves. I closed my eyes and felt the waters suck me under.

I got out of bed and put on proper clothes, cleaned my teeth, brushed my hair. I looked at my face in the mirror and didn't recognize it. I went downstairs slowly, step by step, feeling my way with outstretched fingertips, like a blind woman. I wandered from room to room, and everything was unfamiliar to me. The house seemed to have changed: nothing was in quite the right place; the doorway had shifted sideways, the kitchen sink was lower than I remembered.

I went into the garden, and saw how my feet made prints in the dew. I told myself that nothing lasts for ever. Spring would come. Spring would come again.

25

'Other people cope with the drugs, so why shouldn't I? I just don't feel like me any more. I feel – I feel *grotty*. Bad all over.'

Naomi looked at me for a few moments then stood up. 'Wait here,' she said.

She returned about twenty minutes later, with a large carrier-bag out of which she pulled packets and cartons. Camomile tea. St John's wort. Multi-vitamin tablets, fish-oil, and evening-primrose oil capsules. A bottle of lavender bath salts, with a lavender-scented candle to go with it, sticks of incense. Even a CD of allegedly soothing Pan-pipes music.

'Throw your pills away,' she said.

I stared at her.

'Try it.'

'Don't tell Charlie,' I said.

I waited until Charlie had left the house for his run, then picked up the bottles of pills and held them in my hand. I imagined shaking some out into my palm and swallowing them and even the thought made my throat close up. There weren't many left anyway. They only dole out a few at a time. Just in case, they'd said.

I took them into the downstairs lavatory and pushed open the lids with my thumb. I shook them into the bowl, then flushed and watched the lozenge-shaped capsules swirl and disappear.

At last I was on my own with myself.

I went back into the kitchen, drank the lukewarm tea, washed the mug and, before I could change my mind, went outside into the cold wind. I strode, so quickly that it hurt, to the park where I'd met Charlie that horrible day. I walked round it three times, then home. I even jogged the last bit, although I thought I was going to throw up, and by the end my vision felt a bit blurred. I had a long bath with lavender salts in it. I drank three glasses of water. I slid the CD into the player and listened to the fucking flutes. I tried to concentrate on my inner strength. I waited to see what was going to happen next. I had declared war on myself.

The ghastly dread came slowly, seeping in through the following day. I could feel it as if it were tangible, in my body, in my blood.

In the middle of the second night I heard noises outside, rustling footfalls, and I got up and pressed my face to the windowpane. Was someone out there, lurking among the shadows? I pulled the curtains shut and leaned back against the wall, trembling. I pulled on my dressing-gown and sat on the edge of the bed, trying to think what to do. Call Charlie, that was it. He'd tell me. I opened my mouth and a thin, reedy yell came out.

'Charlie!' I called. Then louder, so my throat hurt. 'Charlie, where are you?'

No reply. He wasn't in the house. Tears welled in my eyes and I mopped at them with the sleeve of my dressing-gown.

Suddenly I wasn't frightened any more. Nothing outside could be as bad as the inside of my own head. I went downstairs, opened the back door into the garden and walked out, over the strip of harsh gravel and on to the half-grown lawn. The grass was muddy and cold under my bare feet; the wind slapped my face.

'Come and get me, then!' I shouted, as loud as I could. 'Come on, Rees or Dean or Stuart or Deborah or whoever you bloody are! I don't care! You'd be doing me a favour.'

I shut my eyes and waited. At least everything would be over soon. This whole mucky business called living.

'Fucking come on, then!' I howled, but I knew no one was out there.

There was the noise of a window opening.

'Most of us are trying to sleep,' came a voice.

I yelled back, just an open mouth and this high sound pouring out.

'Stick your head in an oven,' said the voice.

Go fuck yourself, go top yourself, just go go go.

Where were the words coming from, inside or out? I put my fingers into my ears but the words still swilled round and round my brain. I tottered back inside. The hem of my dressing-gown was soaking and my feet throbbed from the gravel and the cold.

I looked at the stairs and they were too steep to climb. I looked at the phone in the hall, but it was too far away and, anyway, there was a voice inside it that muttered unkind words when I held it to my ears. I held up my hands and they were transparent: I could see the blue veins and the bones like claws. I opened a drawer and looked at all the knives, sharp and silver, glinting up at me with their serrated blades. I slipped off my gown and gazed down in disgust at my white, used-up body. I ran my fingers over my aching ribs, over my hurting breasts, up to my throat. I knelt down on the tiles and laid my forehead against their coldness.

'I can't,' I said. 'I can't I can't I can't I can't.'

I can't go on.

And a kind voice came, from no one, from nowhere: You don't have to, dear heart.

'I don't have to,' I said, aloud this time, relief flooding through me like clear water. 'I don't have to go on. I can stop.'

26

It was like a cool hand on my hot sweating brow. I'd finally acknowledged it. I wanted to be dead.

I was able to consider it with a clarity I hadn't experienced for weeks, and without a shred of doubt. I didn't want pain or messiness. I didn't want to damage anybody else more than was absolutely necessary. I worried about Charlie briefly but it was immediately obvious that he would be better off without me. The world would be a more satisfactory place with me not in it.

If there had been a gun on the premises I would have put it into my mouth and pulled the trigger there and then. Nothing else in the house would quite do the trick. I didn't want to cut my wrists. I wanted to be welcomed into death like an expected guest, not get there by hacking at my skin with a rusty blade. Of course, the scene of my great crack-up had been at London's star suicide location. I'd surely been drawn to the Archway Road bridge by the whiff of death and despair. People came from all over Britain to jump off it and I was just a few minutes' walk away. I wouldn't even need to put on a coat. Yet I wasn't tempted by it. My reasons seemed absurd, almost a form of bad manners, like a child refusing to eat what was on her plate. There were now all sorts of spikes and railings on the bridge to deter people like me and I doubted my ability to get over them. I had an image of cutting myself and tearing my clothes. Worse than that – and this sounded really stupid, even to me – I've always suffered from vertigo. I wanted to drift into death, like a tide going out. I didn't want it to be a rush of horror.

I had an appointment with Dr Thorne. Charlie wanted to come with me, but I told him I'd prefer to go alone. 'After all,' I said, 'this is something I'm going to have to get used to, isn't it?'

Dr Thorne had the results of my last blood test. The lithium levels were on the low side so he told me he was going to increase my dose. He was in a good mood. It was a bright, sunny morning and I was the first patient of his day.

'You look a bit better,' he said.

'I feel better,' I lied brightly. I had dressed with great care and examined myself in the mirror to make sure my clothes were neat, hair brushed, my smile in place.

'Do you feel any side-effects from the medication?'

'No,' I said. Then, because I didn't want to seem excessively cheerful, I added, 'My mouth has been dry and I feel a bit puffy. But it's better than I expected.'

'Excellent,' said Dr Thorne. 'If you drink a bit more than usual, that will sort out the dry mouth.'

'I've been doing that.'

'Good. How is your mood?'

'I feel much calmer.'

'We'll need longer for the lithium to take full effect.'

'I know,' I said.

'And you're coping with the schedule?' he asked.

'Yes,' I said, also untruthfully, of course. I hadn't taken my medication for over three days now. I didn't know how Charlie had failed to notice.

'Good,' he said.

'But I've got a bit of a problem,' I said casually.

'What?'

'Charlie and I thought we might get away for a week or two. We need to spend time alone. I'm not sure where. It might be somewhere remote. I was worried about running out of medication.'

'Don't worry,' said Dr Thorne. 'I'll write you a prescription to cover it. When are you going away?'

It was so easy.

'Charlie's arranging it at the moment,' I said. 'One of these last-minute deals. I hope we'll leave tomorrow, but maybe it'll turn out to be in a week, two weeks. And I'm not sure how long we're away for.'

'Lucky you,' said Dr Thorne, writing busily. 'I hate this time of year. It's the best time for a holiday.'

I've read a lot about people killing themselves almost on impulse, suddenly jumping out of an open window or in front of an oncoming train. For me, it really was like preparing for a secret vacation. Everything had to be settled for the following day, which was a Tuesday, because Charlie had told me he was going to be away for the whole day, on a course he said, although I knew he was lying. He was going out after breakfast and he wouldn't return until early evening. I asked him several times when he was coming back, and he asked me if I would be all right. I smiled and told him I was feeling much better.

After my appointment with Dr Thorne, I went shopping. I bought smoked salmon and brown bread for supper, although I knew I wouldn't be able to eat a thing, and I bought Charlie some new socks and boxer shorts, which I folded neatly into his drawer when I got home. Somehow it made me feel that I was looking after him even as I was leaving him. It was one of the first wifely things I'd ever done for him, and for a few seconds I thought about what our life could have been like together, in another world. But it was too late for all of that now: I knew I was on a frictionless slide towards oblivion and it was as if I had no volition in the matter any more.

We had a calm evening together, and I went to bed early because I wanted the morning to come quickly. I was about to embark on a long journey and I wanted the waiting to be over and to be gone. I slept long and deeply, and when I woke, Charlie had already left. We hadn't even said goodbye, but that didn't matter. How do you say goodbye, anyway? Best just to raise your hand and walk swiftly away, without looking back.

I got up and had a shower, washing my hair. I dressed in loose, comfortable clothes, clean from the drawer. I knew that I was shutting things out of my mind that must not be considered. I was walking across an abyss on a narrow plank. If I didn't think about the deepness below and the narrowness beneath my feet, I would be able to get to the other side. If I let the deepness and the narrowness into the forefront of my consciousness, I would fall.

I found myself making the bed and stopped, seeing the absurdity of it, then finished it anyway, smoothing the duvet. Everything else would be for other people to deal with.

I had to keep going, not stop and think. From the fridge I took a carton of orange juice and a half-full carton of apple juice. I placed them on the kitchen table with a large tumbler. I went to the bathroom. I had more than three weeks' worth of medication. That should easily do it. I was on the edge now. Teetering. Once again, I remembered standing as a little girl on walls, on climbing frames, my father below, his arms outstretched. 'Jump,' he would say, 'jump and I'll catch you.' He would play a game, suddenly withdrawing his arms, as if he was going to let me fall, but then he would catch me at the last minute. I kept thinking about that game. The funny thing was, however hard I tried, I couldn't picture his face any more, or Charlie's. I could picture Meg's, though.

It suddenly seemed to me that Meg was the one who would suffer most from what I was about to do and would feel the most guilt. I had decided not to write a note, but now, at the last minute, I changed my mind. I picked up a pen and got a scrap of paper from the living room and thought for a few seconds. How do you say sorry, when you know that you're going to go ahead with it anyway? How do you say goodbye? I didn't want to talk about her and Charlie and in the end I kept it short: 'My dear and loyal Meg,' I wrote. 'I'm so sorry. So very very sorry. I just want all this to stop. Forgive this, my best and truest friend. All my love, Holly.'

I put the cap back on the pen, laid the note on the kitchen table, and started taking the pills, two at a time, with a gulp of the apple juice and, when that was finished, with the orange juice. It was quick and easy. I went into the hall and noticed that Charlie's keys were still on the hook and for a moment I worried about how he would let himself in this evening. I climbed the stairs slowly and went to lie on my bed, remembering as I did so how I had smoothed the cover with my hand earlier and what a waste of time that had been. I also thought how stupid it was that I had had the best night's sleep I could remember and I wondered whether it would make it hard for me to go to sleep now.

I try to turn over but my movement is sluggish and heavy. I try to think of something, anything outside, anything from the past, something beautiful to think about. I think of a mountain and sunshine and it becomes crumbly and breaks into bits and the bits start to fall downwards and go soft and sludgy and then turn dark and sticky. They get very slow and the sunshine fades and the world becomes cold and sludgy and grey and the grey becomes black and the sun . . . the sun . . .

I am deep deep down at the bottom of a deep deep pit. Shapes move dimly. Coming for me. I feel movement around me. Sickness in me, a slow, rolling, horrible nausea. Soon it will fade and go and be over. And then something happens. I see the face of my father, looking at me, staring. He isn't laughing, in the way he used to so often in my childhood, that rude, boisterous, joyful shout of mirth. And he isn't crying either, crying like a flood that will sweep away the entire world. No. He is just looking into my eyes, very tenderly. Seeing right into me and I don't mind any more. I am naked at last.

'Oh, Daddy,' I say, I try to say, but I am far from speech now. Words fall away, and I know I am descending into silence. I can feel terrible, beautiful life falling away from me: its words, sights, sounds, memories. One by one, I let them go: water falling through cupped hands.

I say to myself, 'Holly, you've let go and you're falling and soon all will be over. The only hell is in being alive.'

At that moment, out of the encroaching darkness, I feel a sudden, agonizing ache of regret. I have a sudden memory: so vivid that I am really there.

I'm abroad and I'm sitting with Meg in a restaurant on a quayside. It's been such a long lunch that the sun is low. On the table are plates and empty shells, bottles, jugs, ashtrays. We were both regular smokers then. The sun is shining at a strange angle so that we can see into the water right to the bottom, and it is clear like blue glass. There are fish in shoals picking around the ropes tethering the fishing-boats. Both of us are wearing dresses. I can't see mine but I can see Meg's, light blue, tight round her breasts. She's leaning forward and giggling but suddenly I've turned serious: 'I'm going to put this away,' I'm saying. 'Like in a bottle. And I'll always have it. In the darkest moments it will be there to help me through.' Now her hand is on mine. I can't hear what she's saying, but I can see her dear, dear face.

There is a thought deep in my mind: call Meg. I move and fall heavily from the bed on to the floor. I pull the phone down with me from the bedside table. There is stickiness on my face. I reach for the phone. I look at the numbers. They go into and out of focus. Slowly, with infinite effort, I push them. I hold the receiver to my ear. Nothing. The phone is dead. I can't think. I don't know what to do. Everything is too heavy, too far away, too hard. My thoughts are so slow, and each one is *heavy, pulled through mud and sludge. I haul myself across the floor, inch by inch, dragging myself, my fingers pulling me along. Where to? What can I possibly do? I try to raise myself and can't. My strength is fading. My eyelids feel so heavy I can't keep them open any longer.*

I make a final effort and see something, a silhouette against the window, a familiar shape. A triangle, a length of wire. The sculpture. That awful sculpture. I have a blind, final impulse, a thought I can hardly recognize. I push myself forward against the table, like a snorting, hoggish animal; my face hurts terribly, but still I push and the table tips and there is a terrible smashing and then a further crashing of glass and then of something further off, outside, that wasn't glass, and then I just fold over and sink into myself, an anchor plummeting into the inky ocean. Down, down, down.

But someone is there. Someone is there and is watching me. I can feel them even though I can't open my eyes any more. I can sense them, standing beside me. Someone.

I try to open my eyes. A narrow slit of wavering light. And in that slit, I see that there are shoes near my face, blurred in their closeness. I cannot get my eyes to focus and an obscene nausea shudders through me.

But someone is there. I know. I can hear them breathing, high above me. In the world I am leaving.

I reach out my hand to touch the shoes and they move back; first one, then the other. They become distant shapes. My hand tries to follow them but it can't.

I try to twist my neck so I can see who is wearing the shoes but I can't. My head is as heavy as a dying planet; ancient, spoiled light dances in front of me, smudged and flickering and about to be extinguished.

I try to say, 'Help,' but my lips won't move, and the breath is drowning in my throat. The tide is going out. Wave after wave rolls back from me and I lie on the deserted shore and feel life ebb away.

And someone is watching me die.

I hear the shoes click away, quite slowly, a final sound before the quiet.

And then the whole world is dark and cold and silent and the last light vanishes.

Dying Twice

27

Her eyes were closed, and her skin was a shade of light grey, blue round her puffy lips. She was thinner than I remembered, and the white sheet that was drawn up over her seemed hardly disturbed by her body. I stared until my eyes pricked and noticed things about her that I'd never seen before. The split ends in her mane of hair, the faintest down on her upper lip, the tiny mole just beneath her left ear, the grazes running in parallel lines along the soft skin of her inner arms. She looked like a wax model in which everything was uncannily correct and yet lacked the animating spirit to bring the form to life. I'd never seen Holly still before. In all the years I'd known her, I'd never seen her asleep or simply restful. Her face changed like a flame flickering in a wind, she threw her hands around dramatically when she talked, tossed back her hair impatiently, leaned forward in her chair, leaned back, tapped pencils against the table, bit the end of her thumb. She was forever jumping up, pacing around, changing position as if she couldn't find a place where she felt comfortable and at home.

Well, she was at rest now. Absolutely still and no trouble to anyone: not to Charlie, not to me, not to the nurses at the front desk who'd shown me to this bed and drawn the curtains carefully to give me privacy. Beyond them, there were all the smells and sounds of a hospital ward, but by her bed there was a hush. I'd come straight from the office, as soon as I received the phone call, leaving everything in the chaos Holly had caused in her final weeks at work. We'd all been trying to undo some of her actions. Sometimes we even had difficulty establishing what she had done, let alone why. But it seemed that no sooner had we placated an angry client than a boxload of madly expensive silk stockings from Italy – presumably one for each woman in the office – or the following day, ten new office chairs, specially and expensively designed to prevent back trouble, had been delivered. I went through recent expenses and settled most of the outstanding invoices. I had a long, complicated meeting with the bank manager, then had to deal with the architect who arrived one morning with his two assistants and beautiful plans for how we could transform the space we worked in, installing glass beams and knocking a shaft through to the floor above us. Apparently Holly had insisted that the company based there, a team of grey-suited, hawk-eyed solicitors, would agree.

I didn't understand how she'd had the time, the hours in her day, to wreak such havoc. Now she lay in front of me so very quietly. I leaned forward and picked up a hand that was lying on the sheet, blue-veined and cold. If she died now, slipped from this deathful sleep, the havoc would die with her. All the restlessness and rage and pain and sheer blinding exhaustion of being her and of knowing her would disappear. A thought was hovering in the margins of my mind, and I made an effort and brought it to the front and looked at it straight on. A part of me wanted her to die and to have done with it and leave us all in peace at last. That was what Holly must have thought as well, when she crammed all those pills into her mouth: that we all wanted her to die, that we'd only be relieved.

I ran my thumb over the bumpy blue veins on the back of her hand. She smelt of disinfectant and vomit. Her lips were slightly open and I saw that her tongue was white. When her eyes opened it was only for a moment. They stared blankly at me, then closed again. When I had first met Holly, and she had come bounding into the office in her preposterous boots, I knew I wanted to be her friend. She was so beguiling, and had this way of really listening to what I said, really looking at me; attending to me, I suppose. It made me feel almost uncomfortable sometimes. In fact, becoming her friend was a bit like embarking on an affair. She bought me presents on the spur of the moment, would ring me up in the middle of the night when she'd had an idea, get angry all of a sudden because of something I'd said or hadn't said. She once told me she loved me, sitting at a table in the South of France eating seafood and drinking wine and looking out over the sea that glinted miraculously in the afternoon sun. I remember I blushed and stuttered something and felt a bit drunk and absurdly English, but she didn't mind. She just giggled and put her hand over mine and said she knew I loved her too; I didn't need to say it; we'd always be friends. She was an impossible adventure.

'Meg?'

'Holly? I'm here.'

'Going to be sick.'

I yanked open the curtains and shouted for a nurse, then watched helplessly as Holly leaned over a plastic bowl and shouted up small dribbles of colourless vomit streaked with blood, then retched air and groans. The nurse seemed unconcerned. When Holly had finished and sunk back against her pillow, she wiped her forehead with a piece of tissue and clicked away with the bowl.

'I could be in prison,' she said.

'Don't be silly,' I said. 'It's not a crime any more.'

'What?'

'You know, trying to . . .' I hardly liked to say the words '. . . kill yourself.'

Slowly she shook her head. 'No,' she said. It was almost a groan. I had to lean close to her mouth to make out the words. She gulped painfully between every phrase. 'You heard? I did another bad thing. Pushed that awful sculpture thing out of the window. Almost landed on an old guy in the street. He dialled 999.' I almost thought I could see a flicker of amusement in her tired eyes. 'I almost kill him and he saves my life.'

She sank back down into the bed. Her eyes closed. I sat silently, holding her hand.

'Then Charlie arrived as well. Poor Charlie. Probably thinks it serves me right,' said Holly, in a whisper.

I tried to make a joke of it. 'It does. You've been a bloody idiot.'

But Holly said, eyes still closed, 'I'm sorry, Meg. Sorry about everything.'

'You don't need to . . .'

'Yes, I do. I'm sorry. So sorry. I've wrecked everything. Everything. Don't deserve to be alive. Feel so sick now.'

'Shall I call the nurse again?'

'Nothing left to come out, just bits of my guts. What a mess.'

'Charlie's downstairs. He went to get some fresh air. Do you want me to get him?'

'No. Don't leave me. Please don't leave me.' Tears oozed from under her lashes.

I waited, watching her puffy grey face, her blue-veined hands fluttering on the hospital sheet. I swallowed hard, breathing in her stale, sickly smell and wanting suddenly to be outside in the cold, clean weather. 'I love you,' I said at last, in a gruff mutter.

'Tried to call you.'

'What?'

'When I was dying. Tried to phone you.'

A shudder passed through me, like a cold ripple of knowledge. I'd never be free of her now. 'You tried to phone me?'

She gave the most tired smile as she spoke, each word an obvious effort. 'Line didn't work. Couldn't get a tone. You know, me and technology, the old story. I tried to leave you a note. Don't tell Charlie. It should have been to him. I don't want to cause unnecessary offence. Or even necessary offence.'

'What did it say?'

'Not much. Sorry, mainly. The police didn't find it, and Charlie didn't see it. Maybe it was in my dream that I wrote it, the kind of waking dream I had when I was dying. I knew you'd think it was your fault that I did it, but it wasn't. I do understand about you and Charlie.'

'Sorry? Me and Charlie?'

'Mmm.'

'God, Holly. You mean you really thought that we . . . that I could ever . . .' I stopped. I picked up one of her cold hands and held it between my own, rubbing warmth back into it.

'It was me,' she said drearily. 'I wrecked everything.'

I grinned down at her, feeling absurdly fond of her. 'You know what? I've got to go in a minute. Because there's someone waiting outside for me right now. He brought me here. His name is Todd, you remember him? I didn't tell you because it was our secret and we didn't want to tell anyone for a bit.'

Holly's eyes opened. She gazed at me through tears that were welling. 'You're really not . . . ?' she said.

'No.'

'You mean, you never . . . ?'

'You're my best friend. I wouldn't do that.'

'I was sure,' she said. 'I thought I'd lost you both, through my own stupid fault.'

'You have been pretty difficult, one way and another.'

'Todd?'

'Yes.'

'Lucky Todd.'

Her voice was slurred. I put her hand back on the cover and stroked it. 'Get some sleep now.'

'Meg?'

'What?'

'I'm happy now.'

'That's good.'

'I'm really, really happy . . .'

Her lips parted a fraction and her breathing deepened. Her eyes pulsed behind her lids. She was dreaming.

Charlie came along the corridor holding a bunch of meagre yellow carnations that he must have bought from the hospital shop downstairs. Although he had obviously shaved that morning and brushed his often unkempt hair, his gait was shambolic, as if he were punch-drunk, and his eyes were on the floor; he was frowning, in his own world.

'Charlie,' I said.

He stopped and stared at me, yet I had the feeling that he was looking straight through me at something else.

'I've just left her. She's asleep again.'

In his way he seemed as tired, as ashen, as Holly in her hospital bed.

'She's been like that,' he said. 'She wakes, she seems barely alive, then she talks until she gets tired and slips back into deep sleep again.'

'She feels guilty,' I said.

'She feels lots of things.'

I felt awkward. I didn't want to compete with him about who best knew what Holly was thinking. 'She's going to be all right, Charlie.'

'Maybe,' he said dully. 'For the time being, maybe.'

'You couldn't have done anything more than you did.'

'Oh, Meg,' he said, meeting my eyes for the first time. 'Of course I could. I left her alone. I should have known.'

'You can't be with her twenty-four hours of the day.'

He didn't say anything, just shrugged and put his face into the carnations. 'I'll be in touch,' he said.

'I'm coming in again this evening after work.'

'Thank you.'

'And you should get some sleep or you'll be ill as well, and that's no use to anyone.'

'Yes,' he said, not meaning it.

*

I returned at seven o'clock that evening but there were too many people wanting to see her: Charlie, in a clean denim shirt; my cousin Luke; Naomi, wearing too much blue eye-shadow; and finally I saw, to my horror, Holly's mother. She sat bolt upright beside the bed, a pinched expression of probity under the gun-metal hair, holding her daughter's hand as if it were an unpleasant object someone had asked her to take care of for a few minutes. Holly lay among them like a corpse, a plastic jug of heavy-scented lilies by her side. Was I the only one who could tell she was only pretending to be asleep?

The next day I was there when Dr Thorne arrived. He was a tall, spindly man with a thin neck and shrewd grey eyes; he looked a bit like a stork, and I warmed to him at once. I stood up to leave.

'Don't go,' said Holly.

'But I —'

'Stay.'

I sat on one side while he looked at Holly's chart, then took a chair and asked her question after question, which for the most part Holly answered briefly, in a soft, subdued voice. Why had she come off her drugs? How long had she planned it? What exactly had made her decide she could no longer bear to go on living? What had been the trigger? Was this the first time that she had tried or considered trying? What about the cuts along her arms? How would she describe her mood at the time leading up to the suicide attempt? He told her to give her mood a colour and Holly thought and then she said, 'Maroon.' How many pills had she taken? Had she discovered as she swallowed them that she wanted to live? How would she describe her feelings now? He asked her to give her present mood a number, on a scale of one to ten, one being the lowest and ten the highest. Holly glared at him with a hint of her old self in the glint of her eyes, and said three and two-fifths and Dr Thorne smiled at her as if he really liked her. The questions went on and on. He looked at her tongue and took her pulse. He asked her if she had heard voices or seen strange things. Holly's eyes slid towards me as if she was suddenly terrified and asking for my help, then away again.

'Maybe,' she muttered. 'How do you know if the voices and the faces are inside your head or outside?'

'Were you scared?'

'Yes.' Her voice had sunk to a whisper. 'Very. Scared of being mad. When I was dying, I thought . . .'

'What did you think?'

'I thought someone was watching me.'

'I think that's quite common.'

'I saw two shoes . . .'

So it continued. I felt I shouldn't be a witness to his precise questions and her murmured answers, and the peeling away of all the layers till we were down to the raw wounds. I sat as quietly as I could, in the sweet stink of lilies.

'Do you wish you had been successful in your attempt?' he asked finally.

Once again, Holly looked at me. There was something in her expression I couldn't read. It was almost sly.

'No,' she said at last. 'I think I want to be alive.'

28

In spite of everything, I was happy, happier than I'd been for many years. Sometimes I felt guilty about that, but I couldn't help it. Every day I woke up and saw Todd beside me and my heart would bound with delight in my chest and the day would spread in front of me like a banner. All the things that used to frustrate me at work now seemed easy. The things that used to bore me were filled with interest. I had a new energy and enthusiasm. I was in love.

Sometimes I'd sleep at his place and sometimes he'd sleep at mine. Our flats were like crime scenes in which we had left more and more and more incriminating pieces of evidence betraying our presence: toothbrushes, underwear, cosmetics, shirts, blouses, paperbacks. I was starting to search for things and then realizing they were at Todd's place. It was fun, never quite being sure where I'd be sleeping at the end of the day. It was a safe adventure.

I knew it would never be quite like this again, whatever happened between us. If it was going to carry on the way I wanted, maybe we would get to a stage where – unimaginably – we would stop thinking about each other all the time, where we would go a day, two, three, without sex, where the other one would be just a familiar part of the furniture. But not now. Now we were endlessly curious about each other. Todd was a maze I wanted to wander in, a puzzle to solve, a magical mystery tour. We talked about our lives, our work, previous lovers, what had gone wrong and what had gone right. We gave each other secrets.

Every day was tantalizingly short because, whatever happened in the future, this intensity and energy would fade. It would have to fade so that we would be able to become normal people again, normal lovers, or partners or, perhaps, just friends, or maybe strangers once more.

But now there was Holly to worry about again. Sitting at breakfast in Todd's flat – he had prepared fruit and coffee and some special kind of muesli – I said that I'd be late seeing him in the evening because I'd have to stop in and see Holly. He just nodded.

'This is all going to take up a lot of time,' I said.

'Of course.'

'I'd understand if you resented it.'

'I don't resent it.'

'I know that when you met Holly it wasn't a complete success . . .'

'You mean *I* wasn't a complete success?'

'It wasn't your fault. To put it mildly.'

'For someone who's meant to be her best friend, don't you think you're a bit scared of her?'

I needed a moment to think about that one. 'Holly's always been high maintenance,' I said.

'Emotionally, I mean. She's been worth it, though. She's driven me mad, she's embarrassed me like you couldn't imagine . . .'

'Oh, but I can,' said Todd.

'But I wouldn't have done half the things I've done without her. That's what she does. She spurs you into things that seem insane and then you think, Well, why not? Lately it went wrong and it was just the insane bit. That's not the real her you've seen.'

'You don't need to convince me.'

I put my hand across and stroked his silky brown hair. 'I do,' I said. 'You more than anyone. As well as destroying herself, Holly put a lot of effort into driving *me* away as well. Maybe that was another way of harming herself, by getting rid of the people who love her.'

I stood up, pulled Todd to his feet and folded my arms round the soft wool of his suit. 'I want you to do me a favour,' I said.

'Of course.'

'Most people would say, "What?" first.'

'Not me, not for you.'

'Oh.' I blinked at him and almost couldn't think what I had been going to say. 'I want you to like Holly now, for my sake. Later, maybe, you'll like her anyway.'

'I'll try.'

'And I'll come round later this evening.'

'That's part of the deal.'

*

272

I sat by Holly's bedside for almost an hour without speaking. Her eyes would flicker open for a few seconds and then she would sleep again. I was almost asleep myself, so that when she spoke I started. I couldn't make out what she said at first. It was just a mumble.

'What?'

'I'm scared.'

'What of? Or do you mean just scared?'

'Of going back.'

'What do you mean?'

'Leaving here. Going back to the world. I'm safe here.'

'Stuart's out on bail now. Charlie told me. But I don't think he'll be after you again.'

'I'm not worried about him. I even keep thinking I shouldn't press charges . . .'

'You should. You must. He could have killed you.'

'He was just the one who got to me first, wasn't he?'

'What do you mean?'

'Well, if it hadn't been him, and if it hadn't been me doing it to myself, it could have been Rees. When I was dying I thought someone was there.'

'There?'

'So many people wanting to kill me. I suppose I was imagining some kind of vengeful witness. You know.'

'Is it Rees you're scared of?'

'Yeah. Well, him and . . .'

'Go on.'

'Promise you won't tell Charlie.'

'So many secrets,' I said.

'Give me water first.'

So I fetched a plastic cup of water and she drank it, flinching with each sip.

'I got involved in a poker game,' she said. 'That night when I came round to yours at dawn and we quarrelled.'

'I remember.'

'Anyway, the thing is, I lost some money to a man called Vic Norris.' She frowned at me. 'Quite a lot of money, actually.'

'How much?' I was expecting her to say a hundred pounds or something: that seemed like a lot to me. The most I've ever gambled was a fiver on the Grand National and that was only once.

'It's going up all the time,' she whispered. 'All the time I don't pay it goes up some more.'

'Just pay.'

'This skinhead comes round,' she said.

'Tell me how much you owe.'

'Meg,' called a voice, 'how're you doing?'

'Eleven thousand,' she hissed at me, and she looked unimaginably distressed. I felt stunned and at the same moment I saw Charlie, walking across the ward weighed down with books and magazines and fruit for Holly. She squeezed my hand frantically.

I went to meet him, taking some of the magazines

that were slipping out of his grasp. He kissed me on both cheeks. 'It's lovely of you to be here. Really good of you. How is she?'

'Better, I think. She –'

But I was cut short by the arrival of a small group of people. Dr Thorne was accompanied by a nurse and a young man with cropped hair in a white coat. The nurse began checking the tubes as if Holly were a troublesome boiler, and while that was going on I touched Dr Thorne's arm to get his attention. 'I want to talk to you,' I said, softly so that Holly wouldn't hear.

'What about?' said Dr Thorne.

'Can we go a bit further off? That's better. We met the other day. My name's Meg Summers. I'm a really close friend of Holly. I'm her work partner as well.'

'Yes, she's mentioned you.'

'I'm worried about Holly.'

'We all are.'

'No, I mean I'm confused. Look, I don't want to get involved in the details of her case but there's something that doesn't make sense.'

'What do you mean?' asked Dr Thorne.

'Holly tried to kill herself, and you're treating her for serious depression.'

'Specifically for a bipolar affective disorder.'

'Which is an illness in her mind.'

'That's right.'

'The point is, I've just had a long talk with Holly. Is it possible that what might look like depression could actually be a perfectly rational reaction to extreme stress?'

'How do you mean?'

I took a deep breath and gave Dr Thorne a brief account of the story I'd got from Holly. 'Don't you see?' I said. 'If I were being hassled like that, I could imagine collapsing as well.'

Dr Thorne looked thoughtful. 'Let's get a cup of coffee,' he said.

I thought he might be taking us to his office for some real coffee, but he meant a coffee machine in the corridor outside the ward. It tasted seriously bad.

'When I was first studying biology,' said Dr Thorne, 'I used to have trouble with the idea of birds' nests and genetics. Birds' nests are so peculiar, and yet so similar within species. How could the bird's genes be responsible for a process that involves finding moss or grass or sticks and using mud or spit? But in fact much of the development of the brain depends on outside stimulus. The human brain is programmed to learn language, but the developing child needs to be exposed to language outside itself in order to stimulate the language areas of the brain. The development of language occurs in the brain using bits of language from outside. One way of looking at a bird's nest is to see it as an extension of the bird's brain, which happens to make use of bits and pieces of the outside world rather than electrical impulses.'

'I don't quite see . . .'

'Holly has talked to me about her fears as well,' continued Dr Thorne.

'What I was asking,' I said, 'is whether these disasters in her life are real or whether they are part of her illness.'

Dr Thorne smiled as if he had solved a particularly tricky quiz question. 'It would be plausible to say that they are real *and* they're part of her illness. That's what I meant by mentioning the bird's nest. Holly's mind is in turmoil, which has partly manifested itself in a form of self-harm. What she has done in the past months is to turn her environment into what can also be seen as an extension of her own mind. You could say that she has externalized her self-loathing by creating situations in which other people feel about her the way she feels about herself. She is a paranoid woman who has manufactured an environment to justify her feelings of paranoia.'

'Are you saying that Holly's fears are all justified?'

'I'm a doctor, not a policeman. What I'm clear about is that it isn't just a matter of treating Holly Krauss's mind with chemicals and giving her psychotherapy, although both of those are important as well. She's not a brain in a vat. She lives in a world and one day, I hope, she's going to have to go out and live in that world again.'

'Yeah, but . . . but meanwhile there are people out there who want to do her harm.'

Dr Thorne looked serious. 'I don't want to say this is going to be easy. I've had other patients who did terrible things. For them recovery was the hardest part because only then did they fully realize the damage they had done when they were ill. I mean people who recovered through treatment only to learn that in their illness they had injured or even killed their own children. Seeing the world clearly can be a mixed blessing. Suddenly you face up to things that your mind has been protecting you from.'

'I'm sorry,' I said. 'I'm none the wiser.'

Dr Thorne allowed himself a slight smile. 'But a little better informed,' he said.

29

It was as if, now that Holly was gone, I was turning into her, filling the space she'd left behind. I was working ten hours a day with sandwiches at my desk for lunch, rushing to the hospital to be with Holly, then staying up late with Todd. Though I've always needed at least nine hours' sleep I was suddenly sleeping six or less and not feeling tired at all. I said something like that to Trish and she laughed.

'What's the matter?'

'No, Meg,' she said, in her emphatic tone that always made me feel a bit frayed at the edges. 'Trust me, you're nothing at all like Holly.'

'I know I'm not really, I just meant I was feeling so energetic all of a sudden.'

'When she was feeling energetic, she was like a comet,' said Trish. 'Or a plane that was about to take off. You couldn't ignore her. Even when she was just sitting at her desk and not moving it was as if she was pulsing and the air around her was turbulent. I could feel it as soon as I opened the door. It would take me about half a second to know if the day was going to be dire or wonderful. I didn't like that because I had no control over it. She was the one who was always in control, even though she was

279

out of control too. You understand what I mean.'

'I guess so.'

'You're her opposite, that's probably why you're such close friends. Chalk and cheese. You're so steady.'

'That makes me sound a bit dreary.'

'No, we like it,' said Trish. 'You make us all feel safe.'

'Do I?'

'Yes. Holly's like a state-of-the-art fun-fair. You're like a – like a . . .' She searched for the right metaphor and I waited. 'A house,' she said at last.

'Is that good?'

'Yes,' she said firmly.

Then she put her small, capable hands on my shoulders and kissed me on both cheeks. I think she was as surprised as I was.

All through that day, rushed and busy as I was, I kept thinking about Trish's words and about Holly; more specifically, about Holly's enemies. What she had said to me, so urgently, and what Dr Thorne had said. Shortly she would be coming out of hospital. I didn't want her to come out into a hostile world. I wasn't sure about Dr Thorne and his birds' nests, but I knew enough to understand that because Holly loathed herself at times, she had created a world in which lots of people wished her ill. I'd seen her do it often enough. She'd tried hard to make everyone give up on her. Even I had come close to doing that and

I was her best friend. I knew I would never be able to understand what Holly had been going through, but I had a glimmer of the hell she'd been in.

Trish said I made people feel safe. It wasn't much. I think I would rather have been compared to a fun-fair than to a house: to be exciting, sexy, glamorous, dangerous, wilful, vulnerable, lovable, maddening and bold like Holly. But it was what I was. And Holly trusted me. It was to me she had written her goodbye note, me she had tried to call when she was dying. I wanted, no, I *needed*, to try to make the world a bit safer for my friend to return to. When I thought of her fragile form in the hospital bed, when I remembered the way she had held on to my arm the day before and gazed at me pleadingly, it felt like my duty. Onerous, unavoidable.

Todd dropped me off at the hospital and said he would meet me there half an hour later. Charlie had just gone but Marcia Krauss was there, and she was arranging a large bunch of flowers in a jug. She was still young – about fifty, at a guess – and probably rather attractive, but it was difficult to see beyond her armour of rectitude. When I'd first met her, a couple of years ago, I'd scarcely been able to believe that she was Holly's mother. Later, I'd come to understand that she was like a negative image of Holly: neat, careful, proper, understated, thrifty, virtuous, controlled and deeply anxious. Having Holly for a daughter must have been scary for her.

I kissed her cheek, then Holly's forehead. 'You're looking better.'

'Liar.'

It was true, though. She was haggard and the fading bruise on her cheek gave her face a lopsided greyness, but her eyes weren't so dull, and she didn't look all washed up and wasted any more.

'Who have you seen today?'

Holly ignored my question. 'We were just talking about Dad,' she said.

'You were talking about him. I wasn't,' said her mother.

'I was asking how he died.'

Holly was certainly feeling better, I thought. Back to being awkward, at least. I felt like cheering.

'He always had a stressful lifestyle,' said Marcia.

'Mum,' said Holly, 'stop fiddling with the flowers and look at me, please. I tried to kill myself.'

'I know,' muttered her mother, into the roses and lilies. 'That's why I'm here.'

'It's just that you haven't mentioned it.'

'I'm here to help you get over all that. And, anyway, Meg's come to visit you now.'

'Meg doesn't mind, do you? Dad was like me, you keep saying so. I just want to know if he killed himself.'

'Holly, this isn't the time.'

'When is the time, then?'

'Not now.'

'He did, didn't he? He was manic-depressive and he killed himself.'

'You can't just put it like that.'

'It's in my blood. From him.'

'Stop it!'

'Oh, never mind,' Holly said. 'There's nothing you can do about it, anyway.'

She sank against the pillow. Her mother picked up her bag, shuffled the flowers one last, unnecessary time, then kissed her daughter, a little peck. 'Don't overtire yourself.'

'No,' said Holly. 'I won't.'

After her mother had left, she turned to me and said, 'I bet she's driving Charlie insane. She doesn't want to be here, and I don't want her to be. It's just one of those things that mothers are supposed to do so that's how it's going to be.'

I sat on her bed, picked up a grape and popped it into my mouth. 'When are you going home, then?'

'Dr Thorne's being evasive. He keeps asking me questions and he says there's another avenue he wants to explore.'

'How's Charlie?'

'Fine, I guess.'

'Can you tell me how to find that gambler man? What did you say he was called? Vic Norris?'

'How did you get from "How's Charlie?" to that?'

'Tell me.'

'Why? Anyway, I haven't got a clue.'

'What about that other guy – Tony? Is that his name?'

It was as if I had become the custodian of Holly's life, knowing more about its details than she did herself.

'Tony Manning. Why?'

'Where's he?'

'Dunno. Actually, I do. He said he was building a new block of flats near Tate Modern. The area's coming up apparently. Why? There's nothing you can do, you know. You can't persuade these people to be nice.'

I didn't have time to reply. Naomi pushed her head round the curtains, calling, 'Hello,' brightly as she did so. Holly mumbled something and closed her eyes.

'I think she's a bit tired,' I said.

'I wanted to give her these.' Naomi put a brown-paper bag on Holly's chest. A yeasty smell filled the air. 'Saffron rolls,' she said. 'Fresh from the oven. They're still warm. Here, try one.'

Holly shook her head.

I don't really like saffron, but she seemed so eager that I didn't want to hurt her feelings, so I picked up a roll and took a small bite. 'Delicious.'

'Good. I thought there were enough flowers and fruit.'

'You've obviously been a great help to Charlie and Holly,' I said.

'Mostly to Charlie,' said Holly, in the same hardly audible mutter.

'It's been a pleasure,' said Naomi. 'They're my friends. And, anyway, I'm a nurse. I know what Holly's been going through. Is still going through,' she added. 'People think she's recovering, but they should bear in mind it's not a virus she's got and she's deep in the thick of it still, aren't you, Holly?'

'I suppose so.'

'She'll need us all to rally round for a long time to come. Isn't that right?'

Holly turned away from both of us and burrowed into her pillow. I bent over and kissed her hollow cheek 'Don't worry any more,' I said softly. 'Not about anything. Everything's going to be fine.'

30

Before I had the time to track down Vic Norris, Rees found me. The very next day, just as I was writing an email to everyone in the office about how expenses should now be submitted properly, not merely scrawled in lipstick on a tissue, he came in through the open door of our office, sauntered up to where I was sitting and dropped a thick brown envelope on the desk in front of me. 'Thought you might like to see some snaps of your little friend before you take her into any more police stations,' he said.

'How do you know about that?'

He smiled.

'I watched you go in,' he said, 'and then I watched you come out again. But I haven't been taken in for questioning, have I? The police didn't want to know, am I right? Who'd believe a word she said, if it came to court? A bit of a fantasist, our Holly. Anyway, look at those snapshots of her – just copies, by the way.'

He turned and walked away. I sat and stared at his receding figure. It took a few seconds for the anger I felt to bubble up inside me.

'It was that guy, wasn't it?' said Lola from behind me. 'That creep who was stalking Holly.'

'Yes. Listen, hold the fort, will you? I'll be back in a minute.'

I was almost amused by the bafflement on her face, open-mouthed like in a cartoon, as I burst past her and ran down the stairs. He had just left the building when I caught him and took him by the sleeve.

'Listen to me,' I said.

'What?'

'I know what you did.'

'You know what Holly said I did.'

'I know what you did,' I ploughed on. 'And I'm warning you, if you ever go anywhere near her again, you won't get away with it a second time.'

'Why would I want to go anywhere near her? She's just . . .' He stopped and searched around for the right word. 'Scum,' he said finally. I could smell the beer on his breath.

'Just keep away. You've no idea of the knife edge she's . . .' I bit down on the words.

'I think I do. She tried to top herself, didn't she? Pity.'

'Pity?'

'That she failed.'

If I had been holding a knife I would have plunged it into Rees's chest, just to take the knowing, vicious smirk off his face.

'And stop harassing her friends.'

'She's sick, isn't she? Sick in the head. Poor old Charlie. Anyway, he's welcome to her. I wouldn't want to fuck a nutcase.'

I took a deep breath, clenching my fists to stop myself screaming and attacking him.

'Keep away,' I said, and left him there in the street. It occurred to me that any onlooker would have assumed we were lovers having a tiff. The thought made me shudder.

Back in the office, I slid my finger under the gummed flap on the brown envelope Rees had dropped on to my desk and pulled out the top photograph. It was a picture of Holly asleep at Luigi's; he must have gone up close, unless he had a zoom lens. She was lying against the table, her head in the crook of one arm, and her eyes were closed, with smudges of mascara round them. Her lipstick was smeared and her skin looked waxy. You could even make out a dribble of saliva running from the corner of her half-open mouth. I couldn't bear the idea of Holly ever seeing this, of her suspecting it existed. I winced and pushed it hastily into the envelope, which I then hid at the back of the filing cabinet's bottom drawer.

At half past eleven, I drove to the building site south of the river. In spite of Holly's vagueness, it proved quite easy to find. I asked a bulky man with a mottled nose and an orange hat if he could point me in the direction of Anthony Manning.

'Tony?'

'Yes, Tony.' I tried to sound businesslike, as if I was expected.

'Not here. He's never here on Thursdays. It's his day at the club.'

'The club?'

'Golf. Schmoozing clients.'

'Which club would that be?'

'In Kingston.'

'Oh. Thanks.'

I thought of giving up, just going back to the office and telling myself I'd done everything that could be expected. But instead I found myself driving to Kingston and asking directions to the golf club, then walking in, trying to look as if I came to this kind of place all the time. At the bar where people were drinking gin and tonic I asked for Anthony Manning, and a man in a hideous brown corduroy suit pointed outside and said he was on the course.

I ordered a tomato juice but was told non-members weren't allowed to drink in the bar. I said I'd just sit in the corner and wait, and was told that non-members weren't allowed even to be in the bar. So I loitered in the hallway, looking at a catalogue full of pictures of checked hats and shoes with tassels. And at last someone said, 'Yes?'

A tall, solid-looking man was before me, jingling change in his pocket. He wasn't wearing the stupid clothes most of the men preferred around here. There was not a hint of a smile in his face, or of curiosity.

'Anthony Manning?'

'Yes,' he said again, a hint of impatience in his voice.

'I'm Meg Summers, a friend of Holly. Holly Krauss.' He didn't say anything; the expression on his face didn't alter. I took a deep breath. 'She's in hospital and not well and I need to track down someone for her. To sort out her debts.'

A tiny smile appeared on his face. 'Do you, now?'

'Yes.'

'And?'

'Where do I find him?'

'You need to visit him at his company headquarters.'

'That sounds grand.'

'It's a shop in Kennington.' He scribbled an address and handed it to me.

'What kind of shop?'

'This and that,' he said, and turned away. But then he added, 'And don't try to beat him down. He's negotiating from a position of strength.'

I thought I should have someone with me so I took Lola. She's really the last person you should involve in a crisis. She's small, innocent, panicky and gullible. But she adores Holly, like a puppy adores its owner. I just wanted her to sit outside in the car and wait for me. What for, I couldn't say.

Cowden Brothers was a pawn shop between a boarded-up travel agent and a barber. In the window was a monocycle, a saxophone, an electric guitar, a grandfather clock and lots of jewellery. Also, a small

sign saying, 'MONEY LENT. GOOD TERMS. CONFI-
DENTIALITY RESPECTED'. I pushed the door and a
bell jangled loudly.

A fat man with a tiny, dainty face sat behind the
counter. He was reading a magazine and smoking.
Behind him a much older man was watching the
racing on TV. 'I'm looking for Vic Norris,' I said.

'And you are?'

'Meg Summers. A friend of Holly Krauss.'

'I don't know who you are and I don't know who
she is.'

'I suppose Vic Norris would know who Holly is.'

He stubbed out his cigarette in an overflowing
ashtray. 'He doesn't work here,' he said.

'I was given this address.'

The man slowly extracted another cigarette from
a packet and lit it. 'What's the nature of your
business?' he said.

'My friend owes Vic Norris some money.
Apparently.'

'Oh dear. And why are you here?'

'She's unwell.'

The man took a deep drag on his cigarette and
gave a wheezy cough. 'What was the name?'

'Holly Krauss.'

'Hang on.' He walked through a door behind the
counter.

The old man turned his head towards me, then
back to the racing.

When the fat man returned, he seemed more affable. 'That's right. Your young lady owes sixteen thousand pounds.'

'Sixteen? I heard it was eleven.'

He chuckled. 'There's interest payments, love,' he said. 'Your friend has been slow in paying.'

'This is completely unfair,' I said. 'She didn't mean any of this. And she's been ill.'

The man didn't seem to have heard me. He just turned to his companion. 'Who won?'

'Nineteen To The Dozen,' said the old man.

'Fuck,' said the fat man.

'I was saying that this is completely unfair.'

'Your friend should be careful where she borrows money,' he said.

'She didn't borrow it. She was lured into a poker game.'

The man shrugged. 'Next week it'll be seventeen, then eighteen. But . . .' Another shrug. He gazed down at his magazine.

'What if she can't pay?' I said. 'What if people can't pay?'

The fat man smiled, showing a gap in the teeth in his upper jaw. 'They always pay,' he said.

I looked at him and at the old man behind him. I looked at the objects arranged on the shelves – old stereos, a drum-kit, shoes, a teapot and matching jug, an exercise bike, several watches, a carriage clock, a clumsy black camera.

'Today's Thursday,' I said. 'I'll come on Tuesday with it. Tuesday before six in the evening.'

'On Tuesday it'll be seventeen thousand.'

'I'll come on Monday. Can I pay with a cheque?'

'There's a service charge for cheques,' he said.

'How much?'

'Thirty per cent.'

'I'll pay cash.'

The door jangled again as I left.

31

I had nearly eleven thousand pounds in the bank, in a special savings account. It had taken me six years to amass that much. I was keeping it to buy a house. Well, probably a poky one-bedroom flat in the outskirts, but a start at least. One day I'd live in a place of my own, with a small garden. Herbs and flowers and an ornamental fruit tree. Maybe a cat, even. Holly had been able to buy her house because there were two of them, and her mother had lent her half the deposit. When we first started the company I dreamed we'd be earning enough to save more quickly, but of course it hadn't been like that.

I put away the thoughts of my fantasy house, my fantasy life. I had eleven thousand, but I still needed to find another five, and I could see no way of raising that at all, let alone by Monday. I had an overdraft limit of five hundred, so I guessed I could call on that. But five thousand?

Late that afternoon I sat at my desk and pondered. At KS Associates we had an agreed overdraft limit of thirty thousand pounds and were only in debt at present to the tune of nineteen thousand, four hundred. That meant I could write out a cheque for cash tomorrow morning and still not have reached the limit. I even took the company cheque book out of the drawer and put it into my bag. But then I glanced round the office, at Lola and Trish and all the others who trusted me – who thought I was safe as a house – and put it back again. I knew I would be signing away everything we'd worked so hard for.

'You'll come with me to my parents for Christmas, won't you?'

It wasn't really a question, more a statement, delivered casually as I was pushing a fork loaded with rice into my mouth. I was suddenly filled with a calm kind of happiness at the steadiness of this relationship, its basic kindness. I laid down my fork. 'That'd be nice,' I replied, trying to keep the wobble of emotion out of my voice. 'If you'd like me to.'

'I'd like you to,' he said. 'And they want to meet you.'

'Do they?' I beamed. 'Yes. I'd like to meet them too.'

We grinned at each other, then returned to our meal. I hadn't looked forward to Christmas for ages. Most years my parents and I had gone to my sister's in Devon. She had a husband, and now two small children, a cat. They lived in a small house in the middle of nowhere, mud churning up to the threshold and the sea not far over the horizon. I always felt a bit of a spare part, the one who arrived late and alone, and played the part of the good daughter and the cheery aunt for a day or two before escaping back to

London. Last year I'd gone to Holly and Charlie's, and stayed up till five in the morning because Holly insisted on a drunken game of charades. I remembered her standing on a table in her spindly shoes, her paper hat askew, giggling helplessly. But this year was different. Todd and I had plans together. We were going to buy a tree together, we were going to go away at New Year together, maybe make resolutions together. The year ahead seemed bright with hopes.

Then I let Holly move from the back of my thoughts into the front once more. She was going to have a strange Christmas this year. I'd talked to Charlie about it and he'd told me that her mother had agreed to stay on until she was out of hospital and settled at home. His mother was also coming for a few days. Naomi was going to cook the dinner. Poor Holly, I thought, lying in her hospital bed, dull and pale and thin, while all around people discussed her and made plans for her.

I had always thought of Holly as bold, the boldest person I'd ever met, but now she was scared. I wondered if she was so afraid because of what was inside her – all the strange, tormenting demons she used to think were part of her character but which now felt like hideous invasions – or of what lay outside, in the real world she would have to return to soon enough. Probably she was afraid of both the inside and the outside: she couldn't escape either, and there was nowhere to hide. Even when she slept, she had told me, she had hideous dreams. I have never felt so sorry for anyone in all my life as I now felt for Holly, nor so responsible. It was as if we'd moved beyond the normal kind of friendship, and she was more like my daughter, my sister, my mother, rolled into one. Like a boulder on my heart, so that even when I was with Todd, a little part of me was thinking of her and worrying. And making plans, like the plan I had for today, which I'd not even told Todd about because I knew he would tell me I was being stupid.

'What's up?' asked Todd. 'Your face has got that frown on it.'

'Has it? I don't know why.'

'What were you thinking about?'

'Oh, nothing.'

'Meg, I'm not blind. Tell me.'

'It's not really my story to tell. It's Holly's.'

'Oh, Holly. I might have known.'

A slight coolness hung between us for the rest of the evening. And in the end, lying in bed, I told him about Holly's debt, my visit to the golf club and to Cowden Brothers.

'You know what I think?'

'You think I'm being incredibly stupid.'

'I think you're the kindest and most loyal and generous friend there's ever been.'

'Oh.' I could feel my cheeks turning pink in the dark. 'Not really.'

'Have you thought this through?'

'I think so.'

'Does Holly appreciate you?'

'I'm not telling her about this. I just want her to be safe when she comes out of hospital.'

'So you're doing it and not even wanting to be thanked. That's positively unnatural.'

'It's gone beyond things like that now,' I heard myself say, realizing as I said it that it was true. 'It feels more like a matter of life and death or sanity and insanity or something. I feel I don't really have a choice.'

There was a silence. He stroked my hair absent-mindedly.

'What are you thinking?'

'I'm thinking you should have told me before.'

'I wanted to, but it was Holly's secret to tell, not mine.'

'You shouldn't have gone there by yourself.'

'I had Lola with me.'

'Great.' He'd met Lola.

'It was fine.'

'You're really going to do this?'

'Yes.'

'Well, then, I was thinking that I can give you four thousand. It's all I've got. A bit more than all I've got.'

'No!' I said. 'No, no and no. That would be all wrong. You don't even know Holly. The only time you met her she was offensive and rude. I wouldn't have told you anything if I'd thought you were going to offer. Now I feel awful.'

'I want to.'

'No.'

'Meg, I *want* to. I've decided.'

'But this is all wrong – I can't take money from you.'

'Why not?'

'I just can't.'

'A loan, then.'

'But . . .'

'But without the weekly interest.'

'Todd.'

'What?'

'I don't know what to say.'

'Why do you have to say anything?'

The remaining thousand pounds I borrowed from Trish and an old schoolfriend who worked in the City, lived in a large house in Camden and spent five hundred on every pair of shoes she bought. I said I'd pay them back after Christmas, without fail; just a slight cash-flow problem. Everyone was a bit embarrassed.

On Monday morning I felt faint with nerves. I made myself go through the motions of working but I couldn't concentrate on anything. I took an hour to answer a few routine emails, then opened the post slowly, trying to look busy. At lunchtime I went to my bank and withdrew eleven thousand five hundred pounds. I now had an overdraft of four hundred and six pounds in my current account, and £1.56 left in my special savings account. I felt a bit tipsy as I pushed the bundles of notes into a plastic bag and then into my shoulder-bag: a mixture of heroic self-sacrifice, sadness, resentment and euphoric strangeness. I wasn't used to doing wild, dramatic things like this. It was as though I had stepped into someone else's life.

I met Todd outside his workplace. He came out looking like a criminal, glancing extravagantly from side to side and holding to his chest a scuffed brief-case I hadn't seen before. A little giggle lodged in my chest. I hugged him tight and kissed his cold cheek.

'Hi,' he half whispered, then smirked at himself.

'Are you hungry? Do you want to grab a bite to eat first?'

'What? Carrying all this cash with us? Christ, Meg, let's just deliver it and get it over with before we lose it or get mugged.'

'Are you all right?'

'I feel peculiar. Illicit. As if we're about to rob a bank or something.'

'If only. We're the ones who are being robbed, remember?'

'Where's the car?'

'Parked on a meter round the corner.'

'Let's go.'

'Todd.'

'What?'

'Thanks.'

'Say that later. Come on.'

It was only the fat man this time, although there were sounds from the back of the shop. He locked the door after we came in and turned the sign to 'Closed'. Then he went back round the other side of the counter and I handed over my plastic bag and Todd's two manilla envelopes. He touched his tongue to his forefinger delicately and started to flick through the notes with practised skill. We both stared at him. I watched his small hands riffling the money and his rosebud lips, which he licked constantly.

'Good,' he said at last.

'Can I have a receipt?'

He tore a piece of paper from a pad, scrawled the figures on it and handed it to me.

'This isn't exactly a VAT receipt,' I said.

'So what?'

'How do I trust you? What if you just denied getting the money? What if you keep on hassling Holly?'

The fat man looked hurt. 'We're a business,' he said. 'What would that do for our reputation? You've settled up. Now go away.'

32

It sounds awful to say but I felt proud of myself.
I had gone out into the awful mess that Holly had
left behind her and I had sorted it out. I wasn't
sure whether I had slain a dragon or just done a bit
of spring-cleaning, but I had made Holly's world a
less hostile place. I looked forward to telling her
about it and teasing a smile out of her; slowly things
would start to get better. It didn't turn out like that.
When I came through the door of her ward, she was
lying in her bed with her back to me. The position
looked unnatural and ominous. I walked round so
that I could look at her face. She was pale, her skin
clammy. At first I thought she was asleep, but then
her eyes opened. They looked dead, like the eyes of
a fish.

'Holly,' I said. 'How are you?'

She mumbled something I couldn't make out so
I leaned closer. It was nonsense, just meaningless
syllables. 'What is it?' I said. 'What's happened?'

In my alarm, I ran for a nurse and almost dragged
her across to Holly's bed. 'Something's terribly wrong
with her,' I said. 'She needs a doctor.'

The nurse frowned and bent over Holly. She took
the chart from the end of the bed. 'Miss Krauss is

resting,' she said. 'She's just got back from her first treatment.'

'What sort of treatment?'

'ECT.'

I almost fought my way past Dr Thorne's secretary on my way in to his office. He was on the phone and looked baffled to see me. I stood there stubbornly until he replaced the receiver. 'I'm Holly Krauss's friend,' I said. 'You talked to me the other day.'

'Yes, Meg, I know who you are.'

'What's the hell's going on? I just came in to see her and she was completely incoherent. And then I discovered she's been given ECT.' I paused. There was no response. 'Well?'

'I ordered the treatment,' he said, 'with the consent of Miss Krauss and her husband.'

'What on earth for?' I said.

'I'm sorry, I really can't discuss the details of her treatment with you.'

'This is a scandal,' I said. 'I'm going to make a complaint.'

Dr Thorne stood up in some alarm. 'Wait,' he said. 'Look. I can't talk about the details of Miss Krauss's case. You can discuss it with her yourself.'

'She's not in a state to discuss anything.'

'That'll be the anaesthetic or the muscle relaxant. It's nothing to do with the ECT.'

'I can't believe you've given her this extreme treatment. It's medieval.'

'It's not in the least extreme,' said Dr Thorne. 'All

303

you know about it probably comes from old movies. I promise you it's nothing like that. It's a safe procedure. We give it to pregnant women in preference to medication. We give it to geriatric patients almost as a matter of course.'

'You're electrocuting her brain,' I said.

He smiled at that. 'Strictly speaking, "electrocuting" means to kill with electricity.'

'Don't play with words. What will it do to her brain?'

'Some patients report a degree of memory loss,' he said, 'but it's usually recovered. The main point is that it is an effective treatment. And in certain patients it can be crucial.'

'You mean severely ill patients?'

He looked uneasy. 'For example, it is almost indispensable in cases where a patient might be considered to be at imminent risk.'

'Do you mean that Holly was suicidal?'

He gave a gesture of helplessness. 'I'm sorry,' he said. 'That's off-limits. All I can say is that you're her friend. You know her. You know what she's been through.'

'This is mad,' I said. 'Ridiculous. She's not severely ill. She was getting so much better. I can't believe that this has suddenly happened now. She told me. She said she wanted to live. She won't try again. I know.'

Dr Thorne was not to be drawn. He sat down again. Clearly our interview was over.

*

When I got back to the ward, Charlie was there and Holly was properly awake. She smiled weakly when she saw me.

'How are you doing?'

'It's a bit fuzzy,' she said. 'Woozy. Dizzy. Words with *Z* in them keep coming into my, er, you know.'

I felt it was my duty to be cheerful about it, at least with Holly.

'I talked to Dr Thorne,' I said. 'He was very positive about it.'

'I was a bit, you know . . . about it. Sort of *Cuckoo's Nest*. Thought you'd come in and find me with a scar on my shaved head. Put a pillow over my face.'

She still made me laugh. I stroked her face. 'You look well,' I said.

We talked for a while, although it was a disjointed conversation. Charlie hovered in the background, not joining in. He fetched coffee for us, fussed with the bed and arranged Holly's things. I felt so sorry for him. He'd spent so much of the past year being a spectator at the Great Holly Show and now he was having to be a nurse as well. I wondered if he resented my presence or whether it was a relief. I looked at my watch and remembered I had a life to lead elsewhere. But I wanted to talk to Charlie first. I nodded at him to follow me away from the bed. We paused in the corridor outside the ward. It was busy with trolleys, nurses, a party of fresh-faced medical students in their white coats. I told Charlie how surprised I'd been. 'I know,' he said. 'It was a difficult decision. But Dr Thorne said it would be for the best.'

'I don't just mean that,' I said. 'He was irritatingly discreet with me. But from what he said it sounded as if he thought Holly was still suicidal.'

There was a pause.

'Yes?' said Charlie.

'But she isn't.'

'What are you talking about, Meg? Are you blind or what? What do you think she's doing here? She died in the ambulance. It's a miracle they got her back.'

'I know, I know,' I said. 'But she's different now. She told me. She said she had discovered she wanted to live.'

Charlie shook his head. 'I wish it were like that. Maybe with you she's still putting on her cheerful-Holly act. With me, it's not like that. She still talks of suicide. She dwells on it. Dr Thorne says that that's a key risk factor.'

'Has she talked about it to him?'

'I don't know,' he said. 'She's talked about it to me and I've talked to Dr Thorne. Does it matter?'

'It just seems so very different from the way she's been with me.'

He looked at me sharply, with narrowed eyes. I was worried that I'd offended him. 'You know Holly, the great pretender. But even with you she talked about you putting a pillow over her face.'

'That was just a joke.'

'Who the hell are you to say whether it's a joke or not?' he said.

'I'm sorry,' I said, startled by Charlie's sudden anger. 'Let's not argue. We're both on the same side.'

'I know. I'm letting it get to me. It's all been exhausting.'

'It must have been,' I said.

'You know what, Meg? I used to worry what people would do to Holly. Now it's what she'll do to herself. Sometimes I feel I've lost her. I think what she wants is to die. If that's true, I don't know what any of us can do to stop it.'

33

The day before Holly came home, I arrived at her house with flowers, only to find it full of extravagant vases of lilies and winter roses that made my small bunch of anemones seem futile. The place was bustling with people. Charlie's mother had just arrived, and was sitting on the sofa, plump and relaxed, smoking a menthol cigarette, while Holly's mother banged pans in the kitchen. Charlie was hanging decorations on an asymmetrical Christmas tree, and Naomi was in the last stages of painting Holly and Charlie's bedroom a soft green. 'We thought we'd give her a surprise,' she said, grinning down at me from the step-ladder, a smudge of paint on her cheek.

I felt a stab of childish jealousy. 'You should have told me. I would have helped.'

'I know how busy you are and, anyway, I like decorating,' said Naomi. She laid her brush carefully on the lid of the paint can. 'Do you fancy a cup of tea? There's some ginger cake I made as well.'

'No, thanks,' I said shortly. 'I can't stop.'

I didn't go round the next day. I thought she'd need to get settled in first. But in the evening, as I was on my way home, my mobile rang and it was her. She told me that everyone was being very attentive and then she snorted derisively and my spirits rose. 'It's a real pain,' she said. 'The two mothers aren't on speaking terms. Charlie's trying so hard to please everybody he's like a dog running between owners. Can you come round? Please!'

'Now, you mean?'

'They wouldn't let you in. I've got to get my rest, apparently. It's enough to send me mad, except of course I'm mad already. Come tomorrow.'

'I don't know if it's –'

'*Please.*'

'All right, then. What time?'

'Come for lunch.'

'I'll bring something.'

'Don't you dare. The kitchen's groaning with food. Everyone's making fucking soup. I know, bring that Todd of yours. It's Saturday, after all.'

'Are you sure?'

'Don't you go treating me like an invalid too. I want to meet him, see if he's good enough.'

'Don't –'

'Don't what? Be rude to him? Me? Don't worry. The pills won't let me.'

I hadn't been going to say that. I'd been going to say, 'Don't steal him.'

We arrived at midday. Charlie opened the door and hugged me, then shook Todd firmly by the hand.

He was wearing an apron and his shirtsleeves were rolled up. There were even more flowers, and get-well cards everywhere, and the Christmas-tree lights were turned on. The house smelt of fresh paint.

I'd expected Holly to be in bed, but she was sitting on the sofa, dressed in old jeans and a flecked, turtle-neck jumper whose sleeves came down over her hands. Her hair was in plaits, and her face bare of makeup. She looked about twelve, and very pale, fragile and sweet. She made me feel huge and clumsy, and I bent down to kiss her cheek carefully. But she put both arms round me and hugged me hard. 'I won't break, you know,' she said. 'I'm a tough old bird.'

She stood up and held out her hand to Todd. 'I think I was a bit rude when we met before,' she said, 'but I've been informed that was a symptom of mental illness. Can we start again?'

'I'd like that,' said Todd, taking her hand awkwardly. 'I'm glad you're better.'

'It all feels a bit like a dream now. Especially since no one in this house mentions it.' She lowered her voice to a melodramatic whisper. '*Dying*, I mean. Trying to die. Or being manic-depressive, as a matter of fact. They just say, "your illness", or "what happened to you", stuff like that. That's why I so badly needed Meg to come round. You know what Meg's like, so . . .'

She searched for a word. I sat glumly on the chair

opposite her and waited for her to say 'solid' or 'safe' or 'comforting'.

'So *true*,' said Holly, at last. 'We've got about twenty precious minutes before Charlie's mother comes back from the supermarket and my mother comes back from whatever mischief she's been up to. God, I wish Christmas was over. It would have been safer to let me stay in hospital until the New Year. Meg, why are you looking at me like that?'

'I'm trying to find new ways of asking how you are,' I said.

'Don't worry,' said Holly. 'I'm not going to try and kill myself again. Anyway, I don't want to talk about myself. I'm fed up with the subject. Tell me about the office. Give me some gossip. Anything.'

I had wanted to tell her about Rees, and about the end of her gambling debts, but now wasn't the time, not with Charlie in the kitchen and Todd looking awkward and willing opposite me, and Holly gabbling like a nervous child. I suddenly felt tired out.

We talked about trivial, lighthearted things. Then she asked me if I'd help her find a Christmas present for Charlie. 'Though I can't think what to give him,' she said. 'Charlie's the kind of man who doesn't want anything.' Suddenly she seemed depressed. She turned to Todd. 'What would you give him?'

'Well . . . I've no idea. What about something to do with his work?'

'I don't think he works any longer. I don't think

he's worked since I went officially mad. And not much before that. He keeps telling me it's not important at the moment, that there are other things to sort out first.'

'He's right,' I said.

'I don't want him to sort me out. That's my job now. I want him to work. He's good at what he does. Really good. You've seen it. When I first met him, I was convinced he could be great. But then I was convinced that I could be great as well. We can't just lock ourselves into our house and not work and drink fucking soup and eat Naomi's ginger cake and forget about the outside world, can we?'

'Maybe not,' I agreed, thinking that perhaps now was the time to tell her about the money.

'How about a dressing-gown?' said Todd.

Holly brightened. 'That's a good idea. That's what I'll get for him. You're brilliant, Todd.'

'He's *nice*,' she whispered, when Todd went to the lavatory.

'Good,' I said. 'I mean, I'm glad you think so, but there are things I need to talk to you about.'

'Let's have a walk later. I've got to get out of here for a bit.'

At lunch Holly fell silent and Charlie kept jumping up and doing unnecessary things at the sink, clattering dishes noisily. The rest of us talked about the possibility of snow and about winter weather, stretching out the topic for far too long. I said something about there being places in the Arctic where you could throw boiling water into the air and it would freeze before it hit the ground, and Todd launched gallantly into a story about skiing in Norway when it was minus twenty-five and his eyelashes froze and icicles formed in his nostrils. I looked across at Holly, fearful that she might say something sarcastic. She looked at me, and there was just the tiniest hint of a raised eyebrow but she remained silent.

The doorbell rang and I saw Holly flinch. I realized that all the time she was sick with apprehension about who might turn up, and I longed to reach over and comfort her. She remained tense until Charlie returned with Naomi, who plonked herself down next to Anthea Carter, his mother, and greeted everyone like family. We all had coffee. Anthea kept dunking chocolate digestive biscuits into hers and losing soggy chunks, fishing them out with her teaspoon and slurping them loudly. She'd had two tankards of wheat beer with her lunch and was decidedly mellow.

Naomi poured milk into her coffee, then a small dribble into Charlie's. Just the amount he liked. Such a trivial thing, but the domestic intimacy jolted me. I stared across at them and saw Charlie slide a glance towards Naomi who looked briefly back at him, before turning away again, demure and bright-eyed.

They're having an affair, I thought. Holly was right after all. She just suspected the wrong woman. Poor

Holly. Poor Holly, poor Charlie, poor all of us. Suddenly it felt almost indecent that we were all sitting round the table like this, chatting, smiling, cheating, lying.

Holly stood up, pushing back her chair with a squeal across the floor. 'I'm going for a walk with Meg and Todd,' she announced.

'Are you sure that's –'

'Quite sure.'

'Do you want me to come?' asked Charlie.

'You stay here. Have a bit of time to yourself, for a change.'

'Wrap up well, then.'

He put her coat on for her, buttoning her into it and tying a bright scarf round her neck. She tilted her face towards him but he avoided her lips and kissed her cheek, as if she was a sick child.

Tactfully Todd dropped us off at the park. It was bitterly cold, with a stinging wind, but Holly didn't seem to mind. And at last I told her that I'd visited Cowden Brothers and that she didn't have to worry any more.

'They just cancelled the debt?' asked Holly, doubtfully.

'In a manner of speaking,' I said.

'Why?'

'I explained that you'd not been yourself on the evening and –'

'Meg, this is me, Holly. Remember? I'm not a

complete idiot and, anyway, I know when you're not telling the truth. You have this funny little furrow between your eyebrows.'

'You don't have to worry,' I said. 'You're safe now. You can concentrate on getting better.'

'You paid it.'

'It's not important.'

'You paid the debt, didn't you? Didn't you?'

'Kind of,' I mumbled.

'How much?'

'Just what you owed.'

'Fucking how much, Meg? Tell me.' She clutched my arm so that I had to stop walking.

'Twelve thousand,' I lied.

She closed her eyes. I could see she was doing some mental arithmetic. 'No,' she said. 'Tell me the real figure.'

'Sixteen.'

'Oh, my God, Meg.'

'The meter was running,' I said. 'It would have been even more by now if –'

'You paid all that?'

'I only did what you would have done in my place.'

'I don't know what to say.'

'I don't want you to thank me.'

'I'm not going to thank you. I'm going to shout at you, you imbecile! What did you think you were up to?' She raised her fist as if she would punch me in the face, but burst into tears instead.

I hesitated, then put my arms round her while

people flowed past us. 'You would have done it for me,' I repeated.

'Where did you get the money?' she sobbed.

'Here and there.'

'You used up all your savings, didn't you? Your house money.'

'This was what it was for, really. This was the rainy day you're meant to save for.'

Holly gave a hiccupy laugh. 'It was my rainy day. Meg, I – I –'

'It doesn't matter,' I said.

We reached the entrance of Golders Hill Park, and headed past the emus towards the goats. 'Nobody can really be unhappy looking at a goat,' I said. And then, without altering my tone, 'How's your brain?'

'That's a blunt question,' said Holly, pushing her gloved hands into her coat pocket.

A tiny kid gave a ridiculously high-pitched bleat.

'I was shocked when I heard about the ECT,' I said, 'but you seem all right.'

'I'm not the person to ask,' said Holly. 'I slept through the whole course. They'd wheel me off and I'd wake up feeling woozy.'

'They said it was an emergency. You were acutely depressed.'

'Yeah, I heard that too,' said Holly.

'You sound like you're talking about somebody else,' I said. 'Don't you know?'

'They said it might affect my memory a bit, but it

hasn't, as far as I know.' She gave a rueful smile. 'Maybe I've forgotten.'

'The funny thing is,' I said, 'that when I talked to you, just before the ECT, you seemed better already. You told me that at the moment you did that . . .' I steeled myself to say the words. 'When you tried to kill yourself, you said that was when you realized you didn't want to die.'

'That's right.'

'I guess I was hoping you were through all that.'

Holly gave a shrug. 'I'm not the most reliable witness. I'm just the person who had the electrodes stuck to my head.'

'I was just surprised.'

'Dr Thorne told Charlie that the major indicators for suicide are, first, having tried it already. Which seems pretty bloody obvious. And then being preoccupied with death. It's not so much about being depressed. You can be incredibly, hopelessly depressed and not suicidal in the least. On the other hand, you can be not depressed at all and suicidal. You can become obsessed with it, as if it was a kind of hobby. It sounds like I was a mixture of both over the last few months and apparently it was something I started talking about again.'

'And now?'

'And now it couldn't be further from my mind.' Holly pulled her coat more closely about her. 'These goats are great,' she said. 'I completely agree with you about their therapeutic qualities. But don't you find that sometimes somewhere indoors and warm with a mug of coffee is even more effective?'

We sat and drank coffee and Holly ate a muffin and we talked over the details of her return to work. When I arrived at her house I had wanted to be able to say of Holly that 'she lived happily ever after'. I saw now that what that would have to mean was that she lived dutifully ever after. The play, the wild adventure, the dream, the romance, the fantasy, they were all over. Now Holly would have to see what life was like when you were sober. She had to lead a career, make her marriage work. It was all about arrangements, appointments, being on time.

Holly seemed reluctant to talk about this in too much detail, as if I were a parent nagging her to do her homework and her music practice. She said that Dr Thorne had told her there was no question of her being able to work for at least a couple of months. He had instructed her that her job now was to recover. Holly said that she was going to get well, she was going to sort out the details of her private life, reorganize her house. Above all, she was going to make things right with Charlie. 'And you, of course,' she said.

That made me laugh. 'You don't need to make anything right with me,' I said.

'I do. You know that note I wrote to you? As far as I can remember in my delirium and with my electrically frazzled brain, it was you I felt I needed to explain things to. Maybe I still do. I'm never going to be completely sensible, you know.'

'We can't go back to that,' I said. 'You can't live again like you did the last few months. You won't survive it. We won't. *I* won't.'

'We'll see,' she said. 'My main task is to get well. No, that's not right. My *main* task is to get Charlie's mother out of the house. Getting well can wait.'

I laughed.

'Is she that bad?'

'Don't you hate the smell of mentholated cigarettes?' she said. 'It's putting things together that shouldn't be put together. It's as if somebody has put out a bonfire by pouring peppermint tea on it.'

'But seriously,' I said, 'I think you mustn't return to work until . . .'

'Let's share some fruit cake.'

'She wasn't what I expected at all. I can see now why you love her,' said Todd.

'I knew you'd like her once you'd met her properly.'

'She's very appealing somehow.'

'Yes, I know. Everyone thinks so. She makes people feel special.'

There was a short silence, then Todd came over to me and put his arms round me. 'What's wrong?'

'Nothing.'

'There is. I can tell.'

'It's nothing, really.' But I couldn't let it go. 'So do you think she's very beautiful?'

'I don't know about beautiful. Lovely, certainly.'

'Most people think she's beautiful.'

'Meg.'

'What?'

'You don't need to worry, you know.'

'I'm not worrying. I don't know what you're talking about.'

'It's you I'm in love with, you're the one I find beautiful.'

'I'm not beautiful.'

'You are to me.'

'"To me". That sounds like pity.'

'More like lust.'

'Really?'

'The real thing. What was it Holly called you? True.'

We put our arms round each other and I pressed my forehead to his. There was a new kind of solemnity to our relationship now, as if both of us knew we were entering something big and grand; that there was no quick turning back any more. After a while, I said, 'Charlie's having an affair.'

'Charlie? Who with?'

'Naomi.'

'How do you know?'

'I just know. They looked at each other.'

'He's had a rough time, you know,' said Todd, after a pause. 'It'll probably fizzle out.'

'Yes. I hope so. So you don't think I should do anything about it?'

'What could you do? Tell her? God, no. Just hope she never finds out.'

34

I didn't see Holly again until the second of January, though I spoke to her on the phone. I was too busy being happy, and although I didn't quite forget about her, I pushed her to the back of my mind. Falling in love makes you selfish and blind.

Todd and I spent two nights over New Year in a remote cottage in Dorset. When we got back, I called on Holly. Charlie was away for the day. Holly had said on the phone that she was trying to sort out all the chaos that had built up over the past few months. It was the least she could do and she wanted to have a sense of purpose over the weeks of convalescence.

'I want to show you something,' she said, as soon as she opened the door.

She was wearing purple tracksuit trousers and a sweatshirt many sizes too large for her with the sleeves rolled up above her elbow. I followed her into the living room. There were packing cases scattered on the floor, half filled with folders, old newspapers and exercise books.

'Are you moving?'

'Just clearing up,' she said, looking around her. 'These are just old things from years ago. There are old essays and projects, which I've kept because they took so long to do but now I think I'll make a celebration bonfire of them. And then there are the books I read as a girl and maybe I'll keep them for, you know, just in case . . .'

'That sounds good,' I said. 'Very good. What is it you wanted me to see?'

'I found these. I don't want to be disloyal and God knows what Charlie's had to put up with, but I had to tell someone.'

She led me to Charlie's work room and gestured to a pile of letters on the desk. 'I found them in the bottom drawer,' she said. 'Don't tell me I shouldn't have been poking around in Charlie's stuff. I know I shouldn't. But I needed to get all the phone bills together so I could do the accounts. I might as well make myself useful in some way. And they were scattered everywhere. Anyway, read them.'

I looked at them one by one, feeling slightly shabby as I did so. All the letters were about work not delivered on time, or not delivered at all.

'He's just stopped,' said Holly. 'I don't think he's produced a single piece of work in months and months. Yet he comes down here and says he's working. He sits at his desk for hours.'

'Poor Charlie,' I said hopelessly.

'Exactly. But why does he pretend to me that he's working? Why doesn't he just talk to me about it? I'll tell you what, Meg, we're up to our necks in financial shit. I've got an overdraft of seven thousand pounds and my bank won't let me withdraw any more cash.

I sold my grandmother's pearl necklace. Not that I ever wore it anyway. Fuck knows what's going on with Charlie's bank. He won't talk about it. He says it's his problem, not mine.'

'He doesn't want to worry you.'

'What does he think's going to happen? Some kind of miracle?'

'It's been a difficult time, for him as well as you. He just wants you to get better.' My voice sounded fraudulent, and I could feel a flush creeping up my neck.

'You're probably right,' said Holly. She rubbed her face. 'It's such hard work sorting everything out. It's all takes so much time and slog. I wish I had a magic pill.' She gave a nervous giggle. 'Well, of course, I *do* have some of those, don't I?'

'You're taking them regularly?'

'Regularly. Religiously. Don't worry. Even those mornings when every atom in me is telling me not to put them into my body I take them. I don't give myself a choice.'

She pushed the letters back into the drawer, then picked up a phone bill from the floor and winced. 'Christ, do we spend that much time on the phone? Look at how many times I phoned you last quarter.'

I glanced at the bill carelessly, seeing my number spreading down the page. Then my eyes were caught by a date. I took the paper from her hand and looked closer. At 15:07 on the day Holly had tried to kill herself there had been a brief call from Holly's number. 'I thought that was when you were, you know, unconscious,' I said, pointing to the digits.

Holly squinted at it and asked for my mobile phone. I handed it across and she dialled the number into it. 'Hello?' she said. 'Sorry, who's that? Oh, God, I'm sorry, I meant to ring, erm . . . you know, Charlie. Sorry. See you soon. 'Bye.' She handed the phone back to me with a puzzled expression. 'Naomi. I must have tried to call her for help as well, mustn't I? I can't remember doing that. But, then, my memories of that are a bit addled.'

I couldn't help myself. I felt a jab of disappointment. Holly had told me that she'd tried to call me; that it had been me she was thinking of as she lay dying. But she'd thought of Naomi as well. She'd actually called her. The evidence was in front of me, and my number wasn't there at all. Maybe she was even making it all up about trying to phone me. Her way of making me feel loved.

'I thought you said the phone was dead,' I said, more sharply than I intended.

'I thought it was. I'm sure it was. But I wasn't in a fit state, Meg. Who knows what numbers I pushed?'

'It was working at 15:07, anyway.'

'Apparently.'

'But then it suddenly wasn't working.'

'Meg, I was dying. Who knows? I may have pressed redial. I don't know.'

'You must feel very close to her.' In my peevishness, I could almost have blurted out the truth.

'Well, I am close to her. She's my next-door neigh-bour. To be honest, I'm not sure if I even like her – she's so . . . so . . . What's the word? *Perky.* You know, always cheerful and helpful. It drives me a bit mad. But maybe that's it. Maybe I thought she could rescue me because she was so close.'

'You know her number by heart?'

'No, of course not.'

'So you went and looked it up while you were falling into a coma?'

'Meg,' Holly said, a bit sharply, 'I'm not going to discuss the technicalities of a phone bill. We shouldn't even be looking at it. I just want to put it away and forget about it.'

'You're right. I'll tell you what,' I said, changing the subject with a clumsiness that made her grin, 'you were going to give me the number for that travel company you told me about. The one that does holidays in remote places.'

'I'd give you the brochure to take with you, ex-cept Charlie wants us to go away together some-where soon. We need to start repairing our marriage, properly talking about everything that's happened. We're just going through the days, one by one, being careful and kind with each other. When I'm not rummaging through his study with a friend, that is.'

Again, it was as if a cloud had passed over her, and she looked tired and low. With a visible effort, she fetched the brochure from the pile of magazines and catalogues stacked up against the wall and tossed it across to me.

'It does look lovely,' I said, flicking through the pages.

I picked up a scrap of paper lying under Charlie's desk, jotted down the phone number and email address, then put it into my wallet.

'When will you go?' I asked.

'Soon, I guess. God knows how we can afford it. But I guess we can't afford not to either. That's what Charlie says.'

I put my hands on her shoulders. 'Everything's going to be fine,' I said, too brightly.

We had been going to sort out bills and gather up receipts to set against tax, but we ended up sifting through Holly's wardrobe. She said she wanted to throw out all the clothes she wasn't going to wear again.

'Like this,' she said regretfully, holding up a small black dress, with the emphasis on 'small'.

'That's what you wore to that party in the Royal Festival Hall! You looked . . .' I hesitated. 'Well, extraordinary.'

'Preposterous, you mean. I know I behaved preposterously. I can hardly bear to think about it. Those days are over. It was fun, though, wasn't it? Maybe I'll keep it to remind me. What about this shirt?'

'It's very dramatic.'

'Bin it or keep it?'

'You decide.'

'If I don't know I'd better keep it. Just in case.'

She ended up by throwing away one skirt with a broken zip and several pairs of laddered tights. That was all. Everything else – all the bright and outlandish garments that were supposed to be tossed out in a gesture of new moderation – were put back into her cupboards. I was oddly relieved.

She wanted me to stay longer, but after a couple of hours I said I had to get back. There were things I had to do.

Holly saw me out, we hugged each other, and she shut the door. I waited for a few moments, then walked the few yards along the road to the neighbouring house, where Naomi had the top floor. She had told me about her living arrangements: a small bedroom, a toilet and a leaking shower, a tiny kitchen, a sitting room that doubled as her study, her own phone line.

I rang the bell and waited, then rang again. At last I heard footsteps and the door opened. An elderly man in a baggy cardigan and slippers peered at me.

'Is Naomi in?' I asked.

'No,' he said. 'They left.'

'Oh,' I said. Something occurred to me. 'Her boyfriend collected her?'

'No, no, nothing like that. She doesn't have a boyfriend.'

I made myself give a relaxed laugh. 'You keep a close eye on her, do you?'

'She makes biscuits for me,' he said. 'Sometimes

we watch TV together in the evening. My wife died two years ago, you see. Shall I give her a message?'

'Who did she go off with?'

'Curious, aren't you?' He chuckled.

'I just wanted –'

'It was only a neighbour.'

'Charlie?'

'That's right. So there's nothing funny going on.'

He invited me in for tea. I think he was lonely, poor man, but my head was buzzing so I could hardly think. I left him as soon as I could.

'It's not very pretty, Meg, but it's what people do,' said Todd. 'The important thing is that Holly's recovery doesn't get knocked off course.'

I frowned. 'You're not getting it,' I said. 'It's not the affair, though God knows I wish that wasn't going on. She tried to phone me that day and couldn't get through. The phone was working for a call she couldn't remember making, then not working for a call she does remember making.'

'Why on earth are you so bothered about something trivial like that when –'

'I've got this terrible idea, Todd. I mean, really, really terrible.'

'Tell me.'

I opened my mouth, then found I couldn't say the words. They were wild, ludicrous, something Holly in her manic state might have dreamed up. 'Never mind, I'm just being paranoid,' I said.

However much he tried to persuade me to talk, I wouldn't. I was embarrassed by my own thoughts.

But I couldn't get it out of my head and I lay awake that night, Todd peaceful beside me, trying to work out what I should do. I kept thinking of Holly's pale, trusting face. Was this it? Was this what I had missed?

35

'I'm at the bar down the road.'

'Down the road from where?'

'From the office, stupid, what do you think? Can you meet me there?'

'I'm on my way now – nothing's wrong, is it?'

'Are you going to spend the rest of your life thinking that whenever I want to see you, something's wrong?'

'No, I just –'

'Nothing's wrong. I just need to see you. There's something I've got for you. Shall I order you a spicy tomato juice?'

'Lots of celery salt and Worcester sauce –'

'– and black pepper and a slice of lemon. Come on, then.'

Whatever Holly had said on the phone, I still thought something was wrong so I dashed out of the office, struggling into my thick coat as I went and shouting apologies to Trish, saying I'd be back as soon as I could and would finish going through the accounts then.

She was sitting in the corner, at our old table, still in her jacket with a scarf wrapped round her neck, idly swilling her water round in its glass. Her face looked drawn and thoughtful, but brightened as I approached.

'There,' she said. 'Tomato juice. And . . .' with a flourish she produced an envelope from her bag '. . . there.'

'What's this?'

'It's for you.'

I took a sip of tomato juice, then opened it. There was a cheque inside, written out to me. Sixteen thousand pounds.

'Holly! No!'

'You didn't think I wouldn't pay you back, did you?'

'I didn't want you to pay me back. It was a gift. Anyway, how on earth did you manage?'

'It was a simple matter – well, a fairly simple matter – of adding it to the mortgage. In all fairness, though, I should warn you that you shouldn't try to pay in that cheque until next week.'

'I don't want this. It's not the right time. It's completely the wrong time. I know what straits you're in and I'd feel awful if I took this.'

'Meg, listen. I don't want to argue about this. It's your money. I'd hate myself if I took it. I know you gave it freely, and I bless you for it and I'll never, ever forget what you did for me. Never.' Tears welled in her eyes and she blinked them away impatiently. 'This is part of my recovery. This is the new me. I'm taking responsibility for what I've done. I need to do this, Meg. I have to. Put it into your bag. Otherwise, who knows what I may do?'

I did as she said, then put my hand over hers and we sat for a moment in silence. A thought struck me. 'So Charlie knows?'

'Oh, yes,' she said grimly. 'He most certainly does.'

'You would have had to tell him in the end.'

'I guess,' she said.

'Was it awful?'

'Not entirely good.'

'That bad?'

'Who can blame him? Just when he thought things couldn't get any worse.'

'What did he say?'

'Not much.' She drank some water. 'He went very, very blank. He retreated into his study. You know, the place where he pretends to work.'

'Oh,' I said blankly.

'He can't take any more. I was remembering something while I was waiting for you to arrive. When I cracked up in the street, attacked those people and was dragged off to hospital, I'd just run away from the house. He didn't know where I was. For all he knew I could have gone off and thrown myself under a bus. The police rang him and told him and he came to the hospital. I was raving like a lunatic . . .' She gave a sour laugh at that. 'What do I mean *like* a lunatic? But when I saw the expression on his face, the anger and despair, there was a sane bit of me that felt so guilty. I knew I'd never be able to make good what I'd done to him. He could shout at me and storm out a thousand times, and it would never be one iota of what I've done to him, day after day and week after week. He should never have met me.'

'Don't say things like that.'

'I wreck everything.'

'Come and stay with us,' I said, suddenly urgent without knowing why. 'Just till things get better. Don't go home, Holly.'

She looked at me and grinned ruefully. 'You keep telling me everything's all right,' she said. 'Are you now saying it isn't?'

'Just for a bit,' I said.

'Finish your tomato juice, my friend,' she said gently, 'and get back to your desk.'

36

I told myself that Charlie was a nice enough man, not a hero but not a villain either, who was having an affair with Naomi. After what he had been through, who could blame him? It was painful to think about Holly struggling to save her marriage while all the time Charlie was having this fling, if that was all it was. I wasn't going to tell her. Whenever I thought of her, it was as someone fragile, with a delicate mechanism that could go wrong at any time, and I knew I mustn't jeopardize her recovery.

I didn't see Holly for several days, but as I sat at my desk, I kept trying to imagine what she would say. It was as if I had her voice inside my head as well as my own. I spoke to her on the phone, just to check she was all right. She sounded fine, quite steady and determined. A date for Stuart's trial had been set for May and she said she felt ambivalent about the whole thing. 'I keep thinking it was my fault.'

'He broke into the house and attacked you.'

'Still,' she said.

'You'll be no good in the witness box.'

'I'll just say what happened. Warts and all.'

She told me she was running and swimming every day. Three times a week she had therapy with a

woman in Muswell Hill. 'It's a pretty narcissistic exist-
ence,' she said. 'I'm just concentrating on looking
after my body and healing my mind. Boring, boring,
boring. I can't begin to tell you how much I long for
work – something outside myself. I'm sure it would
do me good to come back now.'

'You'll be here soon enough,' I said. 'Just a few
weeks now.'

I asked her how Charlie was doing, and she said
he was being 'sweet' again. 'No sex life, though.
Sometimes I think maybe I'll never have sex again.'

'Is it the pills?' I asked, feeling like a traitor.

'It's not me, it's him. He thinks of me as an invalid.'

'It's early days,' I said.

'Maybe I can try and seduce him on holiday,' she
said. 'Pounce and not take no for an answer.'

'When are you going? *Where* are you going, for that
matter?'

'I don't know the answer to either of those questions. Charlie's arranging it all. He's trying to get
some cheap deal.'

'I'll come and see you after this weekend-away
thing with those chartered surveyors, unless you've
gone by then.'

'I wish I could be there too.'

She sounded so wistful. I saw how easy it would
be to say, 'Then come to work now.' Or even, 'Don't
take the drugs, then: go back to your old wild happiness and your days of infinite sadness.' I forced myself
to sound blandly cheerful. 'I bloody wish you could

too. It won't be the same without you. It won't be fun.'

When I put the phone down, I felt a nagging anxiety, like an unreachable itch in my brain, and it didn't go away through all the meetings and tasks. I got a sandwich from the deli for lunch and sat in the empty office, staring at my computer screen but seeing Holly's face.

The phone rang, making me jump: it was our solicitor, asking further questions about Deborah's terms of employment. I pulled open drawers to find the details and, while I was doing so, saw the square brown envelope Rees had dropped on to my desk that day, full of photographs of Holly. I'd stuffed it out of sight, like a dirty secret, but now, after putting the phone down, I took out the sheaf of glossy images. I was amazed and dismayed by how many there were.

They had all been taken secretly. Holly had thought she was alone, free from the gaze of strangers, and all the time she was being spied on and captured on film. I could hardly bring myself to look at them, and yet although it felt almost indecent to do so, I couldn't prevent myself picking each one up and gazing at it, trying to see in Holly's face what she was going through at the time. The pictures were a chronology of her illness, tracing her journey of euphoria, depression and finally florid madness. Views of her that nobody was ever meant to see.

The first one I picked up was a bit blurred, just

Holly, quite close up and in half-profile. She was wearing her suede jacket and a funny little beret with her hair tucked inside it, and on her face was an expression I'd rarely seen: a kind of dreamy, vague pensiveness. Another showed her outside the office, but this time she was further off and I was beside her. I was anxious, hands pushed deep into my coat pockets, head down, frowning. I looked as if I was in a different world from Holly, who had been caught mid-stride and in exuberant conversation. Her open coat flew behind her; her hands were up in a wide, familiar gesture; her hair was snaking down her face; her mouth, painted bright red, was open and grinning. She looked so alive I almost expected to see her move. She also looked hysterical.

There she was again, on the arm of a man I recognized as Stuart and wearing some ridiculous shoes. She wasn't looking at Stuart, who was gazing rapturously down at her, but straight ahead, and her mouth was pursed.

I flicked through them. One of Holly from the back. She was carrying several cans of paint and climbing into a taxi, and a man with a cadaver's face was leaning forward to help her in; there was another figure in the cab, but the photo had been taken at night and it was impossible to make out who it was. One from the distance of Holly walking in the park with Charlie, in a grainy light that might have meant rain. Again, I noted how while his arms were folded, hers were raised in the air. Even in photos you could see how rarely she was still. One of Holly in shapeless tracksuit trousers and greasy hair, looking like an old woman, her shoulders drooping.

And then, suddenly, a picture I almost dropped with the shock of it. For there was Holly looming into view and at first I didn't recognize her: it was like a cartoon version of her, everything recognizable but exaggerated. She was wearing a nightdress and mismatched high-heeled shoes, a scarf trailing from one shoulder on to the pavement. Her hair was a tangle and her mouth was wide open in – what? A scream of terror, an animal howl of pain, a shriek of mindless sexual pleasure? I could scarcely keep my eyes on the intense, terrible intimacy of that picture. I saw now that I had never let myself fully imagine what Holly had experienced over months and years: the torment she had been in.

My eyes glanced over the faces of the people near her. They were almost all staring at her, so that even though she was on the left of the picture, you got the impression she was in the centre. A young man was laughing and pointing at her. I flushed to the roots of my hair, and then I felt angry. Nobody would ever look at this image again, or see my dear friend so mad with pain and grief that she had almost ceased to be human. I held the two edges of the photo between finger and thumb and tore it in half, then dropped it into the bin beneath my desk.

And then, without knowing why, I froze. I had seen something and hadn't seen it. I had a memory of something but I didn't know what it was. I stooped down, and retrieved the two halves. I looked at Holly, at the figures around her – in front of her and behind her. I saw what I had seen without seeing, and known without knowing. I saw him. Just on the edge of the frame, several paces behind Holly, wearing his leather jacket and looking towards the distraught woman with a calm, scrutinizing face quite different from any of the curious, gleeful, pitying faces around him.

Charlie.

I closed my eyes and heard Holly's voice speaking to me: 'When I cracked up in the street, attacked those people and was dragged off to hospital, I'd just run away from the house. He didn't know where I was. For all he knew I could have gone off and thrown myself under a bus. The police rang him and told him and he came to the hospital. I was raving like a lunatic . . .' That's what she'd said. That's what Charlie had told her. But he'd been following her all the time, watching her break down on the bridge. Watching? And waiting? Waiting for her to kill her-self? I stared at the photograph again, and saw how collected he was.

I pulled the phone towards me and called her mobile, but got voicemail. 'Holly,' I said. 'Holly, it's me, Meg, and when you get this, call me. At once, do you hear? Just call me. It's urgent.'

Then I dialled her home number, and listened to the phone ringing and ringing in an empty house.

37

I forced myself to be calm so that I could go over and over it in my mind, although I could almost feel my brain working: sparking, fizzing, crackling with energetic horror. I made a mental checklist of the sort I would do while preparing for a job, just to make sure that everything fitted together, that nothing had been forgotten. So: the way that Charlie had talked about her suicidal mood, about losing her, it had sounded as if he was preparing for something. He had spiralling money troubles caused by Holly. There was Naomi. And now there was the photograph. Any of them on their own might not have been decisive. But put them together. Was it a real pattern or was I, like a child, seeing pictures in the clouds?

And then it struck me like a blow to my skull that Charlie had been in the house while Holly was trying to kill herself. It was he, rather than Holly, who'd called Naomi's number, as his wife lay dying. He had been there and he had done nothing. He must have known suddenly that life for him would be better with Holly dead. Without her he would be free again: not the crushed, shamed husband of his present, but the carefree, handsome man he had been before they met.

But this was Charlie, I reminded myself. I pictured his face in my mind. Charlie, the man I'd almost been in love with once. The man I'd liked, admired, pitied and called my friend, my kindred spirit. I saw his creased, smiling face, the crow's feet round his eyes, his comfortable rumpled clothes. I remembered his expression as he concentrated on some bit of DIY, the way he half frowned but looked so contented. I pictured the way he always smiled when he saw me, laying a warm hand on my shoulder. I remembered him as he'd been at first with Holly, almost dazed with love, basking in the warmth of her passion. No, it couldn't be true. It was ludicrous, repellent, hysterical, insane.

But even as I thought this, I gazed down at the photograph, at his cool, watching face. This was a man I didn't know, a man in the grip of a new, unfamiliar emotion. And I looked, too, at the raw, grotesque image of Holly, out of her skull with self-destructive energy. Fear ran through me in little spasms. I jabbed in Holly's number again, knowing she wouldn't answer.

'Come on,' I said into the phone. 'Pick up.'

Where were they? I tried frantically to recall my last conversation with Holly. Had she said anything that might give a clue? She had talked about their last-minute holiday but nothing had been arranged and it was Charlie who was planning it, not her. Who might know? I rang a couple of friends, but Holly hadn't been in touch with them recently. I rang

Holly's mother, but there was no answer. I felt almost feverish with anxiety, but forced myself to calm down. Finding them shouldn't be so difficult: there had to be an easy answer. Suddenly I remembered the phone number Holly had given me for the brochure. That was it, surely. I fumbled in my purse and found the torn-off piece of paper, folded in half. I noticed that Holly's writing was scribbled across it, even more slapdash than usual, and glanced at it before opening it up for the number: 'My dear and loyal Meg,' I read. That was all. I didn't have time to think about it, only to feel emotion punch me once more in the chest. I was her dear and loyal friend and I had to help her. I jabbed in the number with trembling fingers.

A woman answered. I said that friends of mine had booked a holiday with them and I needed to contact them because of a private emergency. I thought that was a good phrase: it sounded scary but would also discourage too many questions. She was reluctant. She said that it was a matter of policy and that she wasn't allowed to give out customers' details. I very nearly lost my temper, except that when I nearly lose my temper I don't shout. I do the opposite and become very cold and quiet and almost legalistic.

'You're a travel firm not a doctor's surgery,' I said. 'There's been an emergency. I need to contact them to give them some information that is very important to them. If this is a problem for you, could you please pass me on to your supervisor?'

She asked me to wait. I could hear a murmur as she talked to someone.

'I'll see if I can trace the booking,' she said to me finally.

I waited for several minutes.

'I'm sorry,' the woman said. 'I can't find anything.'

'That's not possible,' I said. 'Have you checked under both their names?'

She had and it was hopeless. I almost burst into tears of frustration and rage. A thought came into my mind: Naomi. If anyone knew, she would. I couldn't do this on the phone. It was too important. I had to see her in person and I had to think tactically. Trish was back from lunch. I told her I would be out for a bit and I wasn't sure when I'd be back. I'd ring her. I caught a taxi to the house, thinking all the way of how I was going to handle this. The driver was talking about something, illegal immigrants, I think, but to me he was like an annoying noise in the street. I tuned him out. When I arrived, I rang Charlie and Holly's doorbell in case. Nothing. So I tried next door. As I rang Naomi's bell, it occurred to me for the first time that she might not be there and all this would be a disastrous waste of time when there was no time to lose, and then she opened the door and I felt I was stepping on to a stage under the glare of the lights, with the audience watching and expectant.

'Meg?' she said, surprised.

I walked into the hall, without her inviting me.

'I, er,' I said, forgetting my lines, 'I came to see

Holly about something. Something important. Can I come up?'

'I . . .' she began, but I was already mounting the narrow stairs towards her bedsit.

'Just for a minute or so.'

'I think they've gone away for a few days,' she said, opening the door on to a spotless but depressing room: a beige sofa, a small table pushed against the wall with two chairs beside it, a rubber plant in the corner, swallowing up the light.

'There's something I've got to tell Holly,' I said. 'To do with work. They didn't leave a phone number, did they?'

There was too long a pause and Naomi forced a smile. 'No,' she said. 'Not with me, anyway. Why would they?'

'Charlie has a mobile, doesn't he?'

'Yes,' she said. Then, too hastily, 'But I don't have his number.'

'It's important,' I said.

'I don't have his number,' she repeated.

'Naomi,' I began, but saw the stubborn set of her jaw, her watchful eyes, and stopped dead. It was no use trying to persuade her.

I couldn't think. I didn't know what to do. Then I saw a ring-backed diary on the low table by her sofa. Was it possible? And what could I do about it? I mustn't leave. Not yet.

'So,' I said, 'how do you think things are? With Holly, I mean.'

'Not good,' she said, shaking her head. 'Charlie thinks . . .'

'I know – he thinks she'll try again. Do you?'

'I'm sometimes very scared that . . .'

'Can I have some coffee?'

'Sorry?'

'Coffee, do you have any?'

'I'm in a bit of a hurry,' she said.

'Just instant.'

'I don't have instant.'

'Or a tea-bag.'

'All right,' she said.

We looked at each other, each hating the other, then Naomi left the room.

I waited a moment. 'Can I help?' I shouted.

'Come on through,' she called back, sounding horribly close through the thin walls.

I picked up the diary and flicked through it until I got to the current week. There was something. I'd hoped for an address. It was a phone number, a long area code, not London. Of course, it might be her mum or a builder or anything. Oh, please, God, I thought, please, please, I'll be good for ever and ever. It was too long to memorize. I found a pen on the mantelpiece and wrote it on the back of my hand. I heard footsteps, flicked the book shut and scribbled the last numbers.

'What are you doing?'

She had come into the room behind me. I spun round. 'Ideas,' I said ludicrously.

'What?'

'Ideas come to me and I have to write them down or I'll forget them and I never have a notebook when I need one so I just write them on anything that comes to hand. Such as a hand. I had a thought for a presentation.' I flashed my hand very quickly so she couldn't see there were only numbers. 'But you don't want to hear all this.'

'I was going to ask if you wanted milk,' said Naomi.

'I'm sorry,' I said. 'I've got to go. I've just remembered. A meeting. I'm late. It's already started. I feel terrible. Let's do it again. It's so rude. I'm sorry, I've got to –'

I virtually ran out of the house and along the pavement, searching for a taxi. But this was a residential area. There were no taxis. I looked at the back of my hand. A phone number. What good was that? Well, I could call it. I dialled the number on my mobile. It rang and rang and rang. I didn't know what to think. They could be out on a long, healing walk. Or the phone might be unplugged. I didn't know what to do. You can't look up a phone number in a phone book. I thought of Trish. She knew things like that. I phoned her.

'Trish,' I said, 'if I had a phone number and I wanted to know the postal address, is there anything I could do? Could I buy a CD-Rom or phone someone or is there something on the Internet or –'

'What's the number?'

I read it out to her.

'Hang on,' she said. I heard some tapping. 'Ash Tree House, Corresham, Suffolk. You want the postcode?'

'Yes.'

She gave it to me and I told her I wouldn't be in until tomorrow.

'But the weekend away?'

'I'll be back soon.'

'Is there something I should know?' she said.

'You'll know,' I said. 'One way or the other.'

I rang off and looked at my mobile as if it could tell me something. I could only think of one thing. One person. I punched in some numbers.

'Todd?' I thought of the whole long, messy story and my heart sank. I needed something quicker. 'There was that time a bit ago when I asked if you'd do me a favour and you said of course, without ever asking me what it was? . . . You do? Because I'm asking a favour again. Right now.'

38

'Todd,' I said, as we left London and headed east on an A12 snarled up with early-evening traffic. 'Thank you.'

He gave a sort of grunt but I didn't think he was being cross. Not really. He was being basically calm and steady. Even the patient and unflustered way he drove was designed to settle my nerves. I sat hunched tightly forward in the seat as if I could give us extra momentum.

We didn't talk much. I chewed my thumb furiously at every jam, groaned each time we were forced to a crawl, stared at the map as if I could find a miraculous secret path through the gridlocked cars, looked at my watch, tried to work out how much longer it would take us to get there. Once, we stopped for petrol. I could hardly bear how long it took to fill the tank, and then pay. It felt as though every minute, every second, might count; every queue might mean disaster.

It was nearly dark now, and drizzling. The road ahead was a long string of blurred headlights coming towards us and red tail-lights leading away. Where was Holly now, I wondered. What was she doing? For the hundredth time I pressed the repeat call button on the mobile; for the hundredth time I heard it ring and ring and no one replied. 'Do you think I'm mad?' I asked Todd, yet again.

'Mad?' he said. 'Two weeks ago I gave my entire liquid assets to you to hand to a criminal. Now I'm driving you for hours to scare the life out of your best friend who's on a longed-for holiday with her patient husband. I don't think I'm entitled to accuse anyone in the world of being mad.'

'Oh, Todd, that's lovely of you.'

'And, of course, there is the possibility that the phone number has no connection with Charlie and Holly at all and that we're about to burst in on some total strangers.'

'It can't be,' I said. 'It mustn't be.'

'Oh, good,' he said. 'Then you must be right.'

I leaned forward in silence, feeling fear gnaw at my stomach. I wanted to pray, though I've never believed in God. Let her be all right, let her be all right, please let her be. The windscreen wipers swept back and forth across the screen, clearing semicircles in the glass, instantly refilled with splatters of rain.

Gradually the traffic thinned and Todd put his foot down. It was a dark, moonless night. On the shallow horizon we saw the orange glow of towns. At last we turned off the main road, and down a smaller one, under dripping trees. Cars passed us, dipping their lights. Our own headlights illuminated large, ploughed fields and small woods; old churches in the middle of nowhere with squat towers and coned spires. I bent over the map, trying to trace the quickest route to Corresham, which clustered with other villages in a triangle formed by bisecting larger roads, quite near the coast.

It was straightforward enough at first. We turned left down another B road, marked in yellow on the map, drove through a couple of villages that were where they should be, took another turning.

'We're nearly there,' I said. 'Just a couple of miles. You have to go over a staggered crossroad any minute now.'

A few minutes later, I said, 'I'm sure we should have got there by now. Hang on, we shouldn't be in Foxgrove at all.'

'What do you want me to do?'

'Turn left ahead. No, that's signed to Lenham. I don't understand it. Oh, God. Go straight. Or maybe we should turn round and retrace our route.' I was almost howling by now.

'Here.' Todd pulled over and studied the map. 'Confusing,' he agreed. 'Let's drive to that pub up there and you can run in and ask.'

'Quick, then.'

I got out of the car while it was still moving and ran towards the pub. It had more or less stopped raining, and although it was cold, the air was saturated and oppressive, like an icy blanket lying across everything. I banged open the door and ran to the bar, pushing my way past a couple of men and leaning across to speak to the woman serving. 'Can you tell me how to get to Corresham?'

'Corresham? Let's see.' She considered, lifting up a lump of ice with some metal tongs and dropping it into a tumbler.

'It's urgent,' I said. 'An emergency.'

'She should go down Stone Street,' said one of the men. 'That's a short-cut.'

'Where's Stone Street?'

He gave some needlessly complicated instructions as I backed out of the door.

'Left, right, right, left,' I repeated, as I dashed to the car, splashing through a deep puddle that soaked into my shoes. 'Left, right, right, left. Go!' I said to Todd.

We set off again and soon enough we came to Corresham, a small, straggling collection of houses running along the lane.

'Thank God. Now, Mill House, The Nuttings, Pond Far ... Where the fuck is Ash Tree House? I can't see it.'

'What about that one?'

'It doesn't seem to have a name. Shall I run and see? There's a light on so someone's there.'

I sprinted up the path and hammered on the door with my fists. Maybe Holly would answer, I thought. Or Charlie. But when the door swung half open I had to adjust my line of sight, for it was a tiny girl with hair in plaits, wearing a yellow dressing-gown. 'Is your mother in?' I asked.

'My mother died,' she said gravely.

'Oh, I'm sorry. Well, your father, then?'

'Daddy,' she called, in a high, piping voice. 'Daddy, there's a lady to see you.'

'Ask her who she is, will you?'

'It's an emergency!' I yelled through the door, then pushed it fully open. 'Where's Ash Tree House?'

He came down the stairs. 'Ash Tree House? Why, that's the one in the valley, I think. I'm pretty sure, anyway. Liz!' he called back up the stairs. 'Which one is Ash Tree House? Is it the one with the stream at the bottom of the garden, on the way to the Rose and Crown?'

'Yes. Why?'

'There's a lady here who –'

'Can you just tell me,' I interrupted. 'It's urgent.'

'Up that way and then first on your right down a track,' he said.

Ash Tree House was more of a cottage, whitewashed, standing by itself in a small valley, with a copse behind it. There was no light on, no smoke coming out of its chimney. It looked cold and deserted.

I had to get out a final time to open a gate for the car, then didn't get back in again, simply ran the last few yards down the track to the house. I stood on the doorstep, under a small porch, and banged the knocker. Nothing. I knelt and pushed up the metal flap of the letterbox and tried to peer in but saw only the brush through which letters were pushed. I pressed my face to the window, and in the gloom, lit only by the lights of the car, could make out nothing more than massed shapes in the darkness.

'Holly,' I called. Then louder, shaking hopelessly at the door handle: 'Holly, are you there?'

Todd's feet crunched over the gravel towards me and I turned. 'Nobody's here,' I half sobbed.

Todd looked up at the dark house. Then he bent down, picked up a stone, and threw it through the window. The crash was surprisingly loud. We looked at each other: I was quite sure he had never done anything like this before, and I certainly hadn't. We were rational people, Todd and I, law-abiders and rule-respecters. Todd knocked out the remaining bits of glass, unfastened the sash window from the inside and heaved it up. Breaking and entering. He climbed into the unlit house. I heard him move through it and then he opened the front door. I looked around for signs of life. Together we ran through the rooms, turning on all the lights and calling her name. I stepped into a room and felt as if my breath had been squeezed from my body. Holly's clothes, clothes I had sorted with her, lay spilling out of a suitcase on the floor. On the table by the bed was a phone. Todd picked up the cord. 'Unplugged,' he said.

'Where are they?'

'They must have gone out somewhere,' said Todd.

'Yes. I guess so.'

'But if so,' said Todd, looking out of the back

window, 'they can't have gone far. They've left their car.'

'Where?'

'Look, you can just see it parked behind that old shed.'

'Yes, that's Charlie's car,' I said.

'Shall we go and take a look?' said Todd, and suddenly we gazed at each other, mouths opening.

We ran down the stairs, two and three at a time and burst out through the open door, tripping over the bumpy ground and feeling undergrowth catch at our clothes as we hurtled towards the car. I could feel my heart bumping up and down in my chest and hear myself gasping. And as we came closer we could make out the low rumbling sound of an engine, and something snaking round from the exhaust pipe to the front passenger door. Todd pulled at the tissue paper packing the hosepipe in place and wrenched it free. I pulled desperately at the door, but it was locked.

'Holly!' I screamed, for I could just make out the pale triangle of her upturned face behind the fogged glass. She wasn't moving. 'Holly, we're coming.'

'Here,' said Todd. He scrabbled desperately in the earth for something sharp or heavy and at last found half a mouldering brick.

'Not through the front,' I gasped, as he raised it above his head. 'Through the back or you'll cut her to pieces.'

He thumped the brick into the small side window,

and then again, a jagged hole widening in the glass, and we could smell the gas coming in thick waves at us. Then he thrust in his hand and unlocked the door. I pulled it open.

'Careful not to cut yourself,' Todd said, but it was too late for that. I was plunging into the noxious depths of the car where Holly lay slumped, then heaving her slack body on to the cold ground.

'Holly!' I called. 'Holly!'

I cradled her poor cold body against me. Todd crouched beside us and took her thin wrist between his thumb and forefinger. 'She's still alive, Meg,' he said. He was punching 999 into his mobile as he spoke. 'She's still alive . . . We need an ambulance,' he said into the phone. 'Someone's tried to gas themselves in a car. Ash Tree House, just outside Corresham, on the road to the Rose and Crown. Please hurry. And we need the police too,' he added.

'Ask them what we should do while we wait,' I said.

But they were already telling him and he was relaying it to me. I held Holly's nostrils pinched between my fingers and blew air into her mouth. Her lips felt rubbery and her skin cool, but I could feel her heart faintly beating. Todd and I took it in turns to give her the kiss of life, while the chilly wind blew in gusts through the trees, scattering fat drops of water. I don't know how long we stayed like that. Minutes. Hours. We didn't say anything.

And then two things happened. Over the brow of

the hill, we saw headlights. And as the ambulance and police car came into view, Holly's eyes flickered open. For the briefest moment we looked at each other and I think she even smiled.

After that, it was movement, light, noise and bustle; people bending over her, and talking in quick, clipped voices, giving instructions. A man was talking on a radio. Holly was lifted on to a stretcher, covered with a thick blanket and slotted into the back of the ambulance. Then it was driving away, its blue light flashing eerily across the woods, leaving behind only the police car and two men. Someone else was taking care of everything, so I walked across to Todd on legs that felt as it they were about to crumble into the earth, put my arms round him and hugged him tight. My cheeks were wet, but I couldn't tell if that was with my tears, or his, or simply the rain that had started again. Then, over his shoulder, I saw a silhouetted figure standing at the gate. For a moment, it stood quite still, then walked down the drive towards us, breaking after a few seconds into a ragged run.

'Meg,' said Charlie, as he arrived. 'What's going on?' He turned to the police. 'Where's my wife?'

Then he burst into tears.

39

I looked at Charlie as he gulped back his tears and said again, 'What's going on?' His face in the lights from the police car looked gaunt and ghastly pale; his hands plucked at his jacket and his bloodshot eyes glittered. He was a man in torment, and in the midst of my anger, grief and terror, I felt unwelcome pity for him and a huge, almost crushing weariness.

'It's all right, sir,' said one of the policeman, but I cut him short.

'She's gone in the ambulance, Charlie,' I said, as calmly as I could. 'And you know what's going on.'

'What?' he said wildly. 'What?'

'She's alive.'

'I don't understand.'

'You understand very well,' I said, and walked over to the two police officers, who were in conversation. 'This is the husband. You need to talk to him. This wasn't a suicide attempt. He tried to kill her.'

They looked at me with an expression that was close to embarrassment. I'm not sure if they were more suspicious of Charlie or of me. Charlie gave a jerky gesture and gabbled something about how he couldn't bear it if Holly wasn't all right.

'I'm sorry,' said one of them. 'Miss, er . . . ?'

'I'm Meg Summers, Holly's best friend,' I said. 'My boyfriend and I have just driven up from London. I knew she was in danger. We only just arrived in time.'

'I want to see my wife,' said Charlie. 'I want to see Holly. Can you take me there? Everything else can wait.'

'How could you have done it?' I said. 'How? I know what you've been through. I know about Naomi. I know about everything. You could have left her, just walked away. How could you do this?'

'Miss Summers,' said the officer. 'Please calm down.'

'I'm calm. Am I shouting? Crying? No. I'm calm. Completely calm.'

'Meg darling,' said Todd, and took my hand.

Charlie turned to the police. 'My wife has been suffering from severe depression,' he said. 'She's already attempted suicide. She's received ECT. She's been talking of suicide for weeks.'

'The last bit isn't true.'

'This isn't her first attempt?' the police officer said to Charlie.

'No. She took a massive overdose a few weeks ago. She's manic-depressive. It's been hell for everyone. Look, we can talk about this later. I must see Holly.'

'It's because she's manic-depressive and tried to kill herself that you thought you could kill her and get away with it. The perfect alibi. Everyone's expecting her to do it again, so who'd suspect murder?'

'Meg,' said Charlie, quietly. 'Stop. Please.'

'You used to love her so much. How could it come to this?'

'Don't,' he said. He actually put his hands over his ears. 'I can't listen to this.'

'We can run you to the hospital in a minute, sir,' said one of the policemen to Charlie. 'In the meantime, you'd better go inside.'

The other officer actually patted his shoulder. 'I'm sure there's nothing to worry about, sir,' he said. 'There's probably been some sort of misunderstanding.'

The two of them – Charlie and the brawnier policeman – walked towards the house together. Todd and I were left with the other, who didn't seem suspicious or angry or even very concerned. He just looked a little awkward, as if I'd complicated what should have been a simple situation.

'It's cold out,' said the officer. He was middle-aged. His face was flushed red, probably because of the bitter wind sweeping over the fields from the north. The trees were bending with it. 'We'd all like to get off, wouldn't we? But in the meantime why don't you wait in your car and we'll have a look at things?'

'You don't believe a word I'm saying, do you? How do you explain that I knew she was in danger and raced down here with Todd to save her? How do you explain that? Coincidence?'

He didn't reply.

'Let's wait in the car,' said Todd. 'You don't have

to prove everything at once. You've saved her life. That's the thing, Meg. She would have been dead by now and she's not. She's alive. She's in hospital. She's safe.'

He held open the door and I sat in the passenger seat but didn't close the door in spite of the chill. I sat there and listened to the wind in the trees and felt Todd's strong fingers rub the back of my neck. A few yards away, the officer was examining the car Holly had nearly died in. We could see the strong beam of his torch moving around its dark interior. For a while neither of us spoke. At last the officer left the car and went slowly back to the house, a pool of torchlight marking his way. He was wearing white gloves and carrying something I couldn't identify, something that flapped, like a rag or a small piece of cloth.

'One day,' I said at last, 'we'll look back on this and it will seem like a dream, something that happened to someone else.'

We watched as the same police officer came out of the house and walked towards us.

'I'd like you to come with us,' he said, when he reached my open door. 'There's something Mr Carter would like you to see before we take him to the hospital.'

'I want to go to the hospital too,' I said.

'Please come with me.'

We followed him back to the house and into the living room, where the glass from the smashed window still lay in gleaming shards on the floor. Charlie was sitting in an armchair, his legs splayed apart and his head at a funny angle. He looked half dead with exhaustion, and when he glanced at me his expression didn't change.

'Well,' I said, 'what's this thing we're supposed to see?'

'There was a note,' said the older officer. He looked at me kindly.

'What?' I said.

'We've examined the car. There was a note on the seat beside her. It clearly announced her intention to kill herself.'

'That's not possible,' I said. 'It's a fake. I want to see it.'

'Show it to her,' said Charlie.

The officer stepped forward, removed a piece of paper from a transparent folder and laid it on the table. I recognized Holly's flamboyant handwriting as soon as I saw it. We used to joke about it. She was left-handed and wrote with her hand curled up as if she were trying to stop anyone reading it. It was always hopelessly illegible. After years of experience I was one of the few who could decipher it. I often had to act as an interpreter.

'We could hardly read it,' said the officer.

'I can,' I said, with a sigh. I leaned over. It was a short message, just a couple of lines. The paper had been torn across and the words were written close to the top, as if she had begun what was intended to be a long message, then just stopped, with nothing left to say. 'I'm so sorry,' it said. 'So very very sorry. I just want all this to stop. Forgive this, my best and truest friend. All my love, Holly.'

'No,' I said. 'This isn't true. There's something wrong.'

I felt Todd's reassuring hand on my shoulder. 'This is a mistake,' I said. 'Something's happening. I don't understand.'

'You did the right thing,' said Todd. 'You saved Holly's life.' He looked over at Charlie, and spoke fiercely. 'She did, didn't she?'

Charlie's face was frozen, like a mask. He looked at the police officers. 'I would have got back,' he said. 'I would have saved her.'

'You're a liar and a murderer.'

'Please take your girlfriend away,' said the police officer to Todd. 'She's distressed.'

Without saying any more, Todd led me out and we got into the car. He put the key into the ignition. Before he turned it, he leaned over and kissed me. 'Ready?' he said softly.

'Wait,' I said.

'What do you mean?'

'There's something,' I said. 'Something . . . I can't . . . it's . . .'

'Meg –'

'Shut up. Sorry. But shut up for a moment.'

I held my head, pressing tightly on my temples. Something was coming. I knew it was coming, but

I didn't know exactly what it was. I thought of that moment standing on the platform in the Tube in London when a train is due. At first you don't hear anything. You feel it. A breath of warm air from the tunnel, a few scraps of paper lifted and blown forward, and the train is still half a mile away. There was something in my head and I couldn't quite get at it. And then I could. Yes. Yes.

I pushed my hands into the pockets of my jacket, the one I'd been wearing over the last few days. Yes, it was there. I didn't even need to look at it. I could see it without looking. 'I've got to go back in,' I said.

'No, Meg, don't be ridiculous.'

'I've got to.'

Todd actually ran after me. I think he thought I had gone crazy and he may even have made some attempt to stop me, but I shrugged him off. When the officer opened the door, it was clear from his expression that he was not in the least pleased to see me. They were about to leave. Charlie still had his coat on, the grieving husband, all ready to sit at the bedside. The note was still lying on the kitchen table.

'Miss Summers, did you forget something?'

'No,' I said. 'I remembered something.' I looked at the police officer. 'You found the note?'

'I'm sorry,' he said. 'I thought we were done.'

'You found the note?'

He gave an impatient sigh. 'That's right.'

'Where did you find it?'

'It was on the passenger seat,' he said, with some irritation.

'It was her suicide note.'

'Yes.'

'But not for *this* suicide.'

There was a pause.

'What do you mean?' said the officer.

I took the torn-off slip of paper from my pocket, the one with the phone number on it, the one I'd found under Charlie's desk. I joined the slip to the note on the table. It fitted perfectly.

'"Meg, my dear and loyal friend",' I said. 'That note was written to me.'

'What the hell is this?' said Charlie. 'This is rubbish.'

'No, it isn't,' I said. 'Holly told me she'd written a note to me when she attempted suicide but the note was never found. I assumed it got mixed up in all the chaos and lost. But it didn't. Charlie kept it. You kept it,' I said, looking directly at him. 'It was your Get Out of Jail Free card, wasn't it? Whenever you got round to staging Holly's suicide, you just had to leave that note – of course with my name torn off – and no questions would be asked. But now it does the opposite. It proves you did it.'

There was a long silence. Very delicately the officer took the note by the edge, then my fragment and placed them in the folder.

'Do you hate her that much, Charlie?' I said.

Charlie looked up. 'Hate her?' He sounded almost

as if he were talking to himself, dazed and tormented and listening to the sound of his own words as if he could barely understand them. 'I've been clearing up after her for a year. I've been sober when she's drunk, I've dealt with the people she's fucked around. Or just fucked. She used to say she'd do anything for me, and she meant it. But what did she do? She spent all our money and then she spent money we hadn't got and then she gambled a bit more away just for fun. Every day she did things which if I'd done them just once I would . . . Well, I don't know how I could get over it. She's done to me what my worst enemy couldn't have done. When I met her I was somebody, and in everything she's done since then she's stamped on that. She's destroyed everything I was, everything I thought I was good at. Hate? Love? I don't know the difference any more, Meg. They're just words, after all. I just wanted it to end. I couldn't bear it any more. I wanted to be set free to be myself again.'

I felt any pity ebb away, replaced instead by a kind of disgust: Charlie had enough pity for himself.

'Mr Carter,' said the brawny police officer, 'at this point I need to warn you that anything —'

'Let me see her,' interrupted Charlie.

I turned towards Todd. 'Let's go,' I said.

Hand in hand, we left the room.

40

I heard a voice, a voice I knew, and I stood quite still, letting the memories from that time flood through me.

'I'll take these white roses, please,' was all that she said, but I knew at once who it was.

It was a Friday afternoon in September, one of those gloriously crisp blue autumn days, warm in the sunshine and chilly in the shadows, where summer and autumn meet. I was in Soho, buying things for the party, taking my time, relishing the smells and sounds all around me. I had stopped in front of the flower stall and was hesitating between the bronze chrysanthemums and the freesias. My mind was on a host of other things – the cheese stall, the fruit stall, the people who hadn't replied to the invitations yet, what we were going to eat for supper, the headline about a far-off volcanic eruption I'd just glimpsed in someone else's newspaper – but as soon as she spoke those six words everything disappeared and I was back in the story that I had thought was over for good. Almost reluctantly, I turned round.

I hardly recognized her. She was wearing a thick pink tweed coat and black suede boots with narrow toes and spindly heels. Her hair was longer and straighter. Her clear skin glowed. Everything about her looked expensively and self-consciously chic. She was not like a nurse with an overdraft. But there were her strange, pale brown eyes, staring at me over the flowers. For a tiny moment, I saw a flicker of alarm or hostility, but she forced her mouth into a smile.

'It's Meg, isn't it? Meg Summers.'

'Naomi,' I said. 'How are you?'

'I'm well. At least, as well as can be expected. You don't get over something like that in a hurry, but I told myself I had to be strong and move on, not be dragged down, not be his victim too. It was awful, wasn't it?'

Now she was looking solemn and sad.

'I tried to contact you,' I said. 'Afterwards.'

'Did you? If only I'd known. I couldn't stay in that place, though. I'm sure you understand. I had to get away.'

'Can I buy you a coffee?'

'Well, I would have loved that, Meg. Another time, perhaps, and we can catch up on everything but today I'm in such a hurry and –'

'It won't take long,' I said firmly. I put my hand under her elbow and practically forced her off the crowded street into the nearest café where I ordered coffee for me and herbal tea for her. We sat at a table near the large plate-glass window. With the sun shining straight in on us, it felt oppressively warm so I took off my coat, but Naomi remained firmly buttoned into hers.

'How's Holly?' she asked. 'I would have gone to see her but I thought it would be too painful for her. I heard that she's better, that she's back at work.'

I wasn't going to give her even a whisper of information about Holly. 'Have you heard from Charlie?' I said instead.

'Charlie? No. He sent me letters from prison at first but I didn't open them.' She shuddered. 'You don't think I'd want anything to do with him after what he did to Holly and me, do you?'

'What did he do to you?'

'He used me. He betrayed me. Can you imagine how I felt when I discovered? The man I loved and thought I would be with for the rest of my life.'

I didn't reply and there was a long, painful silence.

'I know what you told the police about me,' she said. 'It was understandable. You were upset. That was only natural. I know you've always adored Holly. Hero-worshipped her, even. I'm sorry, Meg. My relationship with Charlie might not seem . . . The fact is that I pitied him. I thought he was a man at the end of his tether. I thought he needed help. And I let myself fall in love with him.'

'Charlie got seven years,' I said. 'That means he'll be out in four or something ridiculous. If I'd arrived five minutes later, he'd be in for fifteen. When I drove up from London and pulled Holly out of that car, I didn't just save her life, I saved Charlie from eight more years in prison. And when I asked you if you knew where Charlie and Holly had gone, you looked me in the face and said no. Because you knew what Charlie was going to do and you knew he needed time.'

'That's not true.' Naomi took a pair of gloves from her bag and pulled them on, finger by finger.

'What I want to know,' I said, 'is if you ever wake up in the middle of the night and think about it.'

'I sleep fine, thank you.'

I thought she was going to leave, but then something occurred to her and she leaned forward. 'Do you ever think about this?' she said. 'Everyone was doing fine until Holly came along. Charlie was fine. He was a good, kind, talented man and he was happy in his life until he met her. Now he's serving a prison sentence for attempted murder. That woman Deborah was a successful career woman. Now she's lost her job, her flat and most of her sanity, as far as I know. Her boyfriend, Stuart, I read about his trial in the local paper and how Holly behaved as a witness, charming everyone. Still the same old Holly, eh? Stuart only got a suspended sentence but he'll always have a record because of her.'

'Not entirely because of her, surely.'

'No one was bad before they came across Holly. No one was violent or wicked. They were all ordinary people getting on with their lives. They were just unlucky that they were in her way, like being in the way of a tornado. And I was unlucky too.'

'You look as though you're doing all right now,' I said.

She looked at the ring on my finger. 'I can see that you are too,' she said. 'Congratulations. And snap.'

She held up her left hand and I saw a glistening of gold.

41

Todd left the arrangements for the wedding party in my hands. 'I want whatever you want,' he said.

I wasn't quite sure whether to be utterly charmed by that or just a little bit irritated. I decided to be charmed. I was quite clear about what I wanted. I wanted it to be nothing at all like a KS Associates event. It wasn't going to be like a fun-fair or an SAS assault course or the carnival in Rio or the Glastonbury Festival. It was going to be a chance for our friends and family to gather from the corners of the globe and talk and eat and drink and wish us well.

I had some moments of concern about Holly's role in all of this. She had been my witness at the register-office wedding – how could I have chosen anyone else? – and I'd been a little nervous about that as well. I needn't have been. She was perfect. She didn't arrive by parachute. She wasn't dressed as a harlequin. She wore a short blue dress and a pillbox hat with a veil, and she looked demure and almost as happy as I was. She insisted on arranging the lunch after the ceremony for the small group of us, Todd's family, my family, his best friend, Francis. It was perfect, a Spanish restaurant in a small street round the corner where they cooked fish and steaks on an open fire and served too much wine in jugs. At one point in the meal I looked at her chatting to one of my cousins and thought, Well, why not? and she caught my eye and I blushed and she giggled.

She had ideas for my party. She couldn't help herself. She knew some spectacular places. One of the towers of Tower Bridge. A huge glass-fronted room overlooking Oxford Street. An old weaver's workshop in Spitalfields. A canal barge. A closed-down Underground station. The biggest bouncy castle in the entire world. She knew a clown, a magician, a juggler, a hurdy-gurdy man, a puppeteer from the Transvaal. They all sounded wonderful, she was wonderful, but I shook my head. 'No,' I said. 'This is my day and I want absolutely nothing to worry about. There aren't even going to be any speeches. Todd made me promise. It's going to be a grown-up party. People can drink and people can dance and nothing at all can go wrong.'

'What about food?' she said, and she started talking about a chef she'd met who did something involving every single bit of a pig.

'Todd's parents are arranging all that,' I said. 'They insisted.'

'I just want to help,' she said.

'But you'll ask first?' I said. 'I mean, before helping.'

I worried that I might have upset her but she laughed and gave me a hug.

*

One of Todd's friends had a house in Hackney with a large garden that backed on to an even larger garden. There was a gate between them that could be opened to make it into one, improbably large, secret walled city garden, and that was where we held our party. The girls in the office worked on it for a whole day and when I arrived I almost burst into tears. There were garlands of flowers hanging from the branches of trees, and wind chimes tinkling in the breeze and candles everywhere, their soft light growing stronger in the dusk.

There's so much else to say about the party. About how I was worried whether anybody would come, and how I was then worried about whether there was enough to drink, and in the end about whether anyone would ever leave. About how I saw my whole life there in that walled garden, from people I hadn't met since I left primary school to people I saw every day by the coffee machine, from ancient great-aunts to old boyfriends. About how I saw a cross-section of Todd's life, people I would get to know properly over the next months and years, people I would like because he liked them. About meeting Todd's previous girlfriend, who irritated me by being almost six feet tall and then even more by being rather nice, and then soothed my ego by being with a new boyfriend who was clearly, at even the most cursory glance, much less attractive than Todd. But those are other people's stories and this is still a story about Holly.

I mustn't give the impression that I was worrying about her all the time because I didn't need to. Starting again at work had taken enormous courage. She was right back at the bottom of the hill and she had to climb it wearing concrete boots. So much damage had been done. There were clients who came back but quite a few didn't and we had to go out in search of new ones, and even some of the new ones had heard strange rumours on the grapevine. And I could hardly believe it but she had done it: she had got down and dirty and done the grindingly awful work of getting KS Associates back on its feet.

It wasn't quite the same this time round. It couldn't be. There wasn't quite that air of improvisation there had been, or the thirty-six-hour parties, the feeling of being on a tightrope with no safety-net. A lot of it had gone, as maybe it had to. It was the difference between drunk and sober, manic and normal, between being young women too stupid to know what they were taking on and slightly older women who had been made to learn a lesson or two.

But I had a few pangs about Holly at our party, if only because the last wedding party I'd been at with her had been her own. I felt better as soon as I saw her. The rule about not outshining the bride apparently ceased to apply after the wedding ceremony had finished. She had let her hair down so it flowed over her shoulders and she was wearing a scarlet dress expressly designed for reprehensible behaviour. She staggered in carrying a large, elaborately decorated box tied with ribbons. I insisted on opening it there and then. It contained a globe. There was another pink ribbon tied tightly around the equator with a label that bore only the two words 'Your Oyster'. 'As in, "The world is . . .",' said Holly.

Todd came over and gave her a hug. 'I love these things,' he said, spinning it round, like a child. 'Look. Did you know that New York is on the same latitude as Rome?'

'No, I didn't,' I said happily.

'It's useful to be reminded of the world's roundness,' said Holly, 'from time to time.'

Todd carried the globe through to a place of honour. Holly hugged me and looked at me close up. 'I've got through, I think,' she said. 'And it's about ninety-nine per cent due to you.'

'Nine per cent, more like,' I said.

'We can negotiate details like that,' she said.

'I just did what friends are meant to do.'

Holly shook her head. 'I don't think most of them know that all that's part of the deal.' She squeezed my hand. 'Oh, by the way, Charlie sends his regards.'

'You're not serious,' I said.

'He writes to me,' said Holly. 'I give his letters a glance before I pass them on to my lawyer.'

'How can it be allowed?'

'I keep trying to decide if it was my fault and in a way, of course, it was. I think I fell in love with a fantasy, and then God knows what hell I put him through, what nightmare he found himself living in. I wrecked him. If he hadn't met me, he would still be free, still be good. I pushed him into being a man who could murder.' She looked around and saw other people arriving. 'This isn't the time,' she said. 'Oh, there is one thing, something my lawyer told me. You remember Charlie's plan? He kills me, it looks like suicide, one insurance policy pays off the mortgage, another one gives him a fat cheque. But he didn't read the small print. It wouldn't have worked. They didn't – needless to say – pay out in cases of suicide. Poor Charlie. He failed even as a murderer.' She gave my hand another squeeze and disappeared.

From then on I caught a glimpse of her from time to time. There was the inevitable problem with a party of that kind that people stuck in groups, relatives, colleagues, college friends. Holly wasn't like that. Every time I saw her she was in a different part of the garden, talking with all sorts of different people. Then, for a time, I didn't see her at all. I looked around, couldn't find her, wondered if she might have sneaked home, and then I thought of other things, got involved in other conversations, forgot about her for a while.

I was in the kitchen having a delirious reminiscence with a girl from my secondary school when I felt arms round me from behind and found myself held by Todd. 'Having a good time?' he said.

'Wonderful.'

'I'm only just starting to learn what a rich and interesting life you've had,' he said.

'Who the hell have you been talking to?' I asked, in some alarm.

'Everybody,' he said. He looked at his watch. 'You know what time it is?'

'No.'

'It's just about to be midnight. I wanted to –'

He never said what he wanted because there was the most extraordinary explosion and the house shook. In a moment of panic, I wondered if there could have been a terrorist bomb. Then I saw smoke in the garden, billowing in through the french windows. Todd and I ran outside. The crowd in the garden was talking avidly and gesticulating up at the house. We turned and looked up. A top window was open, with smoke pouring out of it, billowing over the sill and tumbling downwards like foamy brown water. Then two faces appeared, their faces black with soot, like chimney sweeps. I turned to the people around me.

'What the . . . ?'

So here they are, then. The people who loved me and hated me, who wanted me to live and who wished me dead, who tried to save me and who let me go. They all look happy. They are gazing at each other, holding hands; some of them are kissing. I can tell that they are making promises to each other for the life ahead. That great journey. Only one is missing.

Sometimes it feels as if Charlie never existed, that he's just a dream I've woken from, a figure fading into nothing inside my giddy head. In a way, that's true. It's like I said to Meg a few minutes ago, the Charlie I fell in love with was a fantasy figure – in the same way that I was for him. He was the man who was going to rescue me from myself. As my therapist says to me about three times each bloody session, 'You're the only person who can help yourself, Holly.' She uses my name in every sentence – 'What do you feel about that, Holly?' 'How do you explain that, Holly?' I want to tell her I've been to that people-management course too, the one that teaches you how to grip someone firmly by the hand when you first meet them, look them in the eye. I want to say that I'm bored to death of talking about me, me, me. That it's all very well looking inside all the time, exploring the dark and secret labyrinths of the mind, but what about the wonderful world outside? What about poetry, music, passion, the lash of the green sea? But then I think of my friends, my family; I think of darling Meg, who even now, on the day of her wedding party, keeps glancing at me to check that I really am all right. I'll keep going. I'll keep on taking the tablets, the exercise, the talking cure. I don't want to die a third time. Not yet, anyway. I'll save death up.

Meg asks me if I miss my moods. She has such an anxious expression on her face that usually I avoid the question. The truth is, of course I do. I miss them like you miss a lover. My wild and swinging self. The inky darkness where demons lurked, and then the glorious light. Falling then flying; crashing down but then hurtling up again until I was so happy and so free I almost wanted to die of the sheer joy of it; a delirium of delight that was very close to terror. The world was mine and I was its.

But the missing is getting better. To begin with, I kept myself on such a tight rein I almost throttled myself. Got up at the same time; went to work at the same time; came home on the dot; sensible food; early bed. Didn't dress up in my favourite clothes, didn't flirt, didn't dance, didn't drink, didn't giggle, didn't howl, didn't stray. Bit by bit, I'm letting myself off the leash.

Tonight I feel good, I feel great, it's almost like the old days when a glorious, uncontainable energy would ripple through me so I could hardly keep my feet on the ground. And look at Meg, her kind and lovely face. She's happy. Never has anyone deserved to be happy as much as Meg, who always puts other people's happiness first. I hope Todd always realizes how lucky he is. I hope I always realize how lucky I am.

I used to think that, in the end, I was profoundly on my

own – and that everyone in this seething world is too. It's a condition of being human. All through your life you search for love and intimacy; you search for unconditional loyalty and recognition. From parents, friends, partners. We all make promises to each other and we believe them, or pretend to believe them. We hang on to the hope that we're not alone. And yet, at moments of great crisis and black despair, the only person who can save you is yourself. No one else can do it. That's what I've always thought, and in a way I think it still, but when I was down and helpless and had given up on myself, Meg was there, like a miracle. She believed in me when I'd lost belief in myself, and made me live when I was ready to die. Put my demons on one side of the scale and Meg on the other, and she outweighs them all. That's what I mean by lucky.

The party is winding down now. People are talking about leaving. I look at my watch and see it's midnight, nearly time. I push my way through the crowds of people, back into the house, and collect the package from where I'd hidden it under coats in the spare bedroom.

A familiar bubble of joy opens in my throat. I know that I am about to do something stupid.

They'd cost me nearly two hundred pounds. The man selling them had been a bit surprised and told me to make sure to read the instructions properly, and there was a woman buying sparklers who'd been downright disapproving. How could I spend that much money, she asked, on something that would be over before you could count to ten, and nothing to show for it? But didn't she understand that that was exactly the point?

To work for days and weeks, then blow it all in a single, dazzling moment.

I sneak out into the garden again. In the kitchen, Meg is leaning against Todd and he's saying something in her ear. They don't notice me. It says on the outside of the pack that they should be planted eighty metres away from people. How ridiculous. Eighty metres would take me through the other house and over the road. So I make do with the end of the garden. It'll be fine. Probably.

The first one goes a bit wrong. Its stake tips sideways at the last moment so that it shoots off at an angle, towards the house. I have a nasty feeling it went through the window. I hear shouts and screams behind me, see smoke. But it's too late to bother with any of that, because a falling spark has already lit the fuse of the second. I watch as the tiny light travels up towards the rocket, then burrows into its base. For a moment it looks as if it has been extinguished, but then there is a short, powerful hiss and the rocket soars fabulously upwards, leaping into the dark sky, its solid body ripping apart and turning into suns and stars and squibs of exploding colour. My gift for my friend.

Time stops. In the secret garden, everyone looks upwards together, at the blossoming flower of perfect shedding light. Its petals of soft fire fall silently towards us.

Twice I died. Now I live.

Read on for a taste of

LOSING YOU

by Nicci French

Available in hardback in February 2007

What is worse than your child going missing? Your child going missing and nobody believing you . . .

Nina Landry is supposed to be taking her two children on holiday today. But her fifteen-year-old daughter, Charlie, has yet to return from a night out . . .

Minute by minute, Nina's unease builds to worry and then to panic. Has Charlie run away? Or has something more sinister happened to her? *And why will nobody take her disappearance seriously?*

As day turns to night on Sandling Island, a series of half-buried secrets lead Nina Landry from sickening suspicion to deadly certainty. The question becomes less whether she and her daughter will leave the island for Christmas – and more whether they'll ever leave it again . . .

Sometimes I still felt that I had fetched up on the edge of the world. The wintry light slanting on to the flat, colourless landscape; the moan of the wind, the shriek of sea-birds, and the melancholy boom of the foghorn far out at sea all sent a shiver through me. But I stamped my feet on the ground to warm them and told myself that in a few hours I would be far away.

Rick dropped the spanner and straightened up from the open bonnet of the car. My car. He rubbed his grazed knuckle. His unshaven face was raw from the cold north-easterly that whipped over us, carrying the first drops of rain, and his pale blue eyes were watering. His curls were damp and lay flat on his head so that I could see the shape of his skull. He blew on his whitened fingers and tried to flash me his boyish smile, but I could see it was an effort.

'Rick,' I said, 'it's kind of you, but you don't need to do this. It was just a rattle in the engine and I thought something had come loose. I would never have called you otherwise. I can take it to the garage after we get back from holiday.'

His wife, Karen, came out of the front door with three mugs of coffee on a tray, three Digestive biscuits laid out neatly beside them. She was a tall woman, almost as tall as Rick, big-boned but thin. Sometimes she looked striking, nearly beautiful, and then I could understand why the pair of them had got together, but too often she seemed gaunt and unfinished, as if she hadn't paid proper attention to herself. Her hair was brown, already peppered with grey, and pulled back in a hasty bun. Her skin was bracketed with worry lines, her nails were bitten down to the ends of her fingers. She rarely wore makeup or jewellery, except for the wedding band on her finger. Her clothes didn't quite fit together. Today it was a strawberry-pink quilted jacket and a thin black skirt that was trailing on the ground. I worried she would trip over it. She had the bossy abruptness of someone who was fundamentally shy, and once, late at night, when she was a bit tipsy, she'd confided to me that life rushed at her out of a fog, constantly taking her by surprise. Maybe that was why she often seemed to talk in non-sequiturs, and her manner often swung between sprightly sarcasm and barely suppressed anger.

'White no sugar, right? How's it going, then? All sorted?'

Rick grimaced at her in exasperation, then down at the ground on which lay the battery from my car and a couple of other parts that I couldn't identify.

A little gleam appeared in her eyes. 'You said when you came back that it would only take a couple of minutes.'

'I know,' said Rick, wryly.

'That was before ten.' She glanced ostentatiously at the watch on her wrist. 'You've been out here for nearly three-quarters of an hour.'

'I know that too.'

'Nina's got a plane to catch.' She cast me an amused smile that said, *Men.* I looked away guiltily.

'*I know.*'

'It's all right,' I said. 'I've done most of the packing for me and Jackson, and Charlie promised she'd be ready by the time I was back.'

Rick's head disappeared beneath the bonnet again. There was the sound of several sharp taps and a mumbled curse. It might have seemed funny but he was so obviously not finding it funny that I bit my lip to forestall even the tiniest hint of a smile. I pulled off my gloves to pick up my coffee mug and wrapped my fingers round it, grateful for the warmth, the curl of steam that licked at my cold face.

'Christmas in the sunshine instead of this endless cold, grey drizzle,' said Karen, and pulled her jacket more closely round her, shivering exaggeratedly. 'What time does your plane go?'

'Not until just before six. I'm picking Christian up on the way to Heathrow.'

I said it casually, but felt a small prickle of nervous happiness in my chest: Christian and I had been friends for nearly eighteen years, lovers for just a few months, and now, for two weeks, the four of us would all be together in the Florida Keys. We would be the family unit I'd thought had been smashed to pieces: going on trips, making plans, collecting shared stories that we could tell and retell later, even eating breakfast together. Except Charlie never ate breakfast: she acted as though toast was immoral. I hoped she would behave herself.

'I think Christmas should be cancelled,' Karen was saying. 'Eamonn has a kind of ideological objection to it it anyway, and is always trying to make us celebrate the winter solstice instead, stand around a bonfire at midnight like witches. Rick tries to make us play board games and Charades and Wink Murder, even though you can't play Wink Murder with just three people, and I . . .' She raised her eyebrows at me. 'I'm the one who drinks too much and burns the turkey.'

Rick came round to the driver's door, leaned in and turned the key in the ignition. 'Right,' he said determinedly. There was a hasty splutter, then silence.

'You *hope* you're picking up Christian,' said Karen, who seemed almost pleased.

Rick pulled a face that was a caricature of confusion, anxiety and distress. This was what he did in life. He helped people, he fixed things; he was unflappably, charmingly capable. People turned to him, just as I had this morning.

'At least you've solved the rattle,' said Karen, gaily, and gave a small, explosive snort.

'What?' said Rick, with a glance at her that she pretended not to see.

'The car won't rattle if you can't switch it on.'

His face went a scary shade of crimson. He looked at his watch and I cast a surreptitious glance at it as well.

'Shall we just call the garage?' I suggested. 'Or the AA? I'm a member.'

'Well,' began Rick. 'It might just be –'

'Don't be ridiculous,' said Karen. 'You've got nothing on today, have you? Just working on your boat. Though God knows why you want to work on your boat on a day like this, and it's the first day of your holiday. You can't just take Nina's car apart and leave it like that. She's got to get to the–'

'I *know*. How old is this car, anyway?' Rick stared at the rusty little Rover as if it was one of his more hopeless pupils.

'About ten years,' I said. 'It was already quite old when I got it.'

Rick gave a grunt as if the car's age was to blame for the situation.

'Can't you work backwards?' said Karen. 'At least you could get it back to the way it was when Nina drove it here.'

'What do you think I'm doing?' Rick asked, with effortful calm.

'Don't worry, Nina,' Karen said reassuringly.

'I'm not worried,' I said, and it was true. I knew that in a few hours, even if I had to get a taxi all the way to Heathrow, we'd be in the air, far from the pinched, icy days of English winter. I imagined sitting beside Christian and gazing out of the window as London became an intricate grid of orange and white lights. I raised my head and looked past Rick and Karen's house to what lay beyond.

For thirty-nine years I had lived in a city where I could go a whole day without seeing the horizon. Here, on Sandling Island, it was all horizon: the level land, the mudflats, the miles of marshes, the saltings, the grey, wrinkled sea. Now it was mid-morning and from where I stood – facing west towards the mainland – I could see only the glistening mudflats with their narrow, oozing ditches of water where waders were walking with high-stepping delicate legs and giving mournful cries, as if they'd lost something. It was low tide. Little boats tethered to their unnecessary buoys tipped at a steep angle to show their blistered, slimy hulls; their halliards chinked and chimed in the wind. From my own house, a bit further round to the south-east, I could make out the sea. Sometimes, when I woke in the morning and opened my eyes on its grey, shifting expanse, I still wondered for a moment where I was, how on earth I'd landed up there.

It was Rory who had wanted to come, who for years of our marriage had dreamed of leaving London, of giving up his job as a solicitor and running a restaurant instead. At first, it had just been a daydream, an if-only that I didn't really share, but bit by bit it had taken on the harder edge of an obsession, until at last he'd found premises on Sandling Island

and dragged his reluctant family with him to begin a new life. It was only sixty miles from London but, rimmed as it was by the tidal estuary and facing out to open sea, it had the feel of a different world, gripped by weather and seasons; full of wild spaces, loneliness, the strange call of sea-birds and sighing winds. It was even cut off from the mainland every so often, when the highest of high tides covered the causeway. From my bedroom, I could hear the waters lapping at the shingle shore, the foghorns booming out at sea. Sometimes at night, when the island was wrapped in the darkness of the sky and of the rising, falling waters, I could scarcely bear the sense of solitude that engulfed me.

Yet I was the one who had fallen half in love with Sandling Island while Rory had been driven mad by it. Somewhere in the dream of the austere restaurant decorated with lobster-pots, nets and etchings of fishing-smacks it had gone wrong. There was an argument with a supplier about the ovens, cash stubbornly failed to flow and the restaurant had never even opened. As he found himself trapped by the fantasy he'd held for so long, he no longer knew what he was for or even who he was. Eventually the only way out was to run away.

'Sorry.' I turned my attention back to Karen, who was saying something.

'It's your birthday, isn't it?'

'That's right.'

'And not just any birthday.'

'Yes,' I said reluctantly. 'Forty. It's one of the ones you're not supposed to be happy about. How did you know?'

She gave a shrug.

'Everyone knows everything about everyone round here. Happy birthday, anyway.'

'Thanks.'

'Do you really mind about it?'

'I'm not sure. A friend of mine once told me –'

'I minded,' she said. 'I looked at myself in the mirror, and I thought, That's you now. No escape. That's who you are. Nothing turns out the way you expect, does it?'

'I think I'm getting there,' said Rick. 'Give me my coffee, will you?'

He had a streak of black grease on his jaw that rather suited him, and a rip in his jacket. I watched as he took a large gulp of cooling coffee, then posted half a Digestive after it. I had a list in my mind that I kept adding to: pack swimming stuff, goggles and sun-cream; remember the Christmas presents, including the snorkel and flippers I'd bought for Christian, who was a marine biologist yet lived many miles from the coast; some dollars; books for the plane; packs of cards. Leave out the dog food and instructions for Renata; the Christmas money for the postman, the milkman, the bin men . . . My toes were getting chilly now; my face felt stiff in the cold wind.

'I've been wanting to ask,' Rick moved closer to

me and spoke in a low tone, 'how's Charlie doing now, Nina? Are things better?'

'I think so,' I said cautiously. 'You can't really tell. At least, I can't with Charlie. She's quite private, you know.'

'She's a teenager,' said Rick. 'Teenagers are meant to be private. Especially with their parents. Look at Eamonn, for Christ's sake.'

'What's this?' asked Karen, moving in closer, a flicker of interest in her eyes.

'Charlie's had a rough time at school,' I said. I didn't want to talk about this because it was Charlie's story, not mine. I didn't want to discuss it lightly, give it a trite meaning. I imagined Charlie's pale, truculent face, its look of withdrawal behind the turbulent fall of her reddish hair. 'Rick found out about it. He talked to the girls who were bullying her, and to their parents. And to me. He was very helpful. As much as anyone can be.'

'Girls can be cruel,' said Karen, with a sweeping sympathy.

'She was at a sleepover at one of their houses last night,' I said. 'Tam's. Maybe that's a breakthrough. I haven't seen her yet. It would be a good way to end the term.'

'She'll be fine, you know,' said Rick, putting down his mug, reluctantly picking up the spanner once more.

Nicci French

about nicci and sean

about *catch me when I fall*

literature about depression
and mental illness

madness in films

books about depression
and bipolar disorder

the books

read more
www.penguin.co.uk

author photo © Mark Read

Nicci Gerrard was born in June 1958 in Worcestershire. After graduating with a first class honours degree in English Literature from Oxford University, she began her first job, working with emotionally disturbed children in Sheffield.

In the early eighties she taught English Literature in Sheffield, London and Los Angeles, but moved into publishing in 1985 with the launch of *Women's Review*, a magazine for women on art, literature and female issues. In 1987 Nicci had a son, Edgar, followed by a daughter, Anna, but by the time she became acting literary editor at the *New Statesman* her marriage had ended. She moved to the *Observer* in 1990, where she was deputy literary editor for five years, and then a feature writer and executive editor.

It was while she was at the *New Statesman* that she met Sean French.

Sean French was born in May 1959 in Bristol, to a British father and a Swedish mother. He too studied English Literature at Oxford University at the same time as Nicci, also graduating with a first class degree, but their paths didn't cross until 1990. In 1981 he won *Vogue* magazine's Writing Talent Contest, and from 1981 to 1986 he was their theatre critic. During that time he also worked at the *Sunday Times* as their deputy literary editor and television critic, and was the film critic for *Marie Claire* and deputy editor of *New Society*.

Sean and Nicci were married in Hackney in October 1990. Their daughters, Hadley and Molly, were born in 1991 and 1993.

By the mid-nineties Sean had had two novels published, *The Imaginary Monkey* and *The Dreamer of Dreams*, as well as numerous non-fiction books, including biographies of Jane Fonda and of Brigitte Bardot.

about nicci and sean

In 1995 Nicci and Sean began work on their first joint novel and adopted the pseudonym of Nicci French. The novel, *The Memory Game*, was published to great acclaim in 1997. *The Safe House*, *Killing Me Softly*, *Beneath the Skin*, *The Red Room*, *Land of the Living*, *Secret Smile* and *Catch Me When I Fall* have since been added to the Nicci French CV. *The Safe House*, *Beneath the Skin* and *Secret Smile* have all been adapted for TV, and *Killing Me Softly* for the big screen.

But Nicci and Sean also continue to write separately. Nicci still works as a journalist for the *Observer*, covering high-profile trials including those of Fred and Rose West, and Ian Huntley and Maxine Carr. Her novel *Things We Knew Were True* was published in 2003, and her second, *Solace*, in spring 2005. Sean's latest novel *Start From Here* came out in spring 2004.

Where did the idea for *Catch Me When I Fall* come from?

Nicci: Several of our books have come from a striking image or initial scene – so, for example, with *Land of the Living* we carried in our head for years a book that started with a woman waking up in the dark, bound, gagged, and with no memory of how she came to be there. Other books start with a 'what if?': with *Killing Me Softly* it was 'what if a woman fell head over heels in love with a stranger and then bit-by-bit discovered that he had a dark past?' Some novels evolve from ideas, as with the controversy over recovered memory with our very first book, *The Memory Game*. But *Catch Me When I Fall* started with the narrator, Holly. Holly is maddening, irresponsible, reckless, generous, impossible. People either love her or hate her. She has friends, but she also has enemies. She behaves badly, and in a sense she is challenging the reader to desert her the way that many of the people in the novel desert her. But gradually, we realise that Holly is not in control of herself. The novel is constructed around her increasingly volatile and destructive moods. In a way, she is the plot, since she creates the danger that she then has to escape.

Sean: It might be that *Catch Me When I Fall* is a culmination of a certain tendency in our books. Our heroines before had been pushed to the edge of sanity or wrongly seen as insane. Abbie in *Land of the Living*, and Miranda in *Secret Smile* are both accused of being mad. In some ways Alice in *Killing Me Softly* gives herself up to a passionate, sexual madness. We thought: what if a heroine really was mad? And then, as the American poet Delmore Schwartz said, 'Even paranoid people have enemies'.

....

Did you worry that readers might not like Holly?

Sean: I worry about everything. Kingsley Amis said an interesting thing about *Brideshead Revisited*. He said that the problem with the book was not that Evelyn Waugh let 'the Marchmains get away with behaving very badly, it's that he let them get away with behaving very boringly'. The problem with real madness, unlike the madness that's usually portrayed in novels or movies, is that it's grindingly boring. Admittedly the manic episodes of bipolar illness often have their exciting aspects. We thought readers would have different responses, which was fine so long as they weren't bored.

Nicci: What we really hope is that while readers might start off disapproving of Holly or being appalled by her, they will come to understand her; they don't have to empathise with her, but they can sympathise. And actually, we came to love her. If she behaves badly to other people, she behaves worse to herself.

Why did you decide to have two narrators?

Nicci: First of all, we felt we needed to get away from Holly! And then, because we wanted to see her and her story from the outside, and to contrast the feverish, intensely subjective world view with something calmer and more rational. Meg's voice and her story is like a counterpoint to Holly's. Also, we wanted to think about friendship. If the novel's a thriller about a woman who courts her own destruction, it's also a novel about female friendship. Meg is unconditionally loyal. She sticks by Holly and however badly she is treated, she won't give up. She's the kind of friend we would all love to have.

Was it important to the story that Holly was a manic depressive?

Sean: We were intrigued by the idea of a woman who was manic depressive but didn't know it. So yes, it was essential.

Nicci: We've read and talked a lot about depression and manic depression. It's one of the conditions which most people feel they can in some way recognise – unlike schizophrenic episodes, which many of us feel are alien and incomprehensible, manic depression has a kind of emotional vocabulary we understand. Indeed, we often glamorize it, seeing it as artistic, romantic and extreme. Yet for those who suffer from manic depression, it can be unendurably painful, grim and numbing. It feels deathly, and it can end in suicide. We wanted to show it realistically, and some of the letters we have most valued about the novel are from those who have experienced manic depression, who feel we have captured its horror. At the same time, there were questions that fascinated us: for example, how much is it an 'illness' that can be cured or contained by drugs, and how much part of what makes us who we are? Are we responsible for ourselves? Holly mourns the self she has lost when she is diagnosed and treated.

Have you had direct experience of it yourselves?

Sean: Didn't Shakespeare say somewhere that writers were just like madmen? (N.B. Yes, he did: 'The lunatic, the lover and the poet/Are of imagination all compact', *A Midsummer Night's Dream*.) We have the ups and downs that go with the job, and perhaps attract you to the job, but real madness is something of a different order.

Shakespeare was fascinated by madness. He repeatedly contrasts feigned madness with the real thing: Edgar and Lear in **King Lear**, Hamlet and Ophelia in **Hamlet**. He raises the question of whether simply doing mad things shows you are mad or whether there is an intrinsic madness which is something else. As Salvador Dali put it, 'The only difference between me and a madman is that I am not mad'.

From the early 19th century, the association between poetry and insanity seemed close. As Wordsworth wrote in his great poem 'Resolution and Independence', 'We Poets in our youth begin in gladness;/But thereof come in the end despondency and madness.' The toll taken by mental illness on modern American poets – Hart Crane, Sylvia Plath, Robert Lowell, John Berryman to name just a few – is terrible to contemplate.

Philip Larkin was very critical of Sylvia Plath's explorations of her own mental disorder: 'How valuable they are depends on how highly we rank the expression of experience with which we can in no sense identify, and from which we can only turn with shock and sorrow.' In no sense? Some of us may think that Larkin's great poem 'Aubade', the last he ever published, about waking in the dark and thinking of death, your own death, is one of the greatest of all evocations of depression from the inside.

The madman has become almost a stock character in modern literature, like the jester in Elizabethan times. Where would the modern thriller be without him? Madness, most famously with Thomas Harris's Hannibal Lecter, becomes almost a sign of superior intelligence.

The use of the insane narrator is a subject in itself, from the great first section of William Faulkner's **The Sound and the Fury** to Mark Haddon's *tour de force*, **The Curious Incident of the Dog in the Night-Time**.

It was important to us when we wrote **Catch Me When I Fall** that Holly's madness wasn't symbolic of anything. Of course, her illness shows itself in her behaviour, so the question of the degree to which it relates to her personality is a difficult one for her, her friends and, we hope, the reader.

But there is a great temptation to allegorise madness. Probably the most famous example is **One Flew Over the Cuckoo's Nest** (1975), an extremely compelling portrayal of madness as a form of revolt, a part of the counter-culture. In this movie, the nurses and doctors are like gaolers; the forms of treatment are forms of punishment and torture. It would be interesting to know how many people were deterred from seeking or accepting treatment, especially ECT treatment, under the influence of Milos Forman's film adaptation of Ken Kesey's book.

There seems to be something irresistible about the idea of the madman as something noble, something special. In **Shine** (1996), David Helfgott's illness is portrayed as inextricable from his musical gift rather than its enemy.

A Beautiful Mind (2001), the true story of the Nobel Prize-winning mathematician and schizophrenic, John Nash, suffers slightly from the same flaw but is nevertheless a remarkable film. It brilliantly attempts to show Nash's disordered mental state from the inside, in the process springing one of the greatest surprises in modern cinema.

Betty Blue (1986) is one of the outstanding portraits of madness in all cinema, because it portrays the complicated way it interacts with normal behaviour. Betty is crazily attractive, until we realize with a shock that she really is crazy. An amazing debut by Béatrice Dalle, which she never came close to matching.

madness in films

The best film ever about madness? An impossible question, but one left-field contender would be Samuel Fuller's amazing **Shock Corridor** (1963). A journalist has himself committed to an asylum to try to solve a murder, however ... But that would be to give the story away.

books about depression and bipolar disorder

The Noonday Demon by Andrew Solomon: A wide-ranging, illuminating, authoritative and beautiful book, written by a man who has himself endured harrowing years of depression, and combining science, history, philosophy, art, self-help and autobiography. Solomon manages to write from inside and out, about despair and hope, suffering and endurance, terrifying illness and possible recovery. It's a measure of Solomon's immense achievement that his book fills one with both sorrow and an unsettling euphoria.

Malignant Sadness by Lewis Wolpert: Several years ago, the distinguished embryologist Lewis Wolpert suffered from a catastrophic bout of depression that left him – despite his happy and successful life – suicidal. In his view, depression is normal emotion pathologized, and in this clear and candid book he combines his own experience of depression with his scientific understanding of the condition, looking at the causes of depression and its possible cures, from therapy to drugs and ECT.

An Unquiet Mind by Kay Redfield Jamison: Jamison has been a manic depressive since her adolescence, although she did not name or confront her condition for many years. She is now one of the leading authorities on bipolar disorders, and **An Unquiet Mind** is her moving and eloquent testimony on the nature of her illness, and an interrogation into the meaning of the 'self' that remains once the condition is treated.

Darkness Visible by William Styron: Styron is a Pulitzer Prize-winning novelist whose descent into depression took him to the brink of suicide. This memoir, written after he had 'trudged upwards out of hell's dark depths', is a clear, spare account of his pain, and a moving description of his recovery.

Depression and How to Survive It by Spike Milligan and Anthony Clare:
This collaboration between the Goon and the psychiatrist is a
disquieting read. Two Milligans emerge: the well and the ill. The former
is funny, generous, full of life; the latter is self-destructive and in a
deathly kind of pain. Through the chapters dealing with facts and
figures, causes and cures, the sheer and brutal grimness of clinical
depression emerges (Milligan himself wrote: 'A thousand grim
winters/grow in my head ... ').

Prozac Diary by Lauren Slater: Slater tried to die several times and
barely survived into adulthood. For a long time she had a horror of the
pharmaceutical cure, but she was saved by Prozac, and became a
psychologist working with the madness and torment of others. In all
her books, she breaks down the boundaries between the mad and
sane, the sick and the healthy, the 'them' and the 'us'.

The Bipolar Disorder Survival Guide by David J. Miklowitz and **Bipolar
Disorder** by Francis Mark Mondimore: both books do what it says on
the cover – provide a practical and comprehensive guide to living with
manic depression, helpful both for sufferers and their families.

THE MEMORY GAME

You remember an ordinary, idyllic childhood.
Then one day you discover that your memory is deceitful.
And possibly deadly ...

When a skeleton is unearthed, Jane Martello is shocked to learn it's that of her childhood friend, Natalie, who went missing twenty-five years ago. Encouraged by a therapist to recover lost memories, Jane hopes to find out what really took place when she was a child – and what happened to Natalie. But in learning the truth about Natalie's and her past, is Jane putting her own future at terrible risk?

'Electrifying' *Harpers & Queen*

THE SAFE HOUSE

You let a traumatized young woman into your home.
And into your heart.
You want to protect her like a member of your own family.
To save her from the darkness that's pursuing her ...

Samantha Laschen is a doctor specializing in post-traumatic stress disorder. She has moved to the coast to escape her problems and to be alone with her young daughter. But now the police want her to take in Fiona Mackenzie, a girl whose parents have been savagely murdered. Yet by allowing Fiona in, Sam is exposing herself – and her daughter – to risks she couldn't possibly have imagined.

'A superior psychological thriller' *The Times*

'Emotionally acute' *Mail on Sunday*

BENEATH THE SKIN

Someone's watching you.
You don't know who and you don't know why.
But *he* knows you ...

Zoë, Jennifer and Nadia are three women with nothing in common except the letters they receive, each one full of intimate details about every aspect of their lives – from the clothes they wear to the way they act when they think they're alone. And if that isn't terrifying enough, the letters also contain a shocking promise: that soon each life will come to a sudden, violent end. Can Zoë, Jennifer and Nadia discover who their tormentor is? And if so, will any of them live long enough to do anything about it?

'A nail-biting, can't-put-it-down read' *Marie Claire*

'Chilling, startling' *Daily Mail*

'Brilliant' *Evening Standard*

THE RED ROOM

The man who almost killed you has been accused of murder.
And you hold the key to his future ...

After psychologist Kit Quinn is brutally attacked by a prisoner, she is determined to get straight back to work. When the police want her help in linking the man who attacked her to a series of murders, she refuses to simply accept the obvious. But the closer her investigation takes her to the truth behind the savage crimes, the nearer Kit gets to the dark heart of her own terror.

'Gripping, chilling, moving' *Observer*

'Absorbing, highly addictive' *Evening Standard*

'French is excellent at building up suspense and elegantly exploiting all our worst fears' *Daily Mail*

SECRET SMILE

You have an affair.
You finish it.
You think it's over.
You're dead wrong ...

Miranda Cotton thinks she's put boyfriend Brendan out of her life for good. But two weeks later, he's intimately involved with her sister. Soon what began as an embarrassment becomes threatening – then even more terrifying than a girl's worst nightmare. Because this time Brendan will stop at nothing to be part of Miranda's life – even if it means taking it from her ...

'Creepy, genuinely gripping' *Heat*

'A must read' *Cosmopolitan*

'Nicci French at the top of her game' *Woman & Home*

LAND OF THE LIVING

You wake in the dark, gagged and bound.
He says he will kill you – just like all the rest.

Abbie Devereaux is being held against her will. She doesn't know where she is or how she got there. She's so terrified she can barely remember her own name – and she's sure of just one thing: that she will survive this nightmare. But even if she does make it back to the land of the living, Abbie knows that he'll still be out there, looking for her.

And next time, there may be no escape.

'Shocking, uncomfortable, exhilarating' *Independent on Sunday*

'Dark, gripping' *Heat*

KILLING ME SOFTLY

You have it all: the boyfriend, the friends, the career.
Then you meet a stranger and on impulse, you sacrifice everything.
You're passionately in love.
And grave danger ...

Alice Loudon couldn't resist abandoning her old, safe life for a wild affair. And in Adam Tallis, a rugged mountaineer with a murky past, she finds a man who can teach her things about herself that she never even suspected. But sexual obsession has its dark side – and so does Adam. Soon both are threatening all that Alice has left. First her sanity. Then her life.

'Compulsive, sexy, scary' *Elle*

'Cancel all appointments and unplug the phone. Once started you will do nothing until you finish this thriller' *Harpers & Queen*

'A real frightener' *Guardian*

TO FIND OUT MORE ABOUT NICCI FRENCH, VISIT
www.niccifrench.co.uk

Get the inside story behind all the novels.

Read fascinating interviews with Nicci Gerrard and Sean French.
Learn more about the authors individually and how they write their novels together.

Extras include a piece from Nicci French's UK editor on the publishing process, and an article from Professor Sue Black on what life is really like for a forensic anthropologist.

Take Nicci and Sean's (not too serious) test and find out if you are a sociopath!